THE DREAM

ÉMILE ZOLA was born in Paris in 1840, the son of a Venetian engineer and his French wife. He grew up in Aix-en-Provence, where he made friends with Paul Cézanne. After an undistinguished school career and a brief period of dire poverty in Paris, Zola joined the newly founded publishing firm of Hachette, which he left in 1866 to live by his pen. He had already published a novel and his first collection of short stories. Other novels and stories followed, until in 1871 Zola published the first volume of his Rougon-Macquart series, which was subtitled 'Natural and Social History of a Family under the Second Empire' and set out to illustrate the influence of heredity and environ-ment on a wide range of characters and milieus. However, it was not until 1877 that the seventh novel in the series, *L'Assommoir*, a study of alcoholism in the working classes, brought him wealth and fame. *The Dream*, the sixteenth novel in the series, published in 1888, offers an unusual hybrid of realism and fairy tale, and tells the story of a young girl, a penniless embroideress given to flights of mysticism, who falls in love with a young nobleman. The last of the Rougon-Macquart novels appeared in 1893 and Zola's subsequent writing was far less successful, though he achieved fame of a different sort in his vigorous and influential intervention in the Dreyfus case. His marriage in 1870 had remained childless, but his extremely happy liaison in later life with Jeanne Rozerot, initially one of his domestic servants, gave him a son and a daughter. He died in 1902.

PAUL GIBBARD is Senior Lecturer in French Studies at the University of Western Australia. He has worked previously as an edi-tor of the *Complete Works of Voltaire* at the Voltaire Foundation, Oxford, and at Monash University and the University of New England.

D0873594

OXFORD WORLD'S CLASSICS

*For over 100 years Oxford World's Classics have brought
readers closer to the world's great literature. Now with over 700
titles—from the 4,000-year-old myths of Mesopotamia to the
twentieth century's greatest novels—the series makes available
lesser-known as well as celebrated writing.*

*The pocket-sized hardbacks of the early years contained
introductions by Virginia Woolf, T. S. Eliot, Graham Greene,
and other literary figures which enriched the experience of reading.
Today the series is recognized for its fine scholarship and
reliability in texts that span world literature, drama and poetry,
religion, philosophy and politics. Each edition includes perceptive
commentary and essential background information to meet the
changing needs of readers.*

OXFORD WORLD'S CLASSICS

ÉMILE ZOLA

The Dream

Translated with an Introduction and Notes by
PAUL GIBBARD

OXFORD
UNIVERSITY PRESS

OXFORD
UNIVERSITY PRESS

Great Clarendon Street, Oxford, OX2 6DP,
United Kingdom

Oxford University Press is a department of the University of Oxford.
It furthers the University's objective of excellence in research, scholarship,
and education by publishing worldwide. Oxford is a registered trade mark of
Oxford University Press in the UK and in certain other countries

© Paul Gibbard 2018

The moral rights of the author have been asserted

First published as an Oxford World's Classics paperback 2018

Impression: 5

All rights reserved. No part of this publication may be reproduced, stored in
a retrieval system, or transmitted, in any form or by any means, without the
prior permission in writing of Oxford University Press, or as expressly permitted
by law, by licence or under terms agreed with the appropriate reprographics
rights organization. Enquiries concerning reproduction outside the scope of the
above should be sent to the Rights Department, Oxford University Press, at the
address above

You must not circulate this work in any other form
and you must impose this same condition on any acquirer

Published in the United States of America by Oxford University Press
198 Madison Avenue, New York, NY 10016, United States of America

British Library Cataloguing in Publication Data

Data available

Library of Congress Control Number: 2018938825

ISBN 978-0-19-874598-3

Printed and bound in Great Britain by
Clays Ltd, Elcograf S.p.A.

CONTENTS

INTRODUCTION

*Those who do not wish to learn details of the plot may prefer
to read this Introduction as an Afterword.*

READERS who pick up a copy of *The Dream* having finished one of
Zola's better-known novels, such as *L'Assommoir*, *Germinal*, or *La
Bête humaine*, may have an impulse, as they wade deeper into it, to
double-check the name of the author on the title page. *The Dream*, the
sixteenth of the twenty novels that make up the Rougon-Macquart
series, is the least 'Zolaesque' among them. Although it is, like the
others, a naturalist novel set in Second Empire France, and linked to
them by the lineage of its main character, it is at the same time a fairy
tale, a romance between naive young lovers that unfolds in the shadow
of a medieval cathedral. The story opens during a snowstorm on
Christmas Day, when the young heroine, Angélique, takes shelter
beneath a cathedral porch. She is found by a childless couple, a pair
of humble embroiderers, who take her in and raise her as their own.
From these beginnings, fairy-tale elements multiply. Angélique falls
in love with Félicien, a lord's son, and their attachment develops
chastely, Zola choosing to steer them away from the sort of frank sexual encounters he had described in some of his earlier novels. *The
Dream* was partly intended by Zola to show critics who had accused
him of obscenity that he could in fact portray the psychology of more
sensitive characters. Rather like an actor playing against type, Zola
enjoys the freedom that this new approach affords him. He places his
characters in a setting suffused with a mood that owes much to the
Middle Ages—a period he had long been fascinated by, and which he
evokes through his descriptions of castle and cathedral architecture,
embroidery, stained glass, and heraldry. He creates in Angélique an
unusual heroine, a girl initially dominated by her passions, who is
gradually reformed through the influence of her environment. He
also hints at his own private anxieties, rarely voiced in the Rougon-
Macquart series, concerning his childless marriage. Radically different from its predecessors, this novel, a hybrid of antagonistic genres,
interweaving realism with fairy tale, reveals a new side to Zola's art
and contains hints of the softening to come in his naturalist stance.

When *The Dream* was published in 1888, reviewers reacted in markedly different ways: there was confusion, disappointment, and scorn—but also a certain amount of admiration. Those who welcomed this 'poem of grace' tended to find points of continuity between it and the lyrical qualities in Zola's earlier works.[1] Some, though, were troubled by the new direction Zola had taken, and found it difficult to classify exactly what it was they were reading. Was *The Dream* a novel or a fairy tale, a prose poem or a piece of whimsy? asked Charles Bigot.[2] Another critic, Jules Lemaître, admitted to feeling bewildered by this 'naturalist fairy tale'—a fantasy composed by Zola using the same painstaking research methods he had deployed for his earlier novels.[3] Anatole France, though, was forthright in his disdain, suggesting that, in this attempt to portray a world of innocence and purity, Zola's talent had deserted him. To the 'winged Zola' of *The Dream*, France much preferred the earthy Zola who went around 'on all fours'.[4] What, then, had propelled Zola to soar free of the tawdry realities of life, which many critics considered his natural element? Why had he written a novel that seemed so uncharacteristic?

The Reaction against Naturalism

By late 1887, when Zola began preparatory work on *The Dream*, it seemed that naturalism had reached a point of crisis. As he mulled over his plans for the novel, he decided that his new book would have to take into account the 'reaction against naturalism' and the current mania for mysticism.[5] Zola's previous novel, *Earth*, published in serial form between May and September 1887, had depicted the harsh lives of the peasants of northern France, and it provoked

[1] Adolphe Brisson, *Les Annales politiques et littéraires* (21 October 1888), cited by Henri Mitterand in '*Le Rêve*: Étude', in Émile Zola, *Les Rougon-Macquart*, ed. Henri Mitterand, 5 vols (Paris: Gallimard, 1960–7), iv. 1651; see also 1653.

[2] Charles Bigot, *La République française* (22 October 1888), cited in Zola, *Les Rougon-Macquart*, iv. 1654.

[3] Jules Lemaître, *La Revue bleue* (27 October 1888), cited in Zola, *Les Rougon-Macquart*, iv. 1656.

[4] Anatole France, *Le Temps* (21 October 1888), [2], adapting a barb Voltaire had used against Rousseau (letter, 30 August 1755, D6451, in Voltaire, *Œuvres complètes* (Oxford: Voltaire Foundation, 1968–), *c.*259).

[5] Preparatory notes for *The Dream*, Paris, Bibliothèque Nationale de France (BNF), nouvelles acquisitions françaises, MS 10323, f. 222.

a critical storm. On 18 August 1887, even before the work had appeared in its entirety, a group of young writers published an open letter to Zola on the front page of *Le Figaro*, attacking *Earth*, its author, and naturalist doctrines. They accused the movement's leader of immorality and obscenity and ridiculed his grandiose artistic theories: the naturalist method for which he had made such great claims in fact offered no advancement, they said, on the realist techniques developed by Balzac, Stendhal, and Flaubert. They announced their separation from the movement: 'the naturalist label, which is automatically stuck onto any book grounded in real life, does not suit us any longer'.[6] In the wake of this letter, other writers and critics ganged up against Zola. Anatole France criticized him for lacking any conception of the inner life of humanity:

Within man, there is an infinite need for love, which exalts him. Monsieur Zola does not understand this. Desire and modesty sometimes mingle with delightful subtlety in the soul. Monsieur Zola does not understand this. [...] There are on earth magnificent forms and noble thoughts; there are pure souls and valiant hearts. Monsieur Zola does not understand this.[7]

Ferdinand Brunetière also condemned Zola for his unfeeling presentation of the peasants. The novel's characters appeared merely in outline, more like 'shop dummies' than nuanced human beings, because Zola, like other naturalists, neglected to deal with questions of 'psychology'. The publication of *Earth*, Brunetière suggested, marked the final failure of the naturalist movement.[8] Although Zola tried to shrug off these attacks, it is clear that he took them to heart, and still had them in mind as he began to flesh out his ideas for *The Dream*. A few years later he confirmed to an interviewer that he was trying to free himself from 'overly rigorous theories' and adopt 'a more sympathetic [...] acceptance of life'.[9]

Zola had first declared his affiliation to naturalism in his preface to the second edition of his novel *Thérèse Raquin* (1868), which features a pair of lovers who carry out a murder, are plagued by remorse, and

---

[6] Paul Bonnetain, J.-H. Rosny, Lucien Descaves, Paul Margueritte, and Gustave Guiches, '*La Terre*: À Émile Zola', *Le Figaro* (18 August 1887), 1.

[7] Anatole France, '*La Terre*', *Le Temps* (28 August 1887), [3].

[8] See Ferdinand Brunetière, 'La Banqueroute du naturalisme', *Revue des deux mondes* (1 September 1887), 218–19, 224.

[9] Jules Huret, interview with Zola, in *Enquête sur l'évolution littéraire* (Paris: Librairie Charpentier, 1891), 173–5.

finally commit suicide. Defending the novel against accusations of
indecency, he claimed: 'My goal has above all been a scientific one
[...] I have simply carried out on two living bodies the investigation
which surgeons perform on corpses', and went on to place his faith in
'the methodical, naturalist school of criticism', aligning himself with
an existing 'group of naturalist writers'.[10] He conceived of literary
naturalism as a more rigorous form of realism, in which the writer
applied a scientific style of observation and analysis to the craft of fiction. He situated his theory in the positivist tradition of the philosopher Auguste Comte and extolled the writings of the literary critic
Hippolyte Taine, who had analysed literary works as a product of
their author's heredity, environment, and period. Alongside *Thérèse
Raquin*, the Goncourt brothers' *Germinie Lacerteux* (1865) and
Flaubert's *Sentimental Education* (1869) are usually counted among
the notable works of early naturalism. In the later 1870s, a group of
naturalist writers formed around Zola, with Guy de Maupassant,
Joris-Karl Huysmans, Paul Alexis, Henry Céard, and Léon Hennique
gathering regularly with 'the Master' at his house in Médan, to the
north-west of Paris. Together they published, in 1880, an influential
collection of stories entitled *Evenings at Médan*. That same year, Zola,
drawing heavily on Claude Bernard's *Introduction to the Study of
Experimental Medicine* (1865), published his most elaborate naturalist
theorizings in *The Experimental Novel*, in which he explicitly compared the novel to a scientific experiment. It was an analogy quickly
ridiculed by both critics and friends. In the last decade of his life, Zola
began to distance himself from naturalism, relinquishing his pro-
fessed naturalist objectivity in favour of a more socially engaged
stance that emerged in his trilogy *The Three Cities* (1894–8) and his
unfinished quartet *The Four Gospels* (1899–1903). The Rougon-
Macquart cycle, however, published between 1871 and 1893, had
explicit naturalist ambitions. The series claimed in its subtitle to be
a 'Natural and Social History of a Family under the Second Empire',
its dual purposes scientific and sociological. Paying particular attention to the interplay between heredity and environment, Zola traced
the spread of degeneracy through the different branches of a family
whose members diffused into all strata of French society. In the

[10] Émile Zola, 'Préface de la deuxième édition', *Thérèse Raquin*, 2nd edn (Paris:
Librairie Internationale, 1868), pp. iii, viii.

'ravenous appetites' of this family, he believed he was capturing the general tendency of the age, 'a strange period of human folly and shame'.[11] To present such a broad expanse of French society convincingly, Zola recognized the imperative of carefully observing and researching his subjects. By late 1887, however, as Zola began composing *The Dream*, he faced a strong current of critical opinion that openly denounced the aims and methods of naturalism.

'*A book that no one expects of me*'

As he made his preparatory notes for *The Dream*, Zola jotted down three aims:

I would like to write a book that no one expects of me. First of all, it must be suitable to be placed in anyone's hands, even the hands of young girls. So no violent passions then, a simple idyll [...]. I'll redo *Paul and Virginie*. What's more, since it's said that I can't do psychology, I'd like to force people to admit that I'm a psychologist. So a bit of psychology then, or what passes for such(!) That is, a moral struggle, the eternal struggle between passion and duty [...]. And, finally, I'd like to work into the book something of the supernatural, the dream, the unknown, the unknowable.[12]

The criticisms of Brunetière and Anatole France seem to be at the forefront of Zola's mind. Firstly, he will avoid any hint of obscenity: the love affair described will be as pure as that found in Bernardin de Saint-Pierre's *Paul and Virginie* (1788), the tale of a boy and a girl who are raised by their mothers side by side in the tropical wilds of the Isle of France (Mauritius) and fall chastely in love. Secondly, the plot will not be typically naturalist. In Zola's novels, characters are generally condemned to their preordained ends by the inexorable action of a particular environment on a particular temperament. There is no free will; determinism prevails. But in *The Dream* Zola will show the mind of a character struggling against her degenerate temperament, trying to exert her will and shape her own fate—a drama, then, of psychology. And, thirdly, he will respond to what he saw as the mood of the time, the contemporary fascination with mysticism, common to symbolists, occultists, and

---

[11] See Émile Zola, 'Preface', *The Fortune of the Rougons*, trans. Brian Nelson, Oxford World's Classics (Oxford: Oxford University Press, 2012), 3, 4.
[12] Paris, BNF, nouv. acq. fr. MS 10323, ff. 217–18.

many in the Catholic Church, and portray the fantasies of a young girl preoccupied by things beyond the material world. Such, at least, were Zola's intentions.

Zola prided himself on the efficiency of his planning for the Rougon-Macquart series. *The Dream*, however, did not feature in the initial outline that Zola drew up in the late 1860s, and its heroine Angélique did not appear on the Rougon-Macquart family tree published in 1878. In response to questions from a Dutch journalist, Jacques van Santen Kolff, as to why Angélique had been left out, Zola admitted that she was a 'new shoot' he had 'grafted on'.[13] A colleague, Paul Alexis, offered an explanation for the gaps in Zola's plan: the author, he explained, deliberately left spaces into which he could insert less ambitious novels. For example, between two major works, *L'Assommoir* (1877) and *Nana* (1880), Zola had published *A Love Story* (1878), a novel narrower in scope. This sort of work served as a sort of pause, a moment of respite, in the onward march of the series. Such interludes also allowed Zola to take advantage of momentary inspirations.[14] When Zola first mentioned his new novel, *The Dream*, to van Santen Kolff in a letter of 14 November 1887, he described it as 'an enormous surprise, a fantasy, a flight of fancy, which I have been thinking over for a long time'.[15] Later Zola suggested to the same journalist that he had conceived it as a counterpart to *The Sin of Abbé Mouret* (1875), not wanting that earlier novel about the religious fantasies and sexual awakening of a young priest to appear thematically isolated in the series. As he explained:

A place was set aside for a study of the supernatural [...], but it's difficult for me to say exactly when. The ideas remain vague until the moment I execute them. But you may be sure that none of this was unplanned. *The Dream* arrived at its appointed moment, just like the other parts of the series.[16]

While the germ of the idea may have predated the furore that greeted *Earth*, *The Dream* only began to take on concrete form in late 1887,

[13] Letter to Jacques van Santen Kolff, 22 January 1888, in Émile Zola, *Correspondance*, ed. B. H. Bakker, 10 vols (Montreal: Presses de l'Université de Montréal, 1978–95), vi. 245.

[14] See Paul Alexis, *Émile Zola, notes d'un ami; avec des vers inédits d'Émile Zola* (Paris: Librairie Charpentier, 1882), 125–6.

[15] Letter to van Santen Kolff, 14 November 1887, in Zola, *Correspondance*, vi. 207.

[16] Letter to van Santen Kolff, 16 November 1888, in ibid., vi. 350.

with Zola reacting at least in part to the recent savaging he had received at the hands of the critics.

A Mid-Life Crisis

The subject matter of *The Dream* was shaped by other concerns of the moment as well. Its composition coincided with a crisis in Zola's life, brought on by age, obesity, and an unhappy marriage. During his years of success Zola had indulged his culinary appetites and grown fat, but in the latter stages of 1887 his despair over his appearance reached a pinnacle. In November, he placed himself on a strict diet, banishing wine, bread, and sweets from his table. By March the following year, he had lost 14 kilograms in weight, much to the astonishment of literary Paris, and he began to look more like the svelte young man he had been in his twenties. His bouts of anguish recurred, and in early 1889 he confided to van Santen Kolff: 'I'm going through a crisis, the crisis of middle age no doubt [...]. For weeks and months on end I'm racked by turmoil, a storm of longing and regret.'[17] His distress arose at least in part from his deep dissatisfaction with his marriage to Alexandrine. They had met and become lovers in 1864 and lived together from the following year. They had married shortly after Zola's 30th birthday in 1870, but their marriage remained childless. Alexandrine, though, had borne a child before she met Zola. In 1859, when just 17, she had given birth to a daughter Caroline out of wedlock, but, lacking the means to support the infant, had given her up to a foundling hospital. It seems that Alexandrine and Zola tried to track down the child in 1877, and learnt that she had been placed in the care of a wet-nurse and taken to Brittany, where she had died aged just three weeks.[18]

While Zola did not usually offer personal reflections in his preparatory notes for his novels, he gave vent to his unhappiness in those he compiled for *The Dream*. The initial outline of its plot featured a lonely scientist of 40 who, tormented by a sense of wasted years and physical decline, falls in love with a girl of 16. The true subject of this story was, in fact, as Zola made clear: 'Me, work, a life consumed by literature, upheaval, crisis, the need to be loved.'[19] After further

---

[17] Letter to van Santen Kolff, 6 March 1889, in ibid., vi. 376.
[18] See Evelyne Bloch-Dano, *Madame Zola* (Paris: Grasset, 1997), 11–19.
[19] Paris, BNF, nouv. acq. fr. MS 10323, f. 221–2.

reflection he decided that the age difference between the protagonists would overcomplicate matters, and so he opted in *The Dream* for two young lovers closer together in age.

Zola's yearning for new love found an object in July 1888, just as he was completing the final chapters of *The Dream*. A 21-year-old maid, Jeanne Rozerot, entered the Zola household, and the writer soon became infatuated with her. When she left their service in October, Zola installed her in a flat in Paris as his mistress. She bore him two children, Denise in 1889 and Jacques in 1891. Alexandrine discovered their liaison only after Jacques's birth and, once her initial rage had subsided, she reluctantly permitted the two households to continue to coexist. The delight Zola took in fatherhood prompted him in the following decade to erect ideas around family and fertility into principles for the regeneration of society—a project he sets out in his novel *Fecundity* (1899). The plot Zola had originally sketched for *The Dream*, about a learned man falling in love with a much younger woman, was incorporated into *Doctor Pascal* (1893), with Zola explicitly identifying Jeanne and himself with that novel's two main characters, the young Clotilde and her ageing lover (and uncle), Dr Pascal. Although Zola's involvement with Jeanne was still to come as he planned *The Dream*, some of the emotions that drew him into this liaison were already present. Zola's frustrations with Alexandrine are perhaps reflected in his portrait of the 'profoundly chaste'[20] relations between Hubert and Hubertine in a 'house made melancholy by their childless sorrow' (p. 12). And when he touches on Angélique's experiences in the foundling hospital, thoughts of Alexandrine's daughter could not have been far from his mind.

Several critics suggested that Zola's decision to people his novel with innocent and virtuous characters arose from another of his concerns of that period: his desire to gain election to the Académie Française. It was a charge he stridently rejected:

It has been said that when I published *The Dream* it was to compel the Académie to take pity on me, that writing it was a way of saying: 'Look, I've become nice and quite reasonable, admit me on the basis of this *ad hoc* book I've just put out!' It would have been a wretched thing to do, and unworthy of me.[21]

---

[20] Ibid., f. 19.
[21] Undated letter to an unidentified addressee, cited in Mitterand, '*Le Rêve*: Étude', *Les Rougon-Macquart*, iv. 1621.

The accusation does not, in any case, make much sense, as in his next novel, *La Bête humaine* (1890), Zola promptly returned to matters of violence and criminality: its protagonist is a psychopathic killer.

Angélique and the Passions

Zola characterizes Angélique as a girl of strong passions: even as a young child she is quick to anger and hates and loves with great intensity. These passions serve several important structural functions in the novel. To create dramatic tension in what might otherwise have been a simple idyll, Zola places an obstacle in the lovers' path, in the form of a refusal by Félicien's father to give his consent to their proposed marriage. Zola then has the opportunity to show that he can write as a 'psychologist' by presenting the conflict within Angélique's mind as she is torn between her passions and her growing sense of duty. Her passions also serve to link this novel to the rest of the Rougon-Macquart series—they constitute Angélique's inheritance from her degenerate forebears. As in the other novels in the series, Zola explores the influence of environment on temperament, but in this case, in a surprising variation, the environment is thoroughly benign.

When Zola devised the Rougon-Macquart series in 1868–9, his ideas were strongly shaped by two works of medical science, Prosper Lucas's *Philosophical and Physiological Treatise on Natural Heredity* (1847–50) and Charles Letourneau's *Physiology of the Passions* (1868). In Lucas's treatise, Zola found the structuring principle of the series: heredity—the process by which mental as well as physical traits could be transmitted from one generation to the next. The main characters in the novels all descend from Adélaïde Fouque (known as Aunt Dide), who has one legitimate child by her husband Rougon, a farm labourer, and two illegitimate children by her lover, the drunkard and smuggler Macquart. Aunt Dide's descendants are governed to different degrees by their inherited characteristics, which range from fierce ambition and neurosis on the Rougon side to alcoholism, vice, and murderous tendencies on the Macquart side.

Lucas set out the complicated mechanisms by which traits supposedly passed from generation to generation in processes such as 'election' (one parent supplying the majority of traits to the child), 'mixture' (separate traits from both parents passing to the child), or 'combination' (two dissimilar traits in the parents combining to form a new one in the child).[22] Lucas never doubted that the passions were just as transmissible as physical features or criminal instincts.[23] Letourneau's focus in the *Physiology of the Passions* was on the way that the passions (or appetites) were produced in the body and he rejected the idea that they came from an intangible source such as the soul. While he felt able to explain how the 'nutritive' passions (to do with circulation, digestion, and respiration) and the 'sensitive' passions (relating to sex and the senses) had their origins in organs and nervous tissues, he admitted that the mechanism by which the nervous system produced the 'cerebral' (moral and intellectual) passions was less well understood. Zola learned from Letourneau that emotions could be understood as 'short-lived passions', and his interest was piqued by Letourneau's suggestion that bodily processes gave rise to emotions and phenomena such as pride, love, and religion.[24] When Zola came to create Angélique's character for *The Dream*, investing her with a predisposition towards anger and religious fervour, the theories of these two medical authorities underlay his grasp of the physiological origin and transmission of the passions.

Angélique's mother, Sidonie Rougon, had featured as a minor character in *The Kill* (1872), the second novel in the series. When Hubert catches sight of her in *The Dream*, she appears as 'a thin, pale woman, of uncertain age and rather sexless, wearing a threadbare black dress covered in all sorts of stains from her dubious activities' (p. 31). She has made ends meet in Paris by selling fruit, olive oil, lace, raincoats, and pianos, among other things, and has found work as a shady sort of go-between, procuring husbands for pregnant girls and girls for lustful men. She is, as her brother recognizes in *The Kill*, a 'true Rougon', possessing the 'hunger for money, the longing for intrigue, which [are] the hallmark of the family'.[25] After her husband's death, Sidonie gave birth to a daughter 'without knowing exactly

[22] See F. W. J. Hemmings, *Émile Zola*, 2nd edn (Oxford: Clarendon Press, 1966), 56–9.
[23] See, for example, Prosper Lucas, *Traité philosophique et physiologique de l'hérédité naturelle dans les états de santé et de maladie du système nerveux*, 2 vols (Paris: J. B. Baillière, 1847–50), ii. 203.
[24] Charles Letourneau, *La Physiologie des passions* (Paris: Germer Baillière, 1868), 8, 26, 77; Zola's notes on Letourneau, Paris, BNF, nouv. acq. fr. MS 10345, ff. 42, 47.
[25] Émile Zola, *The Kill*, trans. Brian Nelson, Oxford World's Classics (Oxford: Oxford University Press, 2004), 54.

where she had got it' (p. 31). No details are offered about Angélique's
father.

In the complete family tree of the Rougon-Macquart, published
five years after *The Dream*, Zola identifies the main principles of
heredity at work in the different characters. Angélique's make-up is
governed by 'inneity'—a principle of difference rather than resemblance. That is, she bears 'no resemblance to her mother or forebears'.[26] It might sound, then, as though Zola is having it both ways.
He anchors *The Dream* in the Rougon-Macquart series by way of
Angélique's maternal line, but supplies Angélique with none of her
family's traits. However, with the 1893 statement, Zola is somewhat
recasting Angélique's inheritance. Earlier, Zola had made it clear that
Angélique is 'proud, passionate, sensual, […] a Rougon-Macquart'.[27]
She inherits the general temperament of her ancestors, even though
it suits the idyll of the novel that Angélique should not share any of
her mother's particular vices.

Angélique's passionate nature expresses itself in a wide variety of
forms in *The Dream*—in rage, disobedience, and sensuality, religious
fervour, love, and a mania for charity. The Huberts encounter this
side of her when they bring her in from the snow to warm her up.
When Hubertine picks up a booklet Angélique has dropped, the child
bursts into rage:

The Huberts watched astonished […]. They no longer recognized the
blonde child with violet-coloured eyes and long neck graceful as a lily. Her
eyes had turned black, her face was twisted with hatred, and her sensual
neck had swollen as the blood pulsed through it. Now that she was warm
she stood tall and hissed like a grass snake that has been rescued from the
snow. (p. 9)

Anger in a young girl is interpreted as a moral flaw: the Huberts think
she must be 'a bad little girl' (p. 10). Such outbursts occur again after
the Huberts install her as their ward, and they view her rage as
a degenerate quality, inherited, no doubt, from vicious parents:

They recoiled with fear before this little monster, horrified by the malign
impulses that stirred within her. Who was she, then? Where had she come

---

[26] Émile Zola, 'Arbre généalogique des Rougon-Macquart (état de 1893)', fold-out in
Les Rougon-Macquart, v; see 'Family Tree of the Rougon-Macquart', p. xl.
[27] Paris, BNF, nouv. acq. fr. MS 10323, f. 8.

from? Foundlings, in most cases, are the children of criminality and vice. (p. 16)

While Angélique's passionate nature manifests itself at times in anger and unruliness, at others her emotions attach themselves to objects of faith. As a little girl she works herself into 'a feverish passion over images, little engravings of holy scenes, and [...] Jesus figurines' (p. 17). Religious passions go hand in hand with sensual passions—as Zola had previously shown in *The Sin of Abbé Mouret*. The 'ardour and intensity' of Angélique's caresses give Hubertine cause for concern, and she catches Angélique on occasion 'kissing her own hands' in a form of sexual experimentation (p. 17). When she turns 12, the child's ardour finds a new object, Jacobus de Voragine's thirteenth-century compilation of the lives of the saints, *The Golden Legend*. Angélique is enraptured by the stories she reads about the saints' miraculous triumphs over Satan, and feels as though she is entering a new world, a 'great dream' emerging from 'the depths of the unknown' (p. 19). Her fervid mysticism, deriving from the same source as her rage, summons forth invisible beings and brings inanimate objects to life around her as she grows older. The passions that create her dream world fire her genius as an embroideress, and she creates a great many 'gleaming, sacred marvels' with her needle (p. 35). She is gripped at times also by an intense 'passion for charity' (p. 25), following the example of St Francis of Assisi and other saints she has read about, on one occasion flinging her clothes out the window to a drunken beggar. This passion is partly virtuous and partly vain—she becomes engaged in a battle with Félicien over who can do the most good, and even offers a pauper girl the shoes from her feet in an effort to prevail.

At 14, as Angélique is 'becoming a woman', her mingled sensual and religious passions grow more intense. The ideal of virginity becomes dearer to her as she develops:

When she read the *Legend*, she heard a ringing in her ears, and the blood beat in the delicate blue veins around her temples; and she was filled now with a tender fellow-feeling for the virgins. (p. 25)

Although Zola had intended *The Dream* to be an innocent idyll, his presentation of Angélique's maturing sexuality is frank enough in its own way—if much less explicit than certain scenes in *Earth*. At 16, as the spring arrives, Angélique feels deeply troubled by the scent of vegetation, her emotions fluctuate wildly, and she has trouble breathing.

In describing her nightly fantasies, Zola uses language that is at once chaste and sensual: 'she had exquisite dreams, shadowy shapes swirled round her, and she swooned in ecstasies she dared not recall on waking, so bewildered was she by the bliss the angels brought her' (p. 48). Around her, inanimate objects come to life: the leaves of the trees, the waters of the stream and the stones of the cathedral all speak to her, and she has 'the sense that the unknown [is] shaping her life, independently of her will' (p. 56). The shadows in the field beyond her bedroom window gradually take on the shape of a young man, Félicien, and, after she meets him in the flesh by the stream on washing day, they fall in love and decide to marry. When Félicien's father, Monseigneur d'Hautecœur, a nobleman and a bishop, forbids the proposed union between his son and a lowly embroideress, Angélique faces a stark choice: whether she should follow her desires or obey her elders. Hubertine, who has long tried to teach Angélique mastery of her passions, urges her ward to choose obedience and duty over pride and passion.

In the chapters that follow, Zola traces Angélique's struggle with this dilemma. It is ultimately resolved in a naturalist fashion, with Zola showing how environment acts on Angélique's inherited passions to mould her fate. Almost against her will, she chooses obedience:

She called to mind her years of toil, such happy, fruitful years, and the calm and honest habits she had gradually acquired, which revolted at the idea of sin. And day after day, the chill little house of the embroiderers, and the hard-working, virtuous life she led there, hidden away from the world, had reformed a little the blood that ran within her veins. (p. 156)

In other circumstances her degenerate inheritance might have propelled her, like her distant relative, the heroine of the novel *Nana* (1880), towards prostitution. For Zola, environment, in this instance, performs a secular function equivalent to Christian grace, redeeming the 'original sin' of the flaw she has acquired from her forebears—her unruly passions.

A Return to the Past

Although *The Dream* is set in Second Empire France, its action unfolding across the years 1860–9, the atmosphere is more redolent of the Middle Ages than the mid-nineteenth century. Much of the research Zola did for the novel went into creating this archaic mood. Not only did he draw heavily on *The Golden Legend*, he read up on the history of embroidery and stained-glass manufacture and on the architecture of cathedrals and castles so as to be able to describe the characters' occupations and surroundings in convincing detail. The methods he had used to impart modern documentary truth to his earlier novels he employs here in the service of anachronism. And yet, oddly enough, there was a contemporary aspect to the novel's medievalism—the Middle Ages had become fashionable again in 1880s Paris, and it was an enthusiasm that Zola shared.

Before he turned to naturalism, Zola's early literary interests lay in the Romantic movement, in authors such as Victor Hugo and Théophile Gautier, who had both been keen medievalists. As Elizabeth Emery points out, Zola went from composing ballads and a story about the crusades in youth to decorating his house at Médan in maturity with an array of medieval objects, ranging from tapestries and suits of armour to stained-glass windows, religious paintings, and church ornaments.[28] When he wrote in his study in Paris, he sat in an armchair bearing the motto of his fictional lords of Hautecœur: 'If God wills, I will.' This thoroughly modern writer had an unshakeable fascination with medieval miscellanea, whether genuine or ersatz. Across the Channel, the Pre-Raphaelite Brotherhood had looked back to the Middle Ages for their artistic inspiration, while William Morris's Arts and Crafts Movement extolled old-fashioned craftsmanship over modern mechanized forms of production. In France, too, by the late nineteenth century, many had grown sceptical about the advantages of science and the modern age, and looked back fondly to the naive faith of earlier eras.[29] Symbolist poets and painters turned away from realism towards the spiritual and ideal, while Joseph Péladan's Order of the Rose + Croix and a resurgent Catholic Church shared common ground in their embrace of mysticism over the positivist doctrines then in vogue.

In *The Dream* Zola uses architecture as one means of reviving the medieval past. The town of Beaumont-l'Église is dominated by its old

[28] See Elizabeth Emery, '"À l'ombre d'une vieille cathédrale romane": The Medievalism of Gautier and Zola', *French Review* 73 (1999), 299; and Emery, 'Bricobracomania: Zola's Romantic Instinct', *Excavatio* 12 (1999), 107–15.

[29] See Henri Mitterand, *Zola, l'histoire et la fiction* (Paris: Presses Universitaires de France, 1990), 160.

cathedral, looming 'enormously over the little heap of low-standing houses, which shelter like a brood of chicks beneath its stone wings. The inhabitants live for it and by it. The artisans toil and the shop-keepers trade simply to nourish, clothe, and maintain the cathedral and its clergy' (p. 14). Although it is only two hours by train from Paris, Beaumont feels cut off from the outside world and 'bathes in an age-old atmosphere of tranquillity and faith' (p. 14). Across the river, the new town of Beaumont-la-Ville is spacious and modern. It owes its prosperity to textile factories and looks back somewhat disdain-fully at its older sibling. Angélique, though, lives out her days in the shadow of the cathedral: her house leans against its wall and trembles when its great bells toll; its vast bulk shuts out the sky above her bal-cony. She develops a connection to this monument that is both phys-ical and emotional. She finds her features mirrored in its ancient sculptures of St Agnes. Through long gazing at the cathedral, she imparts to it a consciousness and enrols it in her dream world, feeling it to be 'as capable of loving and thinking as she herself' (p. 49). The cathedral plays a part in many of the crucial events in her life: she shelters from a snowstorm in its northern porch, summons her lover from its shadows, pleads with the bishop in its chapel and at last mar-ries Félicien before its altar, the edifice rejoicing in the sacrament. The west portal of the cathedral marks the fatal boundary for her between dream and reality, between past and present: it is here that she dies as she walks out of the building on her wedding day. Angélique, who comes to imagine herself a virgin of the primitive Church, is unable to survive this transition into modernity.

Zola offers a precise history of the cathedral's construction: the nave, the reader learns, was begun in 1150 in the Romanesque style and was completed after 1230 in the early Gothic style, while the towers and main façade were finished around 1430 in the late flamboyant Gothic style. These details are important, as the Romanesque and the Gothic styles carry different symbolic meanings. Adapting ideas developed by Victor Hugo in *Notre-Dame de Paris* (1831), Zola associ-ates the squat, heavy Romanesque style with the tyranny of the priest-hood and the vengeful God of the Old Testament, and the lighter, airier Gothic style with the liberation of the people and a movement towards 'a loving and forgiving God' (p. 49). In a striking image, Zola compares the cathedral to a figure at first bowed in prayer (at the Romanesque level) who then turns her face upwards (at the early

Gothic level) and soars towards the heavens (at the late Gothic level). As the final scene in the novel makes clear, the stages of the cathedral symbolize the phases in Angélique's naturalistic development, from a child dominated by the demons of hereditary evil to a young woman set free by the secular grace of a benign environment. Like the mine in *Germinal* or the locomotive in *La Bête humaine*, the medieval cathedral is the emblematic centre of the novel. In modelling his cathedral, Zola relied heavily on the writings of the architectural historian Eugène Viollet-le-Duc (1814–79), and he creates a sort of poetry out of the technical language he acquired, with its voussoirs and tympanums, piers and flying buttresses, spirelets, finials, and pinnacles. The cathedral is, as Zola insists, 'a living thing' (p. 49), and he lyrically evokes its appearance through the changing seasons and shifting patterns of light in a way that seems to anticipate Claude Monet's series of paintings, begun four years later, of Rouen Cathedral in different weathers.[30]

Other buildings in the novel, the Huberts' house and Hautecœur Castle, also date from the Middle Ages and perpetuate the novel's anachronistic atmosphere. Built in the late fifteenth century, the Huberts' house nestles between two buttresses of the cathedral, and offers a refuge from the modern world. The gigantic ruins of Hautecœur Castle, thronged with the legends of the noble family, are visited by the spirits of virgins who died there in the bliss of first love. These medieval property holdings are important to the identities of the two families, as are their coats of arms, Zola seeming to delight in the obscure and archaic language of heraldic description. The Huberts' house and Hautecœur Castle, like the cathedral, have sturdy historical underpinnings. To ensure the authenticity of the first, Zola asked a friend, the architect Frantz Jourdain, to draw up a detailed set of plans for it and then had Jourdain check over his prose descriptions. Zola modelled Hautecœur Castle on the castles of Coucy and Pierrefonds in northern France, drawing on information from Pierre Larousse's *Grand Dictionnaire universel du XIXe siècle* (1865–78).

The crafts practised by the main characters also connect them with the past. The Hubert family, whose ancestors have worked in embroidery for four hundred years, continue to employ the techniques of earlier

---

[30] See Elizabeth Emery, *Romancing the Cathedral: Gothic Architecture in Fin-de-Siècle French Culture* (Albany, N.Y.: SUNY Press, 2001), 59.

centuries, even though the trade is evolving. Zola derived most of his technical information about embroidery from a treatise entitled *The Art of the Embroiderer* (1770) by Charles-Germain de Saint-Aubin (1721–86), who had worked as an embroidery designer for Louis XV and Madame de Pompadour. The initial picture Zola provides of the Huberts in their workshop (pp. 33–34) closely mirrors an illustration from this treatise, showing two women and a man at work on their frames, their tools arranged around them. Embroidery in the novel has a broadly eighteenth-century flavour, though numerous references are also made to medieval techniques and masterpieces. Compared to other workplaces in Zola's novels, such as the coal mine, the food market, or the locomotive cab, the Huberts' workshop is a haven of peace and cleanliness. Embroidery, though, is exacting in its own way: it is physically numbing work, as Zola makes clear, and Angélique's fingers have been deeply scarred by her needle.

Zola ties Angélique's craft closely to her character: she channels her passions into her work, and it, in turn, has a salutary influence on her hereditary flaws. She has a natural genius for embroidering ecclesiastical motifs, and, with a little instruction from the Huberts, becomes an expert by the age of 15: 'Silk and gold thread came alive in her hands, her smallest figures shone with mystical beauty. She gave herself up entirely to her work, which was continually enriched by her fertile imagination and her belief in a world beyond appearances' (p. 35). She takes inspiration from the marvellous and gruesome tales of saintly devotion that she reads in a sixteenth-century translation of *The Golden Legend*, and Zola scatters archaic quotations from this work through his own text. Angélique's embroidered images of the Virgin Mary provoke comparison among connoisseurs with the primitive figures of pre-Renaissance artists. She is the only local embroiderer skilful enough to work in the exacting fifteenth-century technique of 'shaded gold', in which different shades of gold thread are layered over figures embroidered in coloured silk. As with his descriptions of cathedral architecture, Zola uses a technical foundation from which to launch into lyrical description, and he surrounds Angélique with 'a haze of silk, satin, velvet, and gold and silver cloth' (p. 35). At times, Angélique's embroidery seems to merge bodily with her or commune with her morally: in the depths of her illness, for example, the 'red silk of one of the flowers shone bloodily between her white fingers, as though her own blood had seeped out into it, droplet by droplet' (p. 149); and when Félicien begs her to run away with him, an unfinished flower on her embroidery frame seems to counsel her against this. The old-fashioned craft of embroidery has a rare power in the Rougon-Macquart series: it offers a means of redeeming a degenerate trait, and the years Angélique spends labouring with her needle help to repair the vicious side of her nature.

Although Félicien is too wealthy to need to work, he dabbles in repairing stained-glass windows and studiously recreates medieval techniques of glass production. His views on the art form reflect those that Zola found in Larousse's dictionary, which held that the art of the stained-glass window had reached its pinnacle in the crude and naive imagery of the twelfth and thirteenth centuries. Stained glass, embroidery, *The Golden Legend*, heraldry, the cathedral, the castle, the Huberts' house, lineages, and legends – all serve to draw the characters constantly into the past.

Dream and Reality

Although *The Dream*'s hybrid form, part fairy tale and part realist novel, seemed puzzling to certain early critics, it was not the first time that Zola had written in a fairy-tale style. He had experimented with the genre during the penurious years he had spent in Paris in his late teens and early twenties, confessing then to an old schoolfriend that he much preferred to lose himself in hopes and dreams than face the hideous reality of life.[31] His first published collection, *Tales for Ninon* (1864), contained the fables 'The Love Fairy' (1859), 'Simplice' (1863), and 'Sister-of-the-Poor' (1864), which all foreshadow elements of *The Dream*, the first tale featuring a winged guardian who watches over young lovers, the second a fatal kiss between a prince and a water sprite, and the third an orphan girl who performs acts of charity with the help of a magical coin.

Revisiting the fairy tale as a veteran naturalist, Zola expressed somewhat contradictory ideas about how the fantastical might sit alongside the realistic. On the one hand, he declares in his preparatory notes:

---

[31] See letter to Jean-Baptistin Baille, *c*.10 February 1861, in Zola, *Correspondance*, i. 266.

The Dream would be the title of the volume, and that's what I find particularly appealing. I'd like the volume to form the part of the series that deals with dream, fantasy, spirituality, the beyond. And it would be clear, as the title would warn the reader: 'Here's a dream, I'm telling you as much, don't mistake it for anything else.' And then, without overmuch irony, I'd have to stick in life as it never is, as it appears only in dreams, everyone decent, honest, and happy.[32]

And yet, a little further on, he concedes:

I think I'll have to give the work a foundation in reality. If I made it too fantastical and dreamlike, it wouldn't work nearly so well. So I'll have to ground my characters as solidly as I can [...]. It's only by giving a great deal of detail about their lives that I'll make them real.[33]

The fabulist within Zola was brought back to earth by the naturalist. He decided to ground sections of his story in reality by using some of his standard methods of composition. After compiling detailed notes on a variety of subjects, ranging from adoption laws and foundling hospitals to medieval architecture and crafts, he flooded the narrative with this information. Zola later complained to van Santen Kolff about how hard he had had to labour: 'no one will ever appreciate [...] the amount of research I have had to do for such a simple book'[34]—the shortest volume, in fact, of the Rougon-Macquart series.

In *The Dream* Zola veers between the naturalistic and the irrational. In some places, logical explanations are given for fantastical events; in others, miracles stand simply as such. Readers are left in an equivocal position: is the universe of the story governed by positivism or by the supernatural? Zola in fact endorses both. A naturalist explanation is offered for Angélique's visions, which grow out of the interaction between her environment and her temperament. But her dream world is encircled by a broader zone, in which realist elements stand side by side with inexplicable miracles. Naturalist logic and fairy-tale unreality persist together in uneasy cohabitation, until a resolution of sorts occurs in the novel's final scene.

Zola makes it clear that many of the fantastical elements in the story take place simply in Angélique's imagination. Brought up in an atmosphere of piety and tranquillity, and fired by *The Golden Legend*,

---

[32] Paris, BNF, nouv. acq. fr. MS 10323, ff. 226-7.   [33] Ibid., f. 294.
[34] Letter to van Santen Kolff, 25 May 1888, in Zola, *Correspondance*, vi. 289.

Angélique gives free rein to her religious passions. Zola carefully describes the part that this book plays in fostering her mystical beliefs. As she reads about the struggles between the saints and Satan, she begins to live 'entirely in this tragic and triumphant world of marvels' (p. 24) and becomes convinced that miracles and wonders are 'the common rule' (p. 53). Inspired by its example, she invests manmade objects and the natural elements with spiritual presences. To this extent, Zola demonstrates a straightforward naturalist thesis—that mysticism may persist in the modern age through a particular interaction between environment and heredity.[35]

The nature of Angélique's dream is discussed and analysed by the characters themselves. While Hubert, also a dreamer, tends to support Angélique in her flights of fancy, Hubertine does all she can to demolish Angélique's illusions. She sets Angélique menial chores, and tries to convince her that the world is a dark and brutal place. When she finds herself unable to quash Angélique's aspiration to marry beyond her social class, she reproaches herself for having kept the girl 'closeted in the perpetual falsehood of the dream' (p. 120). Angélique herself understands that her dream stems from her ignorance and desires, and that it then rebounds on her day-to-day life, shaping her actual existence.[36] When she is tempted to run away with Félicien, she finds that the spiritual life she has conferred on her surroundings returns to her, directing her towards her duty, and constituting a form of 'grace':

If it is only a dream, a dream I have imparted to the things around me, and which now comes back to me, what does it matter! The dream is saving me, bearing me along unsullied through a world of appearances. (p. 158)

When Angélique opts to remain in her little house peopled with spirits, Félicien tries to discredit her fantasies: 'If there are visions encircling you, it is because you have created them… Come now, if you stop investing the things around you with your spirit, they will fall silent' (p. 158). The narrator, too, suggests candidly at one point that Angélique has been led into a life of error by her dream, even if, in her naive faith, she has become something of a saint (p. 168).

Not all of the mystical elements in the novel fall within the bounds of Angélique's imagination: the fairy tale also exists outside her mind,

---

[35] See Mitterand, *Zola, l'histoire et la fiction*, 157.
[36] See Paris, BNF, nouv. acq. fr. MS 10324, ff. 193–4.

comingling with the naturalist world. There are numerous fairy-tale aspects to the plot: its Christmas-Day opening; an orphan girl as protagonist, abandoned by her mother and taken in by honest, hardworking guardians; the curse of barrenness placed on the Huberts after the death of their first baby; the appearance of a Prince Charming and his marriage offer to a penniless embroideress; her deathbed revival, brought about by a kiss from Monseigneur d'Hautecœur; and her final ascent into the heavens. Zola heightens the fairy-tale mood of the novel through his use of imagery, patterns, and archetypes. The entire novel, for example, is bathed in white, from the snowdrifts of the opening chapter through to the cascades of white silk and flowers at Angélique's wedding. The whitewashed walls of her bedroom glow in the moonlight, the white silks on her embroidery frame and the linen laid out to dry in the Clos-Marie dazzle the eye. Her hair is blonde, her skin like ivory or pale satin. The words 'white' (*blanc*) and 'pale' (*pâle*) and their cognates appear some two hundred times in the novel, at the rate of about one per page, evoking the pallor of innocence and virginity. Faces in the novel are rarely just faces—they are patterned on mythical figures and evoke legendary qualities. Angélique's face mirrors that of St Agnes; Félicien seems to step out of a stained-glass window as St George, and also resembles a 'superb Jesus' (p. 59). Félicien's father, with his majestic bearing and thick white curls, is the image of God himself. In her pale beauty, Angélique is the double of Félicien's mother. Stories recur and multiply.[37] Angélique is abandoned as an infant by her mother, Félicien by his father. The youthful passions of Hubert and Hubertine, and of Félicien's father and mother are reborn in Angélique and Félicien. In her virginal death, Angélique re-enacts the fate of the Happy Dead who float above Hautecœur Castle and the myriad martyred virgins of *The Golden Legend*. Angélique is also a self-conscious fashioner of symbols: she sees an emblem of herself in a sweet-briar that she finds growing wild by the roadside and, after transplanting it to her garden, wonders whether it too will flourish and bear flowers. As patterns and motifs proliferate, the characters seem to become enmeshed in a process of eternal repetition, belonging more to the realm of myth than to the contemporary world.

[37] See Christophe Duboile, 'Les jeux spéculaires dans *Le Rêve*', *Cahiers naturalistes* 76 (2002), 97–103.

The final two chapters in the novel are marked by a series of miracles. Having administered extreme unction to Angélique on her deathbed, Monseigneur d'Hautecœur bends to kiss her on the lips, making the same gesture his forebears had done in previous centuries to cure villagers of the plague. The room seems to fill with bright light and floating white shapes as Angélique miraculously sits up. Have Félicien and Hubertine, who previously denounced Angélique's fantasies, become infected by her delusions? Zola in his notes indicates that a 'miracle' has in fact taken place—he can 'offer no medical explanation' for Angélique's improvement in health.[38] And just before Angélique's wedding, a second miracle occurs when Hubertine, kneeling before her mother's grave, feels a tremor inside her, indicating that the curse of barrenness has been removed and she is pregnant again, many years after she conceived her first child. Finally, on Angélique's wedding day, the third and most striking miracle occurs. As the couple leave the cathedral, Angélique stretches up to kiss Félicien and, in this act, dies. Like the figure of St Agnes on the tympanum, she ascends into the heavens:

[she] soared triumphantly upwards, exultant and pure, borne off in the moment of her dream's fulfilment, swept up from dark Romanesque chapels into flamboyant Gothic vaulting, through vestiges of gold and paint into the paradise of the legends.

Is this simply a vision experienced by Angélique as she dies, or does she actually disappear? The narrator seems to confirm that her body has vanished:

Félicien clasped just a soft and cherished wisp of a thing, the wedding gown made of lace and pearls, a handful of fine feathers left behind by a bird, still warm to the touch. For a long time he had felt that he possessed merely a shadow. This vision, coming out of the invisible realms, had returned to the invisible. It had been a thing of appearance only, generating an illusion and then fading away. All is but a dream. And, at the pinnacle of her happiness, Angélique had vanished in the faint breath of a kiss. (p. 180)

In the 1893 family tree of the Rougon-Macquart, Zola confirms that medical science cannot explain her death: she has died of an 'undetermined illness'.[39] As she leaves the cathedral, she is set to

[38] Paris, BNF, nouv. acq. fr. MS 10323, f. 191.
[39] Zola, 'Arbre généalogique' (1893), fold-out in *Les Rougon-Macquart*, v.

abandon her dream and 'enter reality',[40] but she dies instead, preserving her virginity like the martyred saints she admires. As critics have observed, this ending is strangely ambiguous. While it signals the end of the dream for Angélique, it also seems to suggest that there is, in fact, no possibility for any character to enter reality, since 'All is but a dream.' Zola amplifies the point in his notes: 'Man is a thing of appearance only who dies after creating an illusion.'[41] For all its naturalist elements, the novel ends on an idealist note, suggesting that reality is only an invention of the mind, and that all that has occurred is just a dream. It seems a last-ditch attempt by Zola to resolve the generic tensions in the novel, subsuming the naturalistic once and for all within the irrational. For Zola himself, however, the end of *The Dream* meant a return to positivism, as he set about composing his next novel *La Bête humaine* (1890), a more conventional naturalist study set in the grimy modern world of the railways.

Adaptations of The Dream

The Dream was adapted as an opera in four acts and eight scenes by Alfred Bruneau, with a libretto by Louis Gallet. During rehearsals, a decision was taken to cut the final scene, and so end with Angélique's recovery from illness, rather than the conclusion that appears in the novel. The opera had its debut at the Opéra-Comique in Paris on 18 June 1891, and, although the public was initially disconcerted by its modernist orchestration and its contemporary setting and costumes, it proved a popular success, running for ninety-three performances. It transferred to London later the same year, where it had its premiere at Covent Garden on 29 October. It was warmly received by the English public, and was praised by reviewers, including George Bernard Shaw. The opera was subsequently performed in Brussels, Antwerp, and Hamburg (where it was directed by Gustav Mahler), and in many parts of regional France. In later years Zola turned his hand to writing librettos himself, some original, and some adapted from his own stories, but in the case of *The Dream* his involvement was relatively minor—he cast an eye over Gallet's draft libretto, supplied some small sections of text, and offered comments on the staging. The opera was regularly performed in Parisian theatres until the 1940s.

---

[40] Paris, BNF, nouv. acq. fr. MS 10323, f. 187.   [41] Ibid., f. 188.

Two film versions of the novel were made in the early twentieth century, both directed by Jacques de Baroncelli. The first, a silent film produced by Le Film d'Art, in which Andrée Brabant played the role of Angélique, was released in 1921, and the second, a talking film produced by Pathé-Natan, with Simone Genevois in the principal role, was released in 1931.

TRANSLATOR'S NOTE

THE DREAM was extremely popular during Zola's lifetime, but it seemed to fall out of favour over the course of the twentieth century. By 1903, the year after Zola's death, it featured in the top third of his novels by total sales, having sold some 116,000 copies—several thousand more than *Germinal*. The first English translation of the novel, produced by Eliza E. Chase, appeared in 1893 (London: Chatto and Windus), and by 1911 had sold 132,000 copies. Adaptations of the novel for opera and film were a further testament to its appeal. For all this early popularity, the novel's reputation ebbed during the second half of the twentieth century, in part, no doubt, because its mystical mood seemed so far removed from the stark realism of Zola's best-known works. In the past couple of decades, however, interest in the novel seems to have revived: scholars have begun to examine it more closely, and in 2005 two new English translations appeared: by Andrew Brown (London: Hesperus Press) and Michael Glencross (London and Chester Springs: Peter Owen Publishers).

The present translation, which forms part of the complete set of the twenty Rougon-Macquart novels in Oxford World's Classics, is based on the text of the novel in volume iv (1966) of Henri Mitterand's five-volume edition (Paris: Gallimard, 1960–7) of *Les Rougon-Macquart* in the Bibliothèque de la Pléiade. Zola heightens the anachronistic mood of his novel by offering short passages in archaic French, adapted from the 1549 French translation of Jacobus de Voragine's thirteenth-century Latin compilation of the lives of the saints, *Legenda aurea* ('The Golden Legend'). I have borrowed from a 1527 English translation of *The Golden Legend* in an attempt to replicate this effect.

I would like to record my thanks to the staff and sponsors of the Centre International des Traducteurs Littéraires in Arles, where I completed part of this translation, the University of Western Australia, which granted me study leave to work on it, and the Australian Research Council Centre of Excellence for the History of Emotions, which supported my research into Zola and the passions. I am grateful to staff at Oxford University Press, Judith Luna, Luciana O'Flaherty, and Kizzy Taylor-Richelieu, for all their efforts, and I appreciated the comments offered by the anonymous readers. I would also like to thank the following for various forms of help and advice: Aurélie Julia, Brian Nelson, Margot Nguyen Béraud, Gillian Pink, and Mona de Pracontal.

SELECT BIBLIOGRAPHY

The Dream (*Le Rêve*) first appeared in serial form in *La Revue illustrée*, a periodical published twice monthly, in fourteen issues between 1 April 1888 and 15 October 1888 (issues 56–69). It was released in book form by Librairie Charpentier on 13 October 1888, two days before the final instalment of the serialization appeared. It is included in volume iv of Henri Mitterand's scholarly edition of *Les Rougon-Macquart* in the Bibliothèque de la Pléiade, 5 vols (Paris: Gallimard, 1960–7), and in volume xiii of the Nouveau Monde edition of Zola's *Œuvres complètes*, 21 vols (Paris, 2002–10). Paperback editions exist in the following popular collections: Classiques de Poche, ed. Roger Ripoll (Paris, 2003); Presses-Pocket, ed. Gérard Gengembre (Paris, 1992); Folio, ed. Henri Mitterand (Paris, 1986); GF-Flammarion, introduction by Colette Becker (Paris, 1975).

Biographies of Zola in English

Brown, Frederick, *Zola: A Life* (London: Macmillan, 1996).
Grant, Elliott M., *Émile Zola* (New York: Twayne Publishers, 1966).
Hemmings, F. W. J., *The Life and Times of Émile Zola* (London: Elek, 1977).
Schom, Alan, *Émile Zola: A Bourgeois Rebel* (London: Queen Anne Press, 1987).
Walker, Philip, *Zola* (London: Routledge & Kegan Paul, 1985).

Studies of Zola and Naturalism in English

Baguley, David, *Naturalist Fiction: The Entropic Vision* (Cambridge: Cambridge University Press, 1990).
Baguley, David (ed.), *Critical Essays on Émile Zola* (Boston: G. K. Hall, 1986).
Bell, David F., *Models of Power: Politics and Economics in Zola's 'Rougon-Macquart'* (Lincoln, Nebr., and London: University of Nebraska Press, 1988).
Bloom, Harold (ed.), *Émile Zola* (Philadelphia: Chelsea House, 2004).
Duffy, Larry, *Le Grand Transit moderne: Mobility, Modernity and French Naturalist Fiction* (Amsterdam: Rodopi, 2005).
Harrow, Susan, *Zola, the Body Modern: Pressures and Prospects of Representation* (Oxford: Legenda, 2010).
Hemmings, F. W. J., *Émile Zola*, 2nd edn (Oxford: Clarendon Press, 1966).
King, Graham, *Garden of Zola: Émile Zola and his Novels for English Readers* (London: Barrie & Jenkins, 1978).
Lethbridge, Robert, and Keefe, Terry (eds), *Zola and the Craft of Fiction* (Leicester: Leicester University Press, 1990).

Mitterand, Henri, *Émile Zola; Fiction and Modernity*, trans. and ed. Monica Lebron and David Baguley (London: Émile Zola Society, 2000).

Nelson, Brian, *Zola and the Bourgeoisie: A Study of Themes and Techniques in 'Les Rougon-Macquart'* (London: Macmillan, 1983).

Nelson, Brian (ed.), *The Cambridge Companion to Zola* (Cambridge: Cambridge University Press, 2007).

Nelson, Brian (ed.), *Naturalism in the European Novel: New Critical Perspectives* (New York and Oxford: Berg, 1992).

Wilson, Angus, *Émile Zola: An Introductory Study of his Novels* (1952); 2nd edn (London: Secker & Warburg, 1964).

Studies in English of The Dream

Emery, Elizabeth, ' "À l'ombre d'une vieille cathédrale romane": The Medievalism of Gautier and Zola', *French Review* 73 (1999), 290–300.

Emery, Elizabeth, 'Bricobracomania: Zola's Romantic Instinct', *Excavatio* 12 (1999), 107–15.

Emery, Elizabeth, '*The Golden Legend* in the Fin-de-Siècle: Zola's *Le Rêve* and its Reception', in *Medieval Saints in Late Nineteenth-Century French Culture*, ed. Elizabeth Emery and Laurie Postlewate (Jefferson, N.C.: McFarland Press, 2004), 83–118.

Grant, Elliott M., 'The Bishop's Role in Zola's *Le Rêve*', *Romanic Review* 53:2 (1962), 105–10.

Huebner, Steven, 'Naturalism and Supernaturalism in Alfred Bruneau's *Le Rêve*', *Cambridge Opera Journal* 11 (1999), 77–101.

Kent Bishop, Danielle, 'The Subversive Stitch: Embroidery as a Destabilising Force in *Le Rêve*', *Excavatio* 18 (2003), 169–78.

Matthews, J. H., 'Zola's *Le Rêve* as an Experimental Novel', *Modern Language Review* 52 (1957), 187–94.

Morowitz, Laura, 'Zola's *Le Rêve*: Naturalism, Symbolism and Medievalism in the Fin-de-Siècle', *Excavatio* 9 (1997), 92–102.

Stone, Barbara, 'Family Law in Zola: The Example of the Tutelle', *New Zealand Journal of French Studies* 29:1 (2008), 5–16.

White, Claire, 'Naturalism *in extremis*: Zola's *Le Rêve*', *Romance Studies* 33 (2015), 272–84.

Ziegler, Robert, 'Interpretation as Awakening from Zola's *Le Rêve*', *Nineteenth-Century French Studies* 21 (1992–93), 130–41; repr. in Bloom (ed.), *Émile Zola*.

Historical Background

Emery, Elizabeth, *Romancing the Cathedral: Gothic Architecture in Fin-de-Siècle French Culture* (Albany, N.Y.: SUNY Press, 2001).

Emery, Elizabeth, and Morowitz, Laura, *Consuming the Past: The Medieval Revival in Fin-de-Siècle France* (Aldershot, Hants.: Ashgate, 2003).

Fuchs, Rachel Ginnis, *Abandoned Children: Foundlings and Child Welfare in Nineteenth-Century France* (Albany, N.Y.: SUNY Press, 1984).

Saint-Aubin, Charles-Germain de, *Art of the Embroiderer*, trans. and annotated by Nikki Scheuer, with additional notes and commentaries by Edward Maeder (Los Angeles, Calif.: Los Angeles County Museum of Art, 1983).

Other Works by Zola in Oxford World's Classics

L'Assommoir, trans. Margaret Mauldon, ed. Robert Lethbridge.

The Belly of Paris, trans. Brian Nelson.

La Bête humaine, trans. Roger Pearson.

The Bright Side of Life, trans. Andrew Rothwell.

The Conquest of Plassans, trans. Helen Constantine, ed. Patrick McGuinness.

La Débâcle, trans. Elinor Dorday, ed. Robert Lethbridge.

Earth, trans. Brian Nelson and Julie Rose.

The Fortune of the Rougons, trans. Brian Nelson.

Germinal, trans. Peter Collier, ed. Robert Lethbridge.

His Excellency Eugène Rougon, trans. Brian Nelson.

The Kill, trans. Brian Nelson.

The Ladies' Paradise, trans. Brian Nelson.

A Love Story, trans. Helen Constantine, introduction by Brian Nelson.

The Masterpiece, trans. Thomas Walton, revised by Roger Pearson.

Money, trans. Valerie Minogue.

Nana, trans. Douglas Parmée.

Pot Luck, trans. Brian Nelson.

The Sin of Abbé Mouret, trans. Valerie Minogue.

Thérèse Raquin, trans. Andrew Rothwell.

A CHRONOLOGY OF ÉMILE ZOLA

1840   (2 April) Born in Paris, the only child of Francesco Zola (b. 1795), an Italian engineer, and Émilie, née Aubert (b. 1819), the daughter of a glazier. The naturalist novelist was later proud that 'zolla' in Italian means 'clod of earth'

1843   Family moves to Aix-en-Provence

1847   (27 March) Death of father from pneumonia following a chill caught while supervising work on his scheme to supply Aix-en-Provence with drinking water

1852–8   Boarder at the Collège Bourbon at Aix. Friendship with Baptistin Baille and Paul Cézanne. Zola, not Cézanne, wins the school prize for drawing

1858   (February) Leaves Aix to settle in Paris with his mother (who had preceded him in December). Offered a place and bursary at the Lycée Saint-Louis. (November) Falls ill with 'brain fever' (typhoid) and convalescence is slow

1859   Fails his *baccalauréat* twice

1860   (Spring) Is found employment as a copy-clerk but abandons it after two months, preferring to eke out an existence as an impecunious writer in the Latin Quarter of Paris

1861   Cézanne follows Zola to Paris, where he meets Camille Pissarro, fails the entrance examination to the École des Beaux-Arts, and returns to Aix in September

1862   (February) Taken on by Hachette, the well-known publishing house, at first in the dispatch office and subsequently as head of the publicity department. (31 October) Naturalized as a French citizen. Cézanne returns to Paris and stays with Zola

1863   (31 January) First literary article published. (1 May) Manet's *Déjeuner sur l'herbe* exhibited at the Salon des Refusés, which Zola visits with Cézanne

1864   (October) *Tales for Ninon*

1865   *Claude's Confession*. A *succès de scandale* thanks to its bedroom scenes. Meets future wife Alexandrine-Gabrielle Meley (b. 1839), the illegitimate daughter of teenage parents who soon separated; Alexandrine's mother died in September 1849

1866   Resigns his position at Hachette (salary: 200 francs a month) and becomes a literary critic on the recently launched daily *L'Événement* (salary: 500 francs a month). Self-styled 'humble disciple' of Hippolyte Taine. Writes a series of provocative articles condemning the official Salon Selection Committee, expressing reservations about Courbet, and praising Manet and Monet. Begins to frequent the Café Guerbois in the Batignolles quarter of Paris, the meeting-place of the future Impressionists. Antoine Guillemet takes Zola to meet Manet. Summer months spent with Cézanne at Bennecourt on the Seine. (15 November) *L'Événement* suppressed by the authorities

1867   (November) *Thérèse Raquin*

1868   (April) Preface to second edition of *Thérèse Raquin*. (May) Manet's portrait of Zola exhibited at the Salon. (December) *Madeleine Férat*. Begins to plan for the Rougon-Macquart series of novels

1868–70   Working as journalist for a number of different newspapers

1870   (31 May) Marries Alexandrine in a registry office. (September) Moves temporarily to Marseilles because of the Franco-Prussian War

1871   Political reporter for *La Cloche* (in Paris) and *Le Sémaphore de Marseille*. (March) Returns to Paris. (October) Publishes *The Fortune of the Rougons*, the first of the twenty novels making up the Rougon-Macquart series

1872   *The Kill*

1873   (April) *The Belly of Paris*

1874   (May) *The Conquest of Plassans*. First independent Impressionist exhibition. (November) *Further Tales for Ninon*

1875   Begins to contribute articles to the Russian newspaper *Vestnik Evropy* (*European Herald*). (April) *The Sin of Abbé Mouret*

1876   (February) *His Excellency Eugène Rougon*. Second Impressionist exhibition

1877   (February) *L'Assommoir*

1878   Buys a house at Médan on the Seine, 40 kilometres west of Paris. (June) *A Love Story* (*Une page d'amour*)

1880   (March) *Nana*. (May) *Les Soirées de Médan* (an anthology of short stories by Zola and some of his naturalist 'disciples', including Maupassant). (8 May) Death of Flaubert. (September) First of a series of articles for *Le Figaro*. (17 October) Death of his mother. (December) *The Experimental Novel*

1882   (April) *Pot Luck* (*Pot-Bouille*). (3 September) Death of Turgenev

1883 (13 February) Death of Wagner. (March) *The Ladies' Paradise* (*Au Bonheur des Dames*). (30 April) Death of Manet

1884 (March) *The Bright Side of Life* (*La Joie de vivre*). Preface to catalogue of Manet exhibition

1885 (March) *Germinal*. (12 May) Begins writing *The Masterpiece* (*L'Œuvre*). (22 May) Death of Victor Hugo. (23 December) First instalment of *The Masterpiece* appears in *Le Gil Blas*

1886 (27 March) Final instalment of *The Masterpiece*, which is published in book form in April

1887 (18 August) Denounced as an onanistic pornographer in the *Manifesto of the Five* in *Le Figaro*. (November) *Earth*

1888 (October) *The Dream*. Jeanne Rozerot becomes his mistress

1889 (20 September) Birth of Denise, daughter of Zola and Jeanne

1890 (March) *La Bête humaine*

1891 (March) *Money*. (April) Elected President of the Société des Gens de Lettres. (25 September) Birth of Jacques, son of Zola and Jeanne

1892 (June) *La Débâcle*

1893 (July) *Doctor Pascal*, the last of the Rougon-Macquart novels. Fêted on visit to London

1894 (August) *Lourdes*, the first novel of the trilogy *Three Cities*. (22 December) Dreyfus found guilty by a court martial

1896 (May) *Rome*

1898 (13 January) 'J'accuse', his article in defence of Dreyfus, published in *L'Aurore*. (21 February) Found guilty of libelling the Minister of War and given the maximum sentence of one year's imprisonment and a fine of 3,000 francs. Appeal for retrial granted on a technicality. (March) *Paris*. (23 May) Retrial delayed. (18 July) Leaves for England instead of attending court

1899 (4 June) Returns to France. (October) *Fecundity*, the first of his *Four Gospels*

1901 (May) *Toil*, the second 'Gospel'

1902 (29 September) Dies of fumes from his bedroom fire, the chimney having been capped either by accident or anti-Dreyfusard design. Wife survives. (5 October) Public funeral

1903 (March) *Truth*, the third 'Gospel', published posthumously. *Justice* was to be the fourth

1908 (4 June) Remains transferred to the Panthéon

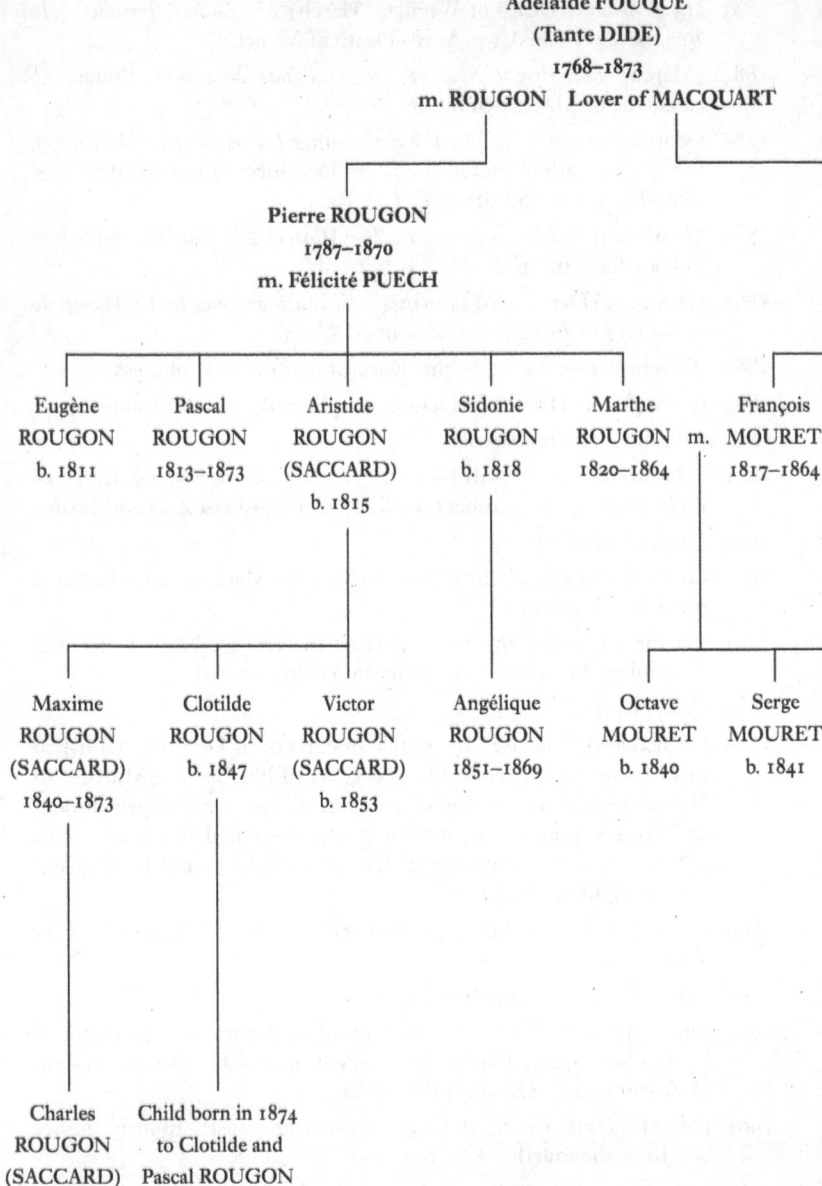

FAMILY TREE OF THE ROUGON-MACQUART

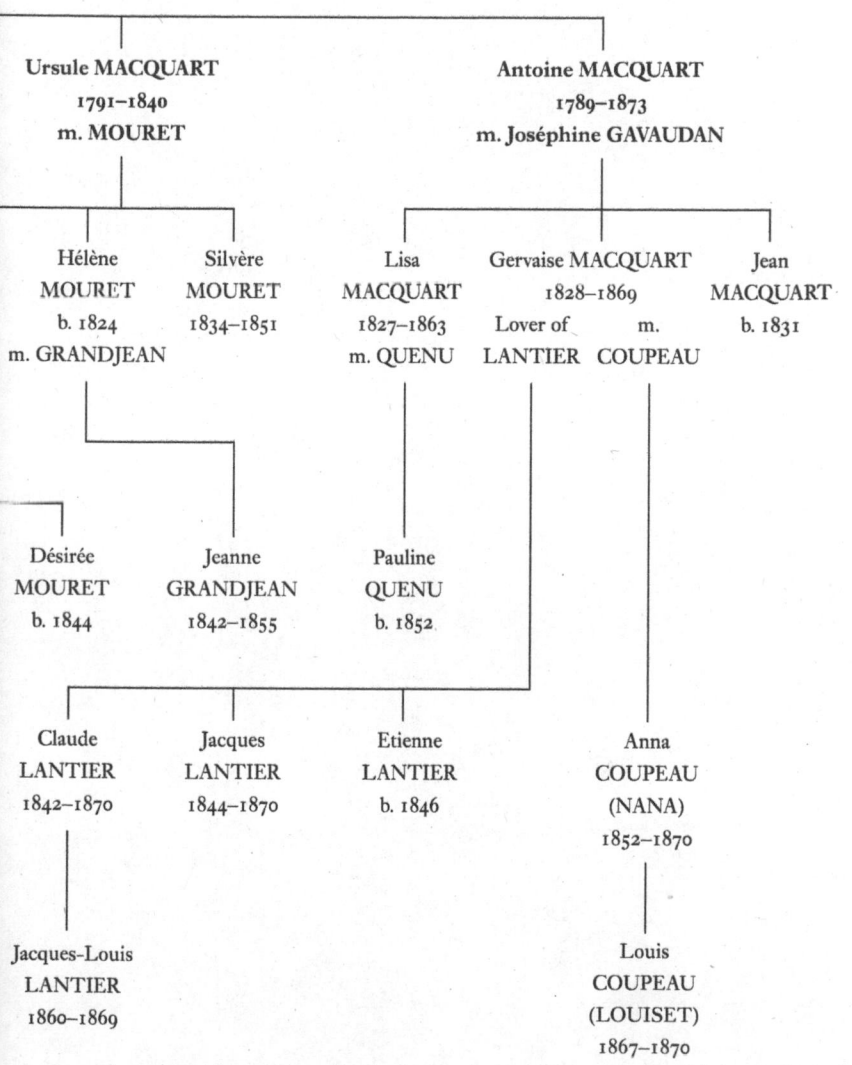

THE DREAM

CHAPTER 1

DURING the bitter winter of 1860 the River Oise* froze over and heavy snowfall covered the plains of Lower Picardy, and on Christmas Day a blizzard blew out of the north-east and almost buried the town of Beaumont. The snow, which had begun falling in the early morning, came down more heavily towards evening, and banked up all through the night. In the upper town, driven by the wind, the snow swept down the Rue des Orfèvres—at the far end of which rises the north face of the cathedral transept, hemmed in by buildings on either side—and beat against St Agnes's door, an ancient Romanesque portal which contains elements of the early Gothic,* elaborately adorned as it is with sculptures beneath a stark gable. By dawn the next morning the snow there lay almost three feet deep.

The street slumbered on, lethargic after the festivities of the previous day. Six o'clock struck. In the darkness tinged blue by the slowly, stubbornly falling flakes, a vague form offered the only sign of life—a little girl of 9, who had taken refuge beneath the arches of the portal, and had shivered through the night, sheltering there as best she could. She was dressed in rags, with a torn scarf wrapped about her head, and her bare feet thrust into a sturdy pair of men's shoes. Doubtless she had ended up there after wandering the town for many hours, and had collapsed, exhausted. She must have felt as though she had come to the ends of the earth, friendless, bereft and utterly abandoned, a prey to gnawing hunger and deadly cold. In her weakened state, choked by the weight of her sorrows, she had ceased struggling and moved only instinctively—shifting her position or burrowing into the old stones whenever a gust of wind sent the snow swirling.

The hours slipped slowly by. For a long time she propped herself against the central pier that divides the double doors of the twin bay, its pillar bearing a statue of St Agnes,* the 13-year-old martyr, a little girl like herself, carrying a palm branch with a lamb at her feet. Above the lintel, the whole legend of the virgin child betrothed to Jesus unfolds across the tympanum,* carved in high relief and suffused with simple faith. It tells how her hair grew down and covered her when the governor, whose son she had refused, sent her naked into houses of ill repute; and how the flames of the pyre turned aside from her limbs and burned the executioners when they set the wood alight. It tells of the miracle of her relics: how Constance, the emperor's daughter, was cured of leprosy;* and of the miracle of one of her painted effigies: how the priest Paulinus,* wracked by the desire to take a wife, on the pope's advice offered an emerald ring to the effigy, which held out a finger, and then withdrew it, keeping the ring (which it still wears)—thereby delivering Paulinus from temptation. At the apex of the tympanum, Agnes appears in a radiant circle of light as she is received into heaven, where Jesus, her betrothed, weds his delicate young bride with a kiss of eternal rapture.

When the wind blew down the street it whipped the snow straight into her face, heaping it into white drifts which threatened to engulf the doorway. And so the child crept to one side and huddled against the virgins that stand in the jambs,* above the stylobate.* These saints are Agnes's companions and her escort: three on her right, Dorothea, who survived in prison on miraculous bread,* Barbara, who lived in a tower,* and Genevieve, whose virginity saved Paris;* and three on her left, Agatha, whose breasts were twisted and torn,* Christina, who was tortured by her father,* and threw pieces of her own flesh in his face, and Cecilia, who was loved by an angel.* Above them, there are still more virgins, rising in three serried ranks along the curves of the voussoirs,* covering the three recessed arches with a great bloom of chaste and exultant flesh; below, they are martyred, crushed, and tortured, and, above, they are greeted by flights of cherubim as they rapturously enter into the company of heaven.

She had long been without shelter by the time eight o'clock struck and day began to break. By then the snow would have reached her shoulders if she had not trodden it down. Behind her the old door was covered with snow, as though cloaked with ermine, as flawlessly white as an altar of repose,* while above it, the grey façade was so smooth and bare that not a single snowflake clung there. The great saints in the jambs were completely coated with snow, from their white feet to their white hair, and shone with pale innocence. Above them, the scenes on the tympanum and the small saints in the archivolts* stood out in vivid relief, drawn with bright strokes against a dark background; and the stonework appeared thus all the way up to that final ecstatic scene, Agnes's wedding, which the archangels seemed to celebrate beneath a shower of white roses. Upright on her pillar, with her white palm branch and white lamb, the statue of the virgin child radiated pale purity, her snow-covered body immaculate in the paralysing cold which had frozen this mystical flight of triumphant virginity all around her. And at her feet, another, a poor, wretched girl, pale also in a mantle of snow, so pale and rigid, in fact, that she seemed to have turned to stone, and could no longer be distinguished from the great virgins.

Along the line of sleeping house-fronts a shutter clattered open, and she looked up. The noise came from her right—from the first floor of the house abutting the cathedral. A dark-haired woman of about 40, well-made and very beautiful, had leant out and seen the child stir. She did not at once draw in her bare arm despite the intense cold. An expression of sorrowful surprise overtook her composed features. She shuddered, and closed the window. The sight she had glimpsed remained with her: beneath the tattered scarf, a blonde-haired girl with violet-coloured eyes, a long face, and a very slender neck that had the elegance of a lily, poised on thin shoulders. But she was blue with cold, her little hands and feet appeared frozen, and that small cloud of breath was the only sign that she was still alive.

The child went on staring dully up at the house. It was an ancient, narrow, two-storey construction, built towards the end of the fifteenth century, and was attached to the wall of the cathedral itself, with buttresses on either side, like a wart that has grown between two toes of a colossus. Supported in this way, the house had been admirably preserved. The ground floor was built of stone, while the upper floor was timber-framed and faced with brick. The roof timbers projected a metre beyond the gable, and at the left-hand corner of the house stood a stair-turret which had a narrow window still with its original leading. On account of its great age, the house had undergone many repairs. The roof tiles must have dated from the age of Louis XIV.* It was easy to identify the work that had been done in that period: a small window had been inserted in the turret head; the original stained-glass windows had everywhere been replaced by wooden-framed windows. On the first floor, the central bay window in a row of three had been bricked up, lending the façade the symmetrical proportions of the other buildings in the street, which were of more recent date. The modifications which had been made on the ground floor were also plain to see: a door of moulded oak had replaced the old one with iron bands under the staircase; and, within the great central arch, the base, sides and summit had been bricked in, leaving just a rectangular opening—a sort of large casement—in place of the ogival bay* which had formerly given onto the street.

The child was still gazing blankly at this venerable building, the well-maintained abode of a master craftsman, and was reading a yellow sign nailed to the left of the door which bore the words *Hubert Vestment-Maker* written in ancient black lettering, when the banging of a shutter once again caught her attention. This time it was the shutter of the rectangular window on the ground floor. A man leaned out, his expression deeply troubled. He had an aquiline nose, a bulging forehead, and a thick head of hair which had already turned white, although he was only 45. He too studied the girl for a while, his broad, gentle mouth creased as though he were in pain. She watched him as he stood behind the little greenish panes. He turned around and made a sign, and his beautiful wife reappeared. Side by side, the couple stood motionless, staring at her sadly.

For four hundred years, generations of Huberts, each son an embroiderer like his father, had lived in the house. A master vestment-maker had built it during the reign of Louis XI;* another had made repairs to it while Louis XIV was on the throne. Like all his ancestors, this latest member of the Hubert line worked as an embroiderer there. At the age of 20 he had fallen so passionately in love with Hubertine, a girl of 16, that when her mother, a magistrate's widow, refused the match, he had run away with the girl and married her. She was marvellously beautiful—and this was the wellspring of their whole romance, their happiness and their misfortune. Eight months later, when she had come to her dying mother's bedside, she was pregnant; her mother disinherited her and cursed her so cruelly that the baby, born that same evening, did not survive. Ever since, the stubborn old lady had refused to grant forgiveness from her coffin in the graveyard, and the couple remained childless, despite their deepest longings. After twenty-four years they still wept for the child they had lost, and despaired of ever swaying the dead woman's resolve.

Unsettled by their gaze, the child had retreated behind the pillar of St Agnes. The street was starting to awaken, and she was greatly perturbed. Shops were opening up and people were venturing out. The Rue des Orfèvres terminates abruptly where it meets the lateral façade of the cathedral; on the apse side it is blocked off by the Huberts' house, and the only egress is by the Rue Soleil, a narrow lane which runs adjacent to the side aisle as far as the cathedral's main façade, where it opens into the Place du Cloître. As they passed by, two pious ladies glanced with surprise at this little beggar-girl whom they had never seen before in Beaumont. The snow continued falling, lightly but stubbornly, and the cold seemed to grow more intense as the wan day advanced. All that could be heard was a distant sound of voices, muffled and deadened by the great white shroud which lay across the town.

Shy of contact, and ashamed of her plight as though of some crime, she shrank back further. And then, all at once, she saw Hubertine—who did without a maid-servant and had stepped out to buy bread—standing in front of her.

'What are you doing there, child? Who are you?'

She did not reply, and simply hid her face. By now her limbs were numb, and she felt as though she were fainting—as though her heart had quite simply turned to ice and stopped beating. After the good lady turned away with a gentle shrug of pity, she sank to her knees, having reached the end of her strength, and collapsed into the snow like a crumpled rag. Snowflakes fell silently, covering her over. When the lady returned carrying her warm loaf, she saw the girl lying on the ground, and went up to her again.

'You can't stay under this porch, child.'

Hubert had come outside now and was standing on the doorstep. He took the bread from his wife, and said:

'Come on, pick her up. Bring her inside.'

Without another word, Hubertine lifted up the girl in her strong arms. The child did not flinch, and was carried off like a dead thing, her eyes shut tight, her teeth clenched, completely cold to the touch, as light as a fledgling that has fallen from its nest.

Once they were inside, Hubert closed the door and Hubertine carried her burden across the front room, which served as a sitting room and looked out into the street. Several panels of embroidery were on display in front of the great rectangular window. She went through to the kitchen, which had in past times been used as a common room, and was preserved almost intact, with its exposed beams, and its flagstones repaired in twenty different places, and its great fireplace and stone mantel. Arranged along the shelves were utensils, pots, kettles, and bowls, all dating from a century or two earlier, along with old earthenware, stoneware, and pewter vessels. In the middle of the hearth, however, stood a modern stove—a large, cast-iron model with shiny copper fittings. It was glowing red, and water could be heard bubbling away in a large kettle. A saucepan containing *café au lait* was warming to one side.

'Goodness, it's much nicer in here than outside,' said Hubert, placing the bread on a sturdy Louis XIII table* which stood in the centre of the room. 'Put the poor little thing in front of the stove to thaw out.'

Hubertine sat the child down and both of them watched as she started to come around. The snow which had lodged in her clothing began to melt and fell in thick droplets. Through the holes in her thick shoes they could see her bruised little feet. The thin dress she wore clung to her stiff limbs and revealed the outline of her pitiful little body which had already endured so much hardship and pain. She shuddered deeply, opening a pair of frightened eyes, and jumped like wild animal that has awoken to find itself caught in a trap. She seemed to try and hide her face beneath the ragged scarf she had tied under her chin. They thought her right arm must be crippled, so stiffly did she hold it across her chest.

'Don't be alarmed, we're not going to hurt you. Where are you from? Who are you?'

The more they spoke, the more frightened she became. She kept turning her head, as though expecting to find someone behind her ready to give her a beating. She cast furtive glances over the kitchen, the flagstones, the beams, and the shiny utensils. And then she looked outside, out through the two irregular-shaped windows which had been inserted into the old bay, and her gaze travelled all around the garden until it reached the white silhouettes of the trees which stood in the grounds of the Bishop's Palace and loomed over the far wall. She seemed surprised to see the cathedral again and the Romanesque windows of the apse chapels at the end of a pathway on the left. She shuddered deeply once more as the warmth from the stove began to spread through her body. And then she turned her eyes to the floor, and sat motionless.

'Are you from Beaumont?... Who is your father?'

Faced by her silence, Hubert imagined that her throat was perhaps too parched for her to speak.

'Instead of asking questions,' he said, 'we would be better off serving her a nice warm cup of *café au lait*.'

It was obviously a sensible idea, and Hubertine at once passed her own cup of coffee to the girl. She then cut two large pieces of bread for her, but the child was still wary, and shrank away. Soon though the torments of hunger proved stronger, and she ate and drank greedily. To avoid disturbing her the couple remained silent. They were distressed to see that the little girl's hand trembled so violently that sometimes she missed her mouth all together. She used only her left hand to serve herself, and held her right arm stubbornly to her body. When she finished, she almost dropped the cup, but wagged her arm lamely, and managed to catch it clumsily in the crook of her elbow.

'Have you hurt your arm?' asked Hubertine. 'Don't be scared, show me, my darling.'

But as Hubertine touched her, the girl reacted violently, leaping up and hitting out. In the ensuing struggle, she moved her arm away from her side, and a small book bound in cloth boards, which she had been hiding against her skin, fell out through a rip in her bodice. She tried to pick it up, and stood with her fists clenched angrily as she watched the two strangers open it and start reading.

It was a record book issued by the Child Welfare Services in the region of the Seine. On the first page, beneath a medallion image of St Vincent de Paul, appeared various printed headings. After 'Surname of child' a simple dash in ink filled the blank. Her 'Christian names' were recorded as 'Angélique Marie'. And as for her dates, she had been born on 22 January 1851, and admitted on the 23rd of the same month, with the registration number 1634. So her father and mother were unknown, and she had no other papers, not even a birth certificate. She had nothing apart from this coldly officious little book bound in pale pink cloth.* She had no one in the wide world, just this record of committal, which numbered and classified her utter abandonment.

'Oh, a foundling!' cried Hubertine.

All at once, Angélique burst into a rage, babbling:

'I'm better than all the rest, I am! I'm better, better, better... I've never stolen anything, but they steal everything I've got... Give me back what you've stolen.'

The Huberts watched astonished as she fervently proclaimed her own superiority, her little body quivering with impotent pride. They no longer recognized the blonde child with violet-coloured eyes and long neck graceful as a lily. Her eyes had turned black, her face was twisted with hatred, and her sensual neck had swollen as the blood pulsed through it. Now that she was warm she stood tall and hissed like a grass snake that has been rescued from the snow.

'Are you really a bad little girl, then?' said the embroiderer gently. 'We only want to find out who you are so we can help you.'

As his wife leafed through the book, he peered at it over her shoulder. The name of the foster mother was given on the second page. 'On 25 January 1851, the infant Angélique Marie was placed in the care of a foster mother Françoise, wife of Monsieur Hamelin, a farmer by profession, who lives in the commune of Soulanges,* in the district of Nevers, said foster mother receiving on their departure a month's food and a set of clothing.'* This was followed by a certificate of baptism, signed by the chaplain of the foundling hospital. There were also medical certificates completed when the child left the hospital and when she arrived at her destination. Four further pages were filled with columns containing details of the quarterly payments made, each one endorsed by the illegible signature of the tax official.

'What? Nevers!' cried Hubertine. 'You were brought up near Nevers?'

Unable to stop them reading the book, Angélique flushed, and sank into a defiant silence. But anger at last unsealed her lips, and she spoke of her foster mother.

'Mamma Nini would have thrashed you, that's for sure. She always stood up for me, even if she slapped me around now and then. I wasn't so badly off there, with all the animals...'

The words caught in her throat. She stammered out incoherent snatches about the meadows where she had taken their cow Red, the wide street where she had played with other children, the cakes she had baked, and a big dog that had bitten her.

Hubert interrupted her, reading aloud:

'In the case of serious illness or mistreatment, the deputy inspector is authorized to move the child to a new foster mother.'

Below it stated that on 20 June 1860, the child Angélique Marie had been placed with Thérèse, wife of Louis Franchomme, who were both artificial flower-makers residing in Paris.

'Now I understand,' said Hubertine. 'You fell ill and were taken back to Paris.'

But that was not it in fact. The Huberts learnt the full story only by drawing it out, little by little, from Angélique. Louis Franchomme, who was the cousin of Mamma Nini, had returned to his village for a month to recuperate from a fever. His wife, Thérèse, had quickly grown fond of the little girl, and had been allowed to take her back to

Paris on the understanding that she would train her as a flower-maker. Three months later her husband had died and, very sick herself, Thérèse had been forced to go and stay with her brother, a tanner named Rabier who worked in Beaumont. She had died there in early December, after entrusting her sister-in-law with the little girl—who had been beaten, bullied and abused ever since.

'The Rabiers,' whispered Hubert, 'you know, I've heard of the Rabiers! They're tanners who live down by the Ligneul,* in the lower town. The husband drinks, and his wife is thoroughly immoral.'

'They treated me like a stray child they'd picked up in the street,' raged Angélique, burning with injured pride. 'They said that a bastard's place was in the gutter. When she'd finished beating me, the woman would put out scraps of food on the floor for me, like I was her cat. Often I went to bed without eating... Oh, by the end, I felt like killing myself!'

She made an angry, despairing gesture.

'Yesterday, Christmas morning, they got drunk and grabbed me and threatened to gouge out my eyes with their thumbs, just for the fun of it. But it didn't work out like out, they started fighting instead and thumped each other so hard they both collapsed on the bedroom floor. I thought they were dead... I'd made up my mind to run away long before. But I wanted my little book. Mamma Nini would show it to me sometimes and say, "That's all you've got, you know, and if you didn't have that, you'd have nothing." And I knew where they hid it after Mamma Thérèse died—at the top of the chest of drawers... So I stepped over them and took out the book. I ran off holding it tight under my arm, next to my skin. But it was too big and I thought everyone would see it and try and steal it. Oh, I ran and ran! When it got dark I started to freeze under that doorway. I was so cold I thought I was going to die. But never mind, I haven't lost it, here it is!'

Just as the Huberts were closing the book to give it back to her, she darted up and tore it from their grasp. And then she sat down, slumping forwards on the table, and started sobbing, cradling the book in her arms, her cheek resting against the pink cloth cover. An agonizing humility overwhelmed her pride, and her whole being seemed to melt before these few, bitter pages with their dog-eared corners; it was a pitiful object, and yet her most treasured possession, offering as it did her only tie to the rest of humanity. She could never empty her heart of such profound despair, and her tears flowed on, unceasingly.

In this abject state, she regained her prettiness and became once again a little blonde child with a pure, almond-shaped face, pale, tender, violet-coloured eyes, and a delicate, elongated neck which gave her the appearance of a virgin in a stained-glass window. All of a sudden she took Hubertine's hand, pressed her eager lips against it and kissed it passionately.

The Huberts felt a surge of compassion and, on the point of tears themselves, stammered, 'Dear, dear child!'

So perhaps she wasn't thoroughly bad after all? It might be possible for them to set her straight, and curb these shockingly ferocious outbursts.

'Don't take me back there, I beg you!' she stuttered. 'Please don't take me back!'

The husband and wife exchanged glances. It just so happened that they had been thinking since the autumn about taking in an apprentice to live under their roof, a young girl who would brighten up a house made melancholy by their childless sorrow. They made up their minds at once.

'What do you think?' asked Hubert.

Hubertine answered calmly and deliberately. 'I think we should.'

They immediately busied themselves with the formalities. The embroiderer went and related the story to the magistrate of Beaumont's north canton, Monsieur Grandsire, one of his wife's cousins, the only relative with whom she still remained in contact. The magistrate took care of everything. He wrote to the Child Welfare Services, which quickly identified Angélique by her registration number, and he obtained permission for her to remain as an apprentice with the Huberts, who were widely recognized as a couple of the utmost propriety. The deputy inspector of the district came by to update her record book, and signed a contract with her new custodian, requiring him to treat the child with compassion, keep her in a state of cleanliness, and ensure that she attended school and church, and had a bed of her own. For its part, the welfare services undertook to pay Hubert the set fees and to issue her with clothing, in accordance with the regulations.

Within ten days, everything was settled. Angélique slept high up in the house in the attic bedroom, which had a view out onto the garden, and a storage room next to it. She had already begun to receive her first embroidery lessons. Before taking her to Mass on Sunday morning, Hubertine opened the old sideboard in the workshop where she kept the gold thread. She picked up the record book and placed it at the bottom of a drawer, saying:

'Look where I'm putting it, in case you ever feel like taking it out. Don't forget now.'

As she went into the cathedral that morning, Angélique found herself once again beneath the portal of St Agnes. There had been a partial thaw during the week and then the bitter cold had returned, and the snow covering the statues had half-melted and then set hard in a great mass of clumps and icicles. Everything was covered with a layer of ice, and the virgins were clad in transparent robes trimmed with glassy lace. Dorothea held a torch whose clear flames flowed downwards from her hands. A silver crown sat on Cecilia's head spilling out brilliant pearls. Agatha bore a crystal breastplate over flesh torn by pincers. And it was as though the scenes in the tympanum and the little virgins on the arches had been preserved like this for centuries behind the glass and jewels of some great reliquary. A courtly cloak, spun from light and embroidered with stars, trailed from Agnes's shoulders. Her lamb wore a fleece of diamonds, and her palm branch appeared a celestial blue. The whole portal gleamed with a pure light in the deep winter cold.

Angélique recalled the night she had spent there under the protection of the virgins. She looked up at them, and smiled.

CHAPTER 2

BEAUMONT* is made up of two completely separate and distinct towns. Perched on a hill, Beaumont-l'Église has an ancient cathedral begun in the twelfth century, and a bishop's palace, dating from just the seventeenth. Its population numbers barely one thousand souls, who live crammed into its narrow and stifling streets. By contrast, Beaumont-la-Ville, a former *faubourg* of the old town, lies at the foot of the hillside on the banks of the Ligneul, and has expanded and grown prosperous thanks to its lace and cambric factories. Its population has swelled to nearly ten thousand, and it can boast wide open squares and an attractive sub-prefecture building, constructed in the modern style. The two cantons, the northern and the southern, have scarcely any dealings with one another, and these are restricted almost entirely to administrative matters. Although it lies only thirty leagues* from Paris, a journey that can be made in two hours, Beaumont-l'Église seems immured within its ancient ramparts, which have in fact all been demolished apart from three gates. It has an unusually sedentary population who have continued to lead the same lives as their ancestors, each generation exactly like the previous, for five hundred years.

The cathedral accounts for everything, has brought everything into being, and preserves everything. A mother and a queen, it looms enormously over the little heap of low-standing houses, which shelter like a brood of chicks beneath its stone wings. The inhabitants live for it and by it. The artisans toil and the shopkeepers trade simply to nourish, clothe, and maintain the cathedral and its clergy. And while you may occasionally run into a few members of the bourgeoisie there, they are the last surviving remnants of a population that has long since departed. The cathedral beats at the centre, each street is one of its veins, and the town breathes only with its lungs. And so it is that the spirit of an earlier age endures, the past piously slumbers on, and the town around it, sequestered from the outside world, bathes in an age-old atmosphere of tranquillity and faith.

And of all the dwellings in this mystical town, the Huberts' house, where Angélique was to live from this time onwards, was the one that stood closest to the cathedral, and was in fact adjoined to its very flesh. Undoubtedly some priest of long ago granted permission for it to be built there, between two buttresses, in an attempt to secure the enduring services of a master vestment-maker and supplier to the sacristy—the ancestor of this line of embroiderers. The colossal mass of the cathedral loomed over the narrow garden, on the southern side; first there were the walls of the side chapels, whose windows looked onto the flowerbeds, and then the soaring body of the nave, supported by the flying buttresses, and finally the vast lead-sheeted roof. The sun never penetrated to the bottom of the garden, and ivy and box were all that flourished there. The great curved roof of the apse cast a perpetual shade, which was at once mild and sweet-smelling, holy, sepulchral, and pure. The cool tranquillity of the greenish half-light was disturbed only by the pealing of the bells which drifted down from the twin towers. The whole house would quiver then; it had merged and fused into the ancient stones, and was nourished by their lifeblood. The simplest of ceremonies would set the house atremble: High Mass, the rumblings of the organ, the choirmen's voices, right down to the troubled sighs of the faithful, would hum through all its rooms, soothing the house with a sacred breath, blown from invisible realms; and sometimes it seemed as though fumes of incense seeped through the warm walls.

For five years Angélique grew up there, as though confined within convent walls, far removed from the world. The only time she went out was on Sundays, when she went to hear the seven o'clock Mass. Hubertine had obtained permission to keep Angélique out of school, as she feared that the child might fall in with bad company. This cramped and ancient building, and its garden, in which a deathly hush prevailed, were Angélique's entire universe. She occupied a whitewashed bedroom under the eaves and came downstairs in the morning to have breakfast, and went back upstairs to the workshop and her embroidery on the first floor. These rooms, along with the turret containing the spiral stone staircase, were the only parts of the house she visited, and were in fact its oldest, not having been altered from one age to the next. She never entered the Huberts' bedroom, and only rarely ventured into the sitting room downstairs; these were the two rooms that had been redecorated according to modern tastes. In the sitting room, the beams had been plastered over and the ceiling ornamented with a central rose and palmette cornices. The wallpaper, which was patterned with large yellow flowers, dated from the First Empire,* as did the white marble chimney-piece and the mahogany furniture—a pedestal table, a sofa, and four armchairs covered in Utrecht velvet.* On the rare occasions when she came downstairs to change the pieces of embroidery that hung on display in the window, she sometimes glanced outside, and saw always the same unvarying scene: the portal of St Agnes blocking off the street; a pious old lady pushing open one of the doors, which then swung softly to; and, opposite, the shops of the goldsmith and the candle-maker with their rows of communion chalices and stout candles, where no customer ever seemed to enter. And all through Beaumont-l'Église—along the Rue Magloire, behind the Bishop's Palace, and the Grand'Rue, off which the Rue des Orfèvres runs, and in the Place du Cloître, dominated by the two soaring towers—a cloistral peace lulled the drowsy air and settled slowly with the pallid daylight onto the deserted cobbles.

Hubertine took it upon herself to complete Angélique's education. She subscribed to the old view that a woman's schooling is more than complete once she has mastered spelling and can do her sums. But she had to battle with the wayward child, who wasted many hours staring out the window, a very meagre diversion, as it was just the garden that lay beyond. Angélique took little interest in reading, and although she attempted many dictation exercises, drawn from a selection of classic authors, she never managed to spell out an entire page correctly. Nevertheless, her handwriting was very charming, and she confidently traced out her slender characters in the erratic style of a *grande dame* of a bygone age. In other areas, such as geography, history, and arithmetic, her ignorance remained untroubled. What was the point of knowledge? It was utterly useless. Later, when it was time for her first communion, she learnt the catechism by heart in such a burst of pious zeal that everyone was amazed by the accuracy of her recall.

Although they treated her gently, the Huberts often had cause to despair during that first year. Angélique displayed all the makings of a very fine embroideress, but bewildered them with her sudden changes of mood and inexplicable bouts of laziness after days of diligent application. She suddenly turned shiftless and sly, and pilfered sugar, her face appearing flushed, with dark rings under her eyes. If anyone tried to scold her, she answered back viciously. Sometimes when they tried to bring her to heel, her pride revolted and she flew into a wild frenzy, quivering tensely, lashing out with kicks and punches, raging to bite and scratch. They recoiled with fear before this little monster, horrified by the malign impulses that stirred within her. Who was she, then? Where had she come from? Foundlings, in most cases, are the children of criminality and vice. On two occasions, filled with sadness, and ruing their decision to take her in, they resolved to be rid of her and return her to the welfare services. But at the end of each of these terrible episodes, with the walls still ringing, the child dissolved in a flood of tears, offering up ardent expressions of remorse, and threw herself to the floor with such eagerness to receive her punishment, that they had to forgive her.

Little by little, Hubertine gained authority over her. With her warm and open nature, her imposing demeanour of calm strength, and her equitable good sense, she was made for instructing the child. She taught her renunciation and submission, setting these against passion and pride. Obedience was the essence of life. One had to obey God, parents, superiors, an entire hierarchy worthy of respect, beyond whose bounds life grew disordered and meaningless. After each act of defiance, she set the child some menial chore as punishment, as a way of teaching her humility—washing the dishes, cleaning the kitchen; and she stayed there until the job was done, ensuring that the child remained bent over the flagstones, raging at first, but in the end subdued. Hubertine was especially concerned by the child's passions, by the ardour and intensity of her caresses. On several occasions she had caught her kissing her own hands. She watched as the young girl worked herself into a feverish passion over images, little engravings of holy scenes, and the Jesus figurines she collected; and then, one evening, she found her in a faint, eyes damp with tears, her head slumped forward on the table, her mouth pressed against the pictures. When Hubertine confiscated these things a terrible scene ensued, the child screaming and weeping as though she were being flayed alive. From that time onwards Hubertine kept a tight rein on her and refused to tolerate her fits of passion, overwhelming her with work, surrounding her with silence and calm when she sensed that the child was starting to grow agitated, her eyes wild, her cheeks burning.

Hubertine found an aid in the book issued by the Child Welfare Services. Every three months when the tax official came to sign it, Angélique remained plunged in gloom until evening. A sharp pain ran through her breast if she chanced to glimpse the book as she fetched a bobbin of gold thread from the sideboard. On a day when she seethed with angry spite, and nothing could calm her, she was rummaging wildly through things at the back the drawer when the sight of the book appeared to stun her. Heaving great sobs, she threw herself at the Huberts' feet, humbling herself before them, stammering that they had been wrong to take her in, and that she was not fit to eat their bread. From that day on, the mere thought of the book was often enough to keep her anger in check.

In this way Angélique reached the age of 12, the age of first communion. The atmosphere of calm that enfolded the little house slumbering in the shadow of the cathedral, fragrant with incense and set quivering by hymns, aided the slow improvement of this wild shoot, uprooted from goodness knows where and replanted in the mystical soil of the narrow garden. Then, too, there was the ordered life they led, working every day, isolated from the outside world, with no sound from the sleepy neighbourhood ever reaching them. But the gentle spirit of the place was shaped above all by the great love the

Huberts shared, which seemed to have been deepened by an incurable remorse. For his part, Hubert spent his days trying to efface from his wife's memory the injury he had done her by marrying her against her mother's will. After the death of their child, he had felt very clearly that she blamed him for this punishment, and he had striven to obtain forgiveness. This had long since been granted; she loved him deeply. At times though he doubted it, and these doubts made him wretched. In order to be certain that the dead woman, her stubborn mother, had indeed relented as she lay there in the ground, he would have liked to have another child. This child of mercy was their sole desire, and he lived at his wife's feet, worshipping her with a conjugal passion that was both ardent and chaste, as though in a state of unending betrothal. Though he did not dare kiss her hair in front of their apprentice, he still entered their bedroom, after twenty years of marriage, troubled by the strong emotions a young groom feels on his wedding night. Their bedroom was styled simply, painted in white and grey, with wallpaper patterned in blue posies, and walnut furniture upholstered in cretonne. No sound ever came from it, but affection emanated from there, warming the whole house. Angélique was surrounded by love, and grew up very passionate and pure.

A book completed the undertaking. As she rummaged about one morning, turning everything on a dusty shelf in the workshop upside down, she discovered among the discarded embroidery tools a very old copy of *The Golden Legend* by Jacobus de Voragine.* This French translation, bearing a date of 1549, must have been bought many years before by some master vestment-maker intending to consult the pictures which were full of very useful information about the saints. For a long time she was interested in little apart from the pictures, old woodcut engravings fashioned with simple faith, which enchanted her. As soon as she was allowed to go off and play, she took the quarto volume, bound in yellow calfskin, and started leafing slowly through it; first came the half-title, in red and black, with the bookseller's address, 'At Paris, in the Rue Neufve Nostre Dame, at the sygne of Saynte Johan Baptest'; and then the title, flanked by medallion images of the four apostles, and framed below by the adoration of the three magi and above by the triumph of Jesus Christ trampling on the bones of the dead. And then the pictures followed on, ornamented letters, and large and middle-sized woodcuts in the running text, across page after page: the Annunciation, an enormous angel showering a frail

little Mary with rays of light; the Massacre of the Innocents, cruel
Herod in the middle of a pile of small corpses; the crib, with Jesus
between the Virgin and St Joseph, who is holding a candle; St John
the Almoner giving to the poor;* St Matthias smashing an idol;*
St Nicholas in bishop's garb with children in a tub* to his right; and
all the female saints, Agnes, her neck pierced by a sword, Christina,
her breasts torn by pincers, Genevieve, with her lambs following her,
Juliana receiving a flogging,* Anastasia being burnt alive,* Mary of
Egypt doing penance in the desert,* Mary Magdalene carrying the
bowl of perfume.* More and yet more of them streamed by, each
inspiring greater terror and pity; it was like one of those tales, at once
appalling and enchanting, that make your heart ache and moisten
your eyes with tears.

Little by little, Angélique became curious to know exactly what the
engravings represented. The two crowded columns of text, which
remained as black as at their first printing on the yellowed paper,
frightened her with their barbaric Gothic letters. However, she grew
accustomed to them, and learnt to decipher the characters and understand the abbreviations and contractions, and became adept at guess-
ing the meanings of expressions and archaic words. And at last she
was able to read them fluently, and rejoiced as though she had resolved
some mystery, and was filled with triumph whenever she overcame
some new difficulty. As she toiled away, a dazzling world emerged out
of the darkness and she entered into celestial splendour. The few classics she owned, cold, dry tomes, ceased to exist for her. It was the
Legend alone that fired her passion, and she would remain hunched
over it, her brow resting on her hands, so entirely absorbed that
ordinary life faded far away, and she was oblivious to time passing.
And all this while, out of the depths of the unknown, she beheld the
great dream blossoming.

God is a kindly figure, and then there are all the saints. They are
born predestined, voices herald them, and their mothers have dazzling dreams. They are all strong, beautiful and triumphant. They
are wreathed in light and their faces are radiant. Dominic has a star
on his brow.* They can read the minds of men and repeat aloud the
thoughts of others. They have the gift of prophecy and their predic-
tions always come true. Their number is infinite: there are bishops
and monks, virgins and prostitutes, beggars and lords of royal blood,
naked hermits living off roots, old men dwelling in caves with does.

They all share the same story: they grow up in the love of Christ, believe in him, refuse to sacrifice to false gods, are tortured and die in glory. Emperors grow weary of persecuting them. Hung upon a cross, Andrew* preaches to twenty thousand people over the course of two days. Mass conversions take place, and forty thousand men are baptized all at once. And if crowds do not convert after witnessing miracles, they flee in terror. Saints are accused of practising magic, they are given riddles which they unravel, and are pitted against learned men who are struck dumb. When they are brought into temples to be sacrificed, idols are overturned by a breath of air and shatter. A virgin ties her girdle around the neck of a Venus, which crumbles to dust. The ground trembles and the temple of Diana collapses, struck by a thunderbolt; people rise up in revolt, civil wars break out. And it is common then for torturers to ask to be baptized, and for kings to kneel at the feet of ragged saints, who have taken a vow of poverty. Sabina flees her father's house.* Paula abandons her five children* and abstains from bathing. They are purified by self-denial and fasting. They abjure wheat and oil. Germanus sprinkles his meals with ashes.* Bernard is unable to distinguish between different foods, and only recognizes the taste of pure water.* Agathon keeps a stone in his mouth for three years.* Augustine despairs of his sins,* such as taking enjoyment in watching a dog run. They disdain health and prosperity, and rejoice in the privations that kill the body. And so they dwell triumphantly in gardens where there are stars instead of flowers and the leaves of trees burst into song. They slay dragons, raise tempests and calm them; they hover in ecstasies two cubits* above the ground. Widows provide for their needs while they are alive, and are told in dreams to go and bury them when they die. Extraordinary events befall them, marvellous adventures, as thrilling as any of the old romances. And when their graves are opened after hundreds of years, sweet odours waft forth.

Facing the saints, there are devils, innumerable devils. 'They flee about us as flyes and fyl the ayer withoute nombre. This ayer is as full of devylles and of wycked spirytes as the sonne bemes ben full of small motes, whiche is small dust or poudre.'* And the battle wages eternally. The saints are always victorious, but they must repeat each victory over and again. The more devils driven away, the more return. Six thousand six hundred and sixty-six of them are counted in the body of a single woman, who is rid of them by Fortunatus.* They wriggle about, and speak and cry out in the voices of the possessed, whose flanks they set wildly aquiver. They get in through noses, ears and mouths, and exit howling after terrible struggles lasting days. At every bend in the road there flounders a man possessed, and a passing saint joins battle. Basil wrestles to save a young man.* After lying down in a graveyard, Macarius spends a whole night defending himself against an onslaught.* At the bedsides of the dead, the angels have no choice but to rain blows on the demons if they wish to take possession of the departing souls. On other occasions, it is a battle of minds and wits. Jokes are played, each tries to outsmart the other; the apostle Peter and Simon the Magician vie to outdo one another with their miracles.* Satan is always on the prowl, adopting any form he likes, disguising himself as a woman, or even taking on the appearance of a saint. But, as soon as he is defeated, his true ugliness appears: 'A blacke catte, whiche was more than a grete dogge, and had grete eyen and flambygne, her tongue longe, brode, and blody, and longe unto the navell. She had the tayle croked and reysed up on hygh, and shewed the after ende, out of whiche yssued a terryble stenche.'* He is all they think about, the great object of their hate. They fear him and they mock him. He is not even treated fairly. However terrible his cauldrons may seem, he remains the eternal dupe. All the pacts he makes are broken, by trickery or violence. Frail women knock him to the ground, Margaret crushes his head beneath her foot,* Juliana staves in his flanks with blows from an iron chain. And the sum of all this is that serenity prevails, along with scorn for evil, since it is impotent, and a conviction in the efficacy of good, since virtue rules supreme. All one has to do is cross oneself, and the devil is powerless: he lets out a howl and vanishes. When a virgin makes the sign of the cross, all the regions of hell cave in.

In the battle between the saints and Satan, many appalling torments are inflicted. Torturers smear martyrs with honey and leave them to the flies. They are made to walk barefoot over broken glass and glowing embers, and are dropped into ditches containing reptiles. They are lashed with lead-tipped whips, and are nailed alive into coffins, which are thrown into the sea. They are hung up by the hair and set on fire; their wounds are doused with quicklime, boiling pitch, or molten lead. They are made to sit in chairs of white-hot bronze; glowing helmets are thrust on their heads. Their flanks are burned with torches, their thighs broken on anvils, their eyes torn out, their tongues cut off, their fingers broken one by one. But their suffering does not matter; the saints remain disdainful, and accept further agonies impatiently, euphorically. A miraculous power protects them at all times, and they drive their torturers to exhaustion. John drinks poison and is none the worse for it.* Bristling with arrows, Sebastian* smiles. On other occasions, arrows hang suspended in mid-air to the martyr's right or left, or turn around and put out the eyes of the archer who had loosed them. They drink molten lead as though it were iced water. Lions lie down and lick their hands like lambs. St Lawrence finds his gridiron* pleasantly cool, and calls out: 'Thou cursed wretche, thou hast rosted the one syde, turne that other and ete, for it hath rosted ynough.'* Cecilia is set in a boiling bath 'whiche her semed was a place colde and well attempered, and she felte not one drope of swette'.* Christina is impervious to all forms of torture: her father has her beaten by twelve men who grow too weary to continue; another torturer takes over, ties her to a wheel, and lights a fire beneath her, and the fire spreads, incinerating fifteen hundred people. He throws her into the sea with a stone tied around her neck, but angels bear her up. Jesus comes and baptizes her himself, and then entrusts her to St Michael,* who brings her back to land. And, at the last, another torturer locks her in a room with vipers, which coil around her neck in a gentle caress, and so he leaves her in an oven for five days, but she just sings, and feels not the slightest discomfort. Vincent, who is subjected to even greater torments, remains untouched by pain: his limbs are broken, his ribs are raked with iron combs until his entrails spill out, he is stabbed all over with long needles, he is thrown onto a brazier whose coals are doused by the blood pouring from his wounds, he is returned to prison and his feet nailed to a post. Dismembered, burnt, his stomach gaping open, he remains alive; and his torments are transformed into the sweetness of flowers, the dungeon fills with dazzling light, and angels accompany him in song, all on a carpet of roses.* 'The swete sowne of the songe, and the swetenes and odour of the floures was smelled out of the pryson. And whan the kepers had seen this that they sawe within, they were converted and turned to the fayth. And whan Dacian herde this he was wood and sayd: What shall we do to hym more, we ben overcomen.'* This is the common cry of the tormentors; and the account always finishes with their conversion or their death. Their hands are struck by paralysis. They perish violently: they choke on fish bones, they are crushed by lightning bolts, their chariots splinter beneath them. The dungeons containing the saints fill with radiance and Mary and the apostles slip effortlessly through the walls. Help is always at hand and apparitions descend from an opening in the heavens, where God appears, holding a gem-encrusted crown. And so death is a thing of joy, which they defy, and parents are elated when one of their own succumbs. On Mount Ararat, ten thousand men expire on their crosses. Near Cologne, the eleven thousand virgins are slaughtered by the Huns. In the circuses, bones crack between the teeth of wild beasts. At the age of 3, Quiricus, who is endowed by the Holy Spirit with the ability to talk like a grown man, suffers martyrdom.* Children at the breast hurl insults at torturers. Disdain and loathing for the flesh, that tawdry human covering, sharpen their pain with exquisite celestial pleasure. It matters little whether the flesh is torn, crushed, or burnt; they welcome torment, endlessly: the flesh can never be violated enough. They all call out for a blade of iron, for a sword-thrust through the throat, which is the only thing that can kill them. Tied to the stake, with a wild, jeering mob all around her, Eulalia inhales the flames* so that she may die more quickly. God grants her wish, and a white dove flies out of her mouth and ascends to heaven.

Angélique was filled with wonder as she read. The litany of horrors, the triumph of joy—she thrilled to all this, so far was it out of the ordinary. But she was fond too of other, gentler aspects of the *Legend*—the animals, for instance, a whole ark's worth, which inhabit it. She was fascinated by the crows and eagles whose task it was to feed the hermits. And how many marvellous stories there were about lions! The helpful lion that digs a grave for Mary of Egypt; the flaming lion that guards the door to the houses of ill repute where the proconsuls bring the virgins; and Jerome's lion, which is given an ass to look after and, after it is stolen, goes off and fetches it back.* And then there is the wolf that is struck by remorse and returns a stolen pig. Bernard excommunicates flies,* which fall out of the air, dead. Remi* and Blaise feed birds at their table, bless them and restore them to health.* Francis, 'full of ryght grete simplycite lyke a dove', preaches to them, and exhorts them to love God.* 'There was also on a tyme a byrde upon a fygge tree besyde his cell, whiche sange oft full swetely, and saynt Fraunceys put forth his hande and called that byrde. And anone the byrde obeyed and came upon his hande. And he sayd to her: Synge my syster and prayse thy Lord. And than anone

she songe, and departed not tyll she had lycence.'* This passage was
an endless source of fascination to Angélique, who had the idea she
might try summoning swallows herself, and was curious to see if they
would come. And then there were the stories she couldn't reread
without laughing herself silly. Christopher, the gentle giant who carried Jesus,* brought tears of hilarity to her eyes. She choked with
mirth over the story of the governor's misadventures with Anastasia's
three chambermaids—he goes into the kitchen to find them, and kisses
the pots and pans, thinking he is kissing the women. 'He was so foule
horryble and blacke that whan he yssued out his meyny that awayted
his comynge supposed that he had ben out of his wytte. And they
bette hym well, and after fledde fro hym for fere, and lefte hym there
alone.'* She laughed deliriously whenever the devil received a beating, especially when Juliana, who was tempted by him in her cell,
gave him such an extraordinary flogging with her chains. 'Whan the
provost commanded to brynge forthe Iulyane before hym, she came
out drawyng after her the devyll. And the devyll cryed and sayd: My
lady Iulyane, I pray you, doo no harme unto me. And so she drewe
hym thurgh the market and afterward caste hym in to the foulest
pytt.'* As she worked on her embroidery, she recounted these legends
to the Huberts, which were far more interesting than any fairy tale.
She had read them so many times that she knew them by heart. There
was the legend of the Seven Sleepers, who fled from persecution,
were walled up in a cave, and slept for three hundred and seventy-
seven years and, when they finally awoke, caused much amazement
to the emperor Theodosius.* And then there was the legend of
St Clement, with its unending series of astonishing and heart-rending
adventures involving an entire family, a father, mother, and three sons,
driven apart by great misfortunes, but finally reunited thanks to the
most wonderful miracles.* Her tears flowed, she dreamt about the
legends at night, and she lived entirely in this tragic and triumphant
world of marvels, a supernatural realm where every virtue is rewarded
with unbounded happiness.

When Angélique made her first communion, she felt as though she
were hovering above the ground just like the saints. She was a young
Christian of the early Church and placed herself in God's hands, having learnt in the book that she could not be saved without grace. The
Huberts worshipped simply: Mass on Sundays and communion on
the great feast days. They did so with the quiet faith of the meek and,

in small part, out of a sense of tradition and for the benefit of their clientele, with all the vestment-makers' sons following their fathers' habit of taking Easter communion. Hubert sometimes left off tightening an embroidery frame to listen as the child read the legends aloud, and trembled just like her, his hair ruffling slightly in a breath of air from the invisible realms. He shared her passion and wept when he saw her in her white dress. That day passed as in a dream and both returned from the church weary and dazed. The ever-sensible Hubertine, who was critical of excess even where good things were concerned, felt obliged to reproach them that evening. From then on, she had to battle against Angélique's zeal and, in particular, the passion for charity that had seized her. Francis had taken poverty as his mistress, Julian the Almoner* called the poor his lords, Gervasius and Protasius* washed the feet of the wretched, and Martin shared his cloak with them.* Following Lucy's example, the child wished to sell up everything and give away the proceeds.* At first she disposed of the little things she owned, and then began to ransack the house. It reached the point where she was giving things away lavishly and indiscriminately to the undeserving. One evening, two days after her first communion, when she was reprimanded for throwing some clothes out of her window to a drunk woman, she relapsed into her old vicious ways, flying into a terrible frenzy. And then, overcome by shame, and unwell, she kept to her bed for three days.

The weeks and months slipped by. Two years later, Angélique had turned fourteen, and was becoming a woman. When she read the *Legend*, she heard a ringing in her ears, and the blood beat in the delicate blue veins around her temples; and she was filled now with a tender fellow-feeling for the virgins.

Virginity is the consort of the angels, the custody of all virtue, the conquest of the devil, and the dominion of faith. It offers grace and is invincible perfection. Lucy is made so heavy by the Holy Spirit that a thousand men and five pairs of oxen cannot fulfil the proconsul's order and drag her off to a house of ill repute. A governor who wishes to kiss Anastasia is struck blind. During their torments, the innocence of the virgins shines brightly and, when iron combs rake their white skin, rivers of milk, instead of blood, stream out. The story of a young Christian woman is repeated in ten different places: she flees her family disguised in a monk's robes and is then accused of wronging a local girl, and bears the calumny without protesting her

innocence, but triumphs at last when she is suddenly revealed to be an
innocent member of the other sex. Eugenia is brought before a judge,
whom she recognizes as her father, and so tears open her robe, revealing herself.* The battle to remain chaste is eternally fought afresh,
and goading desire continually strikes anew. And so it is wise for the
male saints to fear women. The world is strewn with pitfalls, and hermits go to the deserts, where there are no women. They struggle bitterly, flagellate themselves and throw themselves naked into brambles
or snow. A recluse helping his mother to cross a ford wraps his fingers
in his cloak. A bound martyr, tempted by a girl, bites off his own
tongue, and spits it in her face. Francis declares that he has no greater
enemy than his own body. Bernard cries out 'Stop thief!' to defend
himself against the lady of the house. When Pope Leo* administers
the host to a woman, she kisses his hand, and so he cuts it off at the
wrist, but the Virgin Mary restores it. They all extol the idea that
husbands and wives should live apart. Alexis, who is married and very
wealthy, advises his wife to remain chaste, and then goes away.*
Couples marry only as a precursor to dying. Justina is tormented by
the sight of Cyprian, resists, converts him, and walks with him to
their execution.* Cecilia is loved by an angel, and reveals this secret
on her wedding night to Valerian, her husband, who agrees not to
touch her, and to be baptized so that he may see the angel. He found
her 'within her chambre spekyng with an aungell, and this aungell
had two crownes of roses, whiche he helde in his hande, of whiche he
gave one to Cecylye and the other to Valeryan sayenge: Kepe ye these
crownes with an undefouled and a clene body.'* Death is stronger
than love;* it offers up a challenge to life. Hilary* beseeches God to
call his daughter Apia to heaven, so that she may avoid marrying; she
dies, and her mother asks the father to have her called up to heaven as
well; which is done. The Virgin Mary takes the fiancés of women for
herself. A nobleman related to the king of Hungary renounces a young
woman of great beauty as soon as Mary enters the contest. 'Anone
appered tofore hym the gloryous virgyn Marye and sayd to hym: I am
fayre and gracyous. Wherfore levest thou me and takest thou an other
wyfe?'* and he betroths her.

   Among all these female saints, Angélique had her favourites: those
whose lessons touched her heart, and moved her so deeply that she
changed her ways. She was captivated by the wise Catherine, who is
born in the purple, and displays immense learning at the age of 18

when she argues with the fifty orators and grammarians ranged against
her by the emperor Maximian.* She confounds them and reduces
them to silence. 'They were abasshed and wyst not what to saye, but
were styll. And the emperour was replenysshed with felony agaynst
them, and began to blame them by cause they were overcomen so
fouly of one mayde.'* The fifty then declare to him that they are converting. 'And whan the tyraunt herde this thynge he was esprysed
with grete woodnes and commaunded that they all shold be brent in
the myddes of the cyte.'* To Angélique, Catherine seemed the invincible philosopher, whose wisdom was as noble and as dazzling as
her beauty, the one saint she would have liked to be, so that she too
could have converted men, and been fed by a dove in prison, before
having her head cut off. But it was Elizabeth, daughter of the king of
Hungary,* above all, who served as an enduring exemplar. Every time
her pride revolted, or she was seized by violent anger, Angélique
thought about this woman, a model of kindness and simplicity, who is
full of piety at the age of 5, and refuses to play games, and sleeps on
the floor in homage to God; later she is the obedient and abstemious
wife of the landgrave of Thuringia, presenting a cheerful face to her
husband although she weeps floods of tears every night, and at the
last is a chaste widow, happy to live as a pauper after being driven
from her lands. 'Her clothynge was course and vyle, she ware a russet
mantell, her gowne of an other foule colour. The sleves of her cote
were broken and amended with peces of other colour.' The king, her
father, sends out an earl to fetch her back. 'Whan the erle sawe her syt
in suche an habyte and spynnyng, he escryed for sorowe and sayd:
There was never kynges doughter that ware suche an habyte, ne seen
spynnyng woll.'* She is the perfect embodiment of Christian humility, and lives among beggars, eating only black bread, and dresses
their wounds without the slightest repugnance, wears coarse clothing
like them, sleeps on the hard ground, and follows processions in
bare feet. 'She wasshed otherwhile the dysshes and the vessel of the
kechyn, and she hyd her otherwhile that the chamberers shold not let
her. And she wold say: Yf I coude fynde an other lyfe more despysed
I wold have taken it.'* And so Angélique, who had previously stiffened with anger when she was made to scrub the kitchen, now toiled
away at menial chores whenever the brutal urge to bully and humiliate stirred inside her. In the end, one saint was dearer to her than any
other, dearer even than Catherine and Elizabeth, and this was Agnes,

the child martyr. Her heart thrilled whenever she came across her in the *Legend*, for this virgin, with her cloak of long hair, had protected her in the cathedral doorway. How pure the flame of love burns within her when she is accosted at the school gate by the governor's son and turns him down! 'Go fro me thou fardell of synne, nourysshyng of evylles, and morsell of deth, and departe.'* How finely she glorifies her lover! 'I am now embraced of hym of whom the moder is a virgyn, and his fader knewe never woman. The sonne and the mone mervayle them of his beaute, by whose odour deed men ryse agayn to lyf.'* And when Aspasius* commands a soldier to 'put a swerde in her body', she ascends into paradise to be united with her 'whyte and rody spouse'.* For several months now, in times of distress, when the blood was throbbing feverishly in her temples, Angélique had appealed to Agnes, and begged for her help—and all at once she seemed to feel refreshed. Agnes was constantly to be glimpsed around her, and it dismayed her that she often did and thought things that must grieve the saint. One evening when she was covering her own hands with kisses, something she still occasionally liked to do, she suddenly blushed deeply and looked around, ashamed, even though she was alone, for she knew that the saint had seen her. Agnes was the guardian of her body.

At fifteen, Angélique was thus a delightful girl. Admittedly, not even the cloistered, hardworking life she led, the cathedral's peaceful shadow, and the *Legend* with all its lovely saints were enough to shape her into an angel or a creature of absolute perfection. She still flew into violent tempers and new faults reared up unexpectedly from the ungoverned recesses of her soul. Afterwards, however, she was thoroughly ashamed: she was striving so hard to be perfect! And she was, at heart, so compassionate, spirited, unworldly, and pure! On the way home from one of the long walks that the Huberts took twice a year, on Whit Monday and Assumption Day, she had pulled up a sweetbriar, and for fun had replanted it in their narrow garden. She clipped it and watered it, and it grew back straighter, and sprouted larger, sweet-scented roses—for which she had been waiting, with her customary passion, having been loath to make a graft to it, as she wished to see whether by some miracle it would flower. She danced around it, chanting with delight: 'It's me! it's me!' And if anyone teased her about the rosebush that she had plucked from the roadside, she would laugh too, her face a little pale as tears began to well. Her violet eyes were a little more gentle, her lips, parting slightly, revealed small white teeth, and her blonde hair, delicate as sunlight, haloed her long, oval face with gold. She had grown taller, but not thin, and still held her neck and shoulders with proud grace. She had a rounded bust and a supple waist, and was bright, healthy and exceptionally beautiful; her soul was chaste, her flesh innocent, and she bloomed with immense charm.

The Huberts' affection for her deepened with every passing day. The idea of adopting her had occurred to them both, but neither said anything for fear of reviving their perpetual sorrow. And so the morning when the husband came to his decision in the bedroom, his wife collapsed into a chair and burst into tears. Wouldn't adopting a child amount to giving up on ever having one of their own? Of course, at their age, they could never count on it happening; and so she agreed, won over by the lovely idea of making the girl her daughter. When they spoke of this to Angélique, she threw herself into their arms, choking on her tears. It was decided: she would stay with them in this home that she had already filled with her presence, and that had been rejuvenated by her youthful spirit and made merry by her laughter. But as soon as they took the first step, they were dismayed by an obstacle that arose. When they consulted the magistrate, Monsieur Grandsire, he explained that it was completely impossible for them to adopt Angélique, as any adoptee was required by law to be of age. Seeing how much this news upset them, Monsieur Grandsire suggested the expedient of establishing an unofficial guardianship:* any individual over 50 could legally take charge of a minor aged under 15 by becoming the child's unofficial guardian. The ages of the parties were suitable and they took up this suggestion, delighted; and it was even agreed that they would then confer adoption on their ward in their will, as permitted by the civil code. Monsieur Grandsire said he would take charge of the husband's application and the wife's authorization, and then wrote to the Director of Welfare Services, the legal guardian of all children in care, whose consent was required. The matter was investigated, and the documents were at last filed in Paris with the relevant magistrate. Only the final report remained to be delivered, constituting the deed of guardianship, when the Huberts were struck by a belated misgiving.

Before adopting Angélique in this way, shouldn't they make an effort to locate her family? If the mother were still alive, what right had they to decide the girl's fate without knowing for certain whether she had been abandoned? And then there was also that unknown factor, the degenerate stock from which the child perhaps came, which had caused them concern before, and which now returned to worry them. It tormented them so much they could no longer sleep.

Hubert left abruptly for Paris. It was a great disruption in his peaceful existence. He lied to Angélique, saying that he was required in person to make the final arrangements for the guardianship. He hoped to know everything within twenty-four hours. But in Paris the days went by, and obstacles arose at every step. He spent an entire week there, was sent from one official to the next, and traipsed endlessly about, distraught and on the verge of tears. At first he received a very brusque reception at the Child Welfare Services. The administration had a rule that children could not be informed about the circumstances of their birth until they reached the age of majority. He was sent away three mornings in a row. He had to be persistent, and explained his case in four different offices; he grew hoarse presenting himself as her unofficial guardian, until at last a deputy chief clerk, a tall, curt fellow, deigned to inform him that no precise documentation whatsoever existed in the matter. The administration knew nothing: a midwife had brought in Angélique Marie without giving the mother's name. At his wits' end, he was just about to set off for Beaumont again when an idea struck him, and he returned for a fourth time—and asked to see the birth certificate, which would naturally record the midwife's name. Another ordeal ensued. At last he obtained a name—Madame Foucart, and even learnt that in 1850 this woman had been living in the Rue des Deux-Écus.

And so he ran around town once more. One end of the Rue des Deux-Écus had been pulled down, and none of the shopkeepers in the neighbouring streets could remember a Madame Foucart. He consulted a directory, but her name was not to be found. Peering up at the shop signs, he realized he had no choice but to go up and speak to the different midwives; and this was in fact how he found out what he wanted. He had the good luck to come across an old lady who cried out that certainly she knew Madame Foucart! Such a worthy woman, who'd had so many strokes of bad luck! She lived in the Rue Censier, on the other side of Paris. He rushed over there.

Having learnt from experience, he resolved to make a more diplomatic approach. But Madame Foucart, an enormous woman mounded onto two short legs, did not allow him to ask his questions in the careful order he had prepared. As soon as he mentioned the child's Christian names and her date of admission, Madame Foucart broke in and related the whole story in a flood of rancour. Oh, so the little girl was still alive! Well she could be proud to have an utter whore for a mother! Yes indeed, Madame Sidonie,* as she was known since she became a widow, a woman with very good family connections, whose brother was a government minister, it was said—although that didn't stop her from engaging in the most shameful activities! And she explained how she had come to know her—when the slut was running a shop in the Rue Saint-Honoré selling fruit and olive oil from Provence, soon after arriving from Plassans, which she and her husband had left in order to seek their fortune. With her husband dead and buried, she had given birth to a child fifteen months later, without knowing exactly where she had got it, for she was as dry as an invoice, as cold as an overdue notice, and as brutal and uncaring as a bailiff's officer. A mistake can be forgiven, but ingratitude! After the shop had gone under, hadn't she, Madame Foucart, provided for her during her confinement; hadn't she gone so far as to take the child off her hands by placing it with the authorities? And her reward for all this was that when she, in turn, had fallen on hard times, she hadn't even been able to get a month's rent out of her, let alone the fifteen francs she had lent her from her own purse. These days Madame Sidonie had a little shop and three upstairs rooms in the Rue du Faubourg-Poissonnière where, under the pretence of selling lace, she sold all sorts of things... Oh yes, indeed, if you had a mother like that, you were better off not knowing her!

An hour later Hubert was loitering outside Madame Sidonie's shop. He caught sight of a thin, pale woman, of uncertain age and rather sexless, wearing a threadbare black dress covered in all sorts of stains from her dubious activities. Never had any memory of her daughter, born of a chance encounter, warmed her mercenary heart. He made discreet enquiries and learnt things that he never repeated to anyone, not even his wife. Yet still he hesitated, and he came back one last time to walk past the mysterious narrow-fronted shop. Shouldn't he make himself known and obtain her consent? It was up to him, a man of propriety, to decide whether he had the right to sever this tie once and for all. Abruptly he turned around and, that evening, went back to Beaumont.

Hubertine had in fact just learnt at Monsieur Grandsire's office that the legal document granting unofficial guardianship had been signed. And when Angélique threw herself into Hubert's arms, he saw clearly from the expression of pleading enquiry in her eyes that she had understood the real purpose of his journey. So he said to her simply:

'My child, your mother is dead.'

Angélique, in tears, hugged them fiercely. Nobody ever mentioned the matter again. She was their daughter.

CHAPTER 3

THAT year, on Whit Monday, the Huberts took Angélique on a picnic to the ruins of Hautecœur Castle,* which stand above the Ligneul two leagues downstream from Beaumont. And after a day spent running about and laughing in the open air, the next morning, when the old clock in the workroom struck seven, the young girl slept on.

Hubertine had to go up and knock on her door.

'Come on, lazybones!... The rest of us have already finished breakfast!'

Angélique dressed quickly and went down to breakfast by herself. A little later, coming into the workroom where Hubert and his wife had just sat down to their tasks, she said:

'I was in such a deep sleep! And we promised that chasuble for Sunday!'

The workshop, whose windows looked onto the garden, was a single vast room, and had been preserved almost entirely in its original state. In the ceiling, the two main beams and three rows of exposed joists, covered in soot and riddled with wormholes, had never been whitewashed and, in the gap between the joists, the laths could be seen behind flaking plaster. There was a date on one of the stone corbels supporting the beams, 1463, which was no doubt the year of construction. The chimney-piece, its stone now cracked and crumbling, retained a simple elegance, with its slender cheeks, consoles, and hood rising to a crown. The naive figure carved in the frieze seemed to have melted away over the years, though could still be identified: it was St Clair, the patron saint of embroiderers.* The fireplace no longer served its original function; the hearth had been converted to an open cupboard by the addition of shelves, which were piled high with drawings. The room was now heated by a stove, a large bell-shaped model in cast iron, which had a flue that ran along the ceiling and into the hood of the chimney-piece. The doors to the room were very rickety and dated from the time of Louis XIV. Some of the battens in the old parquet floor had almost completely rotted through, and lay alongside newer strips that had been placed, one by one, in the gaps. The old yellow wall-paint had lasted for nearly a hundred years, faded up towards the ceiling, covered in scuff marks lower down, and stained with patches of damp. Every year there was talk of repainting, but no decision was ever taken, out of an aversion to change.

Seated at her embroidery frame, Hubertine looked up from the chasuble that was spread out there and said:

'Do you remember what I said? If we deliver this on Sunday, I'll bring you a basketful of pansies for your garden.'

'Oh, yes, I remember!' Angélique called back, cheerfully. 'I'd better get on with it then! But where did I put my ring-thimble? Our tools just seem to vanish as soon as we put them down.'

She slipped the old ivory ring onto the second joint of her little finger, and sat down on the other side of the frame, facing the window.

No alterations had been made to the workroom since the middle of the previous century. Fashions were changing and the embroiderer's craft was evolving, but, embedded in the wall, a heavy brace—a piece of wood supporting the embroidery frame at one end, as a movable trestle did at the other—remained where it had always been. Old tools slumbered in the corners: a diligent,* with its cogwheels and pins, by which one could transfer spooled gold thread onto a spindle without touching it with one's hands; a hand-held spinning wheel, a sort of pulley, which twisted together different threads that were attached at one end to the wall; and tambours* of all sizes, with their hoops and taffetas,* used for crochet embroidery. An old collection of spangle punches lay on a shelf, alongside a relic, a large traditional copper candlestick that had served the embroiderers of bygone days. In the loops of a rack, made by nailing a strap onto the wall, hung bodkins, mallets, hammers, irons for cutting vellum, and small box-wood chisels used for shaping thread as it was worked. Under the lime-wood cutting table there stood a yarn windle, consisting of two cage-like revolving wicker cylinders, around which a skein of red wool was trained. Chains of brightly coloured silk spools, strung onto a cord, hung by the sideboard. On the floor lay a basket heaped with empty spools. A ball of string had rolled off a chair, unravelling a little.*

'Oh, what a lovely day, what a lovely day!' said Angélique. 'It's a joy to be alive.'

And, before settling down to work, she stared dreamily out of the open window for a few moments longer as the radiant May morning flooded in. A patch of sunlight glanced off the roof of the cathedral and the scent of fresh lilacs rose from the garden of the Bishop's Palace. She sat there in rapture, smiling as the spring flowed all around her. Then, awakening with a start, she said, 'Father, I haven't any gold thread.'

Hubert, who was just finishing the job of pricking out the design for a cope* onto a piece of tracing paper, went and took a spindle from the bottom of the sideboard. He cut the thread into lengths, scratching the gold off the silk at each end. Then he brought the lengths over to her, wrapped in a roll of parchment.

'Is that all you need?'

'Yes, yes.'

She had given a quick look around to make sure that she had everything else: spindles wound with different shades of gold thread, red, green or blue; spools of silk thread of every hue; spangles and coiled gold wires set out in the cut-down crown of a hat that served as a little box; long fine needles, steel pliers, thimbles, scissors and a ball of wax. All these things were laid out on the frame itself, on a sheet of stiff grey paper protecting the taut fabric.

She threaded a needle with a length of gold thread. But as she made the first stitch the thread broke, and she had to rethread it, scratching off a little of the gold which she discarded into a small cardboard waste box, which also sat on the frame.

'Oh, at last!' she breathed, when she had completed her first stitch.

A profound silence descended. Hubert had begun to tighten a frame. He had placed the two side bars opposite one another on the brace and trestle, just far enough apart to accommodate the crimson silk of the cope, which Hubertine had just finished sewing on to the webbing. He inserted the laths into the mortises on the side bars, and fastened them there with four pegs. And after sewing in a series of string loops on the left and right sides, he finished tensioning the frame and took out the pegs. When he tapped with his fingertips on the fabric, it thrummed like a drum.

Angélique had become an expert embroideress, and the Huberts were filled with amazement at her skill and discernment. What she had been taught was only one side of it; she also brought her own passions to bear, which animated her flowers and infused her symbols with faith. Silk and gold thread came alive in her hands, her smallest figures shone with mystical beauty. She gave herself up entirely to her work, which was continually enriched by her fertile imagination and her belief in a world beyond appearances. Several of her embroidered pieces had so impressed the diocese of Beaumont that one priest, who was an archaeologist, and another, a connoisseur of paintings, had come to visit her, and had gone into raptures over her Virgins, which they compared to the naive figures of the primitives. Her work had the same sincerity, the same feeling for a realm beyond this one, all captured in minutely perfect detail. She had a talent for drawing that was frankly miraculous, shaped not by any teacher, but simply by the evening study she had done by lamplight; and so she was able to improve on her models, or simply abandon them, trusting instead to her imagination, and bringing forth astonishing creations with the point of her needle. The Huberts, who had once thought that formal instruction in drawing was essential for any embroiderer, deferred to her, despite their much greater experience. And as time passed they became content to work simply as her assistants, and she was given all the most lavish pieces to do, while they simply prepared the bases.

In the course of the year, how many gleaming, sacred marvels passed through her hands! She spent her days in a haze of silk, satin, velvet, and gold and silver cloth. She embroidered chasubles,* stoles,* maniples,* copes, dalmatics,* mitres, banners, and veils for chalices and ciboria.* But, above all, there were the chasubles, an unending series of them in their five different colours: white for the confessors and virgins, red for the apostles and martyrs, black for the dead and days of fasting, violet for the Innocents, and green for all feast days. Gold too was often used, since it could replace white, red, and green. The same symbols could always be found at the centre of the cross, the monograms of Jesus and Mary, a triangle surrounded by rays of light, the lamb, the pelican, the dove, a chalice, a monstrance,* a bleeding heart wrapped in thorns, while the upright of the cross and its arms were garlanded with ornamental patterns and flowers—all the patterns old-fashioned ones, and all the flowers large blossoms, anemones, tulips, peonies, pomegranates, and hortensias. Not a season passed without her reworking symbolic ears of corn and grapes—in silver on a black background, or in gold on a background of red. For especially costly chasubles she created entire scenes in finely nuanced shades, with the heads of the saints crowding around a central frame showing the Annunciation, the Nativity or the Crucifixion. Sometimes the orphreys* were embroidered onto the fabric itself, and sometimes she sewed stripes made of silk or satin onto gold or velvet brocade. And, piece by piece, this profusion of sacred grandeur flowered from her slender fingers.

At this precise moment, the chasuble Angélique was working on was one of white satin, and its cross was formed by a spray of golden lilies intertwined with bright roses in subtle shades of silk. At the centre of the cross, in a wreath of little roses in matt gold, Mary's richly ornamented monogram gleamed in red and green gold.

In the hour that passed while she was finishing off the leaves of the little gold roses in satin stitch,* not a word was spoken. But her thread broke again, and she reinserted it into the needle by touch alone, under the frame, with much skill. Now that she had looked up, she appeared with one long draught to drink in the mild spring air that was flowing into the room.

'Oh, wasn't it a lovely day yesterday!...' she murmured. 'How nice the sun felt!'

Hubertine, who was waxing her thread, nodded her head.

'I'm all done in—my arms have gone completely numb. I'm not 16 like you any more, and we hardly ever go out!'

Yet immediately she went back to her work. She was preparing the lilies, sewing on cut-outs of vellum in the places that had been marked, so that the flowers would stand out above the level of the fabric.

'And, of course, that first dose of spring sunshine can leave you with a bad headache,' added Hubert, who, with his embroidery frame taut, was about to pounce the orphrey band onto the silk cope.

Angélique still wore a faraway expression, and gazed dreamily at a beam of sunlight reflecting down from one of the cathedral's flying buttresses.

'No, no,' she said softly, 'our day outside left me feeling refreshed, it helped me to relax.'

She had finished the small gold leaves, and began work on one of the large roses. Close at hand lay needles threaded with silk thread of every hue, and she embroidered in split stitches* following the curve of the petals. And, despite the intricacy of the work, memories of the previous day, which she had been silently recalling a few moments before, now tumbled from her lips in such profusion it seemed she might never stop. She recalled their departure, the open countryside, their picnic among the ruins of Hautecœur. They had lunched sitting on the flagstones of a hall, surrounded by crumbling walls, overlooking the Ligneul which glided among willow trees fifty metres below. The ruins of the castle had captured her imagination—its scattered bones, overgrown with brambles, attesting to the immense size of the colossus, which, while it had stood, had commanded two valleys. The keep was still there, rising sixty metres into the air, riven with cracks, its upper section missing, but solid nevertheless on its fifteen-foot-thick foundations. Two towers had also survived, the tower of Charlemagne and the tower of David, which were connected by an almost perfectly preserved curtain wall. Within, a few buildings still stood, the chapel, the hall of justice and a few bedchambers. Everything they came across seemed to have been built by giants: the steps of the staircases, the sills of the windows, and the benches on the terraces were all constructed on a scale vast by modern standards. It had been nothing less than a complete fortified town; five hundred armed men could have withstood a siege of thirty months without running short of munitions or food. For two centuries, wild roses had been prising apart the bricks in the lower rooms, lilacs and laburnums had flowered on the rubble of fallen ceilings, and a plane tree had grown in the guardroom fireplace. At sunset, however, when the shadow of the crumbling keep stretched out across the fields for three leagues, the castle seemed to grow whole once more, colossal in the evening mist, and then one felt again its ancient dominion, its brute resilience—which had made it the impregnable fortress before which even the kings of France had trembled.

'And I'm sure it's inhabited by spirits,' Angélique went on, 'who come back at night. You hear all sorts of voices, animals everywhere stare at you, and just as we were leaving I turned round and saw great white figures floating above the walls... Mother, you know all about the history of the castle, don't you?'

Hubertine smiled serenely.

'Ghosts... well, I've never seen any.'

But she did indeed know the history of the castle, having read about it in a book and, as the young girl pressed her with questions, she was obliged to relate it again.

The territory had belonged to the see of Reims ever since the time
of St Remi, to whom it had been granted by Clovis.* In the early years
of the tenth century an archbishop, Séverin, had built a fortress at
Hautecœur to defend the region against the Normans, who had sailed
up the Oise, the river into which the Ligneul flows. The following
century, one of Séverin's successors gave the territory in fee to
Norbert, a cadet of the house of Normandy, for an annual rent of
sixty sous,* on the condition that Beaumont and its church would be
left unmolested. That was how Norbert I became the first of the marquises of Hautecœur, whose famous lineage throng the annals of history. Hervé IV, twice excommunicated for theft of Church property,
was a highway robber who, in one encounter, slit the throats of thirty
rich commoners with his own hand. He was so bold as to wage war
against Louis the Fat,* who razed his tower to the ground. Raoul I
went on crusade with Philip Augustus and died before the walls of
Acre,* a spear thrust through his heart. But most illustrious of all
was John V the Great,* who rebuilt the fortress in 1225, raising the
redoubtable castle of Hautecœur in under five years and, for a brief
time, within the shelter of its great walls, dreamt of usurping the
throne of France. Having come through the slaughter of twenty
battles, he died in his bed, a brother-in-law to the king of Scotland.
And then there were Félicien III, who walked barefoot to Jerusalem,
and Hervé VII, who laid claim to the throne of Scotland, and many
other powerful and noble figures down through the centuries to
Jean IX, who, under Mazarin, suffered the anguish of witnessing
the castle's demolition.* After the final siege, the vaults of the towers
and the keep were brought down with mines, and the buildings
reduced to ashes. Here Charles VI had sought diversion in his madness* and, nearly two hundred years later, Henri IV had spent a week
with Gabrielle d'Estrées.* All these royal memories now slumbered in
the grass.

Never ceasing to ply her needle, Angélique listened eagerly, as though
the vision of these past grandeurs had drifted out of her embroidery
frame while the rose took shape there in a subtle array of living colours. Her ignorance of history made these events seem even more sen-
sational, as though they belonged to miraculous legends. She trembled
with pious rapture, and in her mind the castle grew whole once more,
towering right up to the gates of heaven, and the Hautecœurs seemed
to rub shoulders with the Virgin Mary.

'And our new bishop, Monseigneur d'Hautecœur*—is he a descendant of that family?' she asked.

Hubertine replied that Monseigneur must belong to the cadet branch, since the senior branch had long been extinct. It was a remarkable turn of events, as for centuries the marquises of Hautecœur had fought with the clergy of Beaumont. In around 1150, an abbot had begun the construction of the church, drawing solely on the resources of his order. As a result, he soon ran short of money, at a point when the building had reached only the level of the vaults in the side chapels. They had had to settle for covering the nave with a wooden roof. Eighty years passed and, after rebuilding the castle, Jean V made a donation of three hundred thousand livres,* which, combined with other sums, allowed work on the church to continue. The nave was completed. The two towers and the main façade were only finished much later, around 1430, and bore all the flourishes of the late Gothic style. To reward Jean V for his generosity, the clergy accorded him and his descendants the right to burial in one of the apse chapels, dedicated to St George, which had ever since been known as Hautecœur chapel. But the good relations could not last. The castle posed a constant threat to Beaumont's franchises, and quarrels continually erupted on questions of tribute and precedence. One matter in particular, the toll that the lords of the castle claimed the right to impose on traffic along the Ligneul, gave rise to endless disputes. It was at this time that the lower town began to grow prosperous on the back of its fine textile mills. From then on Beaumont's wealth grew from day to day, while that of the Hautecœurs declined, until the castle was finally demolished, and the church triumphed. Louis XIV turned the church into a cathedral, the Bishop's Palace was built on the site of the old abbey close, and chance ordained that a Hautecœur should return as bishop to lead a still-thriving clergy, the same body that had defeated his ancestors in a struggle lasting four hundred years.

'But Monseigneur was once married,' said Angélique. 'Doesn't he have a grown-up son of 20?'

Hubertine had picked up her scissors to trim one of the vellum pieces.

'Yes, the Abbé Cornille* told me about it. Oh, it's such a sad story!… Monseigneur was made a captain at the age of 21, during the reign of Charles X. In 1830,* at the age of 24, he resigned his commission, and people say that he led a wild life after that, travelling, adventuring, and duelling, until he was in his forties. And then one evening while staying with friends in the country, he met the daughter of the count of Valençay,* Paule, who was very rich, miraculously beautiful, and had only just turned 19—she was twenty-two years his junior. He fell madly in love with her, and she adored him. They had to marry in haste. It was then that he bought back the ruins of Hautecœur for a song, ten thousand francs, I think, with the aim of repairing the castle where he dreamt of settling with his wife. For nine months they lived hidden away on an old property in Anjou* and refused to see anyone. The hours seemed to rush by all too quickly... Paule had a son, and died.'

Hubert, who was dabbing at his pattern with a pounce-bag containing white powder, looked up, his face ashen.

'Oh, the poor soul,' he murmured.

'They say that he almost died of grief,' Hubertine continued. 'A week later, he entered holy orders. All this happened twenty years ago, and he is bishop now... They also say that for twenty years he refused to see his son—the child who had cost his mother her life. He got rid of the child, placing him with one of her uncles, an old priest. He refused to hear any news of him, and tried to forget the child existed. One day he was sent a portrait of the little boy, and had the impression he was looking again at his dear dead wife. He was found stretched out on the floor, his body rigid, as though felled by a hammer blow. But age and prayer must have eased his great sorrow, for the good Abbé Cornille told me yesterday that Monseigneur has just sent for his son to come and live with him.'

Having finished the rose, which appeared so fresh its scent seemed to drift up from the satin, Angélique gazed once more through the sun-lit window, lost in thought. 'Monseigneur's son...,' she repeated softly.

Hubertine was nearing the end of her story.

'A young man, as handsome as a god, apparently. His father wanted him to join the clergy. But the old priest disagreed, saying the child lacked the calling... And he has millions! Fifty million, they say. His mother left him five million, which was invested in Paris property, and is now worth more than fifty. In short, he's as rich as a king!'

'As rich as a king, as handsome as a god,' repeated Angélique in a vague, dreamy tone.

And mechanically she picked up a spindle of gold thread from the frame, for she was about to begin a large lily in guipure.* After drawing out a strand from the top of the spindle, she sewed down its end with a stitch of silk thread right at the edge of the vellum, which was used to give depth to the figure. And, as she worked on, immersed in vague yearnings, she murmured again:

'Oh, what I'd like, what I'd like…,' without completing her thought.

A profound silence settled once more, broken only by a muffled sound of singing coming from the cathedral. Hubert was painting on his design, using a small brush to go over the dotted lines that had been marked out in powder. In this way the decoration appeared in white on the red silk of the cope. It was he who spoke next.

'Things were splendid in the old days. The lords all wore garments stiff with embroidery. In Lyons, embroidered fabric could fetch up to six hundred livres an ell.* You should read the statutes and ordinances of the master embroiderers, which state that embroiderers of the king have the right to use force of arms to requisition female workers from other masters… And we had a coat of arms: azure, a fesse diapered or, accompanied by three fleurs-de-lis the same, two in chief, one in base…* Ah, those were the days!'

He fell silent, and tapped with his fingernails on the frame to shake off the remaining powder. Then he went on:

'In Beaumont they still recount a legend about the Hautecœurs that my mother often told me when I was little… A terrible plague was ravaging the village, and half the inhabitants were already dead when Jean V, the one who rebuilt the fortress, understood that God had endowed him with the power to combat the plague. And so he went barefooted to the sick, knelt down, and kissed them on the mouth, saying: "If God wills, I will." As soon as his lips touched theirs, the sick were cured. And that is why those words have remained the motto of the Hautecœurs, who were ever after able to cure the plague… Oh, what brave men, a true dynasty! As for Monseigneur, before entering holy orders he was called Jean XII, and his son's Christian name must also be followed by a number, just like a prince's.'

Everything he said nourished and prolonged Angélique's reverie. She said once more, in the same dreamy tone:

'Oh, what I'd like, what I'd like…'

Holding the spindle without touching the thread, she embroidered in guipure, drawing the gold strand from right to left across the vellum, and then back again, sewing it down at each turn with a silk stitch. Gradually the great golden lily began to bloom.

'Oh, what I'd like, what I'd like, is to marry a prince... A prince I'd never seen before, who would come one evening at sunset and take my hand and carry me away to his palace... And what I'd like is for him to be extremely handsome and immensely rich, oh! the handsomest and the richest man who has ever lived! Horses would neigh beneath my window, streams of jewels would cascade into my lap, and showers of gold would pour from my hands, great streams of it, whenever I opened them... And what I'd also like is for my prince to love me madly, and for me to love him, just as madly. And we would remain young, virtuous, and noble for ever and ever!'

Leaving his frame, Hubert came up to her with a smile, while Hubertine affectionately wagged a finger at the young girl.

'Oh, you vain, greedy child—you're incorrigible! You've got completely carried away with the idea of becoming a queen! At least this dream of yours isn't as dreadful as stealing sugar or answering back. But at the root of it all lies the devil—it's pride and passion talking again!'

Angélique looked at her with an amused expression.

'Mother, Mother, what are you saying?... Is it wrong to love whatever is beautiful and rich? I love it precisely because it is beautiful, because it is rich, because, I think, it brings joy to my heart... You know very well that I'm not selfish. Money, ah! you'd see what I'd do with money if I had masses of it. I'd drench the town with it, the poor would swim in it. It would be a great blessing—no more poverty! First of all though I'd make you and father rich; I'd like to see you dressed in brocade like a lord and lady of old.'

Hubertine gave a shrug.

'You're mad!... My child, you're poor, you won't have a sou when you marry. How can you dream of marrying a prince? Would you marry a man richer than yourself?'

'Of course I would!'

She was completely taken aback.

'Of course I'd marry a rich man!... If he had money, why would I need any? I would owe everything to him, and so would love him even more.'

Hubert was delighted by her triumphant logic, and willingly joined the child in this flight of fancy.

'She's right,' he cried.

His wife glanced at him unhappily, and her face grew stern.

'You'll find out how things work later, young lady. You'll learn about life.'

'Life? I know all about life already.'

'Where have you had the chance to learn about life?... You're too young, you know nothing about evil. Listen, evil exists, and it is all-powerful.'

'Oh, evil, *evil...*'

Angélique pronounced the word slowly, as though trying to grasp its full meaning. And in her limpid eyes there appeared that habitual expression of innocent surprise. Evil? She was familiar enough with that—she had read all about it in the *Legend*. Wasn't evil just the devil? And hadn't she seen that, though the devil always returns, he's always defeated? Each battle ended with him lying crumpled on the ground, terribly beaten, a pitiful figure.

'Oh, Mother, if you knew how I scoff at the idea of evil!... To lead a happy life, one just has to control one's passions.'

Hubertine shook her head, looking anxious and perturbed.

'You'll make me wish I hadn't brought you up by yourself in this house, with just the two of us for company, in such an out-of-the-way corner, seeing so little of life... What paradise exactly have you created in your dreams? How do you imagine the world?'

The young girl's face lit up with unbounded hope as she sat there, leaning over the frame, drawing out the thread from the spindle in one continuous movement.

'Do you think I'm being silly, Mother?... The world is full of decent people. If you are honest and hard-working, you will always be rewarded... Oh, I know there are bad people too, a few, anyway. But what do they matter? You just avoid them, and they soon get punished... To me, the world, when I look at it from a distance, appears just like a vast garden—that's right, an immense park bursting with flowers and sunshine. It's so wonderful to be alive; life is so lovely that it can't really be governed by evil.'

She was growing animated, as though uplifted by the sight of all the shimmering silk and gold around her.

'Happiness is something very simple. We are happy living here. Why? Because we love each other. There you have it—it's no more complicated than that... And when the man I'm waiting for comes along, you'll see. We'll recognize each other straightaway. I've never seen him, but I know exactly what he'll be like. He'll walk in and say: "I've come to take you away." And I'll reply: "I was waiting for you. Take me away." And he will take me with him, and we'll be together for ever. We'll go away to his palace and sleep on a gold bed encrusted with diamonds. Oh, it's really very simple.'

'You're mad, stop talking like this!' said Hubertine severely.

And seeing her so excited, and about to soar off into her dream world once more, Hubertine said:

'Stop! You're frightening me... Wretched girl. Once we've married you off to some poor devil, you're going to fall back to earth and break your bones. Happiness for poor people like us can only be found in humility and obedience.'

Angélique continued smiling, stubbornly serene.

'I'm waiting for him, and he will come.'

'But she's right,' cried Hubert, equally excited, his imagination roused. 'Why do you tell her off?... She's so beautiful that a king could come and ask for her hand. Anything could happen.'

Hubertine looked up with sadness in her wise and lovely eyes.

'You mustn't encourage her in her folly. You understand better than anyone else the cost of following your heart.'

He turned very pale, and thick tears gathered on his eyelids. Immediately she felt sorry for having rebuked him, and got up and held out her hands to him. But he broke away, stuttering:

'No, no, I was in the wrong... You must listen to your mother, Angélique, do you hear? We're both completely mad, and she's the only sensible one... I was wrong, very wrong...'

He was too upset to sit down again, and so left aside the cope that he had recently tensioned, and instead set about applying paste to a banner that had been finished and was still in its frame. Taking a pot of Flanders glue* from the sideboard, he used a brush to coat the reverse side of the fabric, so as to reinforce the embroidery. His lips still trembled slightly, and he did not speak.

Angélique fell silent too, in deference to their wishes, but went on quietly dreaming, soaring higher and higher into the empyrean of desire. Her whole appearance gave her away: her lips parted in ecstasy, her eyes reflecting the infinite blue of her vision. And now she embroidered this dream, a poor girl's dream, with her golden thread: it gave rise to the great lilies, and the roses, and the Virgin Mary's monogram which spread across the white satin. The stem of the lily, done with chevron couching,* flew upwards like a beam of light, while the long, slender leaves, fashioned from spangles, each one attached with a strand of purl,* hung down in a shower of stars. At the centre, Mary's monogram dazzled the eye with its thick gold relief, worked in guipure and waffle stitch, blazing out like a burnished tabernacle* aflame with mystical light. And the delicate silk roses sprang with life, and the whole chasuble glowed a flawless white, blossoming with miraculous gold.

After a long silence, Angélique looked up. She gave Hubertine a mischievous glance, shook her head, and said:

'I am waiting for him, and he will come.'

It was a mad chimera, but she clung to it. It would all happen just like that, she was sure of it. Nothing could shake her smiling conviction.

'Everything is going to happen just as I've said, Mother.'

Hubertine decided to have a little fun with her. 'But I thought you didn't want to get married,' she teased. 'Those female saints you're so taken with never married, did they? Rather than going along with it, they converted their fiancés, or ran away from home and got their throats slit.'

The young girl listened to her, startled. And then she let out a great burst of laughter. All her brimming vitality and love of life rang out in her full-throated mirth. The stories of the saints were all from so long ago! Times had certainly changed, and a victorious God no longer asked people to die for him. In the *Legend* it had been the marvels that had fascinated her, rather than any contempt for life or longing for death. Oh yes indeed, she certainly did wish to marry, and love, and be loved, and be happy!

'Be careful!' Hubertine continued, 'or you'll make your guardian Agnes weep. Don't you remember how she turned down the governor's son and chose to die, so she could marry Jesus?'

The great bell in the tower began to toll and a flock of sparrows flew out of a thick knot of ivy that wound around one of the apse windows. In the workroom, Hubert, still sunk in silence, had hung up the damp banner to dry on one of the huge iron nails embedded in the wall. As the sun rose higher, it tracked across the room, lighting up the old tools, the diligent, the wicker cylinders, and the copper candlestick. When it reached the two women, it set ablaze the frame at which they were working, its laths and side-bars polished by use, flames dancing up from all the little things resting on the fabric, the coiled gold wire and the spangles in their small holder, the bobbins of silk, and the spindles of fine gold thread.

As the mild spring sunshine streamed in, Angélique looked at the large symbolic lily she had just completed. And she replied with joyous conviction:

'But Jesus is the one I want!'

CHAPTER 4

ALTHOUGH high-spirited and vivacious, Angélique loved solitude and took great delight in spending time alone in her room in the mornings or evenings. There, she could let herself go and fully savour her escape into the world of dreams. Sometimes, when she was able to dart up during the working day, she was overwhelmed by happiness, as though she had somehow broken free and run far away.

Her vast bedroom took up half the space under the roof, and the store room occupied the rest. Everything in her room was whitewashed, the walls, the joists, and even the exposed rafters. Against all this bare whiteness, the old oaken furniture appeared black. When the sitting room and the bedroom downstairs had been redecorated, all the old furniture, dating from many different eras, had been brought up here: a Renaissance chest, a Louis XIII table and chairs, an enormous Louis XIV bed, a beautiful Louis XV wardrobe.*
A white porcelain stove and a small dressing table covered with an oilcloth stood incongruously among these venerable artefacts. The huge bed, especially, with its drapes of antique pink chintz, patterned with bouquets of heather, the pink so faded that it was barely distinguishable, retained a grandeur commensurate with its great age.

But what Angélique loved most of all was the balcony. Two French windows had formerly opened onto it, but the one on the left had simply been nailed shut, and the balcony, which before had run the length of the whole storey, now ran only in front of the right-hand window. As the joists below were still sound, a new wooden floor had been laid down, and an iron railing screwed in to replace the old rotten banister. It was a delightful little spot, a cosy sort of nest under the tip of the gable, sheltered beneath the roof laths, which had been replaced at the start of the century. If you leant out, you could see the whole of the garden-side façade, looking very dilapidated, with its base course of masonry, the stones cut very small, its timber frame and brick facing, and its broad bay, which had since been narrowed. Down below, the kitchen door was surmounted by a zinc awning. And higher up, the floor beams of the attic, jutting out a metre like the roof timbers, were reinforced by brackets whose feet rested on the string course of the ground floor. The balcony was thus enclosed in a great tangle of timberwork, hidden away in a forest of old wood, which wallflowers and mosses decorated with their greenery.

Since moving into her bedroom, Angélique had spent many hours leaning on the railing, gazing out. Directly below her lay the garden, gloomy beneath the perpetual verdure of the large box trees. In one corner, up against the cathedral, a clump of scraggy lilacs clustered around an old granite bench; while in the other, half-hidden by the ivy that cloaked the whole back wall, stood a small gate that opened into the Clos-Marie, a vast tract of waste ground. The Clos-Marie had once been the monks' orchard. A lively little stream, the Chevrotte, ran across it, in which women from the neighbouring houses were allowed to wash their clothes. A few homeless families squatted in the ruins of an old decrepit mill, but nobody else lived in the field. An alleyway, the Ruelle des Guerdaches, which ran between the high walls of the Bishop's Palace and those of the Voincourt residence, linked it to the Rue Magloire. In summer, the centuries-old elm trees in the two parks hid the narrow horizon behind green crests, while to the south it was obscured by the enormous curve of the cathedral. Enclosed on all sides, the Clos-Marie slumbered in peaceful neglect, overgrown with wild grasses, dotted about with poplars and willows sown by the wind. The Chevrotte leapt and bounded among the stones, burbling an unending crystal song.

Angélique never tired of gazing at this forgotten little spot. And, for seven years, the scene that had greeted her each morning was always the same. The trees in the Voincourt residence, whose façade looked onto the Grand'Rue, were so dense with foliage that it was only in winter that she ever caught sight of the countess's daughter, Claire, a girl of her own age. In the bishop's garden the greenery was even thicker, and she tried in vain to catch a glimpse of Monseigneur's soutane. The old shuttered gate that gave into the close must have been sealed shut long before, for she could never once remember having seen it opened, even just to let a gardener through. Apart from housewives beating their washing, the only people she ever saw there were the same little paupers in rags, lying in the grass.

Spring, this year, was delightfully mild. She was 16, and until now she had always been happy just to watch the Clos-Marie turn green again in the April sunshine. The growth of tender young leaves, the limpid skies of the warm evenings, the earth's fragrant process of renewal—she found it all simply enchanting. But this year, with the arrival of the first buds, her heart had quickened. She felt within her a mounting tumult as the grass sprang higher and the wind bore a more pungent scent of vegetation. At times, for no reason, she suddenly felt as though she could hardly breathe. One evening she threw herself weeping into Hubertine's arms, although she wasn't at all upset—on the contrary, she was brimming with happiness. At night, especially, she had exquisite dreams, shadowy shapes swirled round her, and she swooned in ecstasies she dared not recall on waking, so bewildered was she by the bliss the angels brought her. Sometimes, buried deep under all her bedclothes, she would awake with a start, her hands pressed together and held tightly against her breast, feeling so short of breath that she had to spring barefoot onto the floor and run to open the window, lingering there, trembling and dazed, as the fresh air flowed soothingly around her. She lived in a state of perpetual wonderment, astonished to find that she could no longer recognize herself—her whole being uplifted by joys and sorrows she had never known before, as her womanhood began to burst magically into bloom.

What was going on? Were the unseen lilacs and laburnums of the Bishop's Palace really so sweet-scented that she could not inhale them without a pink flush spreading across her cheeks? Never before had she noticed all the warm fragrances that now caressed her with their living breath. And, in previous years, how had she never spotted the big paulownia in flower, its great sprays of mauve blossoming between two elms in the Voincourts' garden? This year her eyes clouded with emotion when she saw it, so deeply was she moved by its pale violet colour. And she could never remember having heard the Chevrotte chatter so noisily over the pebbles and among the rushes of its banks. Surely the stream was speaking, and as she listened to the vague words it repeated over and over, her agitation grew. Had the field ceased to be what it had always been? Everything in it now filled her with surprise, and seemed to brim with new meaning. Or was it rather she

who had changed, so that now she felt, and saw, and heard life burgeoning in every part of it?

But the cathedral on her right, blocking out the sky with its vast
bulk, surprised her even more. Every morning she felt as though she
were seeing it for the first time, and was moved by a discovery she
made: she understood that the old stones were as capable of loving
and thinking as she herself. There was nothing rational about this
intuition and she could never have explained it: she simply gave herself up to the mystical spirit that suffused the giantess, which had
taken shape across three centuries, and been layered over with the
beliefs of many generations. Lower down, among the Romanesque
chapels of the ambulatory, with their bare, round-arched windows,
adorned with nothing more than slim colonnettes under the archivolts, it was as though the cathedral were kneeling, its head bowed in
prayer. And then its spirit seemed to be drawn upwards, as it turned
its face to heaven, and lifted up its hands—among the ogive windows
of the nave, built eighty years later, tall, graceful windows, with mul-
lions rising up to pointed arches and roses. And finally it soared clear
of the earth, surging rapturously upwards through the piers and flying buttresses of the choir, which had been remodelled two centuries
later in high Gothic style and embellished with spirelets, turrets, and
pinnacles. At the base of the flying buttresses, there were gargoyles
to disgorge rainwater from the roof. A trefoil* balustrade had been
added along the edge of the terrace over the apse chapels. The roof
storey had also been adorned with finials.* And the whole edifice
seemed to blossom out as it soared endlessly upwards towards heaven,
set free from the old priestly terrors, mounting higher and higher
to bury itself at last in the bosom of a loving and forgiving God.
Angélique shared this surging sense of exhilaration, which filled her
with light-heartedness and joy, as though she were singing a pure,
exquisite hymn that drifted up and lost itself on high.

The cathedral was, indeed, a living thing. Swallows in their hundreds had built nests under the band of trefoils and in the hollows of
the spirelets and pinnacles, and mobs of them were forever darting
about the buttresses and piers. There were also wood pigeons from
the elms of the Bishop's Palace, which puffed out their throats as
they strolled at a very leisurely pace along the edge of the terrace.
Sometimes a crow, lost high up in the blue, appearing no bigger than
a fly, could be glimpsed perching on the tip of a spire, smoothing

down its feathers. A great variety of plants, lichens and grasses that grow in the cracks of walls, brought life to the old stones, threading them with the mute toil of their roots. On days when there were heavy downpours, the whole apse awoke and began to roar, as the rains lashed against the lead tiles of the roof, pouring down the channels of the galleries, tumbling from one level to the next with a noise as deafening as a raging torrent. The fearsome gales of October and March filled it with a soul, a voice of anger and woe, as they tore through the forest of gables and arcades, colonnettes and roses. And, eventually, the sun brought new life to it once more in shifting patterns of light—the cathedral appearing pale golden and fresh-faced in the dawn, but falling under a shroud of mystery as the shadows slowly lengthened at evening. The cathedral had its inner life, too, which surged through it like a great pulsing in its veins, and during the ceremonies the whole place vibrated with pealing bells, organ music, and the chanting of the priests. The interior constantly echoed with life: there were muffled noises, the murmurs of Low Mass, the rustle of a woman kneeling, and a faint tremor, barely perceptible—the pious fervour of a prayer, offered with no words and no movement of the lips.

Now that the days were growing longer, Angélique spent a great deal of time in the mornings and evenings leaning on the balcony, alongside her dear friend the cathedral. She loved it still more in the evenings when its vast bulk stood out starkly against the starry sky. Its planes and angles gradually dissolved until she could barely make out the flying buttresses flung out like bridges into the void. She had the sense that it remained awake in the darkness, filled with the contemplation of seven centuries, teeming with all the crowds that had come before its altars in hope or despair. It observed an unending vigil, proceeding from the infinity of past time towards the eternity to come, the mysterious and terrifying vigil of a house where God never slept. And the spot to which her eyes always returned on this dark, motionless but living mass was the window of a choir chapel level with the bushes in the Clos-Marie, the only one that was ever lit up, like a vague eye staring at the night. Behind the window, at the corner of a pillar, there burned a sanctuary lamp. This chapel was, in fact, that which the clergy had in earlier times granted to Jean V of Hautecœur and his descendants, along with the right of burial, as a reward for their generosity. Dedicated to St George, it had a twelfth-century stained-glass window in which was depicted the legend of the saint. As twilight fell, this legend once again took shape in the darkness, luminous as a vision; and that was why Angélique, her eyes dreamy with enchantment, adored it.

The window had a blue background and a red border. Against this rich, dark background, the figures stood out in vivid hues, their naked forms outlined by swirling drapery, each section being made from pieces of coloured glass, shaded with black, and set in lead. Three scenes from the legend were set in the window, one on top of the other, right up to the archivolt. In the bottom one, the king's daughter, arrayed in her royal garments, had been led out of the town to where she should be devoured, and met St George beside a lake, from which the monster's head was already emerging. A banner bore these words: 'Good knyght, perysshe ye not for my sake, for ye may not help me ne delyver me, and wold perysshe with me.' The middle scene contained the battle, the saint on horseback running the monster through with his lance, with this line of commentary: 'George brandysshed his lance, and smote the dragon and hurt hym sore, and threwe hym to the grounde.' And, finally, in the uppermost scene, the king's daughter led the defeated dragon into town: 'George sayd: Bynde your gyrdel about his necke, and be not aferde, fayre mayde. Whan she had done so, the dragon folowed her as it had ben a meke beest and debonayre.'* At the time it was made, the window must have been surmounted by an ornamental design in the rounded section of the arch. But later, when the chapel belonged to the Hautecœurs, they had replaced the design with their own coat of arms. And so, during the dark nights, these brilliant armorial emblems of more recent creation blazed out above the legend. Quartered, one and four, two and three, Jerusalem and Hautecœur: Jerusalem, which is argent, a cross potent or, cantoned with four crosslets the same; Hautecœur, which is azure, a castle or, an inescutcheon sable, a heart argent in fesse point, the whole accompanied by three fleurs-de-lis or, two in chief, one in base. The shield was supported on dexter and on sinister by two chimeras or, and surmounted, in the middle of a plume azure, by a helmet argent, damasked or, full-faced and closed, with eleven grilles—which is the helmet of the marshal dukes of France, titled lords, and the heads of sovereign companies.* And the motto was: 'If Godde willeth I wille.'

Gradually, Angélique, through long gazing at St George as he ran the monster through with his lance, while the king's daughter alongside

raised her joined hands in the air, had developed a passionate attachment to him. At this distance she could not make out the figures clearly,
and saw them only as they were magnified by her imagination—the
girl, slender and blonde, with a face resembling her own; the saint,
pale and magnificent, with the beauty of an archangel. He was in fact
coming to rescue *her*, and she could have kissed his hands with gratitude. This adventure of theirs, which had only a hazy outline in her
dreams—an encounter on a lake shore, a young man more handsome
than the sun coming to save her from great danger, mingled with her
memories of the visit to Hautecœur Castle, as she once more brought
to mind the feudal keep towering starkly against the sky, thronged
with the noble lords of bygone days. The armorial emblems shone
like stars in the summer night sky, she knew them well, and could
read them fluently, in all their sonorous language, familiar as she was
with embroidering blazons. Jean V went from house to house in the
plague-ravaged town, climbing upstairs to kiss the lips of the dying,
curing them with the words: 'If God wills, I will.' Félicien III, learning that illness prevented Philip the Fair from going to Palestine, went
in his stead, barefoot and carrying a candle, for which he was granted
a quarter of the arms of Jerusalem. These emblems conjured up
many, many stories, such as the ones about the ladies of Hautecœur,
the Happy Dead, as they were called in the legend. In this family, the
women died young, in the full flush of happiness. Sometimes two or
three generations were spared before death reappeared with a smiling
face, and carried off the daughter or wife of a Hautecœur in his gentle
arms, the eldest never more than twenty, just at the moment when she
was happiest in love. On the evening of her betrothal to her cousin
Richard, who also dwelt in the castle, Laurette, the daughter of
Raoul I, was sitting at her window and, glancing across from the tower
of David to the tower of Charlemagne, caught sight of him at his own
window. She thought that he was calling to her and, when a moonbeam flung down a bridge of light between them, she started walking
towards him. Reaching halfway, she stumbled, in her haste, her foot
falling wide of the moonbeam's path, and she fell and was dashed to
pieces beneath the towers. And ever since then, when the moon shines
clear in the night sky, she walks the air above the castle, bathing it in
white light as her vast gown sweeps silently over it. Balbine, the wife
of Hervé VII, believed for six months that her husband had been
killed in battle; and then, one morning as she sat waiting for him still

on the heights of the keep, she saw him coming home along the road, and ran downstairs, so overcome with joy that she fell down stone dead on the bottom step. And today, as soon as dusk falls over the ruins, she comes down the stairs, and can be seen running from one floor to the next, slipping along corridors and through rooms, passing like a shadow behind gaping windows, which open onto thin air. They all came back, over and again, Ysabeau, Gudule, Yvonne, Austreberthe, all the Happy Dead, whom death himself adored, carrying them off with a single beat of his wings while they were still young and in the first bliss of love, so as to spare them the burden of living. Some nights they seemed to fill the castle with their pale dove-like fluttering. And thus had things unfolded, right down to the last of them, the mother of Monseigneur's son, who had been found lying beside her son's cradle, where, although desperately ill, she had dragged herself to die, and in the joy of kissing him had breathed her last. These stories haunted Angélique's imagination: she spoke about them as though they were actual events that had only just happened the day before. She had read the names of Laurette and Balbine on the old grave-stones set in the chapel walls. Why then couldn't she die also while still young and happy? The coat of arms blazed with light, the saint descended from his window, and she was borne off to heaven on the faint breath of a kiss.

The *Legend* had taught her this: miracles are the common rule, the ordinary way of things. They can be short-lived or everlasting; they can come into being effortlessly, and at any moment; they can burgeon, proliferate and spread all around; and then, sometimes, they occur for no reason at all, simply for the sake of overturning the laws of nature. People live as equals with God. Abgar, the king of Edessa, writes to Jesus, who writes back to him.* Ignatius receives letters from the Virgin.* The Mother and the Son appear everywhere, adopt disguises, and chat with people very congenially. Stephen treats them with easy familiarity* when he meets them. All the virgins marry Jesus, and the martyrs ascend into heaven to be united with Mary. As for the angels and saints, they are the ordinary companions of men; they come and go, pass through walls, reveal themselves in dreams, speak down from the clouds, are present at births and deaths, sustain the victims of torture, free prisoners from their cells, convey answers, and run errands. Wherever they go, wonders blossom endlessly. Sylvester binds shut a dragon's muzzle with a thread.* The earth rises up to form a seat for Hilary, whose companions sought to humiliate him. A gemstone falls into St Lupus's chalice.*A tree crushes St Martin's enemies,* a dog lets go of a hare and a fire stops burning at his command. Mary the Egyptian walks on water, honeybees fly out of Ambrose's mouth* at his birth. The saints are continually curing eye diseases, paralysed and withered limbs, leprosy, and the plague in particular. No disease can resist the sign of the cross. In a crowd of people, the suffering and the weak are taken to one side, and cured en masse in a flash of lightning. Death is defeated, and resurrections are so common that they simply form part of everyday life. And when the saints themselves have breathed their last, wonders do not cease, but come even faster, and are like everlasting flowers crowning their tombs. Two fountains of oil, a remedy for all ills, flow from the feet and head of Nicholas. A scent of roses drifts up from Cecilia's coffin when it is opened. Dorothea's is full of manna. The bones of the virgins and martyrs unmask liars, compel thieves to return their booty, fulfil the wishes of barren women, restore health to the dying. Nothing is impossible, invisible powers reign, the caprices of the supernatural are the only law. In the temples, enchanters try to join in with their own tricks: sickles reap of their own accord, brass serpents slither, bronze statues burst into laughter, wolves break into song. The saints respond immediately, and overwhelm them: the consecrated host changes into living flesh, blood drips from images of Christ, staves thrust into the ground burst into flower, springs gush forth, loaves of warm bread pile up at the feet of the poor, a tree bows down in adoration of Jesus. And, what's more, severed heads speak, broken chalices repair themselves, rains move away from a church and drench neighbouring palaces, and the robes of hermits never wear out, renewing themselves each season, like an animal's pelt. In Armenia, persecutors throw the lead coffins of five martyrs into the sea, the one containing the remains of the apostle Bartholomew moves to the front, with the other four following behind as a mark of honour; and all, like a squadron in good order, float slowly along in the breeze across vast expanses of sea until they reach the shores of Sicily.*

Angélique was a firm believer in miracles. In her ignorance, she found that she was continually surrounded by wonders: a star rise, or the opening of a humble violet's petals. It seemed foolish to her to think of the world as a machine governed by fixed laws. She understood so little, and felt so weak and lost among powers she could barely reckon with; and she would never even have suspected that these powers existed if she had not occasionally been buffeted by the great gusts they sent forth! And so, like a Christian of the early Church, nourished by her reading of the *Legend*, she placed herself, quiescently, into God's hands, as the only way of effacing the stain of original sin. She had no freedom of her own, God alone could effect her salvation by bestowing grace—and it was indeed grace that had brought her into the Huberts' house in the shadow of the cathedral, so that she might lead a life of obedience, purity and faith. Deep down inside her, she heard it howling still, the demon of hereditary evil. Who knew what would have become of her in her native soil? No doubt she would have fallen into immorality, whereas in this blessed corner she grew with new-found vigour, flourishing more with each passing season. Wasn't this little spot grace itself? Woven out of stories she had learnt by heart, and the faith imbibed with them, and the mystical otherworld that surrounded her, this was a realm of invisible presences, in which miracles appeared perfectly normal and a natural part of her daily existence. Her surroundings armed her for the battle of life, as grace armed the martyrs. And she too was helping to create this little place, without realizing; it grew out of an imagination overheated by fables, out of the unconscious desires of puberty; it was swollen by her ignorance, and was generated by the unknown dwelling in her and in things around her. Everything came out of her, and returned into her; mankind created God to save mankind, nothing existed apart from the dream. Sometimes she grew confused, and anxiously touched her own face, doubting her own materiality. Wasn't she just a thing of appearance, which would conjure forth an illusion, and then vanish?

One May night, while out on the balcony where she spent so many long hours, she burst into tears. She was not in the least bit sad, but rather was overcome by a sense of expectation, even though nobody was due to come. It was pitch dark, and the Clos-Marie appeared like a well of shadows under a star-strewn sky, and she could make out nothing but the great dusky forms of the old elms in the grounds of the Bishop's Palace and the Voincourt residence. The only light visible was the glow of the chapel window. If nobody was coming, why then was her heart pounding like this? For a very long time, since her earliest youth, she had had the feeling that she was waiting, and it had grown only more urgent as she grew older, swelling into the fretful agitation of puberty. Nothing could have surprised her now, as for weeks she had been hearing the hum of voices in this mysterious little place, peopled by her own imagination. The *Legend* had released its supernatural cargo of saints here and miracles were ready to blossom. She understood clearly that every single thing was coming to life, that voices were starting to be heard from things once mute—that the leaves of the trees, the waters of the Chevrotte, and the stones of the cathedral were all speaking to her. But whose arrival did these whispers, coming from the invisible realms, announce? And what intentions did they have for her, these obscure presences that gusted from the vast beyond and hovered in the air? She remained there, gazing into the darkness, as though keeping a one-sided tryst, and she waited and waited until she was drooping with sleep. And all the while she had the sense that the unknown was shaping her life, independently of her will.

For a week Angélique wept like this in the dark of night. She would return to the balcony and simply wait. She had a growing sense that the world was closing in on her, the horizon narrowing and suffocating her. Her heart was heavy, and voices hummed deep inside her skull, although no more clearly than before. All of nature, the earth and the vast sky above, were entering her being, and slowly taking possession of her. At the slightest sound, her hands burned, and her eyes strained to pierce the darkness. Had the long-awaited miracle finally started to occur? No, still nothing, doubtless just some night bird fluttering its wings. And she strained again to hear, and could even make out the different sounds of elm and willow rustling their leaves. Twenty times over, she felt a tremor run through her body, but it was just the sound of a pebble tumbling over in the stream, or an animal out on the prowl sliding down a wall. She leant forward, feeling very faint. Nothing, still nothing.

Finally, one evening, as a balmier darkness settled beneath a moonless sky, something stirred. At first she thought she was mistaken, as this slight noise, a novel one among all those she knew, was so faint as to be almost imperceptible. Silence followed, and she held her breath. Then she heard it again, louder this time, but still indistinct. She would have said the noise was a distant, muffled footfall, a trembling in the air signalling an approach, out of the range of sight and hearing. What she was waiting for seemed to be coming from the invisible realms, emerging slowly from the whole quivering world that surrounded her.

Little by little, it was stepping out of her dream, as though the vague
desires of her youth were being fulfilled. Was it St George from the
window coming towards her, treading through the high grasses with
the silent steps of a painted image? The window was indeed growing
dimmer, and she could no longer clearly make out the saint, who
appeared as just a small purplish haze, dissipating and melting away.
That night, she could make no further sense of things. But the following evening, at the same hour, and in darkness just as profound, the
sound grew louder, and drew a little nearer. It was the sound of footsteps, undoubtedly, the footsteps of a vision lightly brushing over the
ground. They stopped and started, moved here and there, and it was
impossible to tell their exact location. Perhaps they came from the
Voincourts' garden, from someone taking a late night stroll beneath
the elms. Or perhaps they issued from the thick clumps of bushes in
the bishop's garden, from among the tall lilacs, with their heady perfume that troubled her so deeply. She peered vainly into the dark: the
long-awaited miracle impinged only on her hearing and her sense of
smell—the fragrance of the flowers seeming even more intense, as
though mingling with someone's breath. And, over the course of several nights, the footsteps skirted closer and closer to the balcony,
eventually coming right up to the wall below her. There they halted,
and a long silence ensued. She felt as though she were now completely enfolded in the slow, spreading embrace of the unknown, and
she swooned.

On the evenings that followed she saw the slender crescent of the
new moon appear among the stars. But it sank as the day drew to
a close, and disappeared behind the roof of the cathedral like a bright
eye blinking shut. She studied the moon, watching as it waxed a little
fuller every evening, and grew impatient, for this was the torch that
would at last shed light on the invisible. The Clos-Marie emerged
slowly from the darkness, with its old ruined mill, its clumps of trees
and fast-flowing stream. And the process of creation now continued
in the light. What was emerging from the dream materialized into
a shadow; at first she glimpsed just a dim shadow moving in the
moonlight. What was it exactly? The shadow of a branch swaying in
the wind? Sometimes it seemed to vanish, and the field slumbered on
in deathly stillness, and she thought she must have been seeing things.
Then there was no longer any doubt: a dark outline crossed a lit-up
patch of ground, slipping from one willow tree to the next. She lost

sight of it, and then found it again, without ever being able to tell its shape. One evening, she thought she made out a pair of shoulders, retreating rapidly, and she looked immediately across at the window. It appeared grey and empty, as though extinguished by the moon beaming directly onto it. From that time on, she noticed that this living shadow seemed to flatten out onto the ground as it came towards her window, moving from one pool of darkness to the next, approaching through the long grass along the edge of the cathedral. As she glimpsed it drawing nearer, her inner turmoil grew and she felt the nervous disquiet of one who is gazed on by mysterious eyes that themselves remain unseen. Undoubtedly, some presence was waiting there behind the leaves, its glance fixed on her, never looking away. And she felt on her hands and face the physical impression of its scrutiny, a long, lingering gaze that was gentle and shy. She chose not to hide away from it because she sensed that it was pure, coming as it did from the enchanted realm of the *Legend*. And her initial anxiety changed into pleasurable confusion, convinced as she was of happiness to come. Abruptly, one night, the shadow appeared in sharp outline on the pale moonlit ground, the shadow of a man whom she could not see, hidden behind the willow trees. The man did not move, and for a long time she watched the motionless shadow.

Thereafter, Angélique had a secret. It filled every corner of her bare, whitewashed room. She stayed for hours in her great bed, a slender little thing lost in thought, eyes closed, but not asleep, picturing over and over the motionless shadow etched on the bright ground. At dawn, when her eyes opened, she glanced from the great wardrobe to the old chest, and from the porcelain stove to the little dressing table, astonished to find that the mysterious outline was no longer before her, a figure she could have drawn unerringly from memory. In her sleep she had seen it drifting among the pale sprays of heather on the drapes. It filled her dreams as it did her waking hours. This shadow was a companion to her own: she had two shadows, even though she was alone with her dream. And she did not confide this secret to anyone, not even to Hubertine, to whom, until this moment, she had told everything. When Hubertine questioned her, curious to see her so elated, she blushed deeply, and answered that she was happy because of the early spring weather. From morning to evening, she buzzed around like a fly drunk on warm sunshine. Never had the chasubles she embroidered shone with such brilliance of silk and gold. The

Huberts, who were in good spirits themselves, just assumed she was brimming with youthful vigour. Her gaiety mounted as the day drew to a close, and she broke into song when the moon came up. When the appointed hour arrived, she was always leaning there on the balcony, and saw the shadow appear. In the moon's first quarter, the shadow arrived punctually for each tryst, upright and silent, and she learnt nothing further about it, and had no idea to whom it might belong. Was it just a shadow, a thing of appearance only, the saint, perhaps, stepping out from the window, or the angel who had once loved Cecilia, and who now came down to love her, Angélique, in turn? Her pride leapt at this thought, and it was as gratifying to her as a caress from the invisible realms. But she was also impatient to know the truth, and so resumed her wait.

The moon, reaching its full, shone down on the Clos-Marie. When it was at the zenith, the trees, beneath its torrent of perpendicular white beams, cast no shadows, and were like silent fountains streaming with light. The whole field was bathed in the luminous, crystal-clear radiance that spilled from them, and was so brightly lit that even the fine serrations of the willow leaves were clearly visible. The slightest breeze seemed to ruffle this moonlit lake, which slumbered in sovereign peace between the great elms of the neighbouring gardens and the vast curve of the cathedral roof.

Two more evenings went by and, when Angélique came out onto the balcony on the third night, she had a great shock. She could see him standing there in the bright light, facing her. His shadow, like the shadows of the trees, had retreated beneath his feet, and vanished. He was all alone now, and lit up very clearly. At this distance, he was as plainly visible as if he was standing in daylight, aged twenty, blond, tall and thin. He looked like St George, or a superb Jesus, with his curly hair, his sparse beard, his straight, rather strong nose, and dark eyes, which were filled with gentle pride. She recognized him perfectly, and had never imagined him otherwise; it was he, just as she had always expected him to be. The miracle was finally nearing its end: the slow creative work of the invisible realms was about to reach fruition in this living apparition. He was emerging from the unknown, from those tremors that vibrated deep down in things, from the murmuring voices, from the shifting shadows of the night, from all that had enveloped her and almost made her swoon. And he seemed to hover two feet above the ground, as befitted his supernatural coming, while the miracle enfolded him on all sides, floating on the mysterious lake of moonlight. He retained as his escort all the figures of the *Legend*, the male saints whose staves burst into flower, and the female saints whose wounds flow with milk. And the great white company of virgins flocking in the air blotted out the stars.

Angélique continued to gaze at him. He raised his arms and opened them wide to her. She was not afraid, and smiled.

CHAPTER 5

IT was quite an occasion, every three months, when Hubertine did the washing. She hired a woman, Mère Gabet, and for four days embroidery was forgotten. Angélique joined in too, as it was a pleasant break from ordinary work to soap and rinse the linen in the clear waters of the Chevrotte. After soaking it in potash, they wheeled it out in a barrow through the little gate in the wall. They spent the days in the Clos-Marie, out in the sunshine and the open air.

'Mother, I'll wash this time, I really love doing it!'

With her sleeves rolled up above the elbow, and shaking with laughter as she brandished the beetle, Angélique vigorously beat the washing, relishing the healthy exertion of this simple task, which left her spattered with foam.

'This will give me strong arms, Mother, it's doing me good!'

The Chevrotte cut across the field at an angle, flowing sluggishly at first, but later on much more rapidly, as it plunged down a pebbly slope and churned with froth. It emerged from the bishop's garden through a sort of sluice-gate set in the foot of the wall. At the other end of the field, it disappeared into a vaulted arch at the corner of the Voincourt residence, surging underground only to emerge again two hundred metres further on running alongside the Rue Basse, before joining the Ligneul. This meant that a very careful eye had to be kept on the washing, for if one ever let go of an item there was no point in running after it—it was as good as gone.

'Wait a minute, Mother, just wait!... I'm going to put this big stone on top of the towels. We'll see then if she runs off with them, the little thief!'

She set the stone in place, and went back to drag another from the ruins of the mill; it was a joy for her to exert herself, and wear herself out. When she bruised her finger, she simply gave it a shake, saying it was nothing. During the daytime, the family of paupers who lived in the ruins went out begging, scattering along the roadways. The field was left deserted—a lovely, cool, secluded place, with its clumps of pale willows, its tall poplars, and its sea of wild grasses that grew to shoulder height. Silence rippled outwards from the two neighbouring gardens, whose tall trees barred the horizon. At three o'clock, the shadow of the cathedral started to creep over it, mild and meditative, smelling faintly of incense.

And she beat the washing harder, with all the strength of her pale young arm.

'Mother, Mother, I'm going to eat well tonight!... And, you know, you promised me a strawberry tart.'

On the day the rinsing was to be done, Angélique was left to work alone. Mère Gabet had suffered a sudden attack of her sciatica, and had not turned up, while Hubertine was kept at home by other household chores. Kneeling in her straw-lined box, the young girl picked up the pieces of washing one by one, and stirred them all about in the water, spreading dark, soapy trails, until eventually the water ran crystal-clear. She was in no hurry, and had been gripped by a feeling of anxious curiosity since morning, when she had been startled to see an old workman in a grey smock there, setting up some light scaffolding in front of the window in the Hautecœur chapel. Had he come to repair the window? There was a pressing need for this: the figure of St George had gaps in it, and some of the stained glass that had broken over the centuries had been replaced by clear pieces. And yet she was vexed. She was so used to the holes in the saint piercing the dragon, and in the king's daughter leading it with her girdle, that the idea of their repair left her indignant, as though the figures were being deliberately mutilated. It was sacrilege to make alterations to such ancient things. But, all at once, when she came back from lunch, her anger vanished; a second workman stood on the scaffolding, a young man, also wearing a grey smock. She had recognized who it was. It was him.

With cheerful unconstraint, she resumed her earlier position, kneeling in the straw-lined box. Her wrists bare, she once more set to rinsing out the washing in the clear water. It was undoubtedly him: tall, thin, blond, with the springing beard and curly hair of a young god, his skin as pale as it had appeared in the white moonlight. As he was the one tackling it, there was no need to worry about the window; anything he did would only make it more beautiful. She was not in any way disappointed to see him in a smock, a worker like herself— a stained-glass painter,* no doubt. On the contrary, it made her light up with a smile, so absolutely did she believe in her dream of royal destiny. Appearance was all. What was the point of knowing more? One morning he would appear as he must be. A shower of gold streamed down from the roof of the cathedral, a triumphal march burst forth in the distant rumbling of the organ. She did not even stop to consider how he managed to come here, by day and by night. Unless he lived in one of the neighbouring houses, he had to enter along the Ruelle des Guerdaches, which ran beneath the wall of the Bishop's Palace from the Rue Magloire.

And so a charming hour unfolded. As she rinsed the washing, she bent forward until the clear water was almost touching her face. Then, as she picked up each new piece, she raised her head and looked over, a grain of mischief in her glance, for all the commotion in her heart. Up on the scaffolding, he tried to give the impression that he was busily assessing the window, but meanwhile darted sidelong glances at her, and seemed embarrassed when she caught him turning his head towards her. It was remarkable to see how rapidly he blushed, his naturally pale complexion suddenly suffusing with colour. At the slightest emotion, whether of anger or affection, all the blood in his veins mounted to his face. Despite the truculence in his eyes, he was overcome by shyness when he felt her looking at him and became like a small child again, fumbling about with his hands, and stammering out instructions to the older man alongside him. As the water foamed coolly over her arms, she was greatly amused to realize that he was as innocent and as ignorant of everything as she—and had the same greedy passion to taste life for the first time. One doesn't always have to proclaim one's feelings out loud; they are conveyed by invisible messengers, and recounted by silent lips. She looked up, and caught him turning away. The minutes slipped by, and it was utterly delightful.

Suddenly she saw him jump down from the scaffolding, and he began to walk backwards through the grass, as though moving away from the window in order to get a better view of it. But it was so obvious that he was doing this simply in order to come nearer to her that she almost burst out laughing. He had leapt down recklessly, as though ready to risk all, but things had turned touchingly comical. He stood a few paces away from her, stock still, with his back to her, and didn't dare turn around, so mortally embarrassed was he by his hasty action. For a moment she thought he was going to start back towards the window, just as he had come, without giving her a backward glance. He desperately screwed up his courage, and turned to her. Just at that moment she looked up, laughing impishly, their eyes met, and they held one another's gaze. They were both paralysed with embarrassment, all composure vanishing, and they might have stayed like that for ever had a dramatic incident not occurred just then.

'Oh, my God!' she cried out, in alarm.

In her confused excitement, she had been paying little attention to the dimity camisole she was rinsing, and had let go of it. The fast-flowing stream was bearing it away, and in another minute it would disappear into the vaulted archway that swallowed up the Chevrotte at the corner of the Voincourt residence.

For a few seconds, they stared with dismay. He had grasped the situation, and set off in pursuit. The stream leapt and bounded over the pebbles, and the wretched camisole was sailing along faster than he could run. He leant over, thinking he'd just about got it, but snatched only a handful of foam. He missed with two attempts. Trembling excitedly, he plunged into the water like one heroically risking his life, and caught hold of the camisole just at the moment it was about to disappear underground.

Angélique had anxiously followed the rescue, but now felt laughter swell uncontrollably in her lungs. Well, so much for that adventure she had often dreamt about, with the encounter at the lake's edge, and the young man as handsome as the sun delivering her from terrible danger! St George, the champion, the warrior, was none other than this stained-glass painter, this young workman in a grey smock. As she watched him walk back towards her, his legs drenched, the dripping camisole clasped awkwardly in his hands, fully aware of the absurd enthusiasm he had shown in retrieving it from the stream, she had to bite her lip to contain the burst of merriment that tickled her throat.

He gazed at her raptly. She appeared so adorable, so child-like, as she tried to hold in her laughter, her youthful frame quivering all over! Spattered with stream water, her arms chilled by the current, she gave off the pure clean smell of sparkling water as it gushes from a mossy forest spring. She was a picture of health and happiness in the bright sunshine. One could tell she was a good housewife, and a queen too, in her working dress, with her slender waist, and the oval face of a king's daughter, just like the girls in the legends. He had no idea how to go about handing over this piece of washing to her, so overwhelming did he find her beauty—the sort of beauty he encountered in the art he loved. He felt vexed that he should appear so naive to her, for he could see very clearly the effort she was making not to laugh. But he had to do something, and so he handed over the camisole.

Angélique realized that if she unclenched her teeth she would burst into laughter. The poor boy! She felt fondly towards him, but the urge was irresistible. She was overflowing with happiness, and had such a great urge to break into laughter, she could not contain it.

When at last she thought she could speak again, she wanted simply to say:

'Thank you, Monsieur.'

But the laughter returned, and she stammered and stuttered, and couldn't complete a single word. Her laughter rang out very loudly, a shower of harmonious notes echoing like a song to the crystalline accompaniment of the Chevrotte. Disconcerted, he couldn't think of a single thing to say. His pale face suddenly crimsoned, and his boyishly timid eyes flamed like an eagle's. He fled, taking the old worker with him, while she continued laughing, leaning over the clear stream, and was splashed all over with water again as she rinsed the washing on this radiantly happy day.

At six o'clock the next morning they put the washing out to dry; it had been left in a bundle to drain since the previous day. The day was very windy, which would help with the drying. To stop the washing being blown away, they had to weigh down the pieces with a stone at each corner. And so, eventually, all the washing was spread out there, brilliantly white against the green grass, and scented with the clean fragrance of the vegetation, and it was as though the field had suddenly bloomed with snowy drifts of daisies.

After lunch, when she came back to check on it, Angélique was plunged into despair. The wind, gusting even more fiercely, was threatening to blow it all away beneath a sky of blue—which shone with bright clarity as though swept clean by the blasts of air. A sheet had already flown off, and some towels had been whisked away and lay tangled in the branches of a willow tree. She retrieved the towels. But

then some handkerchiefs fluttered away behind her. And there was no
one to help her! She grew frantic. When she tried to lay out the sheet
again, she had to fight it. It wrapped about her, whipping her face and
clacking uproariously, like a flag.

Above the wind, she heard a voice say:

'Mademoiselle, would you like me to help you?'

It was him, and all at once, with no thought other than concern for
her washing, she cried out:

'Of course I would—yes, give me a hand!... Take the end, there!
Hold on tight!'

They stretched out the sheet with their strong arms as it flapped
about like a sail. They laid it on the grass, and placed larger stones at
each corner. It slumped down, subdued, but neither of them stood up.
They remained on their knees, at either end of the sheet, separated by
the great dazzling white cloth.

She broke into a smile of thanks, devoid of any mockery. Emboldened,
he said:

'My name is Félicien.'

'And I'm Angélique.'

'I am a stained-glass painter, and I've been given the job of repairing the window.'

'I live over there, with my parents. I'm an embroideress.'

Their words were carried away by the high wind, which whipped
crisply and spiritedly about them as the warm sunlight shone down.
They chatted together, saying things the other already knew, simply
for the pleasure of it.

'The window's not being replaced, is it?'

'No, no. The repairs won't even be visible. I love it as much as
you do.'

'It's true, I do love it. It has such soft colours!... I embroidered
a St George once, but it wasn't as beautiful.'

'Come now, not as beautiful!... I think I've seen it, if it's the
St George on the red velvet chasuble that the Abbé Cornille was wearing on Sunday. It's a marvel!'

She flushed with pleasure, and then called out sharply:

'Put a stone on the edge of the sheet, on your left there. Otherwise
the wind will carry it away again.'

He hurriedly weighted down the piece of washing, which had
risen up, flapping all about like the wings of a tethered bird trying to

fly again. It stopped moving altogether, and so they both rose to their feet.

She walked along the narrow strips of grass between the pieces of washing, checking on each, while he followed behind, greatly absorbed in the task, and deeply concerned by the possible loss of an apron or a tea towel. It all seemed completely natural. And she chattered on, telling him how she spent her time, and about the things she did and did not like.

'I like everything to be in its proper place… Every morning, at six, I'm woken by the cuckoo clock in the workroom. I sometimes even get dressed in the dark: I keep my stockings here, the soap there, I have a mania for keeping everything just so. Oh, I wasn't born like this, I used to be a very messy creature! Mother used to have words with me about it—very stern ones, at that!… And in the workroom, I couldn't do anything properly if my chair wasn't always in the same spot, facing the window. Fortunately I'm neither right- nor left-handed; I can embroider with either hand, which is a great gift; not everybody can… It's the same with the flowers I like. If I keep a bunch next to me, I always get a splitting headache. Violets are the only ones I can put up with and, funnily enough, their scent actually calms me down. If ever I feel a little out of sorts, I only have to sniff some violets and I feel better.'

He listened, captivated. She had an extremely charming voice, and he was beguiled by its soft, compelling tone and its lingering melody. And he must have been particularly sensitive to this form of human music, as the gentle cadence she gave to certain syllables brought tears to his eyes.

'Oh,' she said, interrupting herself, 'the chemises are almost dry.'

And then she confided a few last things to him, prompted by a naive impulse to reveal more of herself.

'White is always beautiful, isn't it? Some days I feel like I've had enough of blue and red and all the other colours, but I find a joy in white I never tire of. It's never jarring; you feel like losing yourself in it completely… We had a white cat with some tawny markings, and I painted them over. He looked very nice, but the effect didn't last… Now, one thing Mother doesn't know is that I hang on to all the little left-over scraps of white silk. I have a drawer full of them, for no reason really, apart from the pleasure of looking at them and running my fingers over them now and again… I've got another secret too, a really big one! Every morning when I wake up, there's always someone there beside my bed, truly! A pale figure, who quickly flits away.'

He did not doubt this for a moment, and seemed wholeheartedly to believe her. Wasn't it all quite natural and straightforward? A young princess, surrounded by the splendours of her court, could not have conquered him more quickly. In the midst of all this white linen, laid out on the green grass, she radiated charm, good humour, and majesty, and he felt his heart gripped in a tightening embrace. That was that, it was all decided: there would never be anyone else for him but her, and he would follow her until the end of his days. She walked on ahead with tripping little steps, looking back from time to time with a smile; and he followed behind, choked with a feeling of happiness, but with no hope that such happiness could ever fully be his.

A sudden squall burst, and a host of smaller pieces, percale collars and cuffs, cambric scarves and bodices, were lifted into the air and swept a distance away, like a flock of white birds tossed about by a storm.

Angélique started running.

'Oh, my God! Come on, help me!'

The two of them raced off. She pinned down a collar just at the edge of the Chevrotte. He was already clasping two bodices, plucked out of the tall nettles. The cuffs were retrieved, one by one. But in their headlong chase, the pleats of her whirling skirt thrice whipped softly up against him, and each time his heart throbbed wildly and his face flushed. And when he jumped up to try and get the last scarf, which was just out of reach, he brushed softly against her. She stood there, stock still, unable to breathe. The riot of emotions within her stilled her laughter and jokes, and silenced her mockery of this big, clumsy, innocent boy. What was the matter with her—why had her merriment vanished, why did she feel that she was fainting in this exquisite torment? When he passed her the scarf, their hands touched accidentally. They trembled, and stared at one another, wild-eyed. Then she abruptly took a step backwards, and stood there for a few seconds, not knowing what to do after the calamity that had just occurred. And then, suddenly, stricken with panic, she took to her heels, clutching a bundle of washing in her arms, and abandoning the rest.

Félicien tried to call out.

'Oh, for pity's sake... I beg you...'

The wind gusted even more fiercely, snatching the breath from his lungs. Hopelessly he watched her run, and it was as though she were being carried away by the wind. She ran on and on through the white expanse of sheets and tablecloths in the pale golden light of the angling sun, until the shadow of the cathedral swallowed her up. She seemed just about to disappear through the little garden gate, without having given a backward glance, when she turned sharply around, overtaken by a kindly impulse, not wanting to leave him with the impression that she was angry. Smiling self-consciously, she called out:

'Thank you, thank you!'

Was she thanking him for having helped her gather in the washing? Or for something else? She had vanished, and the gate swung shut.

He remained alone in the middle of the field, and strong, invigorating gusts of wind regularly whipped down at him from a clear sky. The elms in the bishop's garden swayed all about, heaving and moaning like a swell on the ocean, while a great clamour swept along the terraces and flying buttresses of the cathedral. But all he heard was the faint flapping of a little bonnet entwined like a white flower in a lilac branch—a bonnet that belonged to her.

From this day onwards, every time that Angélique opened her window she saw Félicien below in the Clos-Marie. The stained-glass repairs were a suitable excuse, and he practically lived there, without making the slightest progress on his work. He whiled away hours lying in the grass on the other side of a bush, watching through the leaves. It was lovely to be able to swap smiles, morning and evening. Brimming with happiness, she asked for nothing more. The washing would be done again only in three months' time, and the garden gate would remain closed until then. But if they could see each other every day like this, surely the three months would simply fly past! Was it even possible to live more happily than this—the day spent in expectation of an evening glance, and the night, awaiting that of the morning?

At their first meeting, Angélique had talked about everything, her daily life, her likes and dislikes, the little secrets that lay in her heart. He had said little: his name was Félicien; she knew nothing more about him. Perhaps that was the way things should be, the woman revealing herself entirely, the man remaining withdrawn and mysterious. She felt no urgent curiosity about him, and a smile came to her face when she mused on the course things must inevitably take. In any case, what she did not know did not matter; the only thing of any importance was to be able to see each other. She knew nothing about him, and yet understood him so well that she could read his thoughts in the expression on his face. He had come, she had recognized him, and they were in love.

They took exquisite pleasure in this mutual possession at a distance. They were continually thrown into new raptures by the discoveries they made. She had long thin hands that he adored, though they were scarred by the needle. She noticed how small his feet were, and was proud of their daintiness. Everything about him delighted her. She was grateful to him for being so handsome, and was overjoyed when she noticed one evening that his fair beard was an even lighter ash blond colour than his hair, which lent his smile a particular sweetness. One morning he went away in a blissful trance after she had leant forward, revealing a brown mole on her delicate neck. They bared their hearts to one another, and discovered many things. The proud and simple way she flung open her window announced that she had the spirit of a queen, even though she was just a little embroideress. Similarly, she could detect the generosity of his soul in the way he trod delicately through the grass. In the first flush of their acquaintance, they glimpsed an endless array of glittering qualities and virtues. Each meeting brought new delights, and it seemed that they could never exhaust the happiness they felt on seeing one another.

However, Félicien soon started to show signs of impatience. He no longer lay for hours stretched out beneath a bush, motionless in perfect contentment. As soon as Angélique appeared at the balcony railing, he grew restive and tried to come nearer. This started to irritate her, as she was afraid that somebody might see him. One day there was a genuine falling out; he came right up to the wall, and so she had to go inside. This was a great shock to him, and he was distraught, his expression so eloquent of obedience and entreaty that she forgave him the next day, and came out onto the balcony at her usual time. But he was no longer happy simply to wait, and resumed his earlier behaviour. Now he seemed to roam all over the Clos-Marie—everywhere at once, filling it with his restless spirit. He emerged from behind every tree trunk, he appeared on top of every bramble patch. Like the woodpigeons that roosted in the tall elms, he seemed to make his home nearby, in the fork of some branch. The Chevrotte seemed to give him a reason for lingering there: he leant out over the stream, appearing to watch the drifting clouds. One day she sighted him over at the ruined mill, standing on the roof-beams of a caved-in shed, elated to have climbed up so high, since he couldn't actually fly right up to her. Another day she stifled a faint cry when she saw him standing high up above her: between two windows of the cathedral, on the terrace over the choir chapels. How could he possibly have reached this gallery, accessible only through a locked door to which the beadle held the key? And how was it that he sometimes appeared silhouetted against the sky among the flying buttresses of the nave and the pinnacles atop the buttress piers? From these heights his gaze could swoop down into her bedroom, like a swallow plunging from the tip of a spire. It had never before occurred to her to hide. But from then on she shut herself away and felt increasingly uneasy at the way he was encroaching on her, and becoming her constant double. But if she was in no hurry herself, why was her heart pounding so violently, like the huge bell in the cathedral tower ringing out at full swing on the great feast days?

Three days passed and Angélique made no appearance, so alarmed was she by Félicien's growing boldness. She vowed never to see him again and convinced herself that she hated him. But his restless mood had infected her and she could not stay still. She found any excuse to get up from the chasuble she was embroidering. Hearing that Mère Gabet was confined to her bed in conditions of the direst poverty, she went to visit her each morning. The old woman lived in the Rue des Orfèvres also, just three doors away. And so Angélique came bearing broth, or sugar, and went out to buy medicine for her from the pharmacist in the Grand'Rue. One day when she came back upstairs carrying various packets and phials, she was startled to find Félicien at the sick woman's bedside. He turned very red, and awkwardly went away. The following day he appeared again, just as she was leaving, and she made way for him, displeased. Did he want to stop her from visiting her poor? She was in the grip of one of her charitable manias, in which she gave herself up entirely to lavishing care on those who had nothing. Her soul melted with fraternal pity at the idea of suffering. She ran all around, paying visits to old Mascart, a blind paralytic in the Rue Basse, whom she fed herself with a bowl of soup she had brought; and to the Chouteaus, husband and wife, an elderly couple in their nineties who lived in a cellar in the Rue Magloire, where she had brought old furniture from the Huberts' store room; and to others also, a great many others—all the poor of the neighbourhood whom she quietly helped with little gifts of things she found around her home. It made her happy to see their faces light up with surprise and delight at some leftover from the day before. But every time she went to visit one of them now, there was Félicien! She had never seen so much of him, even though she had stopped appearing at her window precisely for fear of seeing him again. Her irritation mounted, until she felt ready to burst with anger.

In fact, the worst of this whole business was that Angélique quickly lost her taste for charitable works. The young man spoilt the delight she had taken in doing good. Before this, he had no doubt looked after other poor folk, but not these, as he had never visited them. So he must have spied on her, and then gone in after her and got to know them, in order to steal them from her, one after the other. Now, whenever she arrived at the Chouteaus' with a small hamper of food, there were silver coins lying on the table. One day when she ran over to bring old Mascart ten sous, her entire savings for the week, after he had been whingeing that he had no tobacco money, she found that he had already been enriched by a twenty-franc coin that shone like the sun. And one evening when she visited Mère Gabet, she was asked to go down and change a bank note* for her. It was heartbreaking for her to realize how little she could do for them, being so short of money, while he could dip into his purse at will! She was of course pleased at this windfall for her paupers, but she could no longer take any joy in giving, chastened that she could give so little, while another gave so much. The clumsy fellow understood nothing, and thought he was winning her over by indulging his altruistic urge, whereas in fact he was killing all the joy she took from her good works. On top of this, she had to put up with the continual praise heaped on him by the paupers. He was such a kind young man, and so well brought up! They talked of nobody else, and paraded the gifts he brought, as if to scorn her own. Despite the vow she had taken to forget him, she asked many questions. What had he given them, and what had he said? He was very handsome, wasn't he? Kind-hearted also, and shy! Did he perhaps mention her occasionally? Yes, of course, he talked about her constantly! And she developed an utter loathing for him, for in the end he weighed too heavily on her heart.

Things could not go on like this, and one balmy May evening as twilight was falling, they finally came to a head. It happened over at the ruins of the old mill, which a clutch of beggars, by the name of

Lemballeuse, had made their home. The family was made up solely of women: Mère Lemballeuse, old and wrinkled, Tiennette, her eldest daughter, a big, wild-tempered girl of 20, and her two little sisters, Rose and Jeanne, who had mops of red hair and eyes that already flashed defiance. All four of them spent their days begging along the highway verges, and came home at night, their feet aching with weariness in tattered shoes tied up with string. That evening Tiennette came home in great pain, her ankles bleeding, after her shoes, worn out on the gravel, had finally fallen apart. Sitting at their door in the tall grass of the Clos-Marie, she was picking thorns out of her flesh, while her mother and the two little ones sat by, weeping and wailing.

Angélique arrived just at this moment, holding the bread that she brought them each week hidden beneath her apron. She had come out through the little garden gate, which she had left ajar as she was planning to dash home again. But at the sight of the whole family in tears she stopped short.

'What is it? What's the matter?'

'Oh, kind lady,' groaned Mère Lemballeuse, 'look at the state of this big clot. Tomorrow she won't be able to walk—it's a day wasted… She needs shoes.'

Eyes burning behind their manes of hair, Rose and Jeanne sobbed louder, crying shrilly:

'She needs shoes, she needs shoes!'

Tiennette lifted her head a fraction, her face gaunt and dark-complexioned. Savagely, wordlessly, she plunged a hairpin into her skin, struggling bitterly to remove a long splinter as the blood welled forth.

Overwhelmed by pity, Angélique handed over her gift.

'Here's some more bread for you.'

'Oh, bread!' replied the mother. 'We always need it, of course. But bread won't help her to walk. And it's the Bligny fair tomorrow—every year she gets more than forty sous there… Dear God, dear God, what's to become of us?'

Angélique was rendered mute by shame and compassion. She had five sous in her pocket, that was all. You couldn't buy a pair of shoes with five sous, not even second-hand ones. Once again, her lack of money left her powerless to help. Her exasperation grew when she looked around and saw Félicien standing a few steps away in the deepening shadows. He had probably been there for quite some time and must have heard everything. He was always appearing

like this, and she never knew where he had come from, or how he had
got there.

He's going to offer her some shoes, she thought.

He was already walking forward, in fact. The first stars were starting to come out in the violet sky. A balmy peace poured down, filling
the Clos-Marie with a drowsy hush as the willow trees slowly faded
into the shadows. The cathedral stood out as a dark ridge against the
western glow.

I just know it. He's going to offer her some shoes.

She was plunged into profound despair. He would give them everything they needed—she could never prevail against him! Her heart
pounded as though it were about to burst, and she yearned for great
riches, so that she could show him that she was also capable of making
people happy.

But the Lemballeuses had seen the kind gentleman. The mother
rushed forward, and the two little ones gave a wail and held out their
hands towards him. Their big sister stopped nursing her bloody
ankles, and looked sidelong at him.

'Listen, my good woman,' said Félicien, 'you will go down the
Grand'Rue, as far as the corner of the Rue Basse...'

Angélique understood—that was where the shoemaker's shop was.

She interrupted him roughly, feeling so worked up that she stammered out words at random.

'What a lot of useless running about!... What's the point?... It
would be much simpler to...'

She could not think what this much simpler thing might be. What
alternative could she find or invent to forestall his offer? She would
never have thought that she could feel such deep loathing for him.

'You will say that you have come on my behalf,' resumed Félicien.
'You will ask...'

Again she interrupted him, anxiously repeating:

'It would be much simpler... much simpler to...'

She grew suddenly calm, and sat down on a stone. She quickly
untied her shoes and took them off, and slipped off her stockings.

'There you are! It's all very simple! Why go rushing around?'

'Oh, kind lady, may the Lord reward you for what you have done!'
cried Mère Lemballeuse, examining the shoes, which were almost
new. 'I'll slit open the upper so they fit properly... Tiennette, say
thank you, you big clot!'

Tiennette tore the stockings out of the hands of Rose and Jeanne, who were eyeing them greedily. She never said a word.

At that moment, Angélique realized her feet were bare, and that Félicien could see them. Shame washed over her. She didn't dare move, thinking that if she got up they would be even more on show. She panicked, lost her head, and just started running. Her feet flashed very pale in the grass. The gloom had deepened, and the Clos-Marie was a sea of shadows between the tall trees in the neighbouring gardens and the dark mass of the cathedral. All that could be seen across the dim ground were her small white feet vanishing into the distance, satiny white like the feathers of a dove.

Frightened, and wary of the water, Angélique ran alongside the Chevrotte towards the plank that spanned it. Félicien, however, had cut through the bushes. Previously so shy, he had flushed a deeper red than she at the sight of her pale feet. Spurred on by the flame burning within him, he would have liked to let out a great cry containing all the passion that had consumed him, in all his overflowing, youthful turmoil, since that first day. Then, as she brushed past him, he could only stammer out his confession, one that seemed to scald his lips:

'I love you.'

She stopped, stunned. For a moment, standing to her full height, she stared at him. She had thought she felt only fury and hatred towards him, but these emotions faded, dissolving into a feeling of exquisite pain. What exactly had he said to dumbfound her like this?

He loved her, and she had known it. And yet the word murmured in her ear filled her with fearful amazement. And he, emboldened by laying bare his heart, which had drawn closer to hers during their acts of complicit charity, repeated:

'I love you.'

And she fled once more, in fear of her lover. The Chevrotte was a barrier no longer; she plunged into it like a hunted doe, and her pale little feet darted among the stones through the cold, trembling water. The garden gate swung shut and the feet vanished.

CHAPTER 6

FOR two days Angélique was overwhelmed with remorse. As soon as she was alone, she wept as though she had done something wrong. A dark and disturbing doubt plagued her: had she committed a sin with the young man? Was she lost, like the wicked women of the *Legend*, who yield to the devil? The words 'I love you', so softly murmured, now rang so clamorously in her ears that surely they must come from some terrible being hidden in the invisible realms. But she was not sure, she had no possible way of knowing, having grown up in such ignorance and solitude.

Had she sinned with the young man? She tried hard to remember exactly what had happened, and wrestled with scruples born of innocence. What was sin, then? Was it enough simply to see a man, and speak together, and lie to your parents about it? Surely there was more to evil than that? But why then did she feel as though she couldn't breathe? If she wasn't guilty, why did she have the sense that she was changing, and that a new soul was pulsing inside her? Maybe it was sin swelling there, causing her to faint in silent anguish. Her mind was full of vague, indeterminate fears, a jumble of prospective words and actions that filled her with fear even though she didn't yet understand them. Her cheeks flushed crimson, and the frightful words 'I love you' resounded in her ears. She could no longer think clearly, and burst into tears once more, doubting all that had happened, and fearing the nameless, formless transgressions that lay ahead.

What tormented her most was that she had not confided in Hubertine. If she could just have asked her, doubtless Hubertine would quickly have explained the mystery. Just to talk to someone of her anguish would have soothed her. But the secret had grown too great; she would have died of shame. She resorted to cunning, and put on an air of calm while a tempest raged in her soul. When she was asked why her attention kept wandering, she looked up with a surprised expression, and said that she didn't have anything on her mind. As she sat demurely at the embroidery frame, her hands mechanically plying the needle, she was tormented by a single thought from dawn until dusk. Somebody loved her, loved her! And what about her; was she also in love? It was an impenetrable question, one that, in her unworldliness, she was unable to answer. She kept repeating it to herself until her mind grew numb, words lost their usual meaning, and everything spun into a dizzying whirlpool, sweeping her away. By an effort of will, she regained control of herself and, needle in hand, embroidered away as diligently as before, in the midst of her dream. Perhaps she was coming down with some dreadful illness. One evening, as she went to bed, she had started to shiver, and thought she would never be able to get up again. Her heart beat so fiercely she thought it might burst, and she heard a tremendous ringing in her ears. Was she in love, or was she going to die? She smiled calmly at Hubertine, who was waxing a thread and studying her with concern.

Angélique had sworn in any case never to see Félicien again. She would nevermore venture among the wild grasses of the Clos-Marie, she would not even pay visits to her poor. She was afraid that something dreadful might happen if they ever came face to face again. Her resolution was partly an expression of repentance—she wished to punish herself for any sin she might have committed. On the mornings when she held firm, she never took even a single glance out of the window in case she caught sight of the man she feared down by the Chevrotte. And if she gave in and looked, and then saw that he wasn't there, she was left feeling dejected until the following day.

Now, one morning when Hubert was inking a design onto a dalmatic, a ring at the doorbell brought him downstairs. It must have been a customer with an order, since Hubertine and Angélique could hear the hum of voices through the staircase door, which had been left open. And then they glanced up, startled: footsteps were mounting the stairs, the embroiderer was bringing up his customer—something that never happened. And the young girl was astounded when she recognized Félicien. He was dressed very simply as a workman, a stained-glass painter, though his hands were white. Since she would no longer go to him, he had come to her, after days spent waiting in vain, anxiously and uncertainly telling himself that she must not love him.

'Ah, my child, this is something that concerns you,' explained Hubert. 'Monsieur has come with an order for an exceptional piece. And so I thought it much better to bring him up here to discuss things in peace and quiet... It is to my daughter, Monsieur, that you must show your drawing.'

Neither Hubert nor Hubertine had the slightest suspicion. They went over to stand beside him, curious to see what he was proposing. Like Angélique, Félicien was choking with emotion. His hands shook as he unrolled the drawing, and he had to speak slowly to hide the agitation in his voice.

'It is a mitre for Monseigneur... Yes, well, some ladies of the town, wanting to make him this present, have asked me to draw up the different parts and oversee its making. I am a stained-glass painter, but I also work a great deal with other very old art forms... As you can see, I have simply recreated a Gothic mitre...'

Angélique, who was bending over the large sheet that he had placed before her, let out a soft exclamation.

'Oh, it's St Agnes!'

It was indeed the 13-year-old martyr, the naked virgin covered only by her tresses of hair, from which just her little feet and hands poked out, just as she appeared on her pillar in one of the cathedral portals, as well as inside the cathedral, in an old wooden statue, which had once been painted, but was now a tawny blonde colour, gilded by the years. She filled one entire side of the mitre, standing tall as two angels bore her up to heaven, while below her stretched an intricate distant landscape. The back of the mitre and the lappets were decorated with beautifully drawn lanceolate designs.

'The ladies are offering this gift for the Procession of the Miracle,' resumed Félicien, 'and so I naturally thought I should choose St Agnes...'

'What an excellent idea,' interrupted Hubert.

Hubertine added in turn:

'Monseigneur will be deeply touched.'

The Procession of the Miracle, which took place each year on 28 July, dated from the time of Jean V of Hautecœur, and had been established by him as a way of giving thanks for the miraculous power of healing that God granted him and all his lineage to save Beaumont from the plague. Legend held that the Hautecœurs owed this power to the intercession of St Agnes, whom they greatly revered. And thence derived the ancient custom of taking out the old statue of the saint on the anniversary and parading it solemnly through the streets of the town in the pious belief that it would continue to ward off all sorts of evil.

'For the Procession of the Miracle,' murmured Angélique at last, her eyes fixed on the drawing, 'but that's in twenty days. We'll never have time.'

The Huberts nodded their heads. A piece of this sort required a vast amount of work. Hubertine, however, turned to the young girl.

'I could help you. I'd take care of the decorations, and you would only have to do the figure.'

Angélique was still studying the saint, deeply torn. No, no! She refused, she wished to shield herself from the temptation of accepting. It would be wicked to collude in this matter, for Félicien was undoubtedly lying. She was perfectly well aware that he was not poor and that his workman's outfit was just a disguise. If she mistrusted the simple, unadorned exterior he had assumed, and the improbable story he had invented in order to come up and see her, in her heart of hearts, however, she was delighted and overjoyed, imagining him transfigured, envisioning him as the royal prince he must undoubtedly be, utterly convinced as she was that one day her dream would be fulfilled.

'No,' she repeated very softly, 'we won't have time.'

And, without looking up, she went on, as though speaking to herself:

'For the saint, satin stitch or guipure wouldn't do. It wouldn't be worthy of her... It would have to be embroidered in shaded gold.'*

'That's exactly the type of embroidery I had in mind,' said Félicien. 'I was aware that Mademoiselle had rediscovered all the old secrets of this technique... There is still a rather beautiful fragment in this style in the sacristy.'

Hubert grew more and more excited.

'Yes, yes, it dates from the fifteenth century, and was embroidered by one of my great-grandmothers... Shaded gold, oh, there was no finer sort of work, Monsieur. But it required too much time, it was too expensive, and it was only the true artists who could master it. It's two hundred years since that sort of work has been done... And if my daughter refuses, you might as well give up, as she's the only one capable of doing it today. I don't know anyone else who has a fine enough hand or eye.'

Ever since the talk had turned to shaded gold, Hubertine had been paying close attention.

'Twenty days—that's completely impossible,' she said firmly. 'It requires the most extraordinary patience.'

As she stared at the saint, Angélique had made a discovery that flooded her heart with joy. Agnes looked just like her. In copying the old statue, Félicien had undoubtedly been thinking about her; and the realization that she was constantly on his mind, and that he saw her all around, weakened her resolve to keep him at bay. She looked up at last and saw that he was trembling, his moist eyes brimming with such passionate pleading that she relented. But she had that natural contrariness, that intrinsic guile that all girls develop, however unworldly they may be, and she certainly did not wish to appear to yield.

'That's impossible,' she repeated, handing the drawing back to him. 'I wouldn't do it for anyone.'

Félicien recoiled, deeply discouraged. It was he himself that she was refusing, he understood that. As he made his way to the door, he said to Hubert:

'Regarding the fee—I'll pay anything you ask... The ladies are prepared to offer as much as two thousand francs...'*

They certainly weren't a greedy household. And yet this huge sum took their breath away. The husband looked at his wife. It would be a great pity not to accept such a valuable order!

'Two thousand francs,' said Angélique, softly. 'Two thousand francs, Monsieur...'

The money did not matter to her, but she allowed a teasing little smile to wrinkle the corners of her mouth. It greatly amused her to pretend that she disliked seeing him, and to leave him with a false impression of her feelings.

'Oh, two thousand francs, Monsieur! Well then, I accept!... I wouldn't do it simply to please a customer, but if a customer is prepared to pay... If necessary, I will work all through the night.'

Hubert and Hubertine then wanted to refuse the offer, afraid that she would wear herself out.

'No, no, we can't turn down money like that... You can count on me. Your mitre will be ready the day before the procession.'

Félicien put down the drawing and went out, feeling deeply upset, his nerve failing him. He didn't even bother to try and invent further instructions for her as a way of lingering there. She certainly did not love him, and had pretended not to recognize him, treating him just like an ordinary customer, valued only for his money. He fumed with anger, and in his mind accused her of being mean-spirited. Very well then! It was all over, and he would think no more about her. But then, after endlessly pondering the matter, he forgave her: didn't she live by her work, didn't she have to earn her daily bread? Two days later, sunk in the depths of misery, he began roaming about once more, feeling utterly heartsick that he could not see her. She no longer went out, and made no appearance at the windows. In his despair, he told himself that, even if she did not love him, even if she loved only money, he would nevertheless continue to love her more each day, just in the way that one loves at the age of 20, without reason, at the mercy of the heart's whims, simply for the joy and pain of being in love. He had seen her one evening, and that was that: she was the only one now, there was no other; it did not matter whether she was good or bad, ugly or beautiful, poor or rich. He was going to die if he could not have her. On the third day his suffering became so intense that he returned to the Huberts', despite his vow to forget her.

When he rang the bell, he was met again at the foot of the stairs by the embroiderer, who, having listened to his confused explanations, decided to bring him upstairs once more.

'Monsieur would like to explain some things to you, my child, which I can't say I properly understand.'

'If it's no bother to Mademoiselle,' stammered Félicien, 'I would like to see things for myself... The ladies have asked me to monitor the work in person... That is, unless I would be disturbing you...'

When he had come in, Angélique's heart had lurched violently, rising into her throat, suffocating her. She made an effort to calm her heart, and her cheeks never reddened. With an air of calm indifference, she replied:

'Oh, nothing disturbs me, Monsieur. I work just as well in front of people... It's your design, and it's only natural for you to want to watch how the work is done.'

Quite disconcerted, Félicien would never have dared to sit down, but Hubert invited him to do so, smiling solemnly at this valuable customer. She resumed her work at once, bending forward over her frame, where she was embroidering some Gothic decorations in guipure on the back of the mitre. Hubert, for his part, had just taken down from the wall a completed banner that had been brushed with glue and left to dry for two days, and was now to be removed from its frame. Not a word was spoken, and the two embroideresses and the embroiderer worked away as though nobody else were there.

The young man grew a little calmer, enfolded by such deep tranquillity. Three o'clock struck, the shadow of the cathedral was already lengthening, and a delicate half-light filtered in through the large open window. This was the twilight hour that began at midday in the cool, green-shaded little house at the foot of the colossus. A faint tip-tapping of shoes on the paving stones rose up as girls from the boarding-school were taken to confession. In the workroom, the old tools, the old walls, all those things that never stirred or moved an inch, seemed to slumber on in their centuries-old repose, radiating a deep, cool serenity. A large patch of pure, steady white light fell on the frame as the embroideresses bent forward over it, and their delicate profiles were dappled by tawny reflections dancing up from the gold.

'Mademoiselle, I simply wanted to say,' began Félicien, self-consciously, feeling that he needed to justify his presence, 'I simply wanted to say that for the hair, it would be preferable to use gold thread instead of silk.'

She raised her head. The merriment in her eyes plainly signalled that he should have remained quiet if he had no better advice to offer. She bent forward again, and replied in a gently mocking tone:

'No doubt, Monsieur.'

What a great fool he was, to have only just noticed at this moment that she was working on the hair. Before her sat the drawing he had done, to which watercolour tones and gold highlights had been added, so that it now had the subdued colouring of an old miniature that has grown faded in a book of hours.* And she copied this image with all the skill and patience of a painter working with the aid of a magnifying glass. After duplicating it with slightly coarse strokes on the tightly stretched white satin, with a strong backing cloth in place, she had then covered the satin with lines of gold thread running from left to right, couched simply at either end but otherwise free, with each thread sitting immediately adjacent to the next. Then, using these threads as a sort of weft, she eased them aside with the point of her needle in order to see the drawing traced beneath and, following its pattern, couched the gold thread with silk stitches running at right angles, matching the colour of the thread to the tones of the original image. In the shaded sections, the silk completely covered the gold thread; in the halftones, the silk stitches were spaced more widely; and in the sections of light, gold thread appeared alone, entirely uncovered. This was the technique of 'shaded gold', a golden background varied with shades of silken thread; an image in which the colours seemed to melt and run together, as though heated from below by a golden halo streaming with mystical lustre.

'Ah!' said Hubert all of a sudden, as he was starting to loosen the banner, looping around his fingers the string that had been stitched into the webbing. 'In the old days an embroideress produced her

masterpiece* in shaded gold... As it says in the statutes, she had to
fashion "a single image which is of shaded gold, a sixth of an ell in
height..."* You would have been accepted into the guild, Angélique.'

Silence fell once more. Breaking with custom, Angélique had had
the same idea as Félicien for the hair: not to use silk, but instead to
layer gold over gold. She used ten needles, each threaded with a different shade of gold, from the dark red-gold of a dying fire to the pale
yellow-gold of an autumnal forest. Agnes's hair tumbled down in
a golden cascade, clothing her from neck to ankle. The torrent began
at her nape, swathing her in a thick cloak down to her loins, and
spilled forward over her shoulders in two separate waves, converging
beneath her chin and flowing down to her feet. It was a miraculous
head of hair, a fabulous fleece, with enormous curls, a warm and
living dress that gave off an aroma of naked innocence.

That day, Félicien rarely took his eyes away from Angélique as she
embroidered the curls in split stitches, following the curve of each
coil. He never grew weary of watching the hair lengthen and draw
flame beneath her needle. He was disturbed by its luxuriance and the
great ripple that ran through it as it suddenly unfurled. Hubertine,
who was busy sewing on spangles, hiding the thread that attached
each one beneath a small coil of gold wire, turned around from time
to time, enfolding him in her serene gaze whenever she had to throw
some misshapen spangle into the waste box. Hubert, who had withdrawn the laths so as to unstitch the banner from the sidebars, was
now folding it up carefully. And Félicien, growing more and more
embarrassed as he sat there silently, eventually realized that the wisest
thing to do was to leave, since he could not recall any of the clever
comments he had intended to make.

He rose to his feet, stammering:

'I'll come back later... I made such a poor copy of that lovely drawing of the head, you'll perhaps need me to give you some further
guidance on this.'

Angélique calmly raised her big, clear eyes to his.

'No, no... But come back, Monsieur, come back if you're worried
about our progress.'

He went away, cheered that he had been given permission to return,
but disheartened by her coldness. She did not love him, and she
would never love him, that much was certain. So what was the point?
The next day, and the days after, he returned to the chill little house

in the Rue des Orfèvres. When he was away from it he suffered abominably, riven by his inner struggle and tormented by doubt. He regained his calm only in the presence of the embroideress, and he could accept the fact that she did not like him, and find consolation for his every pain, so long as she was there. Each morning he arrived and chatted about work, and sat down before the frame as though his attendance was vital. He loved to gaze at her steady, elegant profile, bathed in the pale light of her blonde hair, and to follow the agile movements of her supple little hands as they darted about among the long needles. She was very open in her manner, and now treated him like a friend. And yet, for all that, he felt that certain things passed between them which she never mentioned, and which caused him much anguish. She sometimes looked up with an air of mockery, her eyes impatient and enquiring. Then, seeing him grow flustered, she turned cold once more.

But Félicien discovered a way of arousing her enthusiasm, which he exploited unduly. It was by talking to her about her own craft, about the ancient embroidered masterpieces he had seen preserved in cathedral treasure-houses or engraved in books: magnificent copes, the red silk cope of Charlemagne,* which featured eagles with outstretched wings, the Syon cope,* decorated with a whole crowd of saintly figures; a dalmatic considered the most beautiful piece ever made, the imperial dalmatic,* which celebrates the glory of Jesus Christ on earth and in heaven, and shows the Transfiguration, and the Last Judgment, with its multitude of figures embroidered in subtle shades of silk, gold, and silver; a Jesse tree,* also, on a silk-embroidered satin orphrey, which might easily have been taken from a fifteenth-century stained-glass window, with Abraham at the bottom, David, Solomon, and the Virgin Mary above, and Jesus at the top; and superlative chasubles, including one that was striking in its simplicity, a Christ on the cross,* bleeding, splashing red silk onto the golden cloth, with the Virgin at his feet supported by St John; and, finally, the Naintré chasuble,* on which the Virgin Mary is depicted sitting in majesty, holding the naked Infant on her knees, her feet shod. He detailed many, many other wonders, venerable in their great age, overflowing with a faith and naivety we no longer possess, which the tabernacles had imbued with an odour of incense and a mystical gleam of faded gold.

'Ah!' sighed Angélique, 'those beautiful things are all in the past. We just can't match the colours they used.'

With her eyes sparkling, she laid down her work when he told her the stories of the great embroideresses and embroiderers of old, Simonne de Gaules, Colin Jolye,* whose names have resonated through the ages. As she plied the needle once more, she remained transfigured, her face suffused with radiant artistic passion. Never had she appeared so beautiful to him, so fervent or so virginal, burning with a pure flame amid the brilliant gleams of gold and silk, her deep dedication obvious in the precision of her labour, the tiny stitches to which she devoted her soul. He stopped talking and simply gazed at her, until, awoken by the silence, she became aware of the riotous feelings he aroused in her. They embarrassed her, as though she had suffered a defeat, and so she resumed her calmly indifferent manner, and an irate tone of voice.

'Well, that's nice, my silk threads are all tangled up again!... Mother, please stop fidgeting about!'

Hubertine, who hadn't moved in the slightest, smiled peacefully. She had initially been concerned by the attentions the young man was paying to Angélique, and had spoken to Hubert about the matter one evening as they were going to bed. But they liked the fellow, and he was perfectly suitable: why would they oppose meetings that might lead to Angélique's happiness? Hubertine allowed things to carry on, while keeping a careful eye on them. In any case, for several weeks she herself had had a heavy heart as her husband in vain lavished her with his affections. This was the month in which they had lost their child; and each year, at this time, the same regrets and desires revived, and he trembled at her feet, yearning to feel that he was forgiven at last, and she, tender but sorrowful, gave herself to him entirely, losing all hope of overturning the curse. They never spoke of it, and kissed in front of others no more often than was usual; but this heightening of their love poured out from their silent bedroom, and radiated from their bodies in the smallest gesture—in the way that their glances met and they lost themselves for a moment in one another's eyes.

A week passed and work on the mitre advanced. These daily encounters took on a friendly and informal charm of their own.

'The forehead very high, without any trace of an eyebrow. That's right, isn't it?'

'Yes, very high, and not a shadow of an eyebrow, as in the miniatures of the time.'

'Pass me the white silk.'

'Wait, I'll just thread it.'

He helped her out, and working together in this way was very soothing. It grounded them in the reality of everyday life. Although not a single word of affection was spoken, and they were careful never to allow their hands to brush together, the bond between them grew stronger with every passing hour.

'Father, what are you up to now? We haven't heard a sound from you.'

She turned around and saw that the embroiderer was busy loading thread onto a spindle, all the while gazing tenderly at his wife.

'I'm just getting some gold thread for your mother.'

The delivery of the spindle, Hubertine's silent thanks, and Hubert's continual attentiveness towards her all conspired to create a warm, tender atmosphere that enveloped Angélique and Félicien as they bent forward once more over the frame. The workroom itself, the ancient room with its old tools, shadowed with a peacefulness that flowed from an earlier age, was complicit in this. It seemed to lie far distant from the street beyond, as though buried in the depths of a dream, a region peopled by virtuous souls where miracles reign and every happiness is easily attained.

The mitre was due to be delivered in five days, and Angélique, certain now of finishing on time, and maybe even a day ahead, drew breath, and was surprised to find Félicien sitting close beside her, his elbows resting on the trestle. Were they now friends? She no longer defended herself against that conquering side of him, and no longer smiled slyly at all those hidden thoughts of his that she could read so plainly. How was it she had been lulled to sleep, even as she waited so anxiously? And the eternal question recurred, the question she asked herself each evening as she lay in bed: did she love him? Deep in her blankets, she mused on these words for hours, seeking a meaning in them that eluded her. And suddenly, that night, she felt her heart break, and she dissolved into tears, pressing her face into the pillow so that no one would hear. She loved him, she loved him more than life itself. Why? How? She had no idea, and would never understand; but love him she did, and her whole being cried it aloud. The light had dawned, and love burst forth like the rays of the sun. She wept for a long time, filled with ineffable wonder and happiness, although somewhat regretful that she had never confided in Hubertine. Her secret weighed heavily on her heart, and she made a solemn vow to be as ice towards Félicien, and suffer any torment rather than reveal her affection. To love him, to love him and never breathe a word: that was her punishment, an ordeal that would redeem her sin. The pain she experienced was exquisite, and her thoughts ran to the martyrs of the *Legend*; scourging herself in this way, she felt as though she was their sister, and that her guardian Agnes was looking down on her with sad and gentle eyes.

She finished off the mitre the next day. She had embroidered the small hands and feet—the only patches of pale bare flesh to emerge from the majestic golden tresses—in split silk,* using threads finer than the ones that she had used in the piece for the Virgin Mary. She was completing the face, which had the elegance of a lily, the gold thread appearing like the blood of the veins beneath a skin made of silk. And this face rose like a sun above the horizon of the blue plain, borne aloft by two angels.

When Félicien came in, he cried out admiringly:

'Oh! She looks just like you!'

It was an involuntary confession, an acknowledgement of the resemblance he had traced in his drawing. He realized this, and blushed deeply.

'It's true, my girl, she has your lovely eyes,' said Hubert, who had come up to the frame.

Hubertine contented herself with a smile, having noticed this similarity a long time before; but she appeared surprised, and saddened even, when she heard Angélique answer in the voice she had used in the bad old days:

'My lovely eyes—you're making fun of me! I'm hideous, as I'm all too aware.'

She rose then to her feet, shaking out her limbs, overplaying the part of a cold-hearted, grasping young woman:

'Well, it's done now, and I've had more than enough of it. It's a beastly weight off my shoulders!... You know what, I'd never take it on again for that price.'

Félicien listened to her, thoroughly dismayed. What, was she on about money again? For a while she had seemed so earnest, so passionate about her art. Had he been mistaken? Now she seemed entirely consumed by the idea of profit, and callous enough to flaunt her delight at finishing and never having to see him again. For several days he had been mired in despair, trying in vain to come up with some excuse for returning to the house. But she did not love him, and would never love him! Such pain seared his heart that his eyes grew dim.

'Mademoiselle, will you not be assembling the mitre?'

'No, Mother will do that much better... I'll be delighted if I never have to touch it again.'

'Aren't you pleased with your work?'

'I'm not pleased with anything at all.'

Sternly Hubertine told her to be quiet. She begged Félicien to excuse this skittish little girl, and promised him that the mitre would be ready for collection early the following day. It was in effect a farewell, but he did not leave, and instead looked around the peaceful, shadow-crossed old workroom as if he was being expelled from paradise. Although an illusion, the hours he spent there had seemed so blissful, and he now had the painful sense that his heart had been torn from his body, and discarded there. It was a torture to him that he could not explain how he felt, and would carry away this dreadful uncertainty. At last, he had to go.

The door had scarcely closed when Hubert asked:

'What's the matter with you, my child? Aren't you feeling well?'

'Oh no, it's just that I found that boy such a bore. I never want to see him again.'

And Hubertine said, with finality:

'That's fine, you'll never see him again. But there's no reason why you shouldn't be polite.'

Angélique made a hasty excuse, and scarcely had time to flee to her bedroom before bursting into tears. Oh, she was so happy, and yet in such pain! Her poor, dear love, he must have gone away so heartbroken! But she had sworn to the saints that she would love him more deeply than life itself, and he would never know.

CHAPTER 7

THAT same evening, just as she was leaving the table, Angélique said she was feeling very unwell, and went up to her bedroom. The emotional turmoil of the morning and the struggle with her own feelings had left her exhausted. She went straight to bed, and burst once more into tears, pulling the sheet over her head in a desperate longing to vanish, to fade out of existence.

The hours passed, and night fell, a sweltering July night, whose leaden calm seeped in through the open window. Vast multitudes of stars glittered in the black sky. It must have been nearly eleven o'clock, and the moon, now in its last quarter, and already quite slender, was set to rise only around midnight.

In the dark room, Angélique was still weeping, her tears falling in an inexhaustible stream, when a creak at the door made her look up.

There was silence, and then a gentle voice called to her:

'Angélique... Angélique... my darling...'

She recognized the voice of Hubertine, who had doubtless been making ready for bed, with her husband, when she had heard the faint sound of crying and, greatly concerned, had come upstairs, half-dressed, to see what the matter was.

'Angélique, are you feeling unwell?'

Holding her breath, the young girl made no answer. She felt an overwhelming desire to be alone; it was the only thing that soothed her pain. A word of consolation, a caressing hand, even from her mother, would be torture to her. She pictured her standing on the other side of the door, in bare feet, she guessed, from the soft sound her steps had made over the tiles. Two minutes passed, and she sensed that she was still there, bending forward with her ear to the door, pulling her unfastened nightgown around her with her lovely arms.

Hearing nothing further, not even a breath, Hubertine dared not call out again. She was sure that she had heard sobbing, but if the child had at last fallen asleep, what was the point in waking her? She waited for another minute, perturbed by her daughter's hidden sorrows, half-guessing their origin, and full of tender solicitude for her. And she made up her mind to go back down, just as she had come up, her hands feeling familiarly for each curve of the staircase, the soft pat of her bare feet the only sound through the dark house.

Then it was Angélique, sitting up in her bed, who listened. The silence was so complete that she could hear the light pressure of her mother's heels on the edge of every step. The door of the downstairs bedroom opened and closed, and then she heard a faint murmuring, whispers, compassionate and sad, as her parents no doubt conferred about her, discussing their fears and hopes for her, and it carried on interminably, long after they must have put out the light and gone to bed. The nocturnal sounds of the old building had never risen up to her so clearly before. Normally she slept the untroubled sleep of youth, and did not even hear the creaking of the furniture; but now, kept wide awake by her stifled passions, it seemed to her that the whole house throbbed with sorrow and affection. The Huberts must also have been blinking back their tears, choked by the wild and desolate tenderness they shared in their infecundity. Although she couldn't be sure, she sensed that below her in the warm night the couple continued to lie awake, lapped in their deep love and their deep sorrow, in the long chaste embrace of their evergreen union.

As she sat there listening to the sighs and rustles that rose through the house, she could no longer contain herself, and her tears fell once more—but they were silent tears now, a warm, steady stream flowing like the blood in her veins. A single question had been revolving in her mind since morning, tormenting her to the core: had she been right to plant despair in Félicien's mind, to send him away with the belief that she did not love him buried in his heart like a dagger? She loved him, and she had caused him pain, and she was suffering terribly because of it. Why must there be such pain? Did the saints demand tears? Would it have angered Agnes to see her happy? She was racked now by doubts. In the past when she had awaited the one man who must inevitably come, she had arranged things much better in her imagination: he would enter, she would recognize him, and the two would go away together to distant lands, for ever. But now that he had actually come, both he and she wept alone, separated evermore. Why was this so? What had happened? Who had demanded this cruel vow from her lips, to love him but never tell him?

She was especially upset by the thought that it was all her fault, that she had behaved atrociously. Perhaps her old vicious urges were reviving? It was a shock for her to recall how she had feigned indifference towards Félicien, greeted him with mockery, and taken a mean delight in painting a false picture of herself. Her tears flowed with renewed intensity, and her heart melted with immense, unending pity for all the unintended suffering she had caused. She saw him in her mind's eye once more, walking away: she recalled the desolation on his face, the anguish in his eyes, and the way his lips had trembled; and she followed him through the streets to his home, a pallid figure, mortally wounded by her, the blood trickling out of him, drop by drop. Where was he right at this moment? Shivering away, somewhere, in a fever? She wrung her hands in despair, at a loss as to how she could make amends for the suffering she had caused. The idea of inflicting pain—why, it was utterly repulsive to her! She would have liked to perform some act of kindness, there and then, and spread a little happiness around her.

Midnight was about to strike. The great elms in the bishop's garden hid the moon on the horizon, and the room remained plunged in darkness. Her head fell back on the pillow, her mind emptied, and she tried to sleep; but sleep wouldn't come, and tears continued to seep from her closed eyelids. Thoughts began to stir in her mind, and she recalled how for the past fortnight she had found violets on the balcony, in front of the window, when she came up to bed. Every evening there was a new bunch of violets. Undoubtedly Félicien was tossing them up there from the Clos-Marie, for she remembered having told him that violets alone brought her comfort, through some peculiar power they had, while the scents of other flowers caused her the most terrible migraines. In this way, he offered up to her balmy nights of restful sleep, overflowing with pleasant dreams. That night she had the happy idea of taking up the flowers, which she had earlier placed by her bedside, and bringing them into the sheets with her, laying them out next to her cheek so that they might soothe her as she breathed in their perfume. Thanks to the violets, her tears at last dried up. She still did not sleep, but remained with eyes closed, bathed in a fragrance that came from him, happy to lie there waiting in the complete surrender of her being.

Great ripples brushed over her skin. Midnight was striking, and she opened her eyes, startled to find her bedroom bathed in bright light. The moon was slowly rising over the tops of the elms, extinguishing the stars and blanching the sky. Through the window she could see the apse of the cathedral gleaming very white, seeming to cast down a pale shimmer that filled her bedroom with a cool milky light as of the dawn. The white walls, the white joists, the great bare expanse of white, seemed to grow brighter, swelling and expanding as though in a dream. Yet she could still make out the old dark oak furniture, the wardrobe, the chest, and the chairs, the carved figures on them reflecting gleams of light. But it was her bed, her square bed, regal in expanse, that struck her with wonder, as though she were seeing it for the first time, with its rising columns and its canopy of antique pink chintz, enveloped in such a dense haze of moonlight that she had the impression she was lying on a cloud, high up in the heavens, borne aloft on silent and invisible wings. For a brief moment it felt as though the whole bed was swaying; but then her eyes adapted, and she saw that it was in its usual corner. She lay with her head perfectly still in the middle of this moonlit lake, her eyes wandering all around, the bunch of violets by her lips.

What was she waiting for? Why couldn't she sleep? She was certain of it now: she was waiting for somebody. If she had stopped crying, it was only because he was about to appear. This comforting light, which put dark and dismal dreams to flight, heralded his coming. He was about to arrive, the harbinger moon had appeared before him only so as to irradiate them with this dawn-like light. The room was hung with white velvet; they would be able to see one another clearly. So then she got out of bed, and dressed: she put on just a white dress, the muslin dress she had worn on the day of her visit to the ruins of Hautecœur. She did not even tie up her hair, which hung down over her shoulders. Inside her slippers, her feet remained bare. She waited.

At that moment Angélique did not know exactly how he would arrive. He would not be able to come up to her, of course; they would simply see each other at a distance, she leaning on the balcony railing, and he standing below in the Clos-Marie. However, she then sat down, as if she had realized that there was no point in going to the window. Couldn't he simply pass through the walls, like the saints in the *Legend*? She waited, but she was not alone in her vigil, she felt them all around her, the white host of virgins who had encircled her since childhood. They came in with the moonlight, from the tall, mysterious, blue-crested trees in the bishop's garden, and from secluded corners of the cathedral, weaving through its forests of stone. From every part of this familiar and cherished vista, from the Chevrotte, the willows, and the grasses, the young girl could hear her dreams stream back to her—hopes, desires, everything of herself that she had invested in the objects around her as she had gazed at them each day, and the objects were now returning these aspirations to her. Never had the voices of the invisible realms spoken to her so loudly. As she listened intently to these sounds from the beyond, she made out, in the depths of the breathless, stifling night, the slight rustle that was, she sensed, the rippling of Agnes's dress, as the guardian of her body stood beside her. She was cheered to know that Agnes was there, with all the others. She waited.

Time passed, but Angélique did not notice. It seemed perfectly natural when Félicien arrived, swinging his legs over the balcony railing.

His tall figure was silhouetted against the pale sky. He did not come in, but remained standing in the gleaming frame of the window.

'Don't be afraid... It's me, I've come.'

She wasn't afraid of him, she was just thinking that he had turned up on time.

'You climbed up the timbers, didn't you?'

'Yes, up the timbers.'

She laughed at the simplicity of it all. He had at first hoisted himself onto the awning over the door, and had then shinned up the bracket, the foot of which rested on the string-course of the ground floor, and had reached the balcony without any difficulty.

'I was waiting for you. Come close to me.'

Félicien, who had arrived in an agitated mood, full of wild resolutions, did not move, taken aback at this sudden fulfilment of his hopes. Angélique was sure now that the female saints had not forbidden her to love, for she could hear them right beside her, welcoming him with fond laughter that purled as softly as the night breeze. Where had she picked up the absurd idea that Agnes would be angry? Beside her, Agnes was radiant with joy—a joy that seemed to flow down Angélique's shoulders and enfold her like two vast wings. All the women who had died for love had great compassion for sorrowing virgins, and returned to roam the warm night air, keeping invisible watch over the tear-stained passions of girls like her.

'Come to me, I was waiting for you.'

Reeling, Félicien entered. He had said to himself that he wanted her, that he would take her in his arms and clasp her to him, even if she should scream. But finding her in such a gentle mood, he became once more, on entering the pure, white room, shyer and weaker than a child.

He had taken three steps. But he was trembling all over, and fell to his knees, still some distance away from her.

'If you only knew the appalling tortures I've been through! I have never suffered like this before—the only true pain is believing that you are not loved!... I am prepared to lose everything I have, and end up a beggar on the streets, dying of hunger and crippled by illness. But I can't bear to spend a single day more with this pain eating up my heart, thinking that you don't love me... Be kind—spare me...'

She listened to him silently, overwhelmed by pity, but happy at the same time.

'What a state I was in when I left you this morning! I thought that you had changed for the better, that you had understood. And yet you were just the same as on that first day, utterly indifferent to me. You treated me no more kindly than a visiting customer, and cruelly refused to talk to me about anything apart from base matters of money... I stumbled down the staircase. Outside, I started running, and was afraid I would burst into tears. And then, when I got home, I started to go upstairs, but felt I would suffocate if I shut myself away in my room... So I fled into the open countryside, taking roads at random, first one, and then another. Night fell, and I was still walking. But my pain went everywhere with me, gnawing at me constantly. When you are in love, you can never flee the pain... Look! This is where you drove in the knife, and its tip kept burying itself deeper.'

He groaned loudly, remembering all that he had suffered.

'I lay in the grass for a long time, knocked flat by my pain like a tree that's been felled... And nothing else existed, apart from you. I was completely crushed by the thought that I would never have you. I started to go numb all over, and my mind was filled with crazed thoughts... And that's why I've come back to you. I don't remember which roads I took, or how I've come to be in this room. Please forgive me, I would've torn down the doors with my bare hands, I would've climbed up to your window in broad daylight...'

She stood in the shadows. Kneeling in the moonlight, he was unable to see her, or her face which was pale now with repentance and tenderness. She was so choked with emotion that she could not speak. He assumed that she was unsympathetic, and clasped his hands together.

'This all goes back a very long time... One evening I caught sight of you standing here at the window. You were only a vague pale outline, and I could scarcely make out your face, and yet I could see you, I could tell what you were really like. But I was very shy, and wandered about for many nights without finding the courage to come and meet you in broad daylight... And, what's more, I liked this mysterious side of you, and was happy to dream about you, as though you were some unknown person I would never meet... Later, when I found out who you were, it was impossible to resist the lure of knowing and possessing a dream. It was then that my obsession began, and it grew with every meeting. Do you remember the first time, in the field, that morning when I was inspecting the window? I had never felt so clumsy, and you were right to make fun of me... I started to make you feel uneasy then, and my clumsiness continued when I followed you on your visits to the poor. At that stage I was no longer in control of myself, and was surprised and horrified by the things I did... When I showed up with the order for the mitre, I was driven on by some invisible force, as by myself I would never have dared, I was so sure that you didn't like me... If you could only understand how miserable I am! You don't need to love me, but just let me love you. You can be cold, you can be unkind, but I'll still love you exactly as you are. I ask only to be allowed to see you, even if I haven't the slightest hope, just for the joy it gives me to be here, like this, at your knees.'

He fell silent, his courage wavering, no longer believing that he could find words to sway her. He was not aware that a smile was playing on her lips, an invincible smile, slowly spreading. Oh, the darling boy! He was so innocent and trusting—he had just recited this shining, passionate plea, his heart's prayer, adoringly before her, as though before the dream of his youth! And to think that she had at first fought against her desire to see him again, and then sworn to love him without his ever knowing! A profound silence ensued; the saints never forbade love when two people loved like this. Behind her, there was a pulse of brightness, no more than a faint ripple, as the moonlight lapped over the floor tiles. An invisible finger, doubtless that of her guardian, touched her mouth, unsealing her vow. Now she could speak once more, and all the powers and emotions that drifted in the air around her were given voice.

'Ah, yes, I remember, I remember!...'

Félicien was at once captivated by the music of her voice, and he found it so utterly enchanting that his love for her deepened just by listening to it.

'Yes, I remember when you came in the night... You were so far away on those first evenings that the faint sound of your footsteps left me perplexed. Then I recognized you, and later saw your shadow, and then finally one evening you showed yourself, on a beautiful night like this one, lit up by brilliant white moonlight. You emerged slowly out of your surroundings in just the way that I had been expecting all these years... I remember the laughter I tried to hold in, and which burst out from me anyway, when you rescued that piece of washing that had been swept away by the Chevrotte. I remember how furious I was when you poached my paupers from me, giving them so much money that you made me look like a miser. I remember how scared I felt that evening when I was forced to dart away through the grass in my bare feet... Yes, I remember, I remember...'

Her crystal voice faltered, and she trembled as she recalled this last memory, just as though the words 'I love you' had once again brushed her ears. And he listened, enraptured.

'It's true, I've been cruel. We can be very foolish when we know no better! We do what we think we have to, but we're terrified of making mistakes when we listen to our heart. Afterwards, I've been stung by remorse, and have suffered myself, knowing that you were suffering!... I wanted to explain all this to you, but of course I couldn't. When you turned up with your drawing of St Agnes, I was delighted to do the piece for you, and guessed that you would want to come back each day. Try and understand, I pretended not to care because I thought it my duty to drive you from the house... Why do we have to make ourselves miserable? Though I'd have liked to welcome you with open arms, there was another woman, deep within me, who rebelled, who feared and mistrusted you, who enjoyed sowing doubts in your mind, out of a vague notion that she was settling an old quarrel whose cause she'd long since forgotten. I am not always good, there are things inside me that I don't always understand... And, the worst of it, certainly, is that I talked about money. Money, indeed! It's something that never enters my mind. I'm the sort of person who would happily accept cartloads of the stuff, just so I could make it rain down wherever I wanted! I can't think how I took such malicious pleasure in debasing myself in this way. Can you forgive me?'

Félicien was now at her feet, having moved over to her on his knees. It was all so unhoped for, so utterly wondrous.

He murmured:

'Oh, my dearest, what a lovely, pure, exquisite creature you are! Your miraculous kindness has cured me at a stroke. Did I ever even suffer?... No, it's rather up to you to forgive me, for I have a confession to make. I must tell you who I am.'

He began to grow agitated again at the thought that he could no longer continue to hide his identity, since she had confided so openly in him. It would have been unfair. Yet he hesitated, fearing to lose her if she should cast doubt on their future once she knew who he was. She waited for him to speak, a mischievous urge growing in her once more, in spite of herself.

He went on in a very low voice:

'I lied to your parents.'

'Yes, I know,' she said, smiling.

'No, you don't know, you can't possibly know, it all goes back so far... Glass-painting is only a hobby for me, you need to know the truth...'

She swiftly placed her hand over his mouth, stopping his confession.

'I don't want to know... I was waiting for you, and you came. That's enough.'

He made no attempt to speak; the little hand on his lips was almost choking him with happiness.

'I'll find out later, when it's time... In any case, I can assure you that I do know. You are undoubtedly the handsomest, richest and noblest of men, because that's how things are in my dream. I don't mind waiting patiently, as I'm certain it will come true... You're the man I was hoping for, and I am yours...'

She stopped for a second time, as the words she uttered sent a shiver through her body. It was not she alone who was summoning them, they came to her from the beautiful night, from the vast pale sky, from the old trees and the old stones, asleep outside, dreaming her dreams aloud. Behind her, voices murmured them also, the voices of her friends from the *Legend* who peopled the air. But a phrase still remained to be spoken, one that would bring everything together, the long wait, the gradual creation of her lover, the fervid emotion of their first meetings. It rose from her lips like a bird of the morning taking pale wing to meet the daybreak in the virginal whiteness of the bedroom.

'I love you.'

Angélique, her hands resting open-palmed upon her knees, was offering herself. Félicien recalled the evening when she had run barefoot through the grass, looking so lovely that he had chased after her and stammered in her ear: 'I love you.' And he understood that she was only now replying with the same cry: 'I love you', an immortal cry issuing finally from her unlocked heart.

'I love you... Take me, bear me away with you, I belong to you.'

She offered herself up to him entirely. An hereditary flame had been relit within her. Her hands groped around, clutching at the emptiness around, her delicate nape bowed, her head sagging down heavily. If he had held out his arms, she would have fallen blindly into them, yielding to the impulse in her veins, desiring only to melt into him.

And he, who had come here intending to take her, trembled before such innocence and passion. He took her gently by the wrists, and crossed her chaste hands over her breast. He looked at her for a moment, but did not even cede to his desire to kiss her hair.

'You love me, and I love you... Oh, how wonderful it is to know that one is loved!'

In the midst of their rapture, they felt a sudden disturbance. What could it be? Each saw the other lit up in a flood of white light, as though the moon had grown in radiance and was shining like the sun. It was the dawn, and the cloud above the elms in the bishop's garden was flushing crimson. What? Daybreak already! They were bewildered, and could not believe that they had been talking there for hours. She had barely told him anything, and he still had so much left to say!

'A minute, just one more minute!'

A bright dawn was breaking, quite warm already, and presaging a hot summer's day. The stars had gone out one by one, and with them had departed the wandering visions and invisible friends, fleeing astride a moonbeam. And now, in the daylight, the room was white only because its walls and beams were white, and it had been emptied of everything apart from its antique dark oak furniture. The bed stood there, unmade, one of the chintz curtains hanging down, half veiling it.

'A minute, just one more minute!'

Angélique refused, and rose to her feet, urging Félicien to leave. Since day had begun to break, she had been overcome by a sense of shame, which only increased when she saw the bed. She thought she had heard a faint noise to her right, and her hair had rippled slightly, though there was no breeze coming in the window. Could it be Agnes, leaving last, chased away by the day?

'No, leave me, I beg you... It's so light now. I'm afraid.'

Félicien withdrew obediently. To be loved was more than he had hoped. When he got to the window, however, he turned around and looked at her again for a long time, as if he wished to bear away something of her within him. They smiled at each other, bathed in the dawn light, their gazes like a sustained caress.

One last time, he said:

'I love you.'

And she repeated:

'I love you.'

That was all—he was gone already, clambering down the timbers, lithe and agile, as she watched from the balcony railing. She had picked up the bunch of violets, and breathed in their scent to calm her passions. And as he crossed the Clos-Marie he looked up and he saw that she was kissing the flowers.

Félicien had scarcely disappeared behind the willows when Angélique was startled to hear the door to the house opening below. It was just striking four, and nobody in the household was in the habit of getting up until two hours later. Her surprise increased when she saw it was Hubertine, as Hubert was usually the first to go downstairs. She watched as Hubertine wandered slowly along the paths in the narrow garden, her arms hanging listlessly by her sides, her face pale in the dawn light, as though she had fled her bedroom in desperate need of air after a torrid night without sleep. Hubertine still looked very beautiful, dressed in a simple dressing gown, her hair hastily tied up; and she appeared very weary, joyous, and wretched all at once.

CHAPTER 8

THE next day, waking after eight hours' sleep—sleep of that deep, sweet, restorative sort that follows great happiness, Angélique ran to the window. The sky was clear, and it had turned warm again after the great storm that had left her feeling very worried the previous day. She cried out joyfully to Hubert, who was opening the shutters below:

'Father, Father! The sun's come out!... Oh, I'm so glad, the procession's going to be lovely!'

She dressed quickly and went downstairs. It was on this day, 28 July, that the Procession of the Miracle was set to wind its way through the streets of Beaumont. And each year the embroiderers celebrated it as a holiday; they didn't touch their needles, and spent the day tricking out the house with traditional decorations, which had been passed down from mother to daughter for four hundred years.

Angélique drank her *café au lait* hastily, as she was already thinking about the wall hangings.

'Mother, we need to go and check that they're still all right.'

'We have plenty of time,' said Hubertine, calmly. 'We don't need to put them up until midday.'

They were talking about three wonderful panels of antique embroidery, which the Huberts looked after as devotedly as a family relic, and took out just once a year, on the day of the procession. The previous day, in accordance with custom, the ceremoniarius,* the good Abbé Cornille, had gone from door to door informing the townsfolk of the route that would be taken by the statue of St Agnes, behind which Monseigneur would follow bearing the Blessed Sacrament.* The route had remained the same for more than four centuries: the procession set out through the portal of St Agnes, and went down the Rue des Orfèvres, the Grand'Rue, and the Rue Basse, and then, after crossing the new town, it returned by the Rue Magloire and the Place du Cloître and re-entered the cathedral through the main entrance. All along the way, the townsfolk vied fiercely with one another, decking their windows and hanging their walls with their richest fabrics, and strewing rose petals across the cobblestones.

Angélique grew calm only when she was allowed to take out the three panels of embroidery from the drawer where they slumbered the whole year long.

'They're fine, absolutely fine,' she murmured, ecstatic.

Once she had carefully removed the thin sheets of paper that protected them, there they appeared, all three devoted to the Virgin Mary: the Virgin receiving the angel's visit, the Virgin weeping at the foot of the cross, and the Virgin ascending into heaven. They dated from the fifteenth century, and had been fashioned in different shades of silk against a gold background. They were beautifully preserved, and the embroiderers, who had been offered enormous sums for them, were very proud of them.

'Mother, I'll hang them up!'

It was quite a business. Hubert spent the morning cleaning the old façade. He tied a broom on to the end of a stick and dusted down the timber framing and the brickwork, right up to the roof beams. Then he washed down the stonework on the ground floor with a sponge, along with all the parts of the staircase turret that he could reach. The three panels of embroidery were then set in place. Angélique used rings to hang them on to ancient nails, the Annunciation under the left-hand window, and the Assumption under the one on the right; and, as for the Crucifixion, the nails for it were located above the big ground-floor window, and she had to take out a ladder to hang it in its turn. She had already decorated the windows with flowers, and it was as though the ancient building had recaptured its long-lost youth, with the panels of gold and silk embroidery shining in the beautiful holiday sunshine.

After lunch the whole of the Rue des Orfèvres bustled with activity. To avoid the hottest part of the day, the procession set out only at five o'clock; but the town began to put on its finery from midday onwards. Opposite the Huberts', the goldsmith hung his shop with sky-blue drapery edged with silver tassels; while the candle-maker next door used the curtains that cordoned off his bed, red cotton curtains that appeared blood-coloured in the broad daylight. And all the houses were dressed in different hues, festooned in a great profusion of materials—everything that people owned, right down to their bed-side rugs, flapping limply in the slight breeze that stirred the warm afternoon air. The street was all decked out in bright rippling colour, as though transformed into some great gala hall open to the sky. The townsfolk jostled each other, talking loudly as if they were still indoors, some staggering about with their arms full, others clambering up ladders, hammering or shouting. To add to this, an altar of repose was being set up at the corner of the Grand'Rue, sowing consternation among the women of the neighbourhood, who rushed about bringing vases and candelabra.

Angélique ran over to offer the two Empire candlesticks that usually decorated the mantelpiece in the sitting room. She had not paused since morning, but did not feel the slightest bit weary, swept along by great inner joy. And when she came back, her hair blowing about in the breeze, and began to pluck rose petals into a basket, Hubertine joked:

'You'll probably make a lot less effort getting ready for your own wedding... Are you getting married today?'

'Oh, yes, I am!' she replied gaily.

Hubertine smiled in turn.

'In the meantime, with the house looking so lovely, we might as well go up and get dressed.'

'Right away, Mother... My basket's almost full now.'

She finished plucking the rose petals that she was going to keep for herself to throw before Monseigneur's feet. The petals rained down from her slender fingers, and the light, fragrant basket overflowed. She vanished up the narrow turret staircase, calling out with a loud laugh:

'I'm going to make myself look as beautiful as a star in the sky.'

The afternoon was wearing on. The fever of activity gripping Beaumont-l'Église subsided and, with preparations at last complete, gave way to a sense of anticipation, the streets quietly echoing with whispers and faint murmurs. The stifling heat had waned as the sun sank down and, under a fading sky, soft shadows, warm, mild, and serene, spread between the tightly packed houses. A profound mood of reverence filled the old town, as though it were now an extension of the cathedral. The only noise was that of cart traffic drifting up from Beaumont-la-Ville, the new town on the banks of the Ligneul, where many factories had not even closed for the day, disdaining to celebrate this ancient rite.

At four o'clock the great bell in the north tower, whose motion sent a trembling through the Huberts' house, began to toll, and at that moment Angélique and Hubertine reappeared in their finery. Hubertine wore a dress of unbleached linen trimmed with simple lacework and, with her youthful waistline and full, healthy figure, could have been mistaken for the older sister of her adoptive daughter. Angélique, for her part, had put on a white foulard* dress, and that was all: she wore no earrings or bracelets, her hands and neck were bare, and her satiny skin emerged from the delicate fabric like a flower blooming. An unseen comb, hastily affixed, struggled to hold back her rebellious sun-gold curls. She was innocent and proud, unaffected in her simplicity, and as beautiful as a star in the sky.

'Oh, the bell's ringing!' she said. 'Monseigneur has left his palace.'

The bell continued to peal out, high and solemn in the vast unclouded sky. The Huberts settled in at the open ground-floor window, the two women leaning on the cross-bar, the man standing behind them. They had taken up their usual places, and were in a good position to see everything; they were the first to be able to glimpse the procession emerging from the cathedral, and wouldn't miss a single candle passing by.

'Where's my basket?' asked Angélique.

Hubert had to pass her the basket of rose petals, which she cradled in her arms, pressing it tightly against her breast.

'Oh, that bell,' she said, 'it's making everything sway!'

Every part of the little house vibrated, resonating as the bell swung back and forth; the street, and the whole quarter, waited expectantly as these tremors expanded, while the hangings flapped languidly in the evening breeze. The scent of the roses was very sweet.

Half an hour went by. Suddenly the twin doors of St Agnes's portal were flung open, and the inner depths of the cathedral became visible, a darkness stippled with the gleaming points of candle-flames. The cross-bearer emerged first, a subdeacon in a tunicle,* flanked by two acolytes, each holding a large, lighted candle. Behind them, the cere-moniarius, the good Abbé Cornille, came hurrying. After checking that everything in the street was ready, he stopped beneath the porch and cast a quick eye over the procession to make sure that all were in their correct positions. The lay organizations led the way, pious asso-ciations and schools, in order of seniority. There were tiny children, small girls dressed in white like brides, small boys, curly-haired and capless, brimming with excitement and looking like little princes in their Sunday best, who sought out their mothers' eyes in the crowd. A nine-year-old lad walked all by himself in their midst, dressed as St John the Baptist, with a sheepskin* draped over his thin bare shoulders. Four little girls decked in pink ribbons carried a muslin-covered shield on which there stood a sheaf of ripe wheat. Then came the older girls bunched around a banner of the Virgin, and some ladies dressed all in black with a banner of their own, crimson silk embroidered with an image of St Joseph, and then more and more banners, in velvet and satin, swaying on the end of golden rods. The men's confraternities were just as numerous, penitents of every colour, the majority grey penitents, who were dressed in coarse linen and wore hoods, and whose emblem caused a great stir among the onlookers—an enormous cross bearing a wheel, from which there hung the instruments of the Passion.

When the children appeared, Angélique cried out adoringly:

'Oh, the little darlings—look at them!'

One, barely knee-high, and 3 years old at most, tottered proudly by on his little feet, making such a funny sight that Angélique dipped into her basket and threw a handful of petals over him. He was com-pletely covered, he had rose petals on his shoulders, and in his hair. And doting chuckles rippled along the line of onlookers, and flowers rained down from every window. In the quietly humming street, all that could be heard was the muffled tread of the procession as flowers teemed down on the cobblestones in a silent shower. Soon they lay there in drifts.

Although satisfied that the laity were arrayed in good order, the Abbé Cornille grew impatient, concerned by the fact that the procession had not moved for two minutes, and so he hurried back towards its head, giving the Huberts a smile as he passed.

'What's the matter—why aren't they moving?' said Angélique restlessly, as though she were waiting at the far end of the route for the arrival of happiness.

Hubertine replied calmly:

'There's no need for them to rush.'

'There must be a hold-up, maybe one of the altars is still being finished,' Hubert explained.

The Daughters of the Virgin had started to sing a hymn, and their high-pitched voices rose into the air as clear as crystal. Little by little, the procession began to stir, and they set off once more.

Now, in the wake of the laity, the clergy began to emerge from the cathedral, those from the lower ranks issuing first. All were wearing surplices,* and they put on their birettas* as they passed beneath the porch. Each held a burning candle, those on the right in their right hands, and those on the left in their left, beyond the edge of their lines, forming twin rows of tiny flickering flames, almost invisible in the broad daylight. First came those who belonged to the large seminary, the parishes, and the collegiate churches, and next were the clerics and the beneficiaries of the cathedral,* followed by the canons, their shoulders covered by white pluvials.* In their midst, wearing red silk copes, came the choirmen, who had loudly struck up their song, and to whom all the clergy sang a softer response. The hymn *Pange lingua** rose very pure into the air, and the street was filled with a great ripple of muslin, as the wings of the surplices flapped up, and appeared speckled with pale golden stars as the tiny candle-flames burned before them.

'Oh, St Agnes!' murmured Angélique.

She smiled at the saint, whom four clergymen carried on a base of blue velvet trimmed with lace. Each year when St Agnes was brought out from the shadows, where she had maintained her vigil for many centuries, Angélique was astonished by how different she appeared in bright daylight, enfolded in her mantle of long golden hair. She was so ancient and yet so youthful, with her little hands and her slender little feet, and her thin girlish face blackened by age.

Monseigneur was due to follow after her. Already, from the far end of the cathedral, came the jingle of censers swinging back and forth.

There was whispering, and Angélique repeated:

'Monseigneur... Monseigneur...'

And, at that moment, with her eyes fixed on the passing saint, she recalled the old stories, all the great marquises of Hautecœur who had delivered Beaumont from the plague thanks to Agnes's intervention, Jean V and his house who came and knelt in devotion before her image. And she saw them all, lords of the miracle, pass by in procession, like a line of princes of the realm.

A large break had occurred in the procession. The chaplain entrusted with the bishop's crozier moved forward, holding it upright, the curved part towards him. Two thurifers then appeared, walking backwards and swinging their censers through short arcs, each accompanied by an acolyte bearing an incense boat. And the great canopy of purple velvet, fringed with gold, was manoeuvred with some difficulty through one of the bays of the door. Proper order was quickly restored, and the appropriate officials took hold of the rods. Flanked on either side by his deacons of honour, Monseigneur strode along beneath the canopy, his head bare, his shoulders covered with a white stole whose ends he had wrapped around his hands, which bore the Blessed Sacrament without touching it, holding it high above him.

Suddenly the thurifers drew aside, and the censers, which they had been flinging vigorously back and forth, resumed their earlier rhythm, their chains chinking with a soft, silvery note.

Where was it that Angélique had met someone resembling Monseigneur? All the onlookers bowed their heads in reverence. But she, dipping her head only halfway, stared at him. He was tall and thin, noble in bearing and astonishingly youthful for a man in his sixties. His eagle eyes shone, his strong nose accentuated the sovereign authority of his face, which was softened by his thick white curls; and she saw how pale his complexion was, even if a flush seemed to be spreading across it. Perhaps this was only a reflection of the great golden sunburst* that he bore in his stole-wrapped hands, and whose mystical light shimmered down on him.

No, there was no doubt, this face stirred some recollection within her. As he set off, Monseigneur had begun to recite a psalm in his deep voice, enouncing the verses alternately with his deacons. And she trembled when she saw him turn to look at the window where she stood, so severe did he appear, so coldly arrogant and scornful of all vain passions. His eyes had gone to the three ancient panels of embroidery, Mary visited by the angel, Mary at the foot of the cross, Mary ascending into heaven. His glance filled with joy, and then moved downwards and fastened upon her and, as confusion mounted within her, she was unable to tell whether the pale gleam that entered his eyes was kindly or stern. But already his eyes had returned to the Blessed Sacrament and did not waver, glistening in the light that scattered off the great golden sun. The censers swung out and back again, their chains clinking softly, and a small cloud of incense rose into the air.

But Angélique's heart was beating near to bursting. Just behind the canopy she had caught sight of the mitre—St Agnes borne aloft by two angels, the piece she had embroidered thread by thread with all her love, which a chaplain, his fingers wrapped in a veil, was carrying with great piety, as though it were a holy relic. And among the laity who followed behind, in the stream of functionaries, officials and magistrates, she recognized Félicien, in the first row, slender and blond, dressed in a suit, with his curly hair, his strong, straight nose, and dark, gently haughty eyes. She had been expecting him, and was not at all surprised to see that he had changed into a prince. He gave her an anxious look, imploring forgiveness for his lie, to which she responded with a warm smile.

'What on earth!' murmured Hubertine, dumbfounded. 'Isn't that the young man we know?'

She too had recognized him, and grew perturbed when she turned and saw that her daughter was quite transfigured.

'So he lied to us?... Why?... Who is he? Do you know who that young man really is?'

Yes, perhaps she did know. It was as though an inner voice was supplying answers to her recent questions. But she did not dare or wish to delve into these things further. Everything would become clear when the time was right. Feeling that this moment was drawing close, she swelled with pride and passion.

'What's going on?' asked Hubert, bending forward behind his wife.

He was never aware of what was happening. And when she pointed out the young man to him, he was sceptical.

'What an idea! That's not him!'

So then Hubertine pretended that she had made a mistake. It was the wisest course to take, she would look into things later. The procession was about to set off once more, having stopped at the next corner while Monseigneur censed the Blessed Sacrament among the greenery of the altar of repose; and Angélique, who had absent-mindedly laid her hand in the bottom of her basket, still clutching a final ball of rose petals, cast them suddenly into the air, her mind hazy with rapture. Just at that moment Félicien took a step forward. Petals showered down, fluttering about slowly, a couple of them settling in his hair.

It was over. The canopy had disappeared around the corner into the Grand'Rue, and the tail of the procession wound away, leaving the street empty and solemn, as though drowsing in pious reverie, a slightly bitter fragrance rising from the trampled roses. And in the distance, growing ever fainter, you could still make out a silvery jingle of chains whenever the censers were swung.

'Oh, Mother,' cried Angélique, 'can we go into the cathedral and watch them return?'

Hubertine's first impulse was to say no. But she herself felt such a strong compulsion to know for certain that she agreed.

'Yes, in a little while, if it will make you happy.'

But a little patience was necessary. Angélique, who had gone upstairs to put on a hat, could not stay still. She went over to the window every few minutes to study the far end of the street, and then looked up as though wishing to search the very heavens; and she kept up a loud commentary, following the procession along every step of the way.

'They're going down the Rue Basse... Now they must be coming into the square in front of the sub-prefecture... Those big roads in Beaumont-la-Ville stretch on for ever. And all this so that the cloth-merchants can have a good look at St Agnes!'

A delicate pink cloud, latticed artfully with gold, hung in the sky. The stillness in the air gave a sense that ordinary life had been suspended, that God had left his house, and everyone was waiting for him to be returned before resuming their daily occupations. On the other side of the street, the goldsmith's blue drapery and the candle-maker's red curtains still hung over the doorways of their shops. The streets seemed to slumber, and the only thing moving was the slow procession of the clergy, whose progress could be made out from every part of the town.

'Mother, Mother, they're coming into the Rue Magloire, I promise. They're just about to start up the hill.'

She was fibbing. It was only half past six, and the procession never returned before quarter past seven. She was well aware that the canopy was making its way past the lower quays of the Ligneul at that moment. But she was filled with such impatience!

'Mother, hurry up, there won't be any seats left.'

'Well, then, let's go!' said Hubertine finally, unable to suppress a smile.

'I'm staying here,' declared Hubert. 'I'll take down the hangings and lay the table.'

The cathedral appeared empty to them, with God no longer inside. All the doors had been left open, as though it were a house fallen into disarray, awaiting the return of its master. Few people came in; the high altar, an austere sarcophagus in the Romanesque style, alone glimmered with starry candles at the far end of the nave; and through the rest of the vast interior, the side aisles and the chapels, darkness gathered as the dusk settled.

Hubertine and Angélique made a slow circuit around it. The base of the building seemed crushed down by the weight above, squat piers supporting the semicircular arches of the side aisles. They walked past dark chapels, silent as crypts. But when they crossed before the main portal, beneath the organ bay, they had a feeling of release, their glances rising to the lofty Gothic windows of the nave which soared above the heavy Romanesque course. As they continued along the southern aisle, however, the feeling of suffocation returned. Four immense columns at the four corners of the transept crossing rose in a single sweep to support the vault, where a mauve glow still lingered as the daylight ebbed from the rose windows in the lateral façades. They had walked up the three steps leading to the choir, and turned into the ambulatory, which was the most ancient part of the building, begun when the sepulchre was dug. They stopped for a moment before the finely wrought old grille which enclosed the choir on all sides, and stared at the glittering candles on the high altar. The tiny flames were reflected in the antique polished oak of the stalls, a majestic structure burgeoning with elaborately carved figure work. And thus they returned to their starting point and, looking up once more, seemed to feel the nave breathing as it soared upward. And as the shadows deepened, the ancient walls seemed to retreat outwards and loom higher, the last gleams of gold and paint fading into the darkness.

'I knew we would be too early,' said Hubertine.

Angélique did not reply, and simply murmured:

'It's so huge!'

She felt as though she did not know the cathedral, and was seeing it for the first time. Her eyes ranged over the motionless rows of

chairs and into the depths of the chapels, in which the memorial
stones could be distinguished only as a deeper shade of darkness. Her
gaze ran on to the Hautecœur chapel, and she recognized the window,
repaired at last, with its St George figure, as hazy as a vision in the
expiring daylight. And she was filled with great joy.

At that moment a shudder ran through the cathedral as the great
bell began to toll.

'Oh, here they are!' she said. 'They're coming up the Rue Magloire.'

This time it was true. Crowds streamed into the side aisles, and
from minute to minute they could all sense that the procession was
drawing nearer. This feeling grew keener as the bell continued to toll
and a strong gust of wind swept in through the main doors, which
gaped wide open. God was returning home.

Angélique, standing on tiptoes and leaning against Hubertine's
shoulder, trained her eyes on the open doorway, whose curve was
clearly delineated against the pale light of dusk filling the Place du
Cloître. The subdeacon carrying the cross appeared first, flanked
by his two acolytes with their candlesticks; and behind them came
hurrying the ceremoniarius, the good Abbé Cornille, out of breath
and exhausted. On the threshold of the cathedral, each new arrival
stood out for a moment in bold clear silhouette, before dissolving into
the shadows within. These were the members of the laity, schools,
associations, confraternities, whose banners swayed like sails before
being suddenly engulfed by the darkness. The pale band of Daughters
of the Virgin reappeared, and entered singing in high seraphic voices.
The cathedral swallowed up everyone, and the nave was slowly filling,
men on the right, women on the left. Night had at last fallen, and
the square outside sparkled with points of light, hundreds of tiny
moving flames. It was the turn of the clergy now, their burning candles
held beyond the edge of their lines, a double row of yellow flames
passing through the door. There was no end to it, candle following
candle in slow proliferation, the large seminary, clergy of the parishes
and cathedral, choirmen singing the anthem, canons in white
pluvials. And gradually the cathedral grew brighter as it filled with
candle-flames, lit up by hundreds of twinkling stars like a summer
night sky.

Two chairs were empty. Angélique climbed on to one of them.

'Get down,' said Hubertine, 'that's not allowed.'

But Angélique calmly remained standing there.

'Why isn't it allowed? I want to be able to see... Oh, isn't it lovely!'
And her mother finally decided to climb up on the other chair.

The whole cathedral sparkled and blazed now. As the tide of candles swept along, gleams of light darted from the hunched vaults of
the side aisles and the depths of the chapels, where the glass of a reliquary or a golden tabernacle returned a glimmer. Even in the ambulatory and the sepulchral crypts flickering rays were set dancing. The
choir flared with light, the altar flamed, the stalls glowed, and on the
old iron grille the rosettes appeared in dark outline. The nave seemed
to soar upwards even more boldly now; down below, the squat, heavy
piers bore up the rounded arches; above, the sheaves of colonnettes
grew more slender and elaborate, rising to pointed arches. And this
great upswelling of faith and love was like the radiance that spread
heavenwards from the lights below.

Amid the noise of shuffling feet and scraping chairs, the chains
of the censers began to jangle softly once more. And all at once
the organ began to boom and a deafening series of notes swelled
upwards, filling the vaults with a rumble like thunder. Monseigneur,
it seemed, was about to come in from the square. At the same time
St Agnes was entering the apse, borne along on the shoulders of
the clergy, her expression seeming to grow calmer in the candlelight,
evidently happy to return to her dreams, which had lasted for four
centuries. At long last, with the crozier preceding him, and the
mitre coming behind, Monseigneur entered, holding up the Blessed
Sacrament just as he had before, with his stole wrapped around
both hands. The canopy, which was advancing down the centre of
the nave, came to a halt before the choir grille. There were a few
moments of confusion as members of the bishop's retinue closed up
behind him.

From the moment that Félicien had appeared again following the
mitre, Angélique had not taken her eyes off him. It just so happened
that he was carried along to the right of the canopy; and so, for an
instant, she took in the white head of Monseigneur and the young
man's blond head in a single glance. A flame ran across her eyelids,
she clasped her hands together, and said aloud:

'Oh, Monseigneur, and Monseigneur's son!'*

Her secret had slipped out. The cry was an involuntary one—
certainty had finally come to her in the sudden light of their resemblance. Perhaps deep down she had already known, but had never dared

admit it to herself; now the fact blazed out, dazzling her. Memories surged up, from within her and from all around, echoing her cry.

Gripped by confusion, Hubertine murmured:

'That boy is Monseigneur's son?'

People were now crowding on all sides of the two women. The lovely mother in her simple linen dress, and the daughter, radiant as an archangel in her white foulard gown, were known to all, and attracted many looks of admiration. They were very conspicuous, standing on their chairs, and appeared so beautiful that many eyes flew up to them and lingered.

'Yes, of course he is, my good lady,' said Mère Lemballeuse, who happened to be among the throng. 'You mean you didn't know?... Such a handsome young man, and rich too—rich enough to buy the whole town, if he wanted to. He has millions upon millions!'

Hubertine listened, very pale.

'You must surely have heard the story,' continued the old beggar-woman. 'His mother died bringing him into the world, and so Monseigneur entered the priesthood. Today he decided to summon him back home... Félicien VII of Hautecœur—now there's a real prince for you!'

Hubertine's whole body registered her dismay. And delight spread over Angélique's face as she grasped that her dream was coming true. She was not in the least bit surprised; she had been convinced all along that he was the richest, handsomest and noblest of men. And she was filled with a vast unalloyed joy that cared nothing for potential obstacles, and could not in fact conceive of any. He was at last reveal-ing his true self, and offering himself to her in his turn. Gold streamed from the delicate candle-flames, the organ resounded with the pomp of their engagement, and the long line of Hautecœurs emerged from the mist of legend and paraded by in their majesty: Norbert I, Jean V, Félicien III, Jean XII, down to the last of them, Félicien VII, who turned his blond head towards her. He was the descendant of the Virgin Mary's cousins, the master, the superb Jesus, revealing himself in glory beside his father.

Just at that moment Félicien smiled at her, and she did not notice the angry look that flashed across Monseigneur's face as he caught sight of her standing there on the chair, above the crowd, her face flushed with pride and passion.

'Oh, my poor child,' sighed Hubertine, in despair.

But the chaplains and the acolytes had drawn up into lines on the right and left, and the first deacon, having taken the Blessed Sacrament from Monseigneur's hands, placed it on the altar. And there followed the final benediction, choirmen bellowing the *Tantum ergo*,* clouds of incense rising from the censers, and then the sudden, echoing silence of the prayer. And in the middle of the blazing cathedral, overflowing with clergy and townsfolk, Monseigneur approached the altar once more beneath the soaring vaults and, picking up the great golden sun with both hands, moved it thrice through the air, slowly making the sign of the cross.

CHAPTER 9

THAT evening, as she walked back from the cathedral, Angélique thought to herself: 'I will see him soon: he will be in the Clos-Marie, and I will go down and meet him.' The rendezvous had been settled with a glance.

They had a late dinner, at eight o'clock, in the kitchen as usual. Exhilarated by the day's festivities, Hubert prattled on all alone. Hubertine was in a sombre mood, and scarcely answered him. Her gaze remained fixed on the young girl, who ate with great appetite, but quite obliviously, appearing not even to realize that she was bringing the fork to her mouth—so absorbed was she in her dream. And Hubertine could read her every thought, and could follow them as they took shape, one after the other, beneath that innocent brow, translucent as a crystal of the purest water.

At nine o'clock they were surprised to hear a ring at the doorbell. It was the Abbé Cornille. Despite his weariness, he had come to let them know how much Monseigneur had admired the three ancient embroidery panels.

'Yes, he spoke about them while I was with him. I was sure you would be pleased to know.'

At the mention of Monseigneur's name, Angélique pricked up her ears, but fell back to dreaming when talk turned to the procession. A few minutes later she rose to her feet.

'Where are you going?' asked Hubertine.

She was surprised by this question, as though she didn't quite know herself why she had got up.

'Mother, I'm going upstairs. I'm very tired.'

Hubertine guessed the real reason behind this excuse—a desire to be alone with her happiness.

'Come and give me a kiss.'

As she hugged Angélique, she could feel her trembling in her arms. The young girl almost squirmed out of their nightly kiss. Hubertine studied her face very gravely, and read in her eyes the planned rendezvous and her fervid desire to be off there.

'Be good, sleep well.'

But Angélique, after a hasty goodnight to Hubert and the Abbé Cornille, was already climbing upstairs to her bedroom, greatly flustered, so near had she come to spilling her secret. If her mother had held her to her breast for a second longer, she would have told all. After she had shut herself in her bedroom with a double turn of the key, she found the light painful to her eyes, and blew out the candle. The moon was rising later and later each night, and it was very black outside. Without undressing, she sat before the window for several hours, looking out into darkness, just waiting. The minutes passed by, crowded minutes, her mind occupied by a single thought: she would go down and meet him when midnight struck. It would all happen very naturally, and in her mind's eye she watched herself go through with it, every footstep and every gesture, moving in the effortless way one does in dreams. Almost at once she had heard the Abbé Cornille leave. Then the Huberts had gone up to their bedroom. Twice she thought she had heard their door open, and furtive footsteps advance as far as the staircase, as though someone had come to listen there for a moment. After that the house had seemed to subside into a deep slumber.

When the hour struck, Angélique stood up.

'It's time to go, he's waiting for me.'

She opened the door, and went out without closing it. As she passed the Huberts' bedroom on the staircase, she listened carefully, but heard nothing, nothing but tremulous silence. She was in fact very calm and, unmindful of any wrongdoing, felt no anxiety nor any need to rush. Some unseen force drew her along, and it all seemed so simple that she would have smiled at the thought that she was running any danger. Reaching the foot of the stairs, she went out through the kitchen into the garden and, again, forgot to close the door behind her. She walked quickly over to the little gate that led into the Clos-Marie, and left this also wide open in her wake. Once in the field, she did not hesitate, in spite of the pitch darkness, and headed straight for the plank spanning the Chevrotte, and crossed over, feeling her way as though through perfectly familiar surroundings in which every tree was known to her by heart. And turning to the right beneath a willow, she had only to stretch out her hands to meet those of the man who she knew would be waiting there for her.

She was silent for a moment as she clasped his hands tightly. They could not see one another because the sky was shrouded by a sultry haze, as yet unlit by the slender moon, which was just starting to rise. And she began to speak in the darkness, and poured out the great joy brimming in her heart.

'Oh, my sweet lord, I love you so much, and am so thankful to you!'

She was laughing because she had finally learnt who he was, and she was thanking him for being young, handsome, and rich, more than she had dared hope. Happiness rang out in her voice, a cry full of wonder and gratitude at this gift of love offered to her by her dream.

'You're the king, you're my master, and now I'm yours; my only regret is that I'm a thing of such little account... But I'm proud to belong to you, and so long as you love me, I am a queen... Although I waited in complete certainty, my heart has swelled with joy since you took full possession of it. Oh, my sweet lord, I am so grateful to you, and love you so much!'

He put his arm gently around her waist, and drew her away, saying:

'Come home with me.'

He led her through the wild grasses to the far end of the Clos-Marie, and she understood then how he had come in each evening through the old iron gate from the bishop's grounds, which had formerly been sealed shut. He had left the gate open and, with his arm still around her, ushered her into Monseigneur's vast garden. Above, the moon was rising behind a warm veil of thin cloud, lighting it up with a milky transparency. The whole starless vault of the heavens shone with a pale hazy glow and its radiance shimmered down silently in the peaceful night. They walked slowly upstream alongside the Chevrotte, which ran through the grounds; but here it was no swift stream tumbling down a pebbly slope; instead its waters were calm, and meandered languidly between the clumps of trees. Beneath the luminous clouds, the Elysian river, its currents bathing the feet of the floating trees, seemed to wind away like a river in a dream.

Angélique spoke once more, in a joyful tone:

'I feel so proud and happy when you hold me like this.'

Félicien was delighted by her great simplicity and charm, and listened as she expressed her feelings candidly, concealing nothing, saying aloud exactly what she was thinking, in all the innocence of her heart.

'Oh, my darling, it is I who should be grateful that you are prepared to love me a little, and so sweetly... Tell me again about your love for me, and what you thought when you finally found out who I was.'

With a charming gesture of impatience, she interrupted him:

'No, no, let's talk about you, about you alone. Why bother about me? What does it matter who I am or what I think?... You're the only one who exists now.'

She held him tightly, and slowed their pace as they ambled along the banks of the enchanted river. She asked him endless questions; she wanted to know about everything, his childhood, his youth, the twenty years he had spent far apart from his father.

'I know that your mother died when you were born, and that you were brought up by your uncle, an old priest... I know that Monseigneur refused to see you again...'

He began to speak in a low, distant voice, which seemed to rise up out of the past.

'Yes, my father adored my mother, and I was to blame because I came into the world and caused her death... My uncle kept me in complete ignorance of my family, and brought me up harshly, as though I were a pauper's child entrusted to his care. I only learnt the truth much later on, just over two years ago... But I wasn't at all surprised, I had always felt that I had great wealth behind me. Regular work bored me, and all I wanted to do was roam around the countryside. Then I discovered my passion for the stained-glass windows of our little church...'

She started laughing, and he too cheered up.

'I'm a worker just like you. I had decided I would earn my living painting stained-glass windows when all this money fell into my lap... My father was very upset to receive letters from my uncle saying what a little rascal I was, and that I'd never be fit for holy orders! It had been his express wish that I should become a priest; perhaps he thought that I could atone in this way for causing my mother's

death. He relented, though, and asked me to come back to him...
Oh, life, how wonderful life is! The only point of life is to love and be
loved!'

Throbbing with chaste and youthful vitality, his cry rang out in the
peaceful night air. Passion filled his every vein, the passion that had
killed his mother, and had propelled him into this first experience of
love flowering forth from mystery... It was fired by his every attribute,
his wild spirit, his beauty, loyalty, ignorance, and his greedy desire
to live.

'Like you, I was waiting, and the night you appeared at your window I recognized you also... Tell me what your dreams were, and what
your life was like before...'

But she silenced him once more.

'No, let's talk about you, about you alone. I don't want anything
about you to remain hidden from me... I want to possess you and love
you completely!'

She never grew weary of hearing him talk about himself. She was
overjoyed to be able to get to know him, and listened adoringly, like
a holy child at the feet of Jesus. And neither of them ever tired of
repeating the same things, endlessly—how they had fallen in love,
and how they loved one another now. The same words were used over
and over, and yet always seemed new, taking on surprising and unfath-
omable meanings. Their happiness grew as they explored its depths,
or tasted its music on their lips. He confessed how her voice thrilled
him; on hearing it he became so enraptured that he was instantly
her slave. She told him of the tantalizing dread she felt when his pale
skin flushed dark red at the slightest stirring of anger. They had left
the misty banks of the Chevrotte behind, and were plunging into the
dark cluster of great elms, their arms around each other's waists.

'Oh, this garden...,' murmured Angélique, savouring the coolness
that dripped down from the leaves above. 'For years I've wanted to
come here... And now here I am, with you!'

She did not ask where he was leading her. She allowed herself to be
guided by his arm through the gloom enfolding the hundred-year-old
trees. The earth felt soft beneath their feet, and the arches of foliage
fading into darkness high above were like the vaults in a church ceiling. There was not a sound, not a breath of air; all they could hear was
the beating of their hearts.

At last he pushed open the door to a large cottage and said:

'Go on in, you are at my home now.'

It was here that his father had seen fit to keep him, hidden away in a remote corner of the grounds. Downstairs lay a large sitting room; above, expansive living quarters. The huge ground-floor room was illuminated by a lamp.

'As you can see,' he said, with a smile, 'you are in the home of a simple artisan. This is my workshop.'

And it was indeed a workshop, set up at the whim of a wealthy young man whom it amused to dabble in a profession, that of glass painting. He had rediscovered old techniques from the thirteenth century, and could easily imagine himself one of those primitive glass-makers turning out masterpieces using the unsophisticated methods of the time. He made do with just an old table, coated in powdered chalk, on which he drew in red, and where he cut up pieces of glass with a hot iron, disdaining to use a diamond. The muffle kiln,* a small oven he had reconstructed from a drawing, was in use at that moment; the firing of some glass, destined for the repairs to another of the cathedral's windows, was just nearing completion. And in boxes nearby lay pieces of glass of every colour, which he had had to order specially, blues, yellows, greens, and reds, pale, marbled, smoky, dark, pearly or rich in tone. The room was hung with splendid fabrics, and the workshop disappeared beneath the wealth of sumptuous furnishings. At the far end of the room, on an antique tabernacle that served as a pedestal, a tall gilded Virgin smiled through crimson lips.

'And you're working, you're working!' Angélique repeated with childish glee.

She was delighted by the kiln, and asked him to tell her everything about his work; how, following the example of the old masters, he used only glass that had been coloured in the paste,* to which he would merely add black shading; why he confined himself to small, clearly outlined figures, carefully bringing out their gestures and their flowing robes; and his thoughts on the glass-maker's art, which had gone into decline once they had started painting on the glass, using enamel, and making more accurate drawings; and his final word on the stained-glass window—that it ought simply to be a transparent mosaic, the brightest tones ordered in greatest harmony, a delicate floral array erupting with colour. But just at this moment she cared little, deep down, for the glass-maker's art! These things interested her only because they originated with him, and they allowed her to involve herself with him, and formed an intimate part of his life.

'How happy we will be,' she said, 'you doing your glass-painting and I my embroidery!'

He had taken hold of her hands again in the middle of the great room, among whose luxurious furnishings she felt perfectly at ease, as though this were the natural setting in which the grace within her would blossom. For a moment both fell silent. And then it was she who spoke up once more:

'So, is it settled then?'

'What do you mean?' he asked, with a smile.

'Our marriage.'

He hesitated for a moment, his pale face suddenly darkening. She was alarmed.

'Are you angry with me?'

But he had already taken her hands in a clasp that seemed to enfold her entirely.

'It's settled. Every wish of yours will be granted, whatever the obstacles. My only reason for living is to obey you.'

An expression of joy lit up her face.

'We'll get married, we'll always love one another, and we'll never part.'

She had no doubts whatsoever. Everything would unfold exactly as planned the very next day, as effortlessly as in the miracles of the *Legend*. She hadn't the slightest concern that they might encounter any hindrance or delay. Since they loved each other, why would anyone wish to keep them apart a moment longer? People fall in love and then they marry: it's all very simple. The thought filled her with serene and boundless joy.

'It's agreed, then, let's shake on it!' she joked.

He brought her little hand up to his lips.

'It's agreed.'

Fearful of being caught by the dawn, and impatient to divulge her secret, she started to set off, but he was anxious to see her home.

'No, no, we wouldn't make it before daybreak. I can find my way easily enough... Until tomorrow.'

'Until tomorrow.'

Félicien yielded to her wish, and gazed after her as she made off, running beneath the gloomy elms and alongside a Chevrotte now bathed in light. She darted through the park gate and flew through the tall grass in the Clos-Marie. As she ran it occurred to her that she would never be able to wait until sunrise, and that it would be best to awaken the Huberts with a knock on their door, and tell them everything. Happiness swelled inside her, and honesty reared up defiantly: she felt unable to conceal for even five minutes longer the secret that she had kept so long. She ran into the garden, closing the gate behind her.

And there, over by the cathedral, Angélique caught sight of Hubertine, who had sat through the night waiting for her on the stone bench, a clump of straggly lilacs clustering around. Awoken by a pang of dread, Hubertine had gone upstairs and, finding the doors open, had immediately understood. And, sick with worry, uncertain where to go next, and fearing to make things worse, she had decided to wait.

Angélique at once threw her arms around Hubertine's neck, completely unabashed, her heart leaping with joy, laughing gaily now that she no longer had anything to hide.

'Oh, Mother, it's all settled!... We're getting married and I'm so happy!'

Hubertine did not reply at once, and instead studied her closely. At the sight of such blossoming virginity, such limpid eyes and pure lips, her fears dissolved. She remained profoundly sorrowful, however, and tears rolled down her cheeks.

'My poor child!' she murmured, just as she had the previous evening, in the cathedral.

Angélique was astonished by her reaction, since she was normally so even-tempered and never wept.

'Mother!' she cried out. 'What's the matter, are you upset?... It's true that I've behaved badly, and kept my secret from you. But if you only knew how heavily it's weighed on me! I didn't say anything at first, and then I didn't dare to... You must forgive me.'

She had sat down beside her, and had placed an arm affectionately around her waist. The old bench seemed to sink further into this mossy little corner beside the cathedral. The lilacs shaded them above, and nearby spread the sweet-briar which she had planted to see whether it would put forth roses; but having been neglected for some time, it had grown sickly and returned to its wild state.

'Mother, I'm going to tell you everything. Listen closely now.'

In a quiet voice she related the story of the love she shared with Félicien, her words coming in an unending flow as she relived each tiny incident, growing more animated as she did so. She omitted nothing, scouring her memory as though she were at confession. She did not feel any shame, and the blood of passion heated her cheeks, and a proud flame burned in her eyes, but her voice never grew louder, continuing in an ardent whisper.

Eventually Hubertine interrupted her, speaking also in a murmur.

'Oh, there you go again! It's in vain you've tried to mend your ways! You get carried away every time, swept up by the winds of desire... My, you're fiery and proud! You're still the little girl who refused to clean the kitchen and covered her hands with kisses.'

Angélique couldn't stop herself laughing.

'No, don't laugh, soon you won't have tears enough for all your weeping... This marriage can never take place, my poor child.'

At this, Angélique let out a long, musical laugh.

'Mother, Mother, what are you saying? Are you trying to bait me, or punish me?... It's so simple! He's going to talk to his father this evening. And tomorrow he will come and arrange everything with you.'

Was it really possible she thought this could happen? Hubertine had to be brutally honest with her. A little embroideress, without money or name, marry Félicien d'Hautecœur? A young man with a fortune of fifty million? The last in the line of one of France's most ancient houses?

To each new objection, Angélique calmly replied:

'Why not?'

It would be an utter scandal, a marriage that lay outside the ordinary bounds of happiness. A multitude of obstacles would be placed in her path; did she think she could overcome them all?

'Why not?'

Monseigneur was said to be jealous of his name, and scorned caprices of the heart. Did she think she had any chance of swaying him?

'Why not?'

Unshakeable in her conviction, she continued:

'It's funny, Mother, how you only seem to see the bad in the world. And yet I am telling you that everything is going to turn out fine!... Two months ago you chided me and teased me, remember, and yet I was right, everything I said would happen has come to pass.'

'Oh, my poor girl, just you wait and see how things turn out!'

Hubertine was distraught, stricken with remorse at the thought that she had allowed Angélique to remain in such ignorance. She would have liked to offer her some harsh lessons in the realities of life, and enlighten her about the cruelty and brutality that existed in the world, but she found herself tongue-tied, and could not summon up the right words. How awful it would be if one day she had to accept that she was to blame for the child's misfortunes, having raised her in such cloistered confines, closeted in the perpetual falsehood of the dream!

'Come now, my dear, you wouldn't want to marry this young man against our wishes, against even his father's wishes.'

Angélique grew serious, looked her directly in the face, and said in a grave voice:

'Why not? I love him, and he loves me.'

Her mother put both arms around her, and hugged her tightly; and she silently studied her daughter, and felt herself tremble. The veiled moon had sunk behind the cathedral, and the wisps of mist in the sky above were faintly tinged with pink as daybreak approached. The two of them were enfolded in the purity of the morning, in the deep cool silence that was disturbed only by the quiet song of birds awakening to the day.

'Oh, my child, duty and obedience are the only paths to happiness. A single hour of pride or passion can lead to a lifetime of suffering. If you want to be happy, you must submit, renounce, withdraw...'

But she felt her daughter recoil in her embrace, and there slipped from her lips something she had never told her before, something she still hesitated to reveal:

'Listen, you've always imagined that Father and I are very happy. And so we would be, if our lives hadn't been blighted by tragedy...'

Her voice sank lower, quavering as she related their story: the marriage against her mother's wishes, the death of their child, and their futile yearning to have another—a form of punishment for their transgression. Nevertheless, they adored one another, and had put all their energies into their work, and had never been in want. And yet they had been desperately unhappy, and would no doubt have begun to quarrel, and experienced a sort of living hell, and possibly a bitter separation, if it had not been for all the efforts they had made, the kindness in his nature, and her even temper.

'Think about it, my child, do not let anything into your life that will bring suffering later on... Be humble and obedient, and still the urgings of your heart.'

With her defiance faltering, Angélique listened, very pale and on the verge of tears.

'Mother, this is agony to me... I love him and he loves me.'

And her tears began to flow. She was deeply upset, and moved to pity by her mother's secret; and fear showed in her eyes, as though this glimpse of the real world had caused her physical harm. But she did not give up. She would gladly have died for her love!

Hubertine then made up her mind.

'I didn't want to cause you so much heartache all at once. But it is important that you know... Yesterday evening, after you had gone up to your room, I asked the Abbé Cornille some questions, and learnt why Monseigneur, who had for so long refused to summon his son back to Beaumont, finally decided to do so... The young man's spirited nature, his restless desire to lead a life outside the ordinary bounds, were sources of great distress. After painfully abandoning the idea of making his son a priest, he had given up all hope of settling him in an occupation suited to his rank and fortune. He would never be anything other than a madman, an eccentric, or an artist... And then, fearful that his son might develop some foolish entanglement, he brought him back here so that he could be married off at once...'

'Yes, and so?' asked Angélique, who had not yet understood.

'Even before he arrived, plans were being made for his marriage, and it seems that everything has now been settled. The Abbé Cornille told me that the young man is certain to marry Mademoiselle Claire de Voincourt in the autumn... You know the Voincourt residence, over there next to the Bishop's Palace. They have very close relations with Monseigneur. Neither family could wish for more in terms of name or fortune. The Abbé Cornille is very much in favour of this union.'

The young girl was no longer listening to the reasons why the pair were so well suited. An image had suddenly taken shape in her mind, that of Claire, who appeared to Angélique at that moment just as she had sometimes glimpsed her, walking beneath the winter trees in her grounds, or in the cathedral on feast days: a tall, dark-haired lady of her own age, very beautiful, with a beauty more striking than her own, and regal in her bearing. She was said to be very kind, despite her cold manner.

'That tall young lady, who's so beautiful and so rich... He's marrying her...'

She murmured this as though in a dream. But then her heart seemed to rend, and she cried out:

'He's been lying then! He never told me!'

She recalled Félicien's slight hesitation, and the rush of blood that had brought crimson to his cheeks when she had spoken of their marriage. The shock was so severe that the colour fled from her face, and her head slipped down onto her mother's shoulder.

'My darling, my little darling... It's painful, I know. But if you had found out later, it would have been even more painful. You must pull the blade out of the wound at once... And every time your pain revives, you must remind yourself that Monseigneur, the fearsome Jean XII, whose stubborn pride, it seems, is still remembered throughout the town, will never give his son, the last of his line, to a little embroideress who was picked up on a doorstep and adopted by poor people like us.'

As she lapsed into a faint, Angélique heard, and ceased to struggle. What was it she had felt brushing over her face? A cold breath, coming across the rooftops from afar, had sent a chill through her blood. Could it be that she had been touched by the misery of the world, that unhappy reality they had spoken about to her in the same way that a wolf is mentioned to an unruly child? Even though the touch had been a light one, the pain lingered. And yet she had already begun to find excuses for Félicien: he hadn't lied, he had just kept silent. Even if his father wished him to marry that young woman, he no doubt did not want her. But he had not yet dared to confront his father and, though he had not mentioned the match, it was perhaps because he had only just made up his mind to disobey. It was the first collapse of her hopes and, although pale and shaken by this encounter with the harsh reality of life, she remained faithful, and still placed her trust in her dream. Everything would still happen as she imagined, but her pride had been humbled, and so she was reduced again to the humility that is commensurate with grace.

'Mother, it's true that I've sinned, but I shall never sin again... I promise to obey at all times, and to become everything heaven expects of me.'

This was the voice of grace speaking, and the victory lay with the surroundings in which she had grown up and the upbringing she had received there. Why would she have any doubts about what would come tomorrow, since until then everything around her had shown her such kindness and compassion? She wished to retain the wisdom of Catherine, the modesty of Elizabeth, and the chastity of Agnes, bolstered by the support of all the saints, convinced that she could triumph only with their help. And as for her friend the cathedral, the Clos-Marie, the Chevrotte, the Huberts' chilly little house, the Huberts themselves, wouldn't everything that loved her rise up in her defence, sparing her the need to act, allowing her just to remain obedient and pure?

'Well, then, do you promise that you will never do anything against our wishes, and especially not against those of Monseigneur?'

'Yes, Mother, I promise.'

'Then promise me that you will never see that young man again, and that you will no longer entertain the mad dream of marrying him.'

At these words, her heart faltered. One final rebellious impulse almost made her rise up and cry out her love. Then she bowed her head, subdued at last.

'I promise that I won't make any efforts to see him again or encourage him to marry me.'

Moved to her core, Hubertine hugged her fiercely, grateful for this display of obedience. Oh, what agony it was to want what was right, only to bring suffering to those one loves! She felt utterly heartbroken and, getting to her feet, was surprised to find that it was already growing light. The faint notes of birdsong had grown louder, although no birds were yet on the wing. Up above, the clouds were parting like gauze veils, and the sky was turning a limpid blue.

Angélique's glance had settled unseeingly on her sweet-briar, but she eventually noticed it there, holding out its sickly little flowers. She gave a short, sad laugh.

'You were right, Mother, it isn't ready to bear roses.'

CHAPTER 10

IN the morning, at seven o'clock, as usual, Angélique was at work. Day followed day, and each morning she calmly set herself down before the chasuble from which she had risen the previous evening. Nothing seemed to have changed; she kept strictly to her promise, and shut herself away, making no attempt to see Félicien. She did not seem cast down by this turn of events, and appeared always fresh-faced and cheerful, smiling at Hubertine whenever she caught her mother gazing at her with a puzzled expression. And yet, in the silence she cultivated, she thought only about him, all day long. She was filled with unquenchable hope, and was sure that things would turn out as she desired, in spite of everything. And it was this sense of certainty that underlay her proud, courageous, and upright bearing.

Sometimes Hubert scolded her.

'You're working too hard, and seem a little pale to me... Are you sleeping well?'

'Oh, Father, like a log! I've never felt better.'

But Hubertine, too, was worried, and suggested she take a break from work.

'If you like, we'll shut up shop, and all three of us make a trip to Paris.'

'Well, really, Mother! What about our orders?... And haven't I already told you that hard work is good for me!'

In fact, Angélique was quite simply waiting for a miracle, some manifestation of the invisible that would make her Félicien's. It didn't matter that she had promised not to take any steps herself; what would have been the point in any case, since the hidden realms were always acting on her behalf? And so, committed to inaction, whilst projecting an air of indifference, she kept her ears strained, listening to the voices, the mutterings all around her, the low, familiar noises of this little place in which she lived, and which was going to come to her aid. Something was going to happen, without any doubt. Bending over her frame, with the window open, she caught every rustle in the trees, every murmur of the Chevrotte. The faintest sighs of the cathedral reached her ears, amplified by her concentration: she could even hear the shuffling of the beadle's slippers as he put out the candles. She again felt mysterious wings brush against her, and she knew that the unknown realms were helping her. And from time to time she suddenly spun around, thinking that a shadow had mumbled in her ear the secret to her victory. But the days went by, and nothing happened.

At night, so as not to break her promise, Angélique at first stayed away from the balcony, for fear of running down to join Félicien if she saw him below. She waited at the back of her bedroom. Then, as the leaves themselves seemed fast asleep, and made no stir, she ventured forward, and peered into the darkness. Where was the miracle going to take place? Undoubtedly, in the bishop's garden—a flaming hand would signal her to come. Or perhaps in the cathedral, where the organ would rumble out, summoning her to the altar. Nothing would have surprised her, neither the doves of the *Legend* bringing words of blessing, nor the intercession of the saints, passing in through the walls to announce that Monseigneur wished to meet her. There was really only one thing that surprised her, confounding her more each evening: how long it was taking for the miracle to occur. And as the days and nights followed on, still nothing—nothing whatsoever—happened.

By the end of the second week, what surprised Angélique even more was that she had seen no sign of Félicien. She had of course undertaken not to make any attempt to meet him but, without saying so, she was counting on him to do everything in his power to come and see her. However, the Clos-Marie remained empty, and he was no longer to be seen walking through its wild grasses. Not once, in the entire fortnight, during the long hours of the night, did she spy his shadow. This did not shake her faith: if he did not come, it was because he was busy arranging their future happiness. And, yet, she grew more and more confused, and felt the first stirrings of disquiet.

Finally, one evening, after the embroiderers had sat through a gloomy dinner together, Hubert went out under the pretext of an urgent errand, and Hubertine remained alone with Angélique in the kitchen. For a long time she gazed tearfully at her daughter, deeply moved by her great courage. For a fortnight they had not spoken a word about the things that filled their hearts to overflowing, and she was touched by the strength and loyalty her daughter had shown in keeping her pledge. She felt a surge of tenderness, and held out her arms; her daughter flung herself onto her breast, and the two of them silently embraced.

And then, when at last she could speak, Hubertine said:

'Oh, my poor child, I have waited to be alone with you—you need to be told… It's over, it's all over.'

Distraught, Angélique leapt to her feet and cried out:

'Félicien's dead!'

'No, no.'

'If he hasn't come, it's because he's dead!'

And Hubertine had to explain that she had gone to see him, the day after the procession, to ask him, similarly, to promise that he would not return so long as Monseigneur withheld his permission. This separation would be permanent, for she knew that the marriage was impossible. He had been overcome with remorse when she made clear how wrong his actions had been, and how he had compromised this poor, ignorant, trusting young girl, whom he could never marry. And he too had cried out that he would prefer to die of grief, never seeing her again, rather than behave dishonestly. That same evening, he confessed all to his father.

'Now look,' said Hubertine, 'you're so brave, I can tell you all this frankly... Oh, if you only knew, my darling, how sorry I feel for you, and how much I admire you, seeing you so proud and courageous, never saying anything, and always looking so cheerful, while, within, your heart is breaking... But you'll need to be even braver, darling, you'll need every drop of courage... This afternoon I met the Abbé Cornille. It's all over; Monseigneur won't allow it.'

She had expected a storm of tears, and was surprised to see her daughter, her face ashen, sit calmly down. The old oak table had been cleared, and the lamp cast its light across the ancient common room, whose peace was disturbed only by the quiet chattering of a kettle.

'Mother, nothing is over... You must tell me. I have a right to know, don't I? All these things concern me directly.'

And she listened carefully to what Hubertine thought fit to tell her of the things the priest had recounted, skipping over certain details, and continuing to hide the facts of life from this unworldly child.

Since he had summoned back his son, Monseigneur's life had been plunged into turmoil. Having sent him away the day after his wife's death, and refused for twenty years to acknowledge his existence, he was suddenly confronted now by a young man brimming with strength and vitality, a living portrait of the woman he mourned, being the same age as she had been, and possessing the same fair-haired grace that had marked her beauty. The long period of exile, the resentment he had harboured against the child who had robbed him of the mother, had all been well-advised: he felt this now, and regretted going back on his decision. His advancing age, twenty years spent in prayer, the descent of God into his soul—none of these had stopped him from being the man he had always been. And this child of his flesh, the flesh of his beloved wife, had only to rise to his feet with laughter in his blue eyes for the older man's heart to start pounding fit to burst, in the belief that the dead woman had come back to life. He beat his chest with his fist, and wept in futile repentance, crying out that men who had partaken of women, and who were still bound to them by the bond of blood, should be forbidden from the priesthood.

The good Abbé Cornille had related all this to Hubertine in a hushed voice, his hands trembling. Mysterious rumours circulated; it was whispered that Monseigneur locked himself away at dusk, and spent the nights in desperate torment, weeping and wailing so wildly that, despite the muffling draperies, all in the Bishop's Palace were terrified. He thought that he had forgotten the past and mastered his passion; but it had revived in his heart with all the savagery of a tempest. And he remained the fearsome man of earlier years, the reckless adventurer, the descendant of legendary military commanders. Every night, sinking to his knees, a hair-shirt rasping his skin, he tried to drive away the spectre of his much lamented wife, forcing himself to think on the dust lying in her coffin, which was all that must now remain of her. But instead she rose up alive, fresh and exquisite as a flower, appearing exactly as she had done when she was young, and he had loved her with the passionate devotion of a man already in his middle years. The torment began anew, and felt as raw as on the day she had died. He mourned her, and he desired her, and he revolted once more against God, who had taken her from him. It was only at daybreak that he grew calm once more and, deeply wearied, was overcome with self-loathing and contempt for the world. Ah, passion! He longed to slay this vile monster, and slip away again into the peaceful oblivion of divine love!

Emerging from his room, Monseigneur once more assumed a severe demeanour, his expression calm and haughty, his face still a touch pallid. On the morning when Félicien had made his confession, he had listened without saying a word, mastering himself so sternly that not a single fibre of his flesh had quivered. Staring at his son, he was distressed to find him so young, handsome, and passionate, for he saw himself again in this extremity of love. Resentment had given way to an inflexible resolve, a grim sense of obligation to shield his son from an error like the one that still tortured him so bitterly. He would crush his son's passion, just as he wished to crush the passion within himself. This tale, which could have been plucked from the old romances, simply deepened his anguish. What, a poor girl, a girl with no name, a little embroideress glimpsed in the moonlight, transformed into a slender virgin of the *Legend*, and adored in a dream! He had finally uttered just a single word in reply: 'Never!' Félicien then threw himself at his father's feet, imploring him, pleading his own case and Angélique's. Until then, he had always trembled with fear when approaching his father but now, without daring to raise his eyes to this man of God, he begged him not to stand in the way of his happiness. In a subdued voice, he offered to disappear completely, taking his wife so far away that they would never be seen again. He would leave his great fortune to the Church. He wished simply to love and be loved, in obscurity. At these words, a shudder ran through Monseigneur. He had made a pledge to the Voincourts, and would never go back on it. Félicien, at his wits' end, feeling the rage mount within him, had stormed away, alarmed by the flush of blood darkening his cheeks which threatened to plunge him into impious and overt rebellion.

'My child,' concluded Hubertine, 'you must see now that you'll have to stop thinking about this young man, because I'm sure you wouldn't want to go against Monseigneur's wishes... It has all turned out as I predicted. But I prefer to let the facts speak for themselves, rather than place any obstacle in your path myself.'

Angélique had listened calmly, her hands folded in her lap. Staring into space, she scarcely blinked as she imagined the scene, Félicien at Monseigneur's feet, overflowing with tender affection as he spoke about her. She did not reply at once, and remained deep in thought, enfolded in the perfect silence that had spread through the kitchen since the kettle ceased its soft chattering. She lowered her eyes, and looked at her hands, which, in the lamplight, appeared as though of palest ivory. And, then, as a smile of invincible faith rose once more to her lips, she said simply:

'If Monseigneur doesn't yet consent, it's only because he's waiting to meet me.'

Angélique barely slept that night. She turned over and over in her mind the idea that the bishop would alter his stance if only he saw her. There was no personal womanly vanity in this; she believed love to be all-powerful, and loved Félicien so deeply that she felt sure that this would be obvious to his father, and he would change his mind, and no longer hinder their happiness. For a long time she tossed and turned in her great bed, as the same thoughts whirled around in her head. Monseigneur seemed to float before her closed eyes. Perhaps it was within him, and through him, that the long-awaited miracle would occur. The warm night slumbered on outside, and she strained her

ears to make out the voices, trying to catch whatever counsel was flowing from the trees, the Chevrotte, the cathedral, and even the bedroom itself, which thronged with friendly shades. But everything
around seemed to hum and murmur, and she could make out nothing
specific. She grew impatient as certainty of any kind continued to
elude her. But, as she fell asleep, she found herself saying:

'Tomorrow I shall speak to Monseigneur.'

When she awoke, the step she planned seemed perfectly straightforward and necessary. It was sparked by innocent and courageous
passion, and in her valour there mingled great purity and pride.

She was aware that, every Saturday, at around five o'clock in the
evening, the bishop would go and kneel in the Hautecœur chapel,
where he liked to pray alone, immersed in the history of his family
and in his own past, seeking out a solitude that was respected by all
the clergy. And, as it happened, today was Saturday. She quickly
made her decision. If she had gone to the Bishop's Palace, it was possible that she would not have been allowed in to see him; and, in any
case, there were always a lot of people about there, which would have
flustered her. On the other hand, it would be so easy just to wait in the
chapel and introduce herself to Monseigneur when he appeared.
That day she worked on her embroidery with her usual calm diligence;
she felt no great agitation, and was firm in her resolve, confident that
she was doing the right thing. Then, at four o'clock, she said she was
just popping out to see Mère Gabet, and went out, dressed as though
for a visit to the local shops, wearing a simple garden hat knotted
carelessly under her chin. She turned left towards St Agnes's portal
and pushed open one of the padded doors, which swung shut behind
her with a muffled thud.

The cathedral was deserted, and just a solitary penitent lingered in
a confessional in St Joseph's chapel, given away only by her black
skirt trailing out. And Angélique, who had been very calm until then,
began to tremble as she was enveloped in the chill seclusion of this
holy place, the sharp little tap of her footsteps echoing in an alarming
fashion. Why did she feel so apprehensive? She had imagined herself
to be so very strong, and had remained calm throughout the day, convinced that she had a perfect right to seek after happiness! But now
she no longer felt sure, and was blenching as though guilty of a crime!
She slipped along to the Hautecœur chapel, where she had to hold
tight to the grille to support herself.

It was one of the darkest and most sequestered chapels in the ancient Romanesque apse. Resembling a tomb hewn out of solid rock, cramped and stark, with plain ribs running across its low vault, it was lit only by the window, the legend of St George, in which red and blue pieces predominated, creating a purplish gloom. The unornamented altar, made of black and white marble, and mounted simply with a crucifix and a pair of double candelabra, looked like a sepulchre. And the rest of the walls were covered with memorial tablets, the time-worn stones crowding flush against one another from roof to floor, the deeply cut letters of the inscriptions still legible.

Angélique waited, scarcely breathing and perfectly still. A beadle walked right by, but did not see her there, pressed against the inside of the grille. She could still see the skirt of the penitent trailing from the confessional. Her eyes adapted to the half-light and, as her gaze settled mechanically on the inscriptions, she eventually began to pick out letters. She recognized some of the names, which conjured up the legends of Hautecœur Castle, Jean V the Great, Raoul III, and Hervé VII. Her eyes fell on two more, those of Laurette and Balbine, which, in her agitated state, moved her to tears. These were the names of the Happy Dead, Laurette, who had plummeted from a moonbeam on the way to meet her betrothed, and Balbine, who had been struck dead by excess of joy on her husband's return, having thought him killed in battle. It was they who returned at night, their great gowns swathing the castle in billowing white. On the day she had visited the ruins hadn't she seen them hovering above the towers in the pale grey dusk? Oh, she would gladly have died like them, aged 16, in the blissful fulfilment of her dream!

A loud crash, echoing beneath the vaults, made her tremble. It was the priest leaving the confessional in St Joseph's chapel, shutting the door behind him. She was surprised not to see the penitent lady, who had already vanished. And then, when the priest, in turn, went out through the sacristy, she felt absolutely alone in the vast solitude of the cathedral. Hearing that thunderous report as the old confessional banged on its rusty hinges, she had thought that Monseigneur must be drawing near. She had been waiting for him for almost half an hour, unaware of how long it had been. In her trepidation, she was oblivious to the passing minutes.

A new name caught her eye, Félicien III. It was he who had travelled to Palestine carrying a candle, to fulfil a vow made by Philip the

Fair. And her heart beat faster as she saw in her imagination the youthful face of Félicien VII, who was descended from them all, the blond-haired lord whom she adored, and who adored her. The thought filled her with pride and fear. Was it really possible that a miracle was going to occur before her? In front of her there was a more recent marble slab, dating from the previous century, on which she could easily read in black lettering: Norbert Louis Ogier, marquis of Hautecœur, prince of Mirande and Rouvres, count of Ferrières, Montégu and Saint-Marc, and also Villemareuil, baron of Combeville, lord of Morainvilliers, knight of the Four Orders of the King, lieutenant of his armies, governor of Normandy, entrusted with the office of captain general of the hunt and the company of the boar.* These were the titles of Félicien's grandfather, and she had come in all her simplicity, dressed in just her work dress, her fingers scarred by the needle, to marry the grandson of this dead nobleman.

She heard a faint sound, something brushing softly over the flagstones. She turned, and was startled to see Monseigneur there, so silent had his approach been, unaccompanied by the expected thunderclap. He had come into the chapel, appearing very tall and very noble, with his pale face and strong nose, and eyes flashing with youthful vigour. At first he did not see her huddled against the dark grille. Then, as he bowed towards the altar, he discovered her there before him, at his feet.

Angélique's legs had buckled, so overwhelmed was she by dread and terror, and she had sunk to her knees. He appeared to her like God the Father, awful in his absolute mastery over her fate. But she had a valiant heart, and spoke up immediately:

'Oh, Monseigneur, I have come...'

He stood up straight. He remembered her: the young girl he had noticed in the window on the day of the procession and, again, inside the cathedral, standing on a chair, the little embroideress his son was madly in love with. He did not utter a word, or make the slightest motion. He waited, standing tall and rigid.

'Oh, Monseigneur, I've come so that you can see who I am. You rejected me, but you don't even know me. So here I am, look at me, before you dismiss me again... I'm simply the girl who loves your son and is loved by him, I'm nothing more than that. Without love I'm nothing, nothing but a wretched child, found under the porch of this cathedral... You see me at your feet, how small, weak, and humble

I am… You can easily push me aside if I'm a nuisance to you. You could destroy me with your little finger… But, oh, how many tears we've shed! You must understand that we're suffering. We're miserable… I wanted, like your son, to argue my case, Monseigneur. I'm ignorant, I know only that I love, and that I'm loved… Isn't that enough? To love—to love and proclaim it out loud!'

And she went on, speaking in snatches and strangled phrases, revealing her every last thought in an outpouring of innocence and ever more fervent passion. It was love itself making its confession. She had the courage to speak like this only because she was chaste. Gradually, she had lifted up her glance.

'We love one another, Monseigneur. Doubtless he has explained to you how this came about. I've often asked myself the same question, without managing to find an answer… We love one another, and if that's a crime, you must excuse it, because it came to us from afar, from the very trees and stones around us. When I realized that I loved him, it was too late to stop loving him… And why would anyone wish for that now? You can keep him at home, and marry him to someone else, but you will never be able to stop him loving me. He will die without me, as I shall die without him. When he's not with me, I still have the feeling that he's there by my side, and that we shall never be apart, and that each has the keeping of the other's heart. I need only close my eyes, and I can see him, and he is within me… And will you then tear this union asunder? Monseigneur, it is something given by God, I beg you, please don't prevent us from loving one another.'

He looked at her, so fresh and modest, fragrant as a flower, in her simple work dress. He listened as she uttered this hymn to her love in an irresistibly charming voice, which gradually grew steadier. But her garden hat had slipped back onto her shoulders, and her radiant hair formed a delicate golden halo around her face; and she appeared to him like one of the legendary virgins of the old missals,* having, in her passion, something about her that was fragile, primitive, graceful, and passionately pure.

'Be kind, Monseigneur… You are our lord and master, please allow us to be happy.'

Seeing him so cold, motionless, and silent, she pleaded with him and inclined her head once more. Oh, what it was to behold this distraught child at his feet, to inhale the fragrance of youth that rose from her bowed neck! The little blonde curls that he had kissed so wildly long ago were there before him once more. The woman whose memory still tormented him, after twenty years' penance, had had the same youthful fragrance, the same lovely neck, proud and graceful as a lily. She had come to life again: it was she who wept, and who entreated him to show clemency towards passionate love.

With tears now running down her cheeks, Angélique went on, determined to say all that was on her mind.

'And, Monseigneur, I don't love him just for himself, I also love his noble name, and the lustre of his royal fortune... And, yes, I realize that, since I am a nobody and have nothing, it must appear that I want him for his money. And it's true, I do want him for his money, as well... I tell you this because I want you to know everything about me... Oh, what it would be to become rich through him and live with him in opulent splendour; to owe him my every joy, to be free to love as we please, to be surrounded by tears and woe no longer!... For as long as he has loved me, I have imagined myself dressed in brocade, as in olden times. My neck and wrists are hung with glistening jewels and pearls; I have horses, carriages, and vast woods where I can stroll about followed by my page boys... Whenever I think about him, I have this dream. And I say to myself that all this must come to be, that my dream of being a queen has been fulfilled. Monseigneur, is it then so terrible to love him even more because he will gratify all my childhood wishes, and gold will shower down as in the fairy tales?'

She stood proud and tall, and in her simplicity bore herself with all the graceful charm of a princess. She seemed the very image of the other woman, with the same flower-like delicacy, and the same gentle tears that sparkled like smiles. The ecstasy of love spread all around her, and he could feel its warmth ripple through him, mounting to his face—and it was this same warm tremor that welled in his memory every night, causing him to collapse sobbing onto his prie-dieu,* shattering the devout silence of the Bishop's Palace with his laments. Just the night before, he had wrestled once again with his feelings until three o'clock in the morning; and this love affair of theirs, with its roiling passions, inflamed his incurable wound. But his impassive mask was impenetrable; nothing betrayed the efforts he made to master the beating of his heart. If his blood were ebbing from him drop by drop, nobody was able to see where it trickled out: he simply appeared paler and more taciturn.

The profound silence persisted, filling Angélique with despair, and she redoubled her entreaties.

'I place myself entirely in your hands, Monseigneur. Take pity on me, decide my fate.'

But still he did not speak, and terror spread through her as he seemed to loom even taller before her eyes, dreadful in his majesty. As she waited, the deserted cathedral, its side aisles already plunged in darkness, its high vaults flickering with the last traces of the day, seemed to magnify her anguish. In the chapel, the memorial stones had vanished into the gloom, and he was the only thing visible, with his black soutane, and his long pale face, to which the last glimmers of daylight seemed to cling. She could see his eyes gleaming, growing more and more lurid as he stared at her. Was it anger that made them blaze out in this way?

'Monseigneur, if I had not come, I would always have regretted condemning the two of us to everlasting misery, simply for a lack of courage... Speak, I beg you, tell me that I was right, tell me that you give your consent.'

What was the use of talking with this child? He had informed his son of the reasons for his refusal, that was enough. If he chose not to speak, it was because he thought he had nothing to say. She no doubt understood this, and stretched up, trying to kiss his hands. He abruptly drew his hands back; and she was alarmed to see his pale face darken with a sudden flush of blood.

'Monseigneur... Monseigneur...'

At last his lips opened, and he uttered a single word, the same one he had flung at his son:

'Never!'

And without even performing his devotions that day, he fled. His heavy footsteps faded behind the pillars of the apse.

Collapsing onto the flagstones, Angélique sobbed out her heart for a very long time in the vast empty peace of the cathedral.

CHAPTER 11

THAT evening, in the kitchen, after she got up from the table, Angélique confessed everything to the Huberts, telling them how she had approached the bishop and how he had refused her. She was deathly pale, but very calm.

Hubert was greatly distressed. What, his own dear child was in so much pain! She too was deeply upset. Tears filled his eyes, in the kinship of their shared passion, this obsession with the beyond that was apt to carry them away at the slightest gust.

'Oh, my poor darling! Why didn't you ask my advice? I would have gone with you. Perhaps I could have swayed Monseigneur.'

Hubertine silenced him with a look. He could be very foolhardy. Wouldn't it have been better to seize this opportunity to put the impossible marriage behind them for good? She took the young girl in her arms, and kissed her tenderly on the brow.

'It's over now, my darling, isn't it, once and for all?'

Angélique, at first, appeared not to understand. Her response formed slowly, as though coming from very far away. She stared into space, seeming to seek an answer there, and replied:

'No doubt, Mother.'

Indeed, the following day, she sat down at her frame and embroidered away just as she had always done. She resumed her previous life, and did not appear to be suffering. She made no allusion to what had happened, and never glanced over at the window; just a touch of pallor still clung about her cheeks. Her sacrifice appeared complete.

Hubert concluded as much, and bowing to Hubertine's judgement in the matter, made every effort to keep Félicien away. The young man, though not daring to come out in open rebellion against his father, worked himself into a fervour, and in the end broke the promise he had made to wait without trying to see Angélique again. He wrote to her, and his letters were intercepted. He turned up one morning, and it was Hubert who went down to meet him. The ensuing discussion filled both of them with despair, the young man appearing deeply distressed when the embroiderer told him of his daughter's peaceful recovery, and implored him at the same time to remain true to his word, and disappear from sight, so that she wouldn't have to go through the dreadful anguish of the past month again. Félicien agreed once more to remain patient, but vehemently refused to go back on his promise to her. He still hoped to win over his father. He was prepared to wait, and would leave things as they were with the Voincourts, at whose house he dined twice a week so as to avoid being openly disobedient. As he left, he begged Hubert to explain to Angélique why he consented to the torment of not seeing her: he thought only about her, and all his actions were directed to winning her hand.

When her husband related to her what had been said, Hubertine's expression grew solemn. Then, after a silence, she said:

'Will you pass on to the child what he has asked you to tell her?'

'I should.'

She gazed long and hard at him, and finally said:

'Act as your conscience tells you… But he's deluding himself. He'll eventually bow to his father's will, and that will be the death of our poor little girl.'

Faced with Hubertine's misgivings, he was riven by doubt, and hesitated for a time, before making up his mind not to pass on the message. And then, as the days went by, he grew a little easier in his mind whenever his wife pointed out to him how calm Angélique appeared.

'It's clear that the wound is healing… She's starting to forget.'

But she was not forgetting; she, too, was simply waiting. With all human hope destroyed, she returned to the idea of a miracle. A miracle would surely occur if God wanted her to be happy. She needed only to place herself in his hands. She believed that this latest trial was a punishment for having tried to force his will in making her appeal to Monseigneur. In the absence of grace, a person was weak, and could never obtain victory. Her desire for grace made her humble once more, and she could trust only in the help that might come to her from the invisible realms, no longer taking action herself, but allowing the mysterious forces that surrounded her to set things in motion. She resumed reading her ancient copy of *The Golden Legend* by lamplight each evening, and came away from it in a state of enchantment, just as she had done when she was an innocent child. She had no doubt that a miracle was going to take place, firmly convinced that the unknown possessed unbounded power to bring about the triumph of those who are pure in soul.

Just at this time the cathedral upholsterer came to visit the Huberts and ordered a richly embroidered panel for Monseigneur's episcopal throne. A metre and a half wide by three metres high, this panel was to be set into its wooden back, and depict two life-size angels holding a crown above the Hautecœur coat of arms. It would have to be done in low-relief embroidery,* a style that required enormous skill and a great expense of physical effort. At first the Huberts refused, partly for fear of exhausting Angélique, but mainly because they were afraid that Angélique would become mired in gloom if forced to embroider the coat of arms, thread by thread, week after week, her old memories continually reviving. But she had angrily insisted on accepting the order, and set to work every morning with extraordinary energy. It seemed as though she were happy to wear herself out, exhausting her body in an effort to find peace of mind.

Life carried on in the ancient workshop in the same steady way, as though their hearts had never for a moment beat with fiercer passions. While Hubert bustled around the embroidery frames, transferring drawings onto the fabric, tightening and untightening the cloth, Hubertine helped Angélique, and by evening the fingers of both women were bruised and sore. To tackle the angels and the decorations they had to divide each subject into several parts, which they completed separately. For the sections that were to stand out in highest relief, Angélique laid down heavy unbleached thread from a spindle and then sewed over it at right angles with Brittany thread.* As she went along she used a sort of chisel to mould the threads, giving depth to the angels' robes, and bringing out the details in the ornaments. This work was in truth much like sculpture. Once the form had been created, Hubertine and she laid gold thread over it, sewing it down with wicker stitches. It was like a bas-relief done in pure gold, matchless in gloss and brilliance, shining like the sun in the smoke-blackened room. The ancient tools were set out in their time-honoured order, punches, bodkins, mallets and hammers; on the frames, thimbles, needles and little boxes of spangles and offcuts danced about; and, rusting away in the corners, a diligent, a hand wheel, and a yarn windle seemed to slumber on, lulled by the profound calm that flowed in through the open windows.

Days went by, and from dawn until dusk Angélique broke one needle after another, such was the difficulty involved in sewing gold thread through the thick waxed thread. This harsh task seemed to consume her entirely, body and soul, leaving her too exhausted even to think. By nine o'clock she was utterly worn out, and simply climbed into bed and sank into a deep sleep. When work allowed her a minute of reflection, she was surprised not to find Félicien there. Even if she made no attempt to see him, she considered that it was up to him to do everything in his power to come to her. But she was happy that he was being so sensible, and she would have rebuked him if he had tried to hasten things along. He too was doubtless waiting for a miracle. It was the waiting that sustained her now, and every evening she held hopes that tomorrow would be the day. No mutinous ideas had yet crossed her mind. Occasionally, however, she looked up and thought: what, still nothing? And then she would thrust in her needle so force-fully that her little hands bled. She often had to use pliers to pull it out. When a needle broke with a sharp crack like shattering glass, she never gave any sign of impatience.

It worried Hubertine to see her working so doggedly and, since washing time was upon them again, she made Angélique put aside the embroidery panel so that she might spend four days in healthy exer-tions out in the bright sunshine. Mère Gabet, who was untroubled by her usual aches and pains, would be able to help with the soaping and rinsing. A festive mood reigned in the Clos-Marie. The late August weather was utterly glorious, the sky blazed with light, and the shade lay thick and dark. An exquisite chill rose meanwhile from the Chevrotte, its waters icy-cool as they ran beneath the leafy shade of the willow trees. Angélique passed the first day very merrily, beating the washing and plunging it into the water, and took great delight in the river, the elms, the ruined mill, the grasses, all these companion-able things that held so many memories. Wasn't it here that she had first got to know Félicien, who had once appeared so mysterious in the moonlight, and then so adorably awkward that morning when he had rescued the fleeing camisole? After she finished rinsing each item, she could not stop herself from glancing over at the gate to the Bishop's Palace, which had once been sealed shut. She had passed through it on his arm one evening; perhaps he would suddenly fling it open and come and take her away to kneel at his father's feet. This hope lent a charm to her labours among the spatterings of foam.

But the next morning, as Mère Gabet was bringing over the last barrowful of washing for them to hang out, the old woman broke off from her interminable chatter and said, without any malicious intention:

'By the way, did you know that Monseigneur has arranged to marry off his son?'

The young girl, who was busy spreading out a sheet, sank to her knees in the grass, feeling as though her heart had stopped beating.

'Yes, everyone's talking about it... Monseigneur's son will marry Mademoiselle de Voincourt in the autumn. It was all settled the day before yesterday, apparently...'

She remained on her knees, confused thoughts swirling around in her head. She was not at all surprised by the news, and was inclined to think it true. Her mother had warned her, so it was only to have been expected. But what made her legs give way so suddenly was the thought that Félicien, trembling before his father, might marry this other woman one evening in weary despair, even though he did not love her. He would then be lost to Angélique, whom he did love. She had never considered the possibility that he might give in to weakness. In her mind's eye she saw him bend beneath the weight of duty, bringing unhappiness on them both, all for the sake of obedience. And although she still did not move, her eyes ranged over to the gate, and rebellion at last began to stir within her, an urge to go over and rattle its bars, and prise it open with her nails, and run to him and bolster him with her own courage, so that he would never give in.

She was surprised to hear herself reply to Mère Gabet, in a purely instinctive attempt to conceal her distress.

'Oh, it's Mademoiselle Claire he's marrying!... She's very beautiful, and people say she's very nice...'

As soon as the old woman left, she would certainly have to go to him. She had waited long enough, and would now break her promise not to see him, accounting it a mere trifle. What right had anyone to keep them apart like this? Everything around her proclaimed their love—the cathedral, the cool waters, and the old elms, among which they had loved one another. Since it was here that their affection had grown up, it was here that she wished to take him back. And she would cling to him as they fled far away, so far that no one would ever find them again.

'There we go, all done,' said Mère Gabet finally, after hanging the last of the towels over a bush. 'It'll all be dry in a couple of hours... I'll wish you good evening, miss, since you won't be needing me any more.'

Standing among the drifts of washing, which appeared dazzlingly white against the green grass, Angélique thought about that earlier day when they had so innocently given their hearts to one another as the wind had blustered away and the sheets and tablecloths had flapped all around them. Why had he stopped coming to see her? Why hadn't he come to meet her here, amid the clean and cheerful bustle of washing day? But very soon she would hold him in her arms, and then, she knew, he would belong to her alone. There would be no need for her to reproach him for his weakness; as soon as he saw her again he would strive to bring about their joint happiness once more. He would do everything within his power; all she had to do was go to him, and this she would do very soon.

An hour went by, and Angélique walked slowly among the washing, which brilliantly reflected the sunlight, bathing her in white, and a muffled voice rose up within her, growing louder and preventing her from going over to the gate. She became alarmed by the struggle stirring inside her. What was going on? Was there something else inside her in addition to her will? Something else, which had somehow got into her, was stopping her, thwarting her simple, virtuous passion. It was so simple, to run off and go to the man one loved; but she could no longer do it, overcome as she was by tormenting doubts. She had made a promise, so it would perhaps be very wrong to break it. By evening, when the washing was dry and Hubertine had come out to help her bring it in, she still had not made up her mind, and so gave herself the night to think things over. With fresh-smelling, snow-white linen piled high in her arms, she cast an anxious glance back at the Clos-Marie, already sunk in dusk, as though she were looking back at a friendly patch of nature which had refused to offer her solace.

When Angélique woke up the next day her mind was in turmoil. Further nights passed without bringing any resolution. She found haven only in the conviction that she was loved. That had remained unshakeable, and was a source of blissful peace. As long as she was loved, she could wait, she could bear anything. She was seized once more by her mania for charity, her heart melted in the face of the slightest suffering, her eyes welling with tears that seemed ready to gush forth at any moment. Old Mascart wrung gifts of tobacco from her, while the Chouteaus even inveigled jars of jam. But it was the Lemballeuse family who made the most of the unexpected opportunity, and Tiennette was seen dancing at fêtes in a dress that had belonged to the kind-hearted young woman. Then, as Angélique was bringing Mère Lemballeuse some chemises she had promised her the previous day, she glimpsed from a distance Madame de Voincourt and her daughter Claire, accompanied by Félicien, over by where the beggars lived. It was undoubtedly he who had brought them there. She turned about and went home, a chill gripping her heart. Two days later she saw all three going into the Chouteaus', and then, one morning, old Mascart told her about a visit he had received from that handsome young man and the two ladies. And so she abandoned the paupers, who were no longer her own; Félicien had not only taken them away from her, but had handed them over to these ladies. She stopped going out for fear of running into them again, as each time she did so she received in her heart a deeper and more painful wound. And she felt as though something were dying inside her, and her life were ebbing away, drop by drop.

One evening, when she was alone in her room, choking with anguish after one of these encounters, a cry escaped her lips:

'Why, he no longer loves me!'

She could see Claire de Voincourt once more, tall and beautiful with her crown of dark hair; and she saw him beside her, slender and proud. Were they not made for one another, coming from the same stock as they did, and so well matched that one might almost have thought them married already?

'He doesn't love me any more, he doesn't love me any more!'

The words echoed in her mind like the dreadful voice of ruin. With her faith shaken, everything crumbled, and she was unable to compose herself enough to think or weigh things calmly. The day before she had believed, now she believed no longer. All it had taken was the gentlest breath of wind, blowing from who knew where; and suddenly she was plunged into the deepest misery—which is to believe that one is no longer loved. He had in fact told her this very thing once before: that not to be loved was the cruellest pain, the most agonizing torment. Until this moment she had been able to wait resignedly, expecting a miracle. But her strength had vanished with her faith, and she slumped into child-like despair. A bitter struggle began.

At first she mustered up all her self-regard. So what if he no longer loved her—she had too much pride to keep on loving him! And she lied to herself, she made a pretence of having been set free, and hummed a blithe tune while embroidering the Hautecœur coat of arms she had now begun. But her heart swelled up and almost choked her, and she was ashamed to have to admit to herself that she was cowardly enough still to love him, and love him even more deeply. For an entire week, the coat of arms, coming to life thread by thread beneath her fingers, filled her with terrible anguish. Quartered, one and four, two and three, Jerusalem and Hautecœur; Jerusalem, which is argent, a cross potent or, cantoned with four crosslets the same; Hautecœur, which is azure, a castle or, an inescutcheon sable charged with a heart argent in fesse point, the whole accompanied by three fleurs-de-lis or, two in chief, one in base. The colours* were done in silk cord, the metals in gold and silver thread. What agony she felt when her hand trembled, or when she had to bow her head to hide her eyes, which pricked with tears whenever she looked on these flashing emblems! She thought only about him, and adored him in all the splendour of his fabled nobility. And when she embroidered the motto: *If God wills, I will*, in black silk on a silver scroll, she realized that she was in his thrall, and would never be free: her tears prevented her from seeing, but she continued to ply her needle mechanically.

It was a pitiful state of affairs. Angélique loved with desperate passion, struggling in the grip of a hopeless love she could never extinguish. At every moment she yearned to run off to Félicien and fling her arms around his neck, and so win him back; and thus the battle began over again. Sometimes she thought she had won, a profound silence reigned within her, and she appeared a complete stranger to herself, cold in her manner, head bowed like an obedient child, modest in her renunciation. This was no longer her, it was the dutiful young girl into whom she was changing, shaped by her environment and upbringing. But then her blood surged up inside her, making her feel light-headed; her bold vitality and youthful ardour reared up like wild mares; and she recovered her pride and passion, once more under the sway of her harsh and mysterious origins. Why ever should she have obeyed? There was no such thing as duty, there was only untrammelled desire. She was already making plans for her escape, calculating when it would be best to force open the gate to the bishop's garden. But she could also feel her pangs of anxiety returning, a gnawing uneasiness, agonizing doubts. If she gave in to evil, she would suffer eternal remorse. She spent many torturous hours wavering over which course to follow, tossed ceaselessly in this gale from rebellious love to her horror of sin. And each victory over her heart left her weaker.

One evening, just as she was leaving the house to go to Félicien, feeling utterly wretched that she hadn't the strength to resist her passion, she suddenly remembered the record book from her time as a child in care. She took it out from the bottom of the sideboard and leafed through it, torturing herself with the lowliness of her birth as she turned each new page, overtaken by a fierce hunger for humility. Father and mother unknown, no family name, just a date and a number, as utterly neglected as a plant that grows wild at the roadside! Memories flooded back, the lush meadows of the Nièvre and the animals she had tended there, the flat Soulanges road which she had wandered along barefoot, and Mamma Nini who had slapped her face when she stole apples. Certain pages in particular brought back memories—those recording the quarterly visits of the deputy inspector and the doctor, and signatures, sometimes accompanied by notes and remarks: an illness that had almost killed her, a claim from her foster mother relating to scorched shoes, adverse comments about her ungovernable nature. It was the diary of her woe. But then she came to one document that sent the brimming tears spilling down her cheeks: a report describing the removal of a necklet she had worn until the age of six. She remembered having hated it instinctively—a necklet of olive-shaped beads, made out of bone, and threaded onto silk braid, fastened with a silver disk bearing her date of admission and her number. It felt to her like the collar of a slave, and she would have snapped it in her little hands, if not for the terrifying repercussions. When she grew bigger she complained that it was choking her, but they had made her wear it for one more year. And so, finally, what joy when the deputy inspector had snipped the braid in the presence of the mayor of the commune, replacing the identity tag with a formal description on paper, which even then included her violet-coloured eyes and fine golden hair! And yet she continued to have the feeling that the thing remained fastened around her neck, like a collar placed on a domestic animal as a mark of identity: it remained embedded in her flesh, choking her. Turning to this page, on this particular day, she felt all her old feelings of worthlessness come flooding back, and she was driven up to her bedroom in tears, convinced that she was undeserving of love. The record book rescued her on two further occasions. But, after that, it too was powerless against her revolt.

Now it was at the night that she was racked by temptation. Before getting into bed, she made herself reread passages from the *Legend* as a way of purifying her sleep. Despite her efforts, she sat there with her head in her hands, unable any longer to make sense of it: the miracles left her bewildered, and she seemed only to see the fading traces of colourless phantoms. And then, in her great bed, she slept the leaden sleep of the dead, only to wake suddenly in anguish, with darkness all around. Wretched and despairing, she raised herself up and knelt among the sheets she had thrown off, shivering wildly, her temples damp with sweat. She clasped her hands together, and stammered: 'My God, why have you forsaken me?'* What distressed her most at these times was that she was all alone in the dark. She had dreamt about Félicien, and trembled to think that it would be so easy just to get dressed and go to him, no one being there to stop her. Grace was withdrawing from her, God no longer dwelt about her, all the things that surrounded her were abandoning her. She sought desperately to summon up the unknown, and strained her ears for a sound from the invisible realms. But the air remained empty; not a whispering voice or mysterious rustling was to be heard. Everything seemed dead: the Clos-Marie, the Chevrotte, the willows and grasses, the elms of the Bishop's Palace, and the cathedral itself. Nothing was left of the dreams she had set about her; the pale host of virgins had melted away, leaving behind just a sepulchre of scattered remains. She felt herself expiring, impotent and helpless, like a Christian of the early Church struck down by hereditary sin as soon as supernatural protection was withdrawn. In the mournful silence that filled this little spot, she listened as hereditary evil came to life once more, shrieking and howling, triumphing over the upbringing she had received. If no help came from unknown powers in the next two minutes, if presences did not awaken and bring her aid, she would certainly succumb, and go to her ruin. 'My God, my God, why have you forsaken me?' And kneeling in the middle of her great bed, fragile and very small, she felt that she was dying.

But on each occasion so far, in moments of deepest distress, a pure fresh feeling had flooded through her, bringing relief. This was grace taking pity on her, and entering into her to restore her illusions. She leapt down barefoot onto the tiled floor and ran eagerly towards the window; and there she heard the voices once more, invisible wings brushed against her hair, and the inhabitants of the *Legend* issued forth from the trees and stones, and came crowding round her. Her purity and her virtue, all those qualities of hers that had suffused the world around her, returned to her and saved her. After that she was afraid no longer, she knew they were watching over her: Agnes had come back in the company of the virgins, drifting placidly through the trembling air. Encouragement from afar, long murmurings of triumph, wafted their way to her, mingling with the night breeze. For an hour she drank deeply of this mild soothing air, overcome by profound sorrow, strengthened in her resolution to die rather than break her promise. Finally, feeling utterly exhausted, she climbed back into bed and fell asleep again, troubled by anxious thoughts of the struggle that must come the following day, tormented still by the idea that she must eventually succumb to temptation if she continued to weaken like this each time.

A deep lethargy had overtaken Angélique the moment she became convinced that Félicien no longer loved her. She bore the wound in her side,* and she was gradually dying from it, quietly, and without a groan. Its first manifestations were brief spells of exhaustion; she was troubled by shortness of breath, and had to lay down her thread for a minute, her dull eyes staring out at nothing. Then she had stopped eating, and swallowed just a few mouthfuls of milk. She hid her bread, and threw it to the neighbours' hens so as not to arouse her parents' concern. A doctor was summoned but, finding nothing wrong with her, blamed her sedentary way of life, and recommended exercise. It was as if her whole being was fading away, and she was slowly vanishing into thin air. Her body seemed to float as though borne up by two great fluttering wings, and the light of her blazing soul radiated from her emaciated face. Things reached the point where she had to press her hands against the staircase walls to hold herself upright as she staggered down from her room. But she was stubborn, and put on a brave face when anyone looked at her, as she was still anxious to complete the complicated panel of embroidery for Monseigneur's throne. Her slender little hands lacked their former strength, and when she broke a needle she was unable to draw it out with the pliers.

Then, one morning when Hubert and Hubertine had been obliged to go out, leaving her to work by herself, Hubert came home first and found her lying on the floor. She had fallen into a faint while at her frame, and had slid down onto the ground. The task was slowly breaking her; one of the great golden angels remained unfinished. Deeply distressed, Hubert took her in his arms and tried to get her on to her feet again. But she collapsed again, and could not be roused from her faint.

'My darling, my darling... Answer me, for pity's sake...'

At last she opened her eyes, and looked at him forlornly. Why did he want her to live? She had felt so happy in the arms of death!

'What's the matter, my darling? Didn't you tell us the truth—do you still love him?'

She did not answer, but simply gazed at him with an expression of immense sorrow. Hugging her distraughtly, he lifted her and carried her upstairs to her bedroom; and when he had laid the weak, pale girl on her bed, he wept over his unwitting cruelty in separating her from her beloved.

'I would have given him to you myself! Why didn't you tell me?'

But she did not speak, her eyelids slipped shut, and she seemed to sink back into sleep. He remained standing there, staring down at her thin, lily-shaped face, his heart aching with compassion. And then, since she was breathing peacefully, he went downstairs when he heard his wife come home.

Below, in the workroom, they discussed the situation. Hubertine had only just taken off her hat when he told her that he had picked up the child from the floor there, and that she now lay asleep in her bed, mortally ill.

'We were mistaken. Her heart is still set on that boy, and it's killing her... Oh, if you only knew what a shock it gave me. I've been plagued by remorse since I realized; and I had to carry her upstairs in a pitiful state. It's all our fault, we kept them apart with our lies... Would you really allow her to continue suffering? Won't you say anything to save her?'

Hubertine, like Angélique, remained silent, and gazed at him soberly, her face pale with anguish. And he, the more passionate of the two, shaken out of his usual docility by intense suffering, grew more and more agitated, and waved his arms about wildly.

'Well, then, I'll speak to her myself. I'll tell her that Félicien loves her, and that we have acted very cruelly in preventing him from coming back, and in lying to him as well... Every tear she sheds will wound me to the quick. It would be murder, and I'd feel I was to blame... I want her to be happy, yes, happy in spite of all this, whatever it may take...'

He had come closer to his wife, and was boldly voicing the rebellion in his tender heart, his vexation mounting in the face of her melancholy silence.

'Since they love one another, it's up to them to shape their own destiny... Nothing else matters when you love, and you are loved... Yes, happiness by any means is fair!'

At last Hubertine spoke in a measured voice, holding herself upright and perfectly still.

'So he should come and take her away from us, is that it? And then he should marry her, against our wishes, and against those of his father... That's what you advise them to do, you believe they will be happy after that, and that love is all they need...'

And she carried on, without a pause, in the same sorrowful tone:

'On my way home I was passing by the cemetery, and some grain of hope made me wander in once more... I knelt down again on that patch of ground that our knees have worn bare, and I prayed for a long time.'

Hubert turned pale, and his feverish mood subsided. He knew it well, of course—the tomb of her stubborn mother, where they had so often gone to weep and abase themselves, acknowledging their disobedience, and praying that the dead woman might offer them forgiveness from the depths of the earth. And they would stay there for hours, convinced that they would feel this forgiveness blossoming inside them if ever it were granted. What they were entreating, and what they were awaiting, was another child, a child of mercy: the simple sign by which they would understand that they had finally been forgiven. But nothing had come of it: the cold, deaf mother had abandoned them to their punishment without end—the death of their first child, whom she had snatched away from them, and refused to return.

'I prayed for a long time,' Hubertine repeated, 'and listened for the sound of anything stirring...'

Unsettled by her words, Hubert gave her a questioning glance.

'Nothing, nothing at all! Nothing came up from the ground, nothing stirred within me. Oh, that's the end of it, it's too late now, we have brought this misfortune upon ourselves.'

Trembling, he asked:

'Are you blaming me?'

'Yes, it's your fault, and I sinned too when I followed you... We were disobedient, and our whole lives have been ruined.'

'But aren't you happy?'

'No, I'm not happy... A woman without a child is never happy... Love counts for nothing, if it is not blessed.'

He collapsed onto a chair, overwhelmed, and tears swam in his eyes. Never before had she reproached him for this open wound that ran through their lives; and she, who always backed down so quickly and comforted him whenever she had hurt him with some unwitting allusion, this time stood there and watched him suffer, without making any gesture, or taking any step towards him. He wept, and cried out through his tears:

'Oh, our dear child, up there, she's the one you're hurting... You don't want him to marry her in the way that I married you, or for her to suffer in the way that you have suffered.'

She gave a simple nod by way of answer, in all the strength and sincerity of her conviction.

'But you yourself were saying that this would be the death of our poor little girl... Do you really want her to die?'

'Yes, death, rather than a life of sin.'

He had risen trembling to his feet and sought refuge in her arms, and together they wept. They remained in this embrace for a long time. He was giving in to her, and she had to support herself against his shoulder as she gathered her courage. They separated, despairing and yet resolute, enfolded in a thick and agonizing silence, at the end of which lay, should God so will it, the accepted death of their child.

From this day on Angélique was confined to her bedroom. She felt so weak that she couldn't even make her way down to the workroom; her head at once began to spin, and her legs gave way beneath her. At first, she roamed as far as the balcony, supporting herself on the furniture as she went. After that she had to be content with going just from her bed to the armchair. It was a long journey for her, to be ventured only in the morning or the evening, as it left her drained. And yet she carried on working, putting aside the low-relief embroidery, which was too strenuous, and instead embroidering flowers in silks of many hues. She worked from nature, a cluster of scentless flowers, hortensias and hollyhocks, which had a calming effect on her. The blooming flowers stood in a vase, and she often rested for hours just staring at them, as the silk, light as it was, weighed heavily in her fingers. In two days she completed only a single hollyhock, which appeared fresh and dazzling against the satin; but this was a way of life to her, and she would not relinquish the needle until she had breathed her last. Fading away with pain, and appearing ever thinner, she had no more substance than a pure, very lovely flame.

What was the point in fighting on, since Félicien did not love her? She was dying now as a result of one conviction: that he did not love her and perhaps had never loved her. While she had strength, she had struggled against the promptings of her heart, her health and youth, which had all urged her to run to him. Once she found herself confined to her room, she had to resign herself to her fate: it was all over.

One morning as Hubert was settling her into her armchair, swinging her lifeless little feet onto a cushion, Angélique said with a smile:

'Oh well, I'll have to stay here and be good, I suppose, since I can't run away.'

Hubert hurried downstairs, choking with anguish as he tried to hold back the tears.

CHAPTER 12

THAT night Angélique was unable to sleep. Her eyelids smarted as she lay there, wide awake and desperately frail. The Huberts had gone to bed, and it was about to strike midnight, so she decided to get up, despite the great exertion involved, fearing that she would die in her bed if she remained there.

She struggled to breathe as she slipped on a dressing gown and dragged herself over to the window, which she opened wide. Outside, it was a rainy winter's night, mild and damp. After turning up the wick of the lamp, which sat on the small table and was left to burn throughout the night, she sank into her armchair. There in front of her, beside *The Golden Legend*, was the bunch of hollyhocks and hortensias she had been copying. She had the fanciful idea that she might regain her energy by resuming her work, and so drew her frame over and, with shaking hands, made several stitches. The red silk of one of the flowers shone bloodily between her white fingers, as though her own blood had seeped out into it, droplet by droplet.

She had tossed and turned for two hours in vain, wrapped in her burning sheets, but fell asleep almost as soon as she was sitting down. Her head sank against the backrest, and slid down a little towards her right shoulder. She continued to grasp the silk in her motionless hands, and almost gave the impression that she was carrying on with her work. Looking very pale and serene, she slept on in the lamplight, her bedroom as white and peaceful as a tomb. The great royal bed, with its canopy of faded pink chintz, seemed drained of colour in this light. The chest, wardrobe, and chairs of old oak were the only things that stood out in contrast, appearing as black as mourning against the walls. The minutes went by, and she continued to slumber, pale and serene.

At long last a sound disturbed the silence. Félicien appeared on the balcony, trembling all over, and looking as gaunt as she. His face was marked by anguish, and he was just slipping into the room when he saw her, sunk deep in her armchair, a piteous figure, and yet very beautiful. His heart filled with immense pain, and he fell to his knees, losing himself in sorrowful contemplation. So she was no more then, she had been crushed by grief, and lying there, appeared to weigh nothing at all, a mere feather that the wind might carry away. Her bright, slumbering figure revealed to him her suffering and resignation. He recognized her only by her lily-like grace, the delicate line of her neck rising from narrow shoulders, and her slender face, transfigured like that of a virgin ascending into heaven. Her hair was of the same substance as light, and her snow-white soul shone out through skin of translucent silk. She had all the beauty of those saints who have been set free from their bodies, and he was dazzled by her, and filled with despair. He knelt there, stunned and motionless, his hands clasped together. She did not awaken, and he continued to gaze at her.

A faint breath from Félicien's lips must have brushed across Angélique's face. Suddenly her eyes opened wide. She did not move, but gazed at him in turn, smiling as though in a dream. It was he. She recognized him even though he had changed. She thought that she must still be asleep, for she often happened to see him like this as she slumbered, which only intensified her pain on waking.

He held out his hands to her and spoke.

'My darling, I love you. When they told me you were suffering I rushed over... Here I am, I love you.'

She shivered, and instinctively rubbed her eyes.

'You needn't doubt it any longer... I'm here at your feet, and I love you, I love you still.'

She cried out then.

'Oh, it's you... I'd given up waiting for you, and yet here you are...'

Groping around uncertainly, she took hold of his hands—as a way of reassuring herself that he was not a wandering vision summoned by her slumbers.

'You still love me, and I love you, oh, much more than I ever thought I could possibly love!'

They felt dizzy with happiness. It was their first moment of absolute bliss, in which everything was forgotten apart from the certainty of their love, of which they assured one another over and over. Past sorrows and future obstacles all melted away. They did not understand how they had come to be there, but there they were, their sweet tears mingling, their bodies entwined in a chaste embrace, he overwhelmed by pity, and she so wasted by grief that it was as though all he clasped in his arms was a breath of air. In her delighted astonishment she lay there numbly, rapturous and faint-headed in the depths of her armchair, unable to feel her limbs, raising herself up slightly only to slip back again, ecstatic with joy.

'Oh, my dear lord, my sole wish has been fulfilled: I've seen you again before I die.'

He looked up at her in sheer anguish.

'Die!... I don't want you to die! I'm here, and I love you!'

She smiled beatifically.

'I don't mind dying, knowing that you love me. I'm no longer afraid, I'll fall asleep just like this, on your shoulder. Tell me again that you love me.'

'I love you, just as I loved you yesterday, and just as I'll love you tomorrow... You mustn't ever doubt it—I'll love you for all eternity.'

'Yes, we'll love one another for all eternity.'

Angélique gazed out blissfully at the white room. A thought was gradually forming in her mind, causing her to grow solemn. She had started to reflect a little, even in the midst of her immense, overwhelming happiness. And there was something that baffled her in it all.

'If you loved me, why didn't you come?'

'Your parents told me that you didn't love me any more. The news almost killed me. It was only when I found out that you had fallen ill that I made up my mind, even if it meant being turned out of this house whose door was closed to me.'

'My mother told me too that you no longer loved me, and I believed her... When I met you out with that young lady, I thought that you had decided to obey Monseigneur...'

'No, I was waiting. But I was a coward, and trembled before him.'

A silence fell. Angélique had sat up straight, and her face was stern, a furrow of anger creasing her brow.

'So we have both been lied to and misled, in an effort to keep us apart... We were in love, and they tortured us, and nearly killed us... Well, what they've done is dreadful, and it releases us from our vows. We're free.'

Rage and contempt had brought her to her feet. Her illness seemed to fade, and her strength flowed back, as passion and pride reawakened within her. She had thought her dream was dead, and now suddenly it reappeared before her, radiant and alive! To think that they had never tarnished their love, and that the blame lay with others! This restoration of her self-esteem, accompanied by a conviction of certain triumph, filled her with elation, and spurred her towards outright rebellion.

'Come on then, let's go,' she said simply.

She walked spiritedly about the room, bristling with energy and resolve. She was already choosing a coat to put over her shoulders. A lace scarf would do to cover her head.

Félicien had cried out with delight, for she seemed to be anticipating his very own wishes—all he had wanted was to flee with her, but had not been bold enough to say so. Oh, what it would be to go away together, to vanish from sight, and so put an end to all the difficulties and hindrances besetting them! And they had to do this straight away, to forestall any qualms of conscience!

'Yes, let's leave at once, my darling. I was coming to fetch you away—I know where we can find a carriage. We will be far away before daybreak, so far away that nobody will be able to catch up with us.'

She opened drawers, and slammed them shut again, without taking anything out, growing more and more agitated. What on earth! She had been in agonies for weeks, striving to banish him from her memory, and even believed that she had managed to do so! But in fact it had all been a waste of time, and she would have to begin this dreadful undertaking afresh! No, she would never have the strength for it. Since they loved one another, it was quite simple: they would marry; no power on earth would ever prise them apart.

'Let's see, what do I need to take with me?... Oh, how foolish I was, to have such childish scruples. To think that they stooped so low as to lie to us! I could have died, and they wouldn't have asked you to come... Do you think I need to bring linen and clothing? Here's a dress that's a little warmer... They filled my head with a heap of fancies, and a heap of fears. There's good, and there's evil; there are things one can do, and things one can't; it's all so complicated and bewildering! They have been telling nothing but lies; these things simply aren't true. All that matters is to lead a happy life, and to love the one who loves you... Fortune, beauty, youth, you are all these things, my dear lord, and I give myself to you, completely and for all time; you are my only joy, and you may do with me as you please.'

She was filled with exultation as the hereditary fires within her, which seemed to have been extinguished, flared high once more. She thrilled as music rang out; she pictured their royal departure, this son of princes bearing her away to make her queen of some distant realm; and she went with him, clinging to his neck, or lying on his chest, and shuddered with such unworldly passion that her whole body felt faint with bliss. Oh, to be alone together, just the two of them, yielding to the rhythm of galloping hooves; to flee together, and vanish in an embrace!

'I shouldn't bring anything with me, should I?... What would be the point?'

Feverish with impatience, he was already standing by the door.

'No, nothing... Quickly, let's go.'

'Yes, of course, let's go.'

Standing by his side, she turned to take one last look around her room. The lamp burned with the same soft, pale radiance, the bunch of hortensias and hollyhocks still bloomed, and the rose in the middle of her frame, though unfinished, appeared alive, and seemed to await her return. It struck her that the room had never appeared so white, with the white walls, the white bed, and even the air within it all glowing white, as though the room were filled with misty breath.

Something inside her faltered, and she had to clutch the back of a chair to support herself.

'What's the matter?' asked Félicien anxiously.

She did not answer; she was struggling to breathe. She started to shiver and, with no strength left in her legs, had to sit down.

'Don't worry, it's nothing... I'll just rest here for a minute, and then we'll go.'

They fell silent. She looked around the room as though she had left behind some precious object, but could not recall exactly what it was. A feeling of regret, only faint at first, began to swell inside her, and gradually started to suffocate her. She could no longer remember anything. Was it all this whiteness that kept her here? She had always loved white, so much so that she had stolen scraps of white silk just to be able to gaze on them in secret.

'Just another minute, one more minute, and we can leave, my dear lord.'

But she was no longer even trying to stand up. Deeply concerned, he knelt down in front of her once more.

'Are you in pain—is there nothing I can do to help? If you are cold, I'll take your little feet in my hands and I'll warm them up until you can run on them again.'

She shook her head.

'No, no, I'm not cold, I'll be able to walk... Wait a minute, just a minute.'

It was obvious to him that her limbs were held fast by invisible chains, fixing her there so firmly that, in just a few moments, perhaps, it would be impossible for him to wrench her away. If he didn't take her away at once, he knew he would have to face the inevitable struggle with his father the next day, and the final rupture between them that he had been trying to avoid for weeks. And so he grew insistent, entreating her urgently.

'Come now, the roads are pitch-black at this hour. The carriage will bear us away in darkness, and we will travel on and on, cradled in one another's arms, sleeping soundly, as cosily as in any quilt, with no need to fear the night chills. When day breaks we will carry on in sunshine until we reach a land far away, where everyone is happy... Nobody will know who we are, and we will live our lives hidden away at the bottom of some great garden, and will have no care other than to love each other more with each new day. There we will find flowers as big as trees, and fruit that is sweeter than honey. And we will live on nothing in an eternal springtime; we will live only on kisses, my darling.'

She shivered to hear this ardent outpouring of love, which brought warmth to her cheeks. As the happiness he promised rippled over her she felt faint in her whole being.

'Oh, wait just a moment, just a short while!'

'And then, if we grow weary of travelling, we can come back here and raise up the walls of Hautecœur Castle, where we'll live out our days. It's my dream... If necessary, we can lavish our entire fortune on it. The keep will once more command the two valleys. We'll live in the great apartment, between the tower of David and the tower of Charlemagne. We'll restore the whole colossus to its former glory, the curtain walls, the buildings, and the chapel, with all the raw opulence of those bygone days... And I want us to live as in ancient times, with you a princess, and me a prince, attended by a retinue of men-at-arms and pages. We will be cut off from the world by walls fifteen feet thick, and we'll dwell in the realm of legend... The sun will sink behind the hills, and we will return from the hunt on great white horses, villagers falling respectfully to their knees as we pass by. The horn rings out, and the drawbridge is lowered. In the evenings, kings sit with us at table. At night, a dais supports our bed, overhung by a canopy like a throne. In the distance soft music plays as we fall asleep in one another's arms, enveloped in purple and gold.'

Trembling, she smiled now with proud delight, but the pain was already returning, coursing back through her body, erasing the smile from lips that creased in agony. And, as she instinctively waved aside these alluring visions, his fervour intensified, and he tried desperately to seize her in his arms, and make her his.

'Oh, come away, and be mine!... Let's escape and forget everything, and be happy.'

She withdrew abruptly from his embrace, in a movement of impulsive rebellion. And, as she stood there, these words slipped from her mouth:

'No, no, I can't, I can't any longer!'

And, ravaged still by inner conflict, she deplored her fate, hesitating and stammering as she spoke:

'I beg you, be kind, you mustn't press me, you must wait... I'd like nothing more than to obey you, to prove that I love you, and go off arm-in-arm to wonderful faraway lands, and live together in royal splendour in the castle of your dreams. This all seemed so simple to me, and I so often dreamt up different plans for our escape... But what can I say to you? Now, it seems impossible. It's as though the door has suddenly been walled up, and I can't get out.'

He sought to weave his spell over her again, but she waved him to silence.

'No, don't say anything... Isn't it strange! Even as you utter such sweet and tender words, which really ought to win me over, I'm seized by fear instead, and a chill runs through me... My God, what's the matter with me? Your very words are driving me away from you. If you carry on, I'll have to stop listening to you, and you'll have to leave... Wait, wait a moment.'

And she walked slowly around the room, trying to recompose herself, while he remained motionless in despair.

'I had thought I no longer loved you, but no doubt I was simply upset with you, because, a little while ago, when I saw you at my feet, my heart leapt up, and my first instinct was to run off with you and be your slave... But if I love you, why do you fill me with terror? And who is trying to stop me from leaving this room? It is as though invisible hands have seized hold of my body and every hair on my head.'

She had come to a halt beside the bed, turned and came back towards the wardrobe, and then walked on, stopping to stand in front of each piece of furniture in turn. Undoubtedly she felt some sort of mysterious bond with them. Moreover, the pale walls and the pale swathe of the sloping ceiling appeared to wrap her in a gown of purest white, which she would have wept to remove. All these things seemed to have become part of her very being—her surroundings had entered into her. And she understood this more clearly when she came before her embroidery frame, which stood beside the table in the lamplight. Her heart melted at the sight of the rose she had begun, and which would remain unfinished if she went away like a thief in the night. She called to mind her years of toil, such happy, fruitful years, and the calm and honest habits she had gradually acquired, which revolted at the idea of sin. And day after day, the chill little house of the embroiderers, and the hard-working, virtuous life she led there, hidden away from the world, had reformed a little the blood that ran within her veins.

But as he watched her fall once more under the spell of the objects around her, he knew he must try and hasten their departure.

'Come on, the minutes are slipping away, and soon we won't have time.'

But realization burst upon her, and she cried out:

'It's already too late... You can see that I can't go with you. In the past, I was proud and passionate, and would have flung my arms around you, and let you carry me away... But I've been changed by those around me, and I'm no longer the person I was... Can you not hear that everything in this room calls out to me to stay? I now rejoice in being obedient.'

He did not speak or reason with her, but simply tried to drag her off as though she were an unruly child. She dodged away from him, and ran over towards the window.

'For pity's sake, no! A little earlier, I would have followed you. But that was my last impulse of defiance. Without my knowing it, the humility and renunciation instilled in me have gradually grown stronger. And so, with each revival of my original sin, the struggle has become less bitter, and I have mastered myself more easily. Now it's all finished, I have triumphed over myself... Oh, my dear lord, I love you so deeply! Let's not do anything to spoil our happiness. We must submit if we wish to be happy!'

As he took another step towards her, she retreated to the French window, which stood wide open, giving onto the balcony.

'You wouldn't want to make me jump... Listen, now, you must try and understand that everything around me is on my side. These things have been speaking to me for a long time, I've been able to hear their voices, and they have never spoken as loudly as now... Listen, the whole of the Clos-Marie is urging me not to ruin my life and yours by giving myself to you against your father's will. That sound of singing is the Chevrotte, its song so clear and sweet that I seem to have been filled with its crystal purity. That soft, low murmuring, as of a crowd— that comes from the whole expanse of earth before us, from the grasses and trees, and all the living things that flourish peacefully on this holy ground, bringing peace to my life. And voices come from further away, too, from the elms in the bishop's garden, from all those branches blocking out the sky, even the smallest of which is invested in my triumph... And listen now! That great sovereign rumble is my old friend the cathedral, which has been like a tutor to me, ever wakeful through the night. All the stones, all the colonnettes in the windows, all the pinnacles atop the piers, all the flying buttresses of the apse, murmur in a distinctive way, and in a language that I can understand. Listen to what they are saying: that hope endures, even in death. Even in humiliation, love survives, and triumphs... And, finally now, listen! The very air is full of whispering spirits; these are my companions, virgins invisible to the eye, drawing near to us. Listen, listen!'

With a smile on her lips, she had raised her hand in intense concentration. These scattered breaths of air sent a thrill running through her whole being. The virgins of the *Legend* were there, appearing to her imagination just as they had done in childhood, the whole mystical host emerging from that old book lying on the table, its pages filled with naive imagery. First Agnes, her hair falling down around her like a gown, with the engagement ring of the priest Paulinus on her finger;

and then all the others, Barbara with her tower, Genevieve with her lambs, Cecilia with her viol, Agatha with her torn breasts, Elizabeth begging in the street, Catherine prevailing over the learned men. Lucy miraculously grows so heavy that a thousand men and five pairs of oxen cannot haul her away to a house of ill repute. The governor who tries to kiss Anastasia is struck blind. And all of them hover palely on the bright night air, their chests torn open by torturing irons, and streams of milk, instead of blood, pour out. The air turns pale, and the darkness is lit up as though by a shower of stars. Oh, what it would be to die of love like them, to die a virgin, radiant and white, at the first kiss of the betrothed!

Félicien had come up to her.

'I am someone who actually exists, Angélique, and you are rejecting me for your dreams…'

'Dreams,' she murmured.

'If there are visions encircling you, it is because you have created them… Come now, if you stop investing the things around you with your spirit, they will fall silent.'

A thrill of exultation ran through her.

'Oh no, let them speak, let them speak even louder! They are my source of strength, and give me the courage to resist you… This is grace itself, and never has it filled me with such spirit. If it is only a dream, a dream I have imparted to the things around me, and which now comes back to me, what does it matter! The dream is saving me, bearing me along unsullied through a world of appearances… Oh, just give up, and obey like me! I don't want to follow you.'

Weak as she was, she had drawn herself up to her full height, and appeared steadfast and invincible.

'But you were deceived,' he resumed, 'they stooped to telling lies in order to keep us apart!'

'The wrongs of others do not excuse our own.'

'Oh, your affection for me has waned, you don't love me any more.'

'I do love you—I'm only resisting you for the sake of our love and our happiness… Obtain your father's consent, and I will follow you.'

'You don't know what my father's like. Only God could sway him… Well, then, tell me, is it all over? If my father orders me to marry Claire de Voincourt, must I obey him?'

As she staggered beneath this final blow, Angélique could not help complaining:

'This is all too much... Go away, I beg you, don't be so cruel... Why did you come here? I was resigned to my situation, I'd got used to the appalling idea that you didn't love me. And now I learn that you do love me, and I shall have to go through all this suffering again!... What do you expect me to do now?'

Thinking he had found a weak point, he repeated:

'If my father wishes me to marry her...'

She stiffened herself against the pain, and managed to remain standing, even though her heart was on the verge of breaking. Then she dragged herself over to the table, as though to let him pass.

'Marry her, you must obey.'

He made his way over to the window, and was about to leave, since she seemed intent on sending him away.

'But it will be the death of you!' he cried.

She had regained her calm, and murmured with a smile:

'I'm halfway there already.'

He gazed at her for a moment longer, so pale and small, as delicate as a feather that the faintest breath of wind might carry away. Then he shrugged with angry resolve, and disappeared into the night.

She propped herself against the back of the armchair, once he had gone, and thrust out her arms despairingly towards the darkness. Deep sobs convulsed her body, and her face was bathed in mortal sweat. My God, this was the end! She would never see him again. Her malady had retaken possession of her flesh, and her weary legs gave way beneath her. It was only with great difficulty that she managed to regain her bed and lay herself down, triumphant yet scarcely breathing. When they came in the next morning they realized that she was dying. The lamp had burned itself out at dawn in the triumphal whiteness of her bedroom.

CHAPTER 13

ANGÉLIQUE was dying. It was ten o'clock on a crisp, clear morning towards the end of winter, and the sun was glittering in a pale sky. She lay motionless in the great royal bed hung with antique pink chintz, and had not regained consciousness since the previous day. Stretched out on her back, her ivory hands resting lifelessly on the sheets, she had not once opened her eyes; and her profile appeared more pinched beneath her golden cloud of hair; and one might easily have imagined that she was already dead but for the faint breath issuing between her lips.

The previous day, feeling desperately unwell, Angélique had made her confession and taken communion. Towards three o'clock, the Abbé Cornille had brought her the holy viaticum.* And then, in the evening, as the chill of death spread slowly through her body, she had felt an urgent desire for extreme unction, that celestial physic instituted for the healing of body and soul. In her last words before she lost consciousness—a faint murmur that was caught by Hubertine—she had stammered out her wish for the holy oils: oh, at once, while there was still time! But the night was wearing on, and so they had waited for day to come, and the priest, who had been alerted, was finally about to arrive.

The Huberts had finished arranging the room, and everything was ready. As the bright sun struck the windows at this early hour, the room, with its expanse of bare white walls, seemed to glow with the pale light of dawn. They had covered the table with a white cloth. To the right and left of a crucifix, two candles burned in silver candlesticks brought up from the sitting room. They had also placed there holy water and an aspergillum,* a ewer of water in its basin, a towel, and two white porcelain plates, one containing balls of cotton wool, the other white paper cones. They had been to visit all the glasshouses in the lower town, but the only flowers they had been able to find were roses, big white roses with heavy clusters of flowers that made it look as though the table were adorned with rippling white lace. And amid this dazzling sea of white, the dying Angélique drew breath faintly, her eyelids closed.

During his morning visit, the doctor had said that she would not last the day. She might pass away at any moment, without ever regaining consciousness. And so the Huberts waited. For all their tears, it had to be this way. If they willed her death, preferring that the child should die rather than live on in defiance, it was because God willed it also. Now things lay beyond their control, and all they could do was submit. They felt no regret, but were harrowed to the core by grief. Ever since she had come to the verge of death, they had looked after her, and refused all help from outside. They were alone again, in this final hour, and they waited.

Hubert mechanically went over and opened the door of the earthenware stove, which had been making a doleful moan. A hush fell, and the roses appeared duller in the gentle warmth that washed over them. Hubertine had been listening for a moment to the sounds of the cathedral that came from the other side of the wall. A bell was tolling, sending a shiver through the old stones; no doubt the Abbé Cornille was coming out of the cathedral with his holy oils, and so she went downstairs to meet him on the doorstep. A couple of minutes later, a commotion filled the narrow turret staircase. Then, in spite of the warmth in the room, Hubert began to tremble, utterly amazed, and fell to his knees, filled with sacred dread, and a glimmer of hope.

Instead of the old priest they had been expecting, it was Monseigneur who entered: Monseigneur in a lace rochet* and violet stole, bearing a silver vessel containing the Oil of the Sick, which he himself had blessed on Maundy Thursday. He gazed straight ahead with his eagle eyes, and his pale, handsome face, fringed with thick white curls, was full of majesty. And behind him, in the simple role of clerk, walked the Abbé Cornille, a crucifix in one hand, the ritual* tucked under his other arm.

Stopping for a moment by the door, the bishop said solemnly:

'Pax huic domui.'

'Et omnibus habitantibus in ea,'* responded the priest, more softly.

After they had gone in, Hubertine, who had come up the stairs behind them, and was also trembling with astonishment, went over and knelt beside her husband. And both alike, with heads bowed and hands clasped, prayed with all their might.

The day after his visit to Angélique, there had been a terrible confrontation between Félicien and his father. He had forced his way in at first light and bearded the bishop in the oratory, where the older man was still praying after a night spent in terrible struggle against his resurgent past. The dutiful son, held back by fear until now, gave vent to his long-suppressed defiance; and the two men, sharing the same blood, and both swift to anger, clashed fiercely. Rising from his prie-dieu, the old man listened in obstinate and disdainful silence, his cheeks flushing crimson. The young man, his face similarly aflame, poured out his discontent, his voice gradually mounting until he was bellowing. He told his father that Angélique was ill and on the verge of death, and related how, as his mind churned with fear and tenderness, he had made plans to run away with her—and how she had refused to go with him, displaying all the chaste renunciation of a saint. Would it not be tantamount to murder if this obedient child, who would take him only with his father's consent, were allowed to die? When she was finally able to have him, along with his title and his fortune, she had cried out no, struggling with herself until she emerged victorious. And he loved her, too, more than life itself, and he despised himself for not being there by her side, so that the two of them might die together, taking their final breath as one! Could anyone be so cruel as to want them to die so wretchedly? Oh, what did these things count for—pride in one's name, resplendent wealth, stubborn resolve—beside the simple matter of making two people happy? He wrung his trembling hands, twisting one about the other and, beside himself with anguish, demanded his father's consent, threatening him at one moment, and begging him the next. But the bishop deigned to reply only with that single word that resonated with his supreme authority: Never!

Then Félicien rose into a frenzy of defiance, losing all measure of self-control. He spoke about his mother. It was she who was coming back to life within him, claiming what was rightfully owed to lovers. His father could never have loved her and must have delighted in her death if he were prepared to behave so sternly towards lovers who wished to live. It was in vain that he should try to shut himself away with the chilly abnegations of religion; she would come back to haunt him, and torment him, because he was tormenting the child born of their marriage. She was still alive, and wanted to carry on living through her son's children, eternally; and he was killing her all over again by refusing to let his son have his chosen fiancée, the woman who would carry on their line. You could not be married to the Church after you had been married to a woman. Looking directly at his father, who stood still, and seemed to loom taller in the terrifying silence, he called him a betrayer and a murderer. Then, stricken by horror, he staggered away.

When he was alone, Monseigneur turned and sank down, as though a knife had been plunged into his chest, his knees settling onto the prie-dieu. A terrible moan escaped his throat. Oh, what sorrows lay in the heart, and what inescapable weakness in the flesh! That woman, that dead woman who insisted on returning to life, he loved her as much as on that first evening when he had kissed her pale feet. And his son, well! He adored him as though he were an extension of herself, a portion of her living flesh that remained after she had gone. And that young woman, the little working girl he had spurned, he adored her too with all the love his son felt for her. Now his nights were tormented by thoughts of all three of them. Although he could not admit it, she had moved him to pity in the cathedral, the simple little embroideress with her golden hair, and charming neck, and lovely youthful fragrance. She passed before his sight, delicate, pure and enchantingly obedient, and lodged in his core as surely and invincibly as any of his regrets. Although officially he repudiated her, he knew that she held his heart in her humble, needle-scarred hands. While Félicien had been angrily entreating him, he had glimpsed behind his son's blond head those two beloved women, one the object of his tears, the other now dying for his son. And, hollow-cheeked and sobbing, at a complete loss as to how he might ever recover peace of mind, he begged heaven to send him the courage to tear out his heart, since his heart no longer belonged to God.

Monseigneur prayed on until evening. When he reappeared, he was as pale as wax, desolate and yet determined. For his part, there was nothing he could do, and he repeated the awful word: Never! Only God had the right to release him from his vow; and when he had beseeched God, God had remained silent. The suffering had to continue.

Two days went by, and Félicien loitered in front of the little house, wild with anguish, and desperate for any news. Whenever anybody emerged, he grew faint with dread. And so it was, when Hubertine came out that morning and ran over to the cathedral to ask for the holy oils, he knew that Angélique would not last the day. But the Abbé Cornille was not there, and so Félicien scoured the town for him, feeling that the last hope for divine help lay with this man alone. But then, as he returned with the good priest, his hope dissipated, and he was racked by doubts, and filled with anger. What could be done? How could he compel the intervention of heaven? He ran off, and forced his way again into the Bishop's Palace; and, hearing his son's ravings, the bishop was momentarily afraid. But at last he understood: on the verge of death, Angélique was awaiting extreme unction—only God could save her. The young man had come solely to bellow his pain aloud, to sever all relations with his abominable father, and to throw the accusation of murder in his face. But Monseigneur listened to him without anger, his eyes suddenly alight, as though a voice had finally spoken. And he motioned to Félicien to lead the way, and followed on saying:

'If God wills, I will.'

A great shiver ran through Félicien's frame. His father, released from his earlier resolution, was offering his consent, and submitting to the will of the miraculous. They, themselves, were of no account now: God would act. Tears blinded him as Monseigneur took the holy oils from the Abbé Cornille in the sacristy. He went with them in a daze, but dared not go into the bedroom, and fell to his knees on the landing, in front of the open door.

'Pax huic domui.'

'Et omnibus habitantibus in ea.'

Monseigneur had just placed the holy oils between the two candles on the white table, after making a sign of the cross with the silver vessel. He then took the crucifix from the hands of the priest, and bore it over to the sick girl so that she might kiss it. But Angélique was still unconscious and, with her eyelids closed and her hands rigid, resembled a slender stone statue lying stiffly on the lid of a tomb. He studied her for a moment and, seeing by her faint breathing that she was still alive, placed the crucifix to her lips. He waited, his face bearing the august expression of a minister of penance, no human emotion playing across his features as he perceived that her delicate profile and lucent hair remained untroubled by the slightest tremor. She was still alive though, and that was enough for the remission of her sins.

Monseigneur then took from the priest the small bowl containing the holy water and the aspergillum and, with the priest holding the ritual open before him, he sprinkled holy water on the dying girl as he read out the Latin words:

'Asperges me, Domine, hyssopo, et mundabor; lavabis me, et super nivem dealbabor.'*

The droplets flew out, and the great bed was bathed in freshness, as though by a fall of dew. The droplets showered down on fingers and cheeks, and trickled away, one by one, as though running down lifeless marble. And the bishop then turned towards the others who were present, and sprinkled them in turn. Hubert and Hubertine, kneeling side by side, and desperate to feel their faith burn higher, bowed down beneath these waves of blessing. And the bishop carried on, blessing the room, the furniture, the white walls, all its bare white expanses, until, coming to the doorway, he found himself before his son, huddled there on the threshold, overwhelmed by anguish, sobbing into his burning hands. Three times the bishop slowly raised the aspergillum, and sent a gentle rain down upon him, cleansing him. Scattered all around like this, the holy water was intended to drive out the evil spirits that flew about invisibly in their millions. Just at this moment a pale ray of winter sunlight struck the bed, bringing to life a whole host of dust motes, an innumerable crowd of darting speckles, which streamed down from a corner of the window to bathe the cold hands of the dying girl in their warm flood.

Monseigneur came back to the table, and recited the prayer 'Exaudi nos'.*

He did not make haste. Death was there, among the old chintz curtains, but he sensed that it was not in any hurry, and would wait. And although the child, in the depths of her prostration, could not hear him, he spoke to her, asking:

'Is your conscience troubled by any matter? Confess your torments, my child, and unburden yourself.'

Stretched out there, she remained silent. After waiting in vain for her to respond, he began to exhort her in the same sonorous voice, seemingly unaware that not a single one of his words was reaching her.

'Gather your thoughts, and from deep within yourself ask forgiveness from God. The sacrament will cleanse you and bring you new strength. Your eyes will become clear, your ears chaste, your nostrils fresh, your mouth holy, and your hands innocent...'

He spoke the set piece through to the end, his eyes fixed upon her as her breath scarcely came and not a lash on her eyelids trembled. Then he commanded her:

'Recite the Creed.'

After waiting for a moment, he recited it himself:

'Credo in unum Deum...'*

'Amen,' responded the Abbé Cornille.

Félicien was still gasping out great sobs out on the landing, his mind deranged with hope. Hubert and Hubertine continued to pray, their postures at once zealous and fearful, as though they sensed strange and awful powers flowing down. There was a brief pause, filled with whisperings of prayer. And then the litanies set down in the ritual began to unfold, invocation was made to all the saints, and *Kyrie eleisons** soared upwards, calling on the whole host of heaven to come to the aid of wretched humanity.

And then all the voices fell suddenly quiet, and a profound silence ensued. Monseigneur washed his fingers in a few drops of water that the priest poured from the ewer. At last he picked up the vessel containing the holy oils, removed the lid, and went over and stood before the bed. In this way the sacrament was borne solemnly to her side—that last sacrament whose efficacy erases all unpardoned mortal and venial sins remaining in the soul after the other sacraments have been received: remnants of old forgotten sins, sins committed unawares, sins of languor, which have prevented one from truly recovering the grace of God. But where did those sins come from? Did the sins come from outside, carried along on this ray of sunlight that swarmed with motes of dust and seemed to carry the seeds of life right into the great royal bed, which this virginal death had turned pale and cold?

Monseigneur paused for a moment to contemplate Angélique once more, making sure that her faint breathing had not ceased. He forbade himself from feeling any emotion as he noticed how thin and insubstantial she had grown, appearing now as beautiful as an angel. His thumb was steady as he dipped it gently into the holy oils, and began to anoint the five parts of her body in which the senses reside—the five windows through which evil enters the soul.

Firstly, the eyes—with his thumb he lightly traced the sign of the cross on her closed eyelids, the right, and the left, saying:

'Per istam sanctam unctionem, et suam piissimam misericordiam, indulgeat tibi Dominus quidquid per visum deliquisti.'*

And the sins of sight were repaired, lustful glances, prurient curiosity, wanton spectacles, unwholesome reading, tears shed over guilty passions. Yet she had known no book other than the *Legend*, no horizon other than the apse of the cathedral, which blocked out the rest of the world. And she had wept only when the struggle between obedience and passion raged within her.

The Abbé Cornille took one of the balls of cotton wool, wiped both her eyelids, and then folded it into one of the white paper cones.

Monseigneur anointed her ears next, just on the lobes, which were as translucent as mother-of-pearl, the right one, and then the left, and the sign of the cross left scarcely any trace of moisture.

'Per istam sanctam unctionem, et suam piissimam misericordiam, indulgeat tibi Dominus quidquid per auditum deliquisti.'*

And all the abominations of hearing were redeemed, all corrupting words and music, gossip, slander, blasphemy, lewd remarks indulgently received, a lover's lies leading to neglect of duty, profane songs exalting the flesh, violins weeping sensually beneath chandeliers. And yet, during all her years of seclusion, she had never once overheard the crude chattering of the women in her street or a carter's oaths as he whipped his horses. Her ears were filled entirely with the music of sacred hymns, the rumble of the organ, and murmurings of prayer, which vibrated through every part of the chill little house, huddled against the flank of the old cathedral.

After wiping her ears with a ball of cotton wool, the priest placed it in one of the white paper cones.

Monseigneur turned his attentions to the nostrils next, which were like two small white rose petals, and traced with his thumb the sign of the cross on the right one, then the left one, purifying them.

'Per istam sanctam unctionem, et suam piissimam misericordiam, indulgeat tibi Dominus quidquid per odoratum deliquisti.'*

And so her sense of smell returned to its first innocence, washed of all its stains. It was cleansed not simply of the carnal shame that lies in luscious fragrances, and the crude allure of sweetly scented flowers, and the perfumes that drift scattered on the air, sending the soul to sleep, but also of the sins of the inner olfactory sense, the poor examples set to others, and the contagious corruption of scandal. And yet, being so upright and pure, she had in the end become a lily among lilies, a great lily whose scent brought strength to the weak, and joy to the strong. And she was so delicate and pure, in fact, that she had never been able to bear fiery carnations, musky lilacs, or febrile hyacinths, and felt easy only among calmer blooms, violets and primroses.

The priest wiped her nostrils, and slipped the ball of cotton wool into another of the white paper cones.

Then Monseigneur moved down to her closed mouth, which opened slightly with each faint breath, and he traced the sign of the cross on her lower lip.

'Per istam sanctam unctionem, et suam piissimam misericordiam, indulgeat tibi Dominus quidquid per gustum deliquisti.'*

And her whole mouth became a simple whorl of innocence, and this time pardon was granted for the base pleasures of taste, for gluttony and the sensual delights of wine and honey, and for the crimes of the tongue particularly, which was unendingly culpable, a provoker, a poisoner, an instigator of arguments, wars, errors, and untruths that darken heaven itself. And yet gluttony had never been her vice and, like Elizabeth, she had come to a point where she ate without noticing what food she had before her. And if she lived in error, it was her dream that had led her there, the aspirations she had towards the beyond, the consolations she found in invisible realms: the whole enchanted world her ignorance had created, making of her a saint.

The priest, having wiped her mouth, folded the ball of cotton wool into the fourth of the white paper cones.

And then Monseigneur anointed the palms of her small ivory hands, the right, then the left, which lay facing upwards on the sheet, and he erased their sins with the sign of the cross.

'Per istam sanctam unctionem, et suam piissimam misericordiam, indulgeat tibi Dominus quidquid per tactum deliquisti.'*

Her whole body was white now, cleansed of its last stains: those of touch, which are the most defiling, robberies, assaults, and murders, along with the sins of other body parts so far unmentioned, the chest, the loins, and the feet, which this unction also redeemed; everything that burns and howls in the flesh, our rages, our desires, our disordered passions, the charnel houses to which we hasten, the forbidden pleasures that make our limbs cry out. And as she had been lying there, brought to the point of death by her victory, she had conquered her violent impulses, her pride and passion, as though she had carried original sin within her solely for the glory that came with triumphing over it. And she was no longer aware that she had ever felt desire, or that her body had groaned with love, or that those deep throbbings that had coursed through her in the night-time could have in any way been blameworthy, so stoutly did ignorance armour her, leaving her soul white—an utterly pristine white.

The priest wiped down her hands, and tucked the ball of cotton wool into the last paper cone, and then cast the five cones into the stove to burn.

The ceremony was over. Monseigneur was washing his fingers before saying the final prayer. All that remained for him to do was to exhort the dying girl once more, placing a symbolic candle in her hand to drive away the demons and show that she had recovered her baptismal innocence. But she was lying there rigidly, her eyes closed, dead. The holy oils had cleansed her body, and the signs of the cross were still traced upon the five windows of her soul, but had not been able to restore any hint of life to her cheeks. The miracle they had hoped for and entreated had not occurred. Hubert and Hubertine remained kneeling side by side, but were no longer praying, and instead gazed at her intently, as though they had been frozen in that position permanently, like the figures of donors* awaiting the resurrection in the corners of old stained-glass windows. Félicien, still on his knees, had dragged himself over to the door, and craned his head up so that he too could see. He was no longer weeping, angered that God remained deaf.

Monseigneur went over to the bed one last time, followed by the Abbé Cornille, who was holding the lighted candle that was to be placed in the hand of the sick girl. And the bishop, stubbornly intent on proceeding to the very end of the rite, so as to allow God time to act, spoke the appointed words:

'Accipe lampadem ardentem, custodi unctionem tuam, ut cum Dominus ad judicandum venerit, possis occurrere ei cum omnibus sanctis et vivas in saecula saeculorum.'*

'Amen,' responded the priest.

But when they tried to open Angélique's hand and place it around the candle, it fell back lifeless upon her chest.

A great shudder then ran through Monseigneur's body. His feelings, which he had fought against for so long, overflowed within him, sweeping away the rigid formality of his priestly calling. He had loved this child from the day she had come and wept at his feet. And now she looked quite piteous, as pale as the grave, and so distressingly beautiful that he could not turn his gaze towards the bed without his heart secretly melting with sorrow. He made no further attempt to control his emotions, and two large tears swelled on his eyelids, and ran down his cheeks. She couldn't be allowed to die like this. On her deathbed, she cast an irresistible spell over him.

And Monseigneur, remembering the miracles performed by his ancestors and the healing powers that heaven had bestowed upon them, thought that God must undoubtedly be awaiting his paternal consent. He invoked St Agnes, to whom all his forebears had made their devotions and, just as when Jean V of Hautecœur had gone to pray at the bedside of plague victims, and kissed them, he prayed, and kissed Angélique on the mouth.

'If God wills, I will.'

All at once, Angélique opened her eyes. Awoken from her long swoon, she looked at him without a hint of surprise, a smile playing on her lips, which were still warm from his kiss. All of these things had been destined to occur, perhaps once again she had simply dreamt them. She found it perfectly natural for Monseigneur to be there to marry her to his son, since the moment had finally arrived. Without any help, she sat up in the middle of the great royal bed.

The bishop, the radiant light of the miracle shining before him, repeated the formula:

'Accipe lampadem ardentem...'

'Amen,' responded the priest.

Angélique had taken the lighted candle and, with a steady hand, held it straight. Life had returned to her, and the flame burned very brightly, driving away the spirits of the night.

A great shout filled the room, and Félicien was on his feet, as though raised up by the power of the miracle; while the Huberts, stunned by the same force, remained on their knees, their eyes wide and their expressions rapturous after what they had just witnessed. The bed, it seemed to them, had been enveloped in bright light, and white shapes, like white feathers, were still floating up along the ray of sunlight. The white walls, and everything in the white room, shone as dazzlingly as snow. In the middle, like a lily given water and standing straight on its stem once more, Angélique was the source of this radiant light. Her fine golden hair formed a bright halo about her head, her violet-coloured eyes sparkled celestially, and her pure face shone with glorious vitality. Félicien, seeing her restored to life, and overwhelmed by the grace of heaven, went up to her, and knelt beside the bed.

'Oh, my darling! You can recognize us, you're alive... I'm yours now, my father wills it, since God has willed it.'

She bowed her head, and gave a merry laugh.

'Oh, I knew all along, I was just waiting... Everything I have seen in my dream must come to pass.'

Monseigneur, who had recovered his lofty air of calm, placed the crucifix to her lips again, and this time she kissed it, as an obedient servant. With great sweeps of his hand, he dispensed his final blessing across the whole room, and over all their heads, while the Huberts and the Abbé Cornille wept.

Félicien had taken Angélique's hand. And in her other little hand she held the candle of innocence, whose flame burned very high.

CHAPTER 14

THE wedding was set for early March. Angélique was still very weak, although joy radiated from her whole being. At first she had wanted to go back down to the workroom, in the very first week of her convalescence, and seemed stubbornly intent on completing the panel of low-relief embroidery for Monseigneur's throne. It was her last job as a worker, she said gaily, and you shouldn't abandon an order when you were in the middle of it. But, exhausted by the effort involved, she had been forced to keep once more to her bedroom. She passed the hours there quite cheerfully, without however regaining the full health of earlier times, still as pale and insubstantial as when she had been anointed with the holy oils. She wandered slowly back and forth, visions peopling her mind, or rested for hours in a dream after some long march—from her table to the window. And the wedding was put back, and it was decided that they would wait until she was fully recovered, which, with proper care, would not be long.

Félicien went up to see her every afternoon. Hubert and Hubertine were there, and they spent delightful hours together going over and over the same plans, endlessly. Even from her armchair she appeared lively and high-spirited, and was the first to speak about their future life together, their travels, the restoration of Hautecœur, and all the happiness that awaited them. She seemed completely out of danger now, her strength growing as the early spring weather wafted in through the open window, each day a little warmer than the one before. It was only when she was alone, and knew that no one was watching, that she fell into more sombre thoughts. At night-time, voices caressed her and the earth called out to her, all around; and things became clear—she understood that the miracle was persisting solely to fulfil her dream. Wasn't she in fact already dead? And if she continued to exist in the realm of appearances, wasn't this because those presences about her had granted her respite? In her hours of solitude, this thought was infinitely sweet and soothing, and she felt no regret at the prospect of being carried off in the midst of joy, certain that she would taste her anticipated happiness to the full. Whatever evils lay ahead would wait. And, with this, she grew a little more solemn in her gaiety, and in perfect stillness let herself drift away until she could no longer feel her body, and she seemed to float up into a realm of pure bliss. It was only when she heard the Huberts opening her door, or Félicien coming in to see her, that she sat up and pretended to be well once more, and spoke, with much laughter, about the years they would share together, far off in the future.

Towards the end of March, Angélique's spirits seemed to lift further. On two occasions she had fainting fits while alone. One morning she had fallen down at the foot of her bed just as Hubert was bringing her up a cup of milk and, to fool him, she blithely suggested from the floor that she was looking for a lost needle. Then, the following day, she gaily proposed that they hasten the wedding, and bring it forward to the middle of April. But they protested at this: she was still so weak, why not wait? There was no hurry! But she grew vehement: it had to happen right away, without any delay. Startled, Hubertine felt a glimmer of suspicion at this urge for haste, and studied Angélique a while, turning pale at the chill breath that faintly grazed her cheek. But the frail girl had already grown calm again, mindful to sustain an illusion of good health in front of the others, even though she knew that she was about to die. Hubert and Félicien, absorbed in their adoring thoughts, had seen and sensed nothing. Raising herself to her feet by an effort of will, and walking gracefully about as of old, she was a picture of loveliness, and assured them that the ceremony would complete her recovery, with all the joy it promised. In any case, it was up to Monseigneur to make the decision. When the bishop came to call that same evening, she looked steadily into his eyes as she explained her wish to him, her glance never wavering, her gentle voice conveying an earnest entreaty whose reasons she left unspoken. Monseigneur heard, and understood. He fixed the wedding for mid-April.

So then the house filled with commotion as elaborate preparations were made. Even though he was Angélique's unofficial guardian, Hubert had to ask for consent from the Director of Welfare Services, who was the representative of the board of guardians, since Angélique was still under age. And Monsieur Grandsire, the justice of the peace, took care of these formalities, so as to spare Hubert and the young girl any distress. But when Angélique realized that these things were being kept from her, she had her record book brought up, and was determined to hand it over herself to her fiancé. She had now reached a state of perfect humility and wished him to know all about the lowly origins from which he was raising her up, enveloping her in the glorious lustre of his legendary name and fortune. For her, this administrative document, a record of committal showing just a date and a number, was akin to a title of nobility. She leafed through it once more, and then gave it to him without any sense of shame, exhilarated by the thought that she was a nobody and all she was becoming was due to him. He was profoundly moved, and knelt down and tearfully kissed her hands as though she were the only one to offer up a gift, the royal gift of her heart.

For two weeks the preparations kept all of Beaumont busy, throwing the upper and the lower towns into disarray. Twenty women were said to be working day and night on the trousseau. The wedding dress alone took up the efforts of three, and there were to be gifts to the bride worth a million francs, cascades of lace, velvet, satin, and silk, a stream of gemstones, diamonds fit for a queen. But what caused the greatest stir were the considerable sums being distributed as alms, since the bride wished to give to the poor the same amount as she herself was receiving, and so another million tumbled down on the town in a shower of gold. She was at last satisfying her long-standing desire to give with largesse, which she was permitted by the abundance of the dream, and she opened her hands wide, allowing a river of wealth, a flood of prosperity, to flow down on the poor. In her small bare white room, where she was confined to her old armchair, she laughed rapturously whenever the Abbé Cornille brought her the lists of donations. More, more! She was never happy with how much was being given. She would have liked to see old Mascart sit down to a feast fit for a king, the Chouteaus ensconced in palatial luxury, and Mère Gabet recover her health and youth with the help of money; and as for the Lemballeuse family, the mother and her three daughters, she would have simply showered them in dresses and jewellery. The hail of golden coins beat faster on the town, as in a fairy tale, far exceeding what was required to meet daily needs, its purpose now just beauty and delight and the splendour of gold, falling in the street and gleaming in the bright sunlight of benevolence.

Finally, on the eve of the great day, everything was ready. Félicien had bought a grand old house in the Rue Magloire, behind the Bishop's Palace, and had just finished furnishing it in lavish style. Its vast rooms were adorned with beautiful draperies, and filled with the finest furniture. The sitting room was hung with ancient tapestries, and the boudoir decorated in a blue as soft as the morning sky, but most impressive of all was the bedroom, a nest of white silk and white satin, nothing but white—delicate and ethereal, shimmering like light itself. But, even though a carriage was organized to come and fetch her, Angélique refused to go and see these wonders. She listened as people talked about them, and smiled with pleasure, but she did not give any instructions, and was unwilling to involve herself in any of these arrangements. No, no, all that was happening very far away in those unfamiliar realms that she had never yet visited. Since people who loved her were preparing these delights for her so carefully, she wanted to enter like a princess who has travelled from fantastical lands and arrives in the true kingdom of her reign. And, likewise, she refused to see the marriage gifts which were being kept there as well—the trousseau of fine linen stitched with the monogram of her marquisate, the heavily embroidered evening gowns, the ancient jewellery, an entire, groaning cathedral treasure-house worth, and the modern jewellery, intricately set marvels of craftsmanship and clusters of brilliants of the purest water. For her dream to prevail, it was enough that this fortune should await her at the house, glimmering with the impending reality of life. The only thing that was brought to her was her wedding dress, on the morning of the ceremony.

And that morning, awakening in her great bed before the others, Angélique was overcome for a moment by a feeling of terrible weakness, and feared that she would not be able to stand up. When she tried, she felt her legs buckle beneath her and, giving the lie to the serene courage she had displayed for weeks, her whole being screamed out in appalling torment one last time. However, as soon as Hubertine came in, glowing with joy, Angélique was surprised to find herself able to walk and, since she had no strength herself to do so, help must surely be coming from invisible realms—friendly hands were bearing her up. Her mother dressed her. She weighed nothing, and her mother found her so astonishingly light that she jokingly told Angélique that she must keep still if she didn't wish to float away. And as she was being decked in her attire, the Huberts' chill little house, alive in the cathedral's flank, quivered with the giant's deep exhalations and rumblings, as the clergy rushed feverishly about their preparations, and the bells pealed out, a constant clamour of joy that set the old stones trembling.

For an hour the bells in the upper town had been ringing, just as they did on great feast days. The sun had risen glittering into a clear April morning, and the spring sunlight streamed down, alive with the echoing calls that had roused the townsfolk. The whole of Beaumont was rejoicing in the marriage of the little embroideress, who had won over all their hearts. The beautiful sunshine pouring down onto the streets was like the shower of gold, the fairy-tale alms, that cascaded from her frail hands. And beneath this rhapsody of light, the crowds were moving as one towards the cathedral, filling the side aisles and overflowing into the Place du Cloître. The great façade rose up like a cluster of ornate stone flowers, carved in the most florid Gothic style above the severe Romanesque course. The bells continued to peal from the towers, and the façade seemed a glorious manifestation of the marriage itself—a penniless girl borne aloft on the wings of miracle, everything blazing and soaring upwards, the open lacework, and the lily-like flowering of slender columns, balustrades, arcades, and saints' niches surmounted by canopies, gables hollowed into trefoils, adorned with crossettes and finials, and immense rose windows unfolding their mystical stone tracery.

At ten o'clock the organ began to boom and Angélique and Félicien entered, walking slowly towards the high altar between the packed rows of the congregation. A fond and admiring sigh rippled through the crowd. Brimming with emotion, Félicien advanced with a proud and solemn air, as blond and handsome as a young god, and even more slender than usual in a severe black tail-coat. But it was Angélique who touched their hearts, looking so ethereal and lovely, a mysterious and enchanting vision. Her dress was of white watered silk, overlaid simply with fine old Flanders lace fastened with pearls, strings of fine pearls trimming the bodice and flounces. A veil of antique lace in English point,* attached to her hair by a triple crown of pearls, flowed down to her heels. And she was adorned with nothing else, not a flower or a jewel, and her exquisite little figure—that of a stained-glass virgin, violet-eyed and golden-haired—was enfolded in this cascade of gossamer, this rippling cloud, as though in a pair of delicately beating wings.

Two chairs of crimson velvet had been placed before the altar for Félicien and Angélique; and behind them, as the organ's welcoming phrases swelled, Hubert and Hubertine knelt down on the family prie-dieux. The day before, something had happened to fill their hearts with joy, and they still moved about in a sort of daze, unable to find enough ways to give thanks for their new-found happiness, coming on top of their daughter's. Hubertine had gone to the cemetery again, her mind filled with sad thoughts of how lonely they would be in the small empty house once their beloved girl had left, and for a long time she had plied her mother with humble entreaties. And then suddenly she had felt a great shudder inside her body, and she had risen to her feet, trembling, her wish granted at last. After thirty obstinate years, the dead woman was offering her forgiveness from beneath the soil, and was sending them the child of mercy they had desired for so long, and so long awaited. Was this a reward for the kindness they had shown in rescuing a poor abandoned wretch from the cathedral doorstep one snowy morning, a child who was today marrying a prince in great pomp and ceremony? They remained on their knees, and offered no prayer or formulaic phrase, overjoyed and immensely grateful, their whole beings radiating infinite thanks. And on the other side of the nave, seated on his episcopal throne, Monseigneur, now also a part of their family, appeared full of the majesty of God, whose representative he was. Gloriously arrayed in sacred vestments, he wore an expression of lofty calm, seeming detached from the passions of this world, while above his head on the embroidery panel a pair of angels bore up the brilliant coat of arms of the Hautecœurs.

The ceremony began. All the clergy were present, the priests having come from their parishes to honour their bishop. Among the mass of white surplices crowding within the railings there gleamed the golden copes of the choirmen and the red gowns of the choirboys. The eternal darkness of the side aisles, beneath the crushing weight of the Romanesque chapels, was brightened that morning by limpid April sunshine lighting up the stained-glass windows, in which points of red gleamed like smouldering gemstones. A mass of candles flared in the gloomy nave, candles as numerous as stars in the summer night-sky; and, in the middle, the high altar was ablaze with them, a symbolic burning bush aflame with the soul's fire, which burst out also in torches, candle-stands and chandeliers. In front of the young couple, two great candelabra, branching into circles, shone like two suns. Banks of green plants transformed the choir into a living garden that bloomed with great clusters of white azaleas, white camellias and white lilacs. Right to the far end of the apse, glints shot out among the greenery, flashes of gold and silver, half-glimpsed panels of velvet and silk, a distant burnished tabernacle. And, above this flickering blaze, the nave soared upwards, the four huge pillars of the transept rising to support the vault, and the quivering currents of air sent up by the thousands of small flames made the daylight shimmer in the high Gothic windows.

It had been Angélique's wish to be married by the good Abbé Cornille, and when she saw him coming towards her in his surplice and white stole, followed by two clerks, she smiled. She was at last fulfilling her dream: she was marrying wealth, beauty, and power beyond all hope. The cathedral sang out through its organ pipes, shone forth in its candle-flames, and lived through its congregation and priests. Never before had this ancient nave gleamed with such splendid ceremonial, as though, among all this sacred majesty, it were swelling with happiness. And Angélique smiled, aware that amid all this joy she carried death within her, even as she celebrated her victory. When she had entered, she had glanced over at the Hautecœur chapel where Laurette and Balbine, the Happy Dead, lay sleeping, carried off in the blush of youth and the full bliss of love. On the threshold of death she had come to her perfection, having mastered her passions, mended her errors, and changed her ways, and did not even take pride in her triumph, accepting the fact that her soul would take flight during the hosanna of her friend, the cathedral. When she knelt down, it was as a very humble and obedient servant, completely cleansed of original sin; and she was filled with joy by her renunciation.

Stepping down from the altar, the Abbé Cornille gave the exhortation in a kindly voice. He offered as an example the marriage that Jesus had contracted with the Church, and he spoke of the future, of days to be lived in faith, and children to be brought up as good Christians. Once again, such prospects made Angélique smile, while Félicien, beside her, trembled at the idea of so much happiness, feeling it now to be assured. Then came the ritual questions, the answers that bind for a lifetime, the decisive 'I will' which she uttered, moved to the depths of her soul, and which he said more loudly, his tone tender and solemn. It was now irrevocable, the priest had joined their right hands together as he uttered the phrase: 'Ego conjungo vos in matrimonium, in nomine Patris, et Filii, et Spiritus Sancti.'* But he had still to bless the ring, which is the symbol of inviolable fidelity, and of the everlasting nature of the bond; and this took some time. The priest waved the aspergillum about, making the sign of the cross over the gold ring sitting in its silver bowl. 'Benedic, Domine, annulum hunc...'* And then he gave it to the groom in witness of the fact that the Church was placing a seal on his heart, where no other woman could enter; and the groom placed it on the finger of his bride, to instruct her in turn that he alone among men existed for her from this day forward. The ring stood for their close and everlasting union, a symbol of her subordination that she would wear as a constant reminder of the faith she had sworn; it also contained the promise of the long years they would share together, as though this small circle of gold bound them together until the grave. As the priest addressed them once more, after the final prayers, Angélique wore her bright smile of renunciation. She alone knew what was to come.

The organ boomed out jubilantly behind the Abbé Cornille as he withdrew with the clerks. Motionless in his majesty, Monseigneur lowered his eagle eyes to gaze tenderly at the couple. Still kneeling, the Huberts looked up, blinded by happy tears. And the immense strains of the organ rumbled above, giving way at last to a hail of short, shrill notes, which pattered down beneath the vaults like the dawn song of a lark. A deep tremor ran through the crowds of worshippers packed into the nave and the side aisles, and fond murmurings rippled all about. Garlanded with flowers, and glittering with candles, the cathedral rejoiced in the sacrament.

And there followed two further hours of majestic ceremonial, a sung Mass with incensings. The celebrant appeared wearing the white chasuble, and was accompanied by a ceremoniarius, two thurifers bearing the censer and the incense boat, and two acolytes carrying the great lighted golden candelabra. Monseigneur's presence complicated the rite, with its salutations and kisses. Every few moments the wings of the surplices were set flapping by bows and genuflexions. In the old, ornately carved stalls, the entire chapter would rise to their feet, and then, at times, it was as though the breath of heaven swept through the crowded apse, prostrating all the clergy. The celebrant sang at the altar, and then, as he fell silent and returned to his seat, the choir began, and continued for a long time, the low strains of the older men mingling with the delicate tones of the choirboys, light and ethereal as the flutes of archangels. A voice very pure and beautiful rose into the air, a voice exquisite to the ear, the voice, so the word went around, of Mademoiselle Claire de Voincourt, who had wanted very much to sing at this miraculous wedding. She was accompanied by the organ, which soughed out long and tender exhalations, utterly serene, as though it were pure and joyous of soul. Sudden silences fell, and then the organ rumbled forth mightily once again. And meanwhile the ceremoniarius guided the acolytes back with their candelabra and led the thurifers up to the celebrant, who blessed the incense in the boats. Great clouds of incense rose constantly into the air, and the chains flashed brightly and gently chinked together. The air filled with fragrant blue smoke as a thurifer censed the bishop, the clergy, the altar, and the Gospel, each individual and object in turn, and finally the massed ranks of the congregation, swinging thrice, to the right, to the left, and to the front.

Kneeling, Angélique and Félicien listened devoutly to the Mass, which is the mysterious consummation of the marriage of Jesus and the Church. Each had been given a burning candle to hold, a symbol of virginity preserved since baptism. After the Lord's Prayer, they remained beneath the veil in sign of their submission, modesty, and humility, while the priest, standing on the Epistle side,* read out the appointed prayers. They continued to clasp the burning candles, which are also an admonition to think on death amid the righteous joy of the wedding. And then it was over, the offering had been made, and the celebrant had begun to move away accompanied by the ceremoniarius, the thurifers, and acolytes, after prayers had been said that God might bless the newly married couple so that their children should increase and multiply down to the third and fourth generations.

At that moment the whole cathedral filled with rejoicing. The organ burst into a triumphal march so thunderous that the old building shook. Trembling, the crowd rose to their feet and craned to see; women climbed onto chairs, and massed rows of faces stretched all the way to the back of the dark side chapels. Smiles appeared everywhere, and every heart beat faster. For this final farewell, thousands of candles seemed to burn higher, long tongues of flame stretching upwards, seeming to set the vaults dancing above. The final hosanna of the clergy rose from among the flowers and the greenery, the splendid decorations and glittering sacred vessels. But all of a sudden, over beneath the organ, the twin doors of the great portal opened, and a blade of bold daylight pierced through the dark wall. Beyond lay the bright April morning, the vibrant spring sunshine, and the Place du Cloître with its cheerful white houses. Awaiting the couple outside were an even larger crowd, eager and adoring, who had already begun to wave and cheer. The candles grew dim, and the thundering organ drowned out the noises of the street.

Angélique and Félicien walked slowly down the aisle, between the two banks of the faithful, towards the door. After her triumph, she was emerging from the dream, advancing to where she would at last enter reality. Throbbing with raw light, the doorway opened into a world she knew nothing about; she slowed and contemplated the overflowing houses and the bustling crowd, all that was about to greet her and lay claim to her. She felt so weak that her husband almost had to carry her. And yet she continued to smile, and thought about the princely house that awaited her, filled with jewellery and clothing fit for a queen, and the wedding chamber hung with white silk. She was having trouble breathing and came to a halt; but she summoned up the strength to take a few steps more. Her glance had lighted on the ring on her finger and she smiled at this everlasting bond. And then, on the threshold of the great portal, at the top of the steps that led down into the square, she staggered. Had she not experienced all the happiness there was to know? After this, surely life held no further joy? With a final effort she strained upwards and put her mouth to Félicien's. And with this kiss, she died.

But it was a death without sadness. Monseigneur, with his customary gesture of pastoral blessing, helped her soul gain release, feeling completely at peace himself now that he had sunk back into godly oblivion. The Huberts, having been granted forgiveness, were returning to ordinary life and had the blissful sensation that a dream was coming to an end. Great celebrations engulfed the cathedral and the entire town. The organ groaned more loudly, the bells pealed out and in glorious spring sunshine the crowds cheered on the loving couple poised on the threshold of the mystical cathedral. And Angélique soared triumphantly upwards, exultant and pure, borne off in the moment of her dream's fulfilment, swept up from dark Romanesque chapels into flamboyant Gothic vaulting, through vestiges of gold and paint into the paradise of the legends.

Félicien clasped just a soft and cherished wisp of a thing, the wedding gown made of lace and pearls, a handful of fine feathers left behind by a bird, still warm to the touch. For a long time he had felt that he possessed merely a shadow. This vision, coming out of the invisible realms, had returned to the invisible. It had been a thing of appearance only, generating an illusion and then fading away. All is but a dream. And, at the pinnacle of her happiness, Angélique had vanished in the faint breath of a kiss.

EXPLANATORY NOTES

ABBREVIATIONS

AE   Charles-Germain de Saint-Aubin, *Art of the Embroiderer*, trans. and annotated by Nikki Scheuer, with additional notes and commentaries by Edward Maeder (Los Angeles, Calif.: Los Angeles County Museum of Art, 1983), with a facsimile of the original French edition (Paris: L.-F. Delatour, 1770).

GL   Jacobus de Voragine, *The Golden Legend: Readings on the Saints*, trans. William Granger Ryan, with an introduction by Eamon Duffy (Princeton and Oxford: Princeton University Press, 2012).

GT   Orby Shipley (ed.), *A Glossary of Ecclesiastical Terms* (London: Rivingtons, 1872).

LA   Jacobus de Voragine, *Thus endeth the legende, named in Latyn Legenda aurea that is to saye in Englysshe the golden legende*, trans. William Caxton (London: Wynkyn de Worde, 1527).

LD   Jacobus de Voragine, *La Légende dorée*, ed. Gustave Brunet, 2 vols (Paris: Librairie de Charles Gosselin, 1843).

LS   Jacobus de Voragine, *The Golden Legend, or Lives of the Saints*, trans. William Caxton, ed. F. S. Ellis, 7 vols (London: J. M. Dent, 1900).

ODE   *Oxford Dictionary of English*, electronic edn (Oxford: Oxford University Press, 2009).

OED   *Oxford English Dictionary*, 2nd edn, rev., online edn (Oxford: Oxford University Press, 2009), <http://www.oed.com/>.

3 *River Oise*: rising in Belgium, the Oise runs in a roughly south-westerly direction through northern France and joins the Seine to the west of Paris.

ancient Romanesque . . . early Gothic: the Romanesque style of architecture prevailed in Europe *c*.950–1200, and is characterized by 'round arches and massive vaulting, and by heavy piers, columns, and walls with small windows'. The Gothic style evolved out of the Romanesque in the twelfth century, and commonly features 'pointed arches, rib vaults, and flying buttresses, together with large windows and elaborate tracery' (*ODE*). Each style has a specific symbolic significance for Zola: see 'Introduction', pp. xxi–xxii.

St Agnes: according to legend, Agnes (*c*.291–*c*.304) was born to a noble Roman family and brought up a Christian. Pursued by several suitors, she refused marriage because of her devotion to Christ, and was denounced to the authorities for her religion. She was executed during the great persecution of Diocletian, which began in 303 (*GL*, 101–4). By the mid-fourth century a basilica dedicated to her had been erected over her tomb beside the Via Nomentana, near Rome. Owing to her name, she was associated with the lamb (Latin: *agnus*).

3 *tympanum*: the vertical recessed space above a door. Zola modelled his portal after two sources: the main entrance to the Romanesque abbey at Vézelay in Burgundy (constructed in the late twelfth century) and the portal of the Coronation of the Virgin (completed in the early thirteenth century), which is the north portal in the west façade of Notre-Dame Cathedral in Paris, and features three episodes from Mary's death and Assumption described in *The Golden Legend* (*GL*, 535–44).

4 *Constance . . . leprosy*: Constantina, or St Constance (d. 354), eldest daughter of the Roman emperor Constantine the Great and his second wife, Fausta. Constantina is said to have gone to pray at Agnes's grave, seen the saint in a vision, and been cured of her disease (*GL*, 104).

Paulinus: a priest serving in the church of St Agnes in Rome (*GL*, 104).

jambs: in Gothic cathedrals, the jambs, or upright supports to the doors, are normally splayed outwards—that is, emerge at an oblique angle from the face of the wall—and are often decorated with sculptures.

stylobate: a continuous base serving as a support to features such as columns. In the portal of the Coronation of the Virgin at Notre-Dame, statues of the saints and angels stand atop slender columns over the stylobate.

Dorothea . . . bread: born of a noble family, Dorothea (d. *c*.304) is said to have fled with her family from Rome to Caesarea in Cappadocia, where she was baptized. Having promised herself to Christ, she rejected the proconsul Fabricius's offer of marriage. He had her placed in a barrel of burning oil, from which she emerged unscathed. He then imprisoned her without food or drink, but she was fed by 'angels' food of our Lord'. He tortured her further and eventually had her beheaded (*LS*, vii. 42–7).

Barbara . . . tower: Barbara was locked in a tower by her father, Dioscorus, so that her great beauty should not be seen by men. After converting to Christianity, she was said to have been tortured and beheaded under Maximian (r. 286–305) (*LS*, vi. 198–205). Although she does not seem to have been venerated in antiquity, her cult was popular in late medieval France.

Genevieve . . . Paris: patron saint of Paris (d. *c*.500). Genevieve is said to have become a nun at the age of 15, and to have been admired for her piety and charitable works. When Attila's army threatened Paris in 451, she urged the women of the city to pray and fast, causing the Huns to move on to Orléans. During a later siege by the Frankish king Childeric I, she broke through the lines in a boat and brought back provisions for the famished citizens (*LS*, iii. 284–304). She was buried in an abbey built for her by Clovis I (466–511), king of the Franks. Louis XV had a new church built in her honour, which was secularized during the French Revolution and renamed the Panthéon.

Agatha . . . torn: after refusing the Roman official Quintianus, Agatha of Sicily was sent to live in a brothel, but remained devoted to Christ and continued to rebuff Quintianus's advances. She was tortured and had her breasts cut off, and died in prison in the mid-third century (*GL*, 154–7).

Christina . . . father: owing to her great beauty, Christina is said, like Barbara (see above), to have been locked in a tower by her father, in Tyro, Italy, and there converted to Christianity. She refused to worship the pagan gods, and so her father tore off her flesh with hooks and broke her limbs. After her father's death, Roman officials continued to torture her, and she is said to have died from arrow wounds in 287 (*LS*, iv. 93–7).

Cecilia . . . angel: born into a noble Roman family, Cecilia was raised as a Christian. After marrying Valerian, she confessed to him that she had a lover, an angel of God who watched over her, and she refused to consummate their marriage. Valerian converted to Christianity, and was executed by the prefect Almachius. Cecilia refused to sacrifice to the pagan gods, and so Almachius tried to boil her alive in a bath, and then to have her beheaded, but in vain. She is said to have died *c*.220 (*LS*, vi. 247–53). It was only in the sixteenth century that she became venerated as the patron saint of musicians.

voussoirs: a voussoir is a 'wedge-shaped masonry unit in an arch or vault whose converging sides are cut as radii of one of the centres of the arch or vault' (Cyril M. Harris (ed.), *Illustrated Dictionary of Historic Architecture* (New York: Dover Publications, 1977), 567).

altar of repose: either the altar on which the consecrated host is set aside on Maundy Thursday for use on Good Friday, or the altar on which the host rests during a pause in a procession. An altar of the second type features below in chapter 8.

archivolts: the curved part of an arch above the level of the jambs.

5 *Louis XIV*: Louis XIV, the 'Sun King', r. 1643–1715.

6 *ogival bay*: a bay having a vault that rises to a point, as in a Gothic arch.

Louis XI: king of France, r. 1461–83.

8 *Louis XIII table*: Louis XIII was king of France from 1610 to 1643. Furniture of this period is typically large and robust, and the tables commonly featured legs turned on a lathe.

9 *book bound in pale pink cloth*: Zola based his description on an actual record book, supplied to him by his friend Gabriel Thyébaut in December 1887.

10 *Soulanges*: a name presumably adapted by Zola from that of the commune of Coulanges, which lies just upstream from the town of Nevers on the Nièvre river, in Burgundy.

foster mother . . . set of clothing: in the mid-nineteenth century, a woman seeking to take in a foster child would travel to the foundling hospital in Paris, armed with a certificate from her local mayor attesting to her morals and suitability. If her application there was successful, she would collect the child, an initial payment, and an allowance of food and clothing, and travel back with the child to her home—by cart or railway, sometimes making the final leg of the journey on foot. See Rachel Ginnis Fuchs, *Abandoned Children: Foundlings and Child Welfare in Nineteenth-Century*

France (Albany, N.Y.: SUNY Press, 1984). The distance from Paris to Nevers is around 240 kilometres.

11 *the Ligneul*: the name of this fictional river is taken from an embroidery term meaning 'waxed thread'.

13 *Beaumont*: modelled after several different towns in northern France: Cambrai, near the Belgian border, renowned for its cambric industry, along with Coucy and Chauny in the Aisne region.

faubourg: in its historical sense, this term denotes part of a town situated outside its gates or wall.

thirty leagues: the length of the land league (as distinct from the nautical league) varied widely according to region and usage before the Revolution, and was still not fixed after integration into the metric system. By the mid-nineteenth century, though, it was commonly accepted as measuring 4,000 metres. Beaumont is thus 120 kilometres from Paris.

15 *the First Empire*: the period of Napoleon's rule as emperor of the French, from 1804 to 1814/15.

Utrecht velvet: 'a strong, thick kind of plush made of worsted, mohair, or mohair and cotton' (*OED*).

18 *The Golden Legend by Jacobus de Voragine*: the Dominican Giacomo, or Jacopo, da Varazze (1228/30–98), archbishop of Genoa from 1292, compiled the *Legenda aurea*, or *The Golden Legend*, in the 1260s from a wide range of patristic and medieval sources. The book contains a collection of the lives of the saints, along with information about holy days and seasons. It was one of the most popular religious works of the Middle Ages, and was translated into most of the Western vernaculars.

19 *St John the Almoner . . . poor*: born in Cyprus, John was patriarch of Alexandria from *c*.610 to 617, and many anecdotes celebrated his generous almsgiving (*GL*, 113–18).

St Matthias . . . idol: replaced Judas Iscariot as an apostle after the latter's suicide (Acts 1:23–6; *GL*, 166–71). Zola describes the image in greater detail in his notes: 'St Matthias has broken an idol which is falling, and he is run through by a spear which has been thrust into his back and is coming out of his chest' (Paris, Bibliothèque Nationale de France, nouvelles acquisitions françaises, MS 10324, f. 69). This description does not illustrate any story about Matthias in *The Golden Legend*.

St Nicholas . . . tub: bishop of Myra in Asia Minor in the fourth century. The image relates to a story in which Nicholas restores three boys to life after they have been cut up and pickled in a salting-tub by a butcher, a story that does not feature in *The Golden Legend*.

Juliana . . . flogging: said to have lived during the reign of Diocletian (284–305), Juliana refused to marry her betrothed, Eulogius, prefect of Nicomedia, unless he converted to Christianity. She was beaten by her father, and then tortured and imprisoned by the prefect. The devil visited her in her cell, and Juliana whipped him with her chains. Then, when she was released, she dragged him through the town by her chains and threw him into a sewer. The prefect had her beheaded (*GL*, 160–1).

Anastasia . . . burnt alive: born of a noble Roman family, Anastasia was raised a Christian by her mother and was married to a young man named Publius. She feigned illness to keep him away, and was imprisoned when he discovered her ruse. She was later passed from one prefect to another, but could not be swayed in her faith, and so was burnt at the stake during the persecutions of Diocletian (*GL*, 43–4).

Mary of Egypt . . . desert: at the age of 12, Mary (5th century) is said to have run away to Alexandria, where she worked as a prostitute for seventeen years. After travelling to Jerusalem to pay homage to the cross of Christ, she was stopped by an invisible force from entering the church that housed it. She realized that this was because of her sins, and so, after asking forgiveness from the Virgin Mary, she went into the desert and spent forty-seven years doing penance. She died there and was buried by a lion (*GL*, 227–9).

Mary Magdalene . . . perfume: the Gospels recount an incident in which a woman anoints Jesus with perfume while he is still alive, as though, he suggests, in anticipation of his burial. Identified as 'Mary' and 'a sinner', this woman became associated with Mary Magdalene, and the bowl of perfume came to form part of the latter's iconography.

Dominic has a star on his brow: when Dominic (*c*.1170–1221), founder of the Order of Preachers, or the Black Friars, was baptized as an infant, his grandmother lifted him from the font and it 'seemed to her that he had on his forehead a brilliant star which shed its light over the whole world' (*GL*, 431).

20 *Hung upon a cross, Andrew*: an apostle, a fisherman, and brother of Simon Peter, Andrew is said to have travelled widely after Jesus's death, preaching and performing miracles, and was himself crucified *c*.60 by the proconsul Aegeus at Patras in the northern Peloponnese (*GL*, 13–21).

Sabina . . . house: Sabina (or Savina) was the daughter of a Roman nobleman. Her brother Sabinian converted to Christianity and was executed at Troyes in France by the emperor Aurelian (r. 270–5). Without telling her father, she set out for Rome, where she was baptized by Pope Eusebius, and performed miracles there and elsewhere. She died on reaching the site of her brother's martyrdom (*GL*, 527–9).

Paula . . . children: a member of the Roman nobility, Paula bore her husband, Toxocius, four daughters and a son. Widowed at 32, and further grieved by the death of her eldest daughter, Blaesilla, she converted to Christianity and fell under the influence of Jerome. Despite the entreaties of her family, she left Rome (with one daughter, Eustochium) to visit the sites of the Holy Land, living very simply. She settled in Bethlehem alongside Jerome, where she established a monastery and convent, and she remained there until her death in 404 (*GL*, 121–6).

Germanus . . . ashes: born of noble Romano-Gaulish parents in Auxerre, Germanus (*c*.378–*c*.448) studied in Rome and was appointed bishop of

Auxerre. He was renowned for his charitable works and austere way of life: 'He never ate wheaten bread or vegetables, drank no wine, did not flavour his food with salt. [...] He began a meal by swallowing some ashes, following this with a barley loaf; and he fasted always, never eating before evening' (*GL*, 413).

20 *Bernard . . . water*: born near Dijon, Bernard (*c*.1090–1153) joined the Cistercian order of monks and after several years was appointed abbot of Clairvaux, where he lived very frugally: 'He had so mastered the cravings of gluttony that he had largely lost even the ability to distinguish different tastes. [...] He used to say that the only thing he tasted was water, and that was because it cooled his cheeks and throat' (*GL*, 487). He played an active role in Church affairs, combated the theology of Pierre Abelard, and preached in favour of the Second Crusade.

Agathon . . . three years: an Egyptian abbot who was said to have kept a pebble in his mouth for three years 'until he learned to keep silence' (*GL*, 740).

Augustine . . . sins: in his *Confessions*, Augustine of Hippo (354–430), one of the most influential early Christian theologians, reproaches himself for various slight sins which have distracted him from meditation and prayer. He 'accuses himself, with regard to the sense of sight, [...] of taking too much pleasure in watching a dog run, or of enjoying, as he walked through the fields, the sight of hunters hunting, or of spending too much time at home watching spiders trap flies in their webs' (*GL*, 510). See also St Augustine, *The Confessions*, trans. Henry Chadwick, Oxford World's Classics (Oxford: Oxford University Press, 1998), 212.

two cubits: a cubit is an ancient measure of length derived from the forearm, equating to roughly half a metre.

'They flee . . . or poudre': Zola modified passages of a sixteenth-century French translation of *The Golden Legend* and incorporated them into his novel; on the way that these have been rendered into English, see the 'Translator's Note', p. xxxi. The lines here are drawn from 'The feast of St Michael' (*LA*, f. 256r; *GL*, 591); *as the sonne bemes ben*, 'as the sun beams are'.

Six thousand . . . Fortunatus: bishop of Todi in Tuscany, and a friend of Gregory the Great, Fortunatus (d. 537) used prayer to drive the devils from a woman who had sinned by sleeping with her husband the night before attending the dedication of a church to St Sebastian (*GL*, 101).

21 *Basil . . . young man*: Bishop of Caesarea and a Doctor of the Church, Basil the Great (*c*.330–379) grasps hold of a slave whom the devil and a horde of demons seek to bear away, the slave having sworn in writing to serve the devil in return for help in winning the love of a nobleman's daughter (*GL*, 108–13).

Macarius . . . onslaught: Macarius the Great (*c*.300–390), founder of an abbey in the Scetis desert, near the Nile delta, was renowned for his skill in 'outwitting the deceits of the demons' (*GL*, 89).

Peter . . . miracles: in Acts 8:9–24, Peter rebukes Simon, a sorcerer living in Samaria, for offering to pay the apostles to acquire the power to perform miracles. In later accounts, Peter and Simon confront one another in various places, such as before the emperor Nero in Rome, and vie over such feats as resurrecting the dead, commanding the behaviour of dogs, and flying through the air (*GL*, 341–4).

'A blacke catte . . . terryble stenche': 'The Life of St Dominic' (*LA*, f. 193*v*; *GL*, 438); *grete eyen and flambynge*, 'huge, flaming eyes'.

Margaret . . . foot: at the age of 15, Margaret of Antioch aroused the lust of a passing prefect, and was imprisoned and tortured for rejecting him in favour of Christ. When the devil appeared in her cell, she 'grabbed him by the head, pushed him to the ground, planted her right foot on his head, and said: "Lie still at last, proud demon, under the foot of a woman!"' (*GL*, 369) After suffering further tortures, and having converted five thousand men, she was beheaded under Diocletian.

22 *John . . . for it*: during his travels through Asia, John the apostle (*c*.6–*c*.100) was challenged by a high priest named Aristodemus to drink poison in order to prove that his master was the true God; John did so and was unharmed (*GL*, 53).

Bristling . . . Sebastian: Sebastian (d. *c*.300) joined the Roman army, and, although secretly a Christian, rose to the position of captain in the Praetorian Guard under Diocletian and Maximian. When Diocletian discovered that Sebastian had been helping fellow Christians, he ordered that he be tied to a post and shot full of arrows. Sebastian miraculously reappeared before the emperor a few days later, and was beaten to death with clubs (*GL*, 99–101).

St Lawrence . . . gridiron: born in northern Spain, Lawrence (*c*.225–58) was appointed deacon of the Church in Rome by his friend Pope Sixtus II. During the persecution of Valerian (or Decius in some accounts), he was asked to deliver up the treasure of the Church, and so assembled the poor and declared to the prefect of Rome that these were its riches. For this he was placed on a gridiron and roasted to death over hot coals (*GL*, 449–60).

'Thou cursed wretche . . . rosted ynough': 'The Life of St Lawrence' (*LA*, f. 200*r*; *GL*, 453).

'whiche her semed . . . drope of swette': 'The Life of St Cecilia' (*LA*, f. 328*v*; *GL*, 709).

St Michael: the archangel (*GL*, 387, 587–93).

Vincent . . . roses: Vincent (d. *c*.304) was a deacon under Valerius, bishop of Saragossa, and both were brought to Valencia, where they were imprisoned during the persecution of Diocletian. Vincent spoke belligerently to the governor Dacian, and remained defiant as he was subjected to ever more gruesome tortures and cast into a dungeon. When his cell filled with light, song, and lovely scents, and the guards converted, he was transferred by Dacian to a soft bed, where he died (*GL*, 105–8).

'The swete sowne . . . we ben overcomen': 'The Life of St Vincent' (*LA*, f. 77*r*; *GL*, 106–7); *sowne*, 'sound'; *wood*, 'furious'; *we ben overcomen*, 'we have been beaten'.

23 *Quiricus . . . martyrdom*: Julitta, or Julietta, brought her 3-year-old son Quiricus (d. *c*.304) from Iconium to Tarsus (southern Turkey) to escape persecution, but was whipped by the governor Alexander when she refused to sacrifice to the gods. Alexander sought to soothe her weeping child, who scratched and bit him, declaring: 'I too am a Christian.' Alexander cast the child down, dashing out his brains, and had the mother flayed, boiled, and beheaded (*GL*, 323–4).

Eulalia . . . flames: Eulalia of Merida (d. *c*.304) was said to have been the daughter of a noble family in Hispania. Aged only 12, she was so outraged after reading the edicts of Diocletian that she ran away from her home and paid a visit to the governor Dacian, reproaching him for denying the true God. She was threatened with torture, but responded by spitting on an idol, and then breaking it. Dacian had her tortured and then burnt alive (*LD*, i. 359–60).

Jerome's lion . . . back: while living in Bethlehem, Jerome (*c*.341–420), Church Father and translator of the Bible into Latin, was visited by a lion with a wounded paw, which he dressed carefully. Afterwards he set the lion to watch over an ass, but one day the ass was stolen by passing merchants while the lion slept. Ashamed, the lion searched for its friend, and, sighting it at the head of a camel train, drove all the animals back to Jerome (*GL*, 599–600).

Bernard excommunicates flies: a swarm of flies had invaded a monastery, making life there unbearable (*GL*, 490–1).

Remi: elected bishop of Reims at the age of 22, Remi, or Remigius (*c*.437–533), is celebrated for having baptized Clovis I, king of the Franks, and thousands of his followers. Remi was 'so gentle that the birds came to his table and ate crumbs of food from his hands' (*GL*, 86).

Blaise . . . health: elected bishop of Sebaste in Cappadocia, Blaise retired to a cave during a period of persecution, and lived as a hermit. 'Birds brought him food, and wild animals flocked to him [. . .], if any of them were ailing, they came straight to him and went away cured.' When Blaise refused to worship false gods, the prefect of the region had him thrown into a lake, which turned into firm ground. Blaise was then beheaded (*GL*, 151–3). His death is said to have occurred in 316 under the emperor Licinius.

Francis . . . love God: although the son of a wealthy cloth merchant, Francis of Assisi (1181–1226) chose the life of a wanderer and beggar, and over the years attracted numerous followers, eventually founding the Franciscan order of friars. He was renowned for his humility and love of nature, and in many stories he commands the obedience of animals (*GL*, 606–16).

24 *'There was also . . . she had lycence'*: 'The Life of St Francis' (*LA*, f. 264v; *GL*, 611); *tyll she had lycence*, 'until she had permission'.

Christopher . . . carried Jesus: reputed to have lived during the persecutions of Decius (249–51), Christopher (meaning 'Christ-bearer') is said to have been twelve feet tall, and was advised by a hermit to go and live by a river to help people cross. On one occasion, a child he was carrying grew as heavy as lead, only to reveal himself as Christ, saying: 'You were not only carrying the whole world, you had him who created the world upon your shoulders.' Later, in Lycia, a king asked Christopher to renounce God, but he refused, and was tortured and beheaded (*GL*, 396–400).

'He was so foule . . . there alone': 'The Life of St Anastasia' (*LA*, f. 52r; *GL*, 44).

'Whan the provost . . . foulest pytt': 'The Life of St Juliana' (*GL*, 161).

Seven Sleepers . . . Theodosius: wealthy Ephesians, the seven sleepers fled into the hills and hid in a cave during the persecutions of Decius. Enraged, the emperor had them walled in there, and they awoke centuries later to find their city Christian. During a visit from Theodosius II (r. 408–50), they lay down and died. *The Golden Legend* calculates that the duration of their sleep was, in fact, 195 years (*GL*, 401–4).

St Clement . . . miracles: Clement of Rome (d. 99), Pope Clement I, is said to have remained in Rome as a child while his mother set off to Athens with his two brothers. Their ship was wrecked, and the mother washed up on an island where she remained a beggar for twenty years until found by St Peter. Clement's two lost brothers were also located by Peter, who introduced all three to an old astrologer, whom they recognized as their father. Clement followed Peter, Linus, and Cletus as the fourth bishop of Rome. Sent into exile by Trajan, Clement performed miracles and attracted many converts, and was martyred at last by being thrown into the sea with an anchor tied to his neck (*GL*, 709–18).

25 *Julian the Almoner*: an error. Zola no doubt means 'John the Almoner', whom he mentions above, on p. 19.

Gervasius and Protasius: twins said to have been martyred in Milan in the first or second century (*GL*, 326–8).

Martin . . . with them: born in Pannonia (central Europe), Martin of Tours (*c*.316–397) followed his father into the Roman army. Encountering an almost naked beggar near Amiens, he cut his cloak in two with his sword, and offered the pauper half. After leaving the army he set up several monasteries, and was ordained bishop of Tours in 372 (*GL*, 678–86).

Lucy's example . . . the proceeds: born to a noble Sicilian family, Lucy (d. 304) miraculously healed her mother after seeing St Agatha in a vision, and in gratitude gave away all her property to the poor. Angered, her betrothed denounced her to the consul Paschasius as a Christian. Paschasius intended to offer her up to a crowd who would rape her, but the Holy Spirit made her body too heavy to move, and she died where she lay (*GL*, 27–9).

26 *Eugenia . . . revealing herself*: daughter of the prefect of Alexandria, Eugenia (d. *c*.258) studied the Greek philosophers, but renounced their teachings in favour of Christianity. Putting on a monk's habit, she joined a monastery, and became known as Brother Eugene. A noblewoman made advances on her, thinking her a man and, after being rebuffed, accused Eugenia of

having tried to rape her. Brought before her father in court, Eugenia
opened her robe to reveal her sex and identity. She converted her family,
and was later martyred in Rome under Valerian (*GL*, 551–3).

26 *Pope Leo*: Leo I the Great (d. 461), pope from 440, renowned for his success in extending the influence of the papacy and personally intervening to
defend Rome against barbarian invasion, was associated with a number of
miracles (*GL*, 339).

Alexis . . . goes away: the son of noble Roman parents, Alexis urged his
bride on their wedding night to retain her virginity, and then left her and
travelled to Edessa, where he lived as a beggar under a church porch for
seventeen years. Returning to Rome, he was taken in by his family as
a poor pilgrim, and lived with them, unrecognized, until his death in
c.400, when his identity was miraculously revealed (*GL*, 371–4).

Justina . . . execution: after converting to Christianity, Justina of Antioch
was pursued by the magician Cyprian, who summoned a series of shape-
changing demons to help in her seduction. She repelled them all with the
sign of the cross. Cyprian converted and was later ordained bishop of
Antioch. The two saints were tortured and beheaded under Diocletian
(*GL*, 578–81).

'within her chambre . . . clene body': 'The Life of St Cecilia' (*LA*, f. 327*v*;
GL, 705); *undefouled*, 'undefiled'.

Death is stronger than love: a recasting of the Song of Solomon 8:6: 'Love
is as strong as death'.

Hilary: born of wealthy pagan parents, Hilary (*c*.315–368) married and
had a daughter, and after long study converted to Christianity. He was
ordained bishop of Poitiers *c*.353 and at synods and councils he staunchly
criticized the Arian heretics, who denied the divinity of Christ. He is said
to have been snubbed at one meeting by the pope, and denied a seat; then
when he sat on the ground, it 'rose up and put him on the same level with
the other bishops' (*GL*, 88).

'Anone appered . . . an other wyfe': 'The Conception of Our Lady' (*LA*, f. 47*r*;
LS, ii. 128).

27 *Catherine . . . Maximian*: a Christian princess, Catherine was reputedly
born during the reign of the emperor Maximian (*c*.250–310; r. 286–305,
306–10), though the legends normally identify her tormentor as his son
Maxentius (*c*.283–312; r. 306–12). She is said to have confronted the
emperor when he ordered Alexandrians to make sacrifices to the gods.
A gifted orator, she argued with his learned counsellors 'by syllogistic
reasoning as well as by allegory and metaphor, logical and mystical infer-
ence' (*GL*, 721). Her cult seems to have begun only in the ninth century.

'They were abasshed . . . one mayde': 'The Life of St Catherine' (*LA*, f. 337*v*;
GL, 722); 'They were astonished, and did not know what to say, and fell
silent. And the emperor was furious with them, and railed at them for
allowing themselves to be beaten so shamefully by a young girl.'

'And whan the tyraunt . . . myddes of the cyte': 'The Life of St Catherine' (*LA*, f. 337*v*; *GL*, 723); 'And when the tyrant heard this, he was filled with great rage and ordered that they should all be burnt in the middle of the city.'

Elizabeth . . . king of Hungary: Elizabeth of Hungary (1207–31), daughter of King Andrew II of Hungary, married Louis IV, landgrave of Thuringia (central Germany), in 1221. After her husband died in 1227 on his way to join the Sixth Crusade, she built a hospital at Marburg and devoted herself to helping the poor and sick (*GL*, 688–704).

'Her clothynge . . . other colour'; *'Whan the erle . . . spynnyng woll'*: 'The Life of St Elizabeth' (*LA*, f. 321*v*; *GL*, 695); *he escryed for sorowe and sayd: There was never kynges doughter that ware suche an habyte, ne seen spynnyng woll*, 'he cried out with sorrow and said: Never has a king's daughter worn such clothing, or been seen spinning wool.'

'She wasshed . . . have taken it': 'The Life of St Elizabeth' (*LA*, f. 322*r*; *GL*, 696); 'She washed the dishes and other kitchen utensils, at times hiding from the chambermaids, who otherwise would not have let her. And she said: If I had been able to find a more menial life, I would have taken it.'

28 *'Go fro me . . . and departe'*: 'The Life of St Agnes' (*LA*, f. 74*v*; *GL*, 102); 'Get away from me you millstone of sin, who encourage wickedness, bearer of death, go!' For Agnes see note to p. 3.

'I am now embraced . . . agayn to lyf': 'The Life of St Agnes'(*LA*, f. 74*v*; *GL*, 102); 'I now love one whose mother is a virgin and whose father has never known a woman, whose beauty fills the sun and moon with wonder, and by whose sweet scent dead men rise again to life.'

Aspasius: deputy prefect of Rome (*GL*, 103).

'whyte and rody spouse': a reference to the Song of Solomon 5:10: 'My beloved is white and ruddy', a verse cited in 'The Life of St Stephen' (*LA*, f. 54*v*; *GL*, 49). The two lovers of the Song are sometimes considered to be an allegory of Christ and his 'bride', the Church.

29 *unofficial guardianship*: this legal bond was established in French law in 1803, and imported into the Civil Code (Book 1, Title 8, Chapter 2), as a way of sanctioning a relationship that was more than simple benefaction but did not extend as far as adoption. The ward was not legally a member of the unofficial guardian's family and received no rights of inheritance. This provision was designed as a preliminary to adoption, as the government sought to prevent the over-hasty adoption of children before their characters had become apparent. Adoption could occur only once the child had reached 21, the age of majority. The guardianship is 'unofficial' in the sense that the Director of Welfare Services legally remained the child's guardian, as is made clear below.

31 *Madame Sidonie*: Sidonie Rougon features in earlier novels by Zola, *The Fortune of the Rougons* (1871), *The Kill* (1872), and *The Masterpiece* (1886). Born in 1818 in Plassans, she had married a lawyer's clerk named Touche and come to Paris and set up a fruit shop. The various shady dealings she

pursues after her husband's death are described in *The Kill*, and Zola places in Madame Foucart's mouth several phrases used by the narrator in that earlier novel. The fortunes of Sidonie's opportunistic brother Eugène, who rises from mediocrity to become a minister in the imperial government, are traced across several novels in the series, and he is the central figure in *His Excellency Eugène Rougon* (1876). In *Doctor Pascal* (1893), the final novel in the series, it is revealed that Sidonie, having grown tired of her dubious practices, is working for a charity sheltering unmarried mothers.

32 *Hautecœur Castle*: this fictional castle is an amalgamation of the castles of Coucy and Pierrefonds in northern France, on which construction began in the early thirteenth and late fourteenth centuries respectively. Both were repaired by the architect Eugène Viollet-le-Duc in the nineteenth century. The stories about the lords of Hautecœur that appear later in this chapter are based on those of the lords of Coucy.

St Clair . . . embroiderers: a number of saints bearing the name Clair are associated in different accounts with embroiderers: Clair, bishop of Nantes in the third century; Clair of Vienne (d. *c*.660), abbot of Saint-Marcel; and Clair, originally from England, who became a hermit in the diocese of Rouen and was martyred in *c*.875.

33 *diligent*: a small hand-turned machine invented in 1773 for winding gold thread quickly and evenly onto a spindle (*AE*, 69).

tambours: a tambour is a circular frame, consisting of two hoops, one fitting tightly within the other; the material for embroidering is stretched over the inner hoop and held in place by the outer one. Some models were attached to stands; others were held on the knees.

taffetas: excess material would be tucked into a piece of taffeta fitted around the edge of the tambour.

34 *No alterations . . . unravelling a little*: Zola's description of the embroiderers' workshop is closely modelled on a drawing that appears in Saint-Aubin's *Art of the Embroiderer*, right down to the ball of string that has rolled off the chair (*AE*, 23).

cope: a liturgical garment in the form of a long cloak, fashioned from a semi-circular piece of material, worn open or fastened with a clasp at the front.

35 *chasubles*: a chasuble is 'a kind of sleeveless mantle covering the body and shoulders, worn [. . .] by the celebrant at Mass or the Eucharist' (*OED*).

stoles: a stole is vestment consisting of a long strip of material, worn over the shoulders and hanging down in front to the knees or lower.

maniples: a maniple is a strip of material, around a metre in length, worn over the left arm near the wrist by the priest celebrating the Eucharist.

dalmatics: a dalmatic is a 'vestment, with a slit on each side of the skirt, and wide sleeves, and marked with two stripes, worn in the Western Church by deacons and bishops on certain occasions' (*OED*).

ciboria: a ciborium is a vessel, usually shaped like a cup, in which the host is placed.

monstrance: 'An open or transparent vessel of gold or silver, in which the host is exposed' (*OED*); see also note to p. 104.

36 *orphreys*: ornamental borders or bands on ecclesiastical vestments.

satin stitch: 'Close, parallel, over-and-over stitches', which produce a smooth satiny effect (Mary Brooks Picken, *A Dictionary of Costume and Fashion, Historic and Modern* (New York: Dover Publications, 1999), 284).

split stitches: 'Outline stitch in which the needle is brought up through the thread itself' (Brooks Picken, *A Dictionary of Costume and Fashion*, 318).

38 *The territory . . . Clovis*: on Remi and Clovis, see note to p. 23.

sixty sous: the *sou* was a coin with a value equivalent to a twentieth of a *livre*. The *livre* was a unit of account against which coins of different denominations were valued, and was not itself represented by a specific coin. The value of the *livre* had originally been set at that of a pound of silver.

Louis the Fat: Louis VI, king of France (r. 1108–37), spent much of his reign suppressing the unruly robber barons in the royal lands of Île-de-France and the Orléanais.

Philip Augustus . . . Acre: Philip II, king of France (r. 1180–1223), joined forces with Richard I the Lionheart of England for the Third Crusade to the Holy Land, during which they conquered the port city of Acre in 1191.

John V the Great: Zola models his career on that of Enguerrand III de Boves (d. 1242), lord of Coucy, who fought with Philip II against the English and took part in the Albigensian Crusade. Enguerrand consolidated his power by building a number of castles in the Aisne region, and was rumoured to have plotted to overthrow the young Louis IX.

Mazarin . . . demolition: Jules, Cardinal Mazarin (1602–61; original Italian name Giulio Mazarini), was, after Cardinal Richelieu's death in 1642, first minister of France. During the minority of Louis XIV, he overcame the rebellious nobles who rose up against the crown in the second Fronde (1650–3). In his notes, Zola places the destruction of the castle in 1652.

Charles VI . . . madness: nicknamed both 'the Well-beloved' and 'the Mad', Charles VI (1368–1422) was crowned king of France at the age of 11, and exercised power only intermittently—firstly because of his youth, and later owing to periodic bouts of insanity, which began in 1392 and continued until his death. In 1420 he signed the infamous Treaty of Troyes which disinherited his offspring and recognized Henry V of England as his legitimate successor. In his notes, Zola places Charles VI's visit in 1393.

Henri IV . . . Gabrielle d'Estrées: Gabrielle d'Estrées (1573–99), mistress of Henri IV, king of France, from 1590 until her sudden death due to eclampsia, was an important advisor to the king, and bore him three children while he was married to Marguerite de Valois.

39 *Monseigneur d'Hautecœur*: 'Monseigneur' is a title given in France to bishops, archbishops, cardinals, and princes.

three hundred thousand livres: on the *livre*, see note to p. 38.

the Abbé Cornille: 'Abbé' is a title given in France to lower-ranking clergy.

1830: in the wake of the July Revolution of 1830, Charles X (1757–1836), who had ascended the throne in 1824 on the death of Louis XVIII, abdicated and went into exile, bringing an end to the rule of the House of Bourbon in France. Louis Philippe of the House of Orléans, a more popular and liberal figure, seized the crown from Charles's nominated successor, the 9-year-old Henri, duke of Bordeaux. In his notes, Zola suggests that the marquis of Hautecœur despises the new 'bourgeois monarchy' (Paris, BNF, nouv. acq. fr. MS 10323, f. 206).

40 *count of Valençay*: a fictional nobleman. The historical lords of Valençay had their seat at the château of the same name, south of Orléans, but their line was extinguished during the eighteenth century. Charles X revived the title 'duke of Valençay' in 1829, bestowing it on his nephew.

Anjou: a historical region of north-western France, whose capital was Angers in the Loire valley.

guipure: 'A sort of embroidery which is made with fine gold applied over vellum or thread stitch padding. The strands of gold are smooth and evenly spaced, one next to the other. They are attached by means of silk stitches at the edges of the vellum' (Nikki Scheur, 'Introduction', *AE*, 72).

41 *ell*: the length of an ell (French: *aune*), an old unit for measuring cloth, varied in France from region to region, but generally equated to a little under 120 centimetres. The Parisian ell was around 118.8 centimetres, the Lyons ell slightly shorter.

coat of arms . . . one in base: Zola adapts a description of the coat of arms of the master embroiderers, supplied to him by his friend Henry Céard, a fellow novelist and a curator at the Musée Carnavalet in Paris. Concerning the heraldic terms: *fesse*, 'a broad horizontal stripe across the middle of the shield' (*ODE*); *diapered or*, decorated with a golden geometric pattern; *fleurs-de-lis*, the fleur-de-lis is a stylized lily, a symbol associated with the French monarchy; *in chief*, in the uppermost section.

44 *Flanders glue*: a glue preferred by painters and clothiers because, though weaker than common glue, it was transparent and did not flake.

chevron couching: in chevron couching, 'two or three strands of gold [are] applied with a spindle and sewn flat next to each other. The gold is held in place with tiny silk stitches forming the desired shapes of lozenges, shells or chevrons, etc.' (*AE*, 67)

45 *purl*: 'Thread or cord made of twisted loops [. . .] of gold or silver wire' (*OED*).

tabernacle: an 'ornamented receptacle or cabinet in which a pyx containing the reserved sacrament may be placed in Catholic churches, usually on or above an altar' (*ODE*).

46 *Louis XIV bed, a beautiful Louis XV wardrobe*: furniture in the Louis XIV style (*c.*1670–1700) was grand and luxurious, and made innovative use of materials such as tropical woods, tortoiseshell veneers, and inlays of ivory, brass, or pewter. Pieces might feature bronze gilt mounts or be gilded all over. The Louis XV style (*c.*1720–1750) emerged as a reaction against this style, and furniture became smaller, more modest, and more comfortable. It was characterized by its supple curving lines and delicate rococo ornamentation, often featuring pebble and shell motifs.

49 *trefoil*: 'an ornamental design of three rounded lobes like a clover leaf' (*ODE*).

finials: carved ornaments placed on the apex of a roof or pinnacle, usually modelled after flowers or foliage.

51 *'Good knyght . . . perysshe with me'*; *'George brandysshed . . . to the grounde'*; *'George sayd . . . meke beest and debonayre'*: see 'The Life of St George' (*LA*, f. 111v; *GL*, 239); *debonayre*, 'gentle'.

coat of arms . . . sovereign companies: Zola modelled the Hautecœur coat of arms on that of Eudes Le Maire (known as Chalo de Saint-Mars), at the suggestion of his friend Henry Céard. According to one story, Philip IV the Fair (1268–1314), king of France from 1285, had vowed in 1313 to go on crusade, but fell sick, and Chalo went to the Holy Land in his stead. Concerning the heraldic terms: *argent*, silver; *cross potent or*, a golden cross with crossbars at the four ends (a form also known as a crutch cross); *cantoned*, appearing in the same quarter; *inescutcheon*, a small scutcheon or shield within the larger one; *sable*, black; *dexter*, the right; *sinister*, the left; the heraldic *chimera* has the head of a woman, the body of a goat, the legs and mane of a lion, and the tail of a dragon; the helmet should appear surrounded by mantling (ornamental drapery) rather than by a *plume*, which normally appears above the helmet; *damasked or*, patterned with gold; *sovereign companies*, judicial bodies established by the authority of the king.

53 *Abgar . . . back to him*: King Abgar V Ukkama of Osroene (r. 4 BC–AD 7, and AD 13–50), who had his capital at Edessa in Mesopotamia, is said to have written a letter to Jesus in which he acknowledged Jesus's divinity, asked to be cured by him, and offered him refuge in Edessa. According to legend, Jesus wrote back commending him for his faith, but explained that he was busy with his own works, and after his Ascension would send a disciple to cure him (*GL*, 646–7).

Ignatius . . . the Virgin: bishop of Antioch (d. *c.*107), whose authentic letters provide much insight into the early Church. It is said that he wrote to Mary asking her to 'strengthen and console' him, and received a heartening reply (*GL*, 140–1). He was executed under Trajan.

Stephen . . . easy familiarity: the Church's first martyr, Stephen (d. *c.*35), was one of the seven deacons appointed by the apostles to preach and to distribute alms. He made a spirited defence of the Christian faith to the judges of the Sanhedrin, who grew angry, and had him taken out and stoned to death (Acts 6–7). During his oration he praised Moses's friendship with God (*GL*, 46). Zola noted: 'familiarity with God' (Paris, BNF, nouv. acq. fr. MS 10324, f. 38). In assigning 'familiarity' to Stephen, Zola may have transposed Moses's attribute, or may be referring to the way in which Stephen addresses God and Christ directly at the moment of his death.

53 *Sylvester . . . a thread*: Sylvester was pope from 314 until his death in 335, but little is known about his life. In later legends, he was falsely said to have converted and baptized the emperor Constantine the Great, and to have been granted supreme spiritual and temporal power by him. It was also claimed that Sylvester subdued a ferocious bull and a dragon (*GL*, 62–71).

54 *gemstone . . . St Lupus's chalice*: born in the Orléanais, Lupus (*c.*573–*c.*623) was ordained archbishop of Sens in *c.*609. When Chlothar II conquered Burgundy, he sent Lupus into exile, where the saint preached and performed miracles until he was recalled. Further miracles occurred when Lupus visited Paris: prison doors flew open so that the inmates could meet him, and one Sunday, while Lupus was celebrating Mass, 'a jewel fell from heaven into his sacred chalice' (*GL*, 530).

A tree crushes St Martin's enemies: Martin (see note to p. 25) wished to cut down a pine tree dedicated to some devils, but the local pagans would only agree to this if they could test his faith by cutting it so that it would fall on him. As the tree came down Martin made the sign of the cross and it 'fell in the opposite direction, almost crushing the people who had taken a place they thought was safe' (*GL*, 681).

honeybees . . . Ambrose's mouth: while Ambrose (*c.*339–397), the infant son of a Roman prefect, lay asleep in his cradle, a swarm of bees 'flew in and covered his face and mouth so completely that the bees seemed to be moving in and out of their hive' (*GL*, 229). During service as a judge, Ambrose was asked by the people of Milan to become their bishop, and reluctantly took up this position. He put an end to Arianism in that city, and played an important role in the politics of the empire, advising emperors from Gratian to Eugenius.

Bartholomew . . . Sicily: one of the twelve apostles, Bartholomew is mentioned only briefly in the Synoptic Gospels (Matthew, Mark, and Luke), and is thought by some to be the same person as the apostle Nathaniel mentioned in John's Gospel. In later accounts Bartholomew is said to have travelled as a missionary to Egypt, India, Persia, and Armenia, meeting his end in Albanopolis, where he was flayed and then crucified or beheaded (*GL*, 495–502). The story of the flotilla of coffins was probably devised to explain why some of his relics could be found on Lipari, a small island north of Sicily.

62 *stained-glass painter*: the general term for an artist who made stained-glass windows.

71 *silver coins . . . a bank note*: at this time silver coins ranged in value from 20 centimes to 2 francs. The old unit of currency the *sou*, a twentieth of a *livre* (see note to p. 38), disappeared when decimal currency was introduced

during the French Revolution; however, people continued to use the term *sou* to refer to the 5 centime coin (a twentieth of a franc). The 'ten sous' Angélique offers are thus worth 50 centimes. The 20 franc coin shines like the sun as it was gold in colour. In the mid-1860s, coins were made of different metals in the following denominations: bronze, 1, 2, 5, 10 centimes; silver, 20, 50 centimes, 1, 2 francs; gold, 5, 10, 20, 50, 100 francs. The paper note of the smallest value was the 50 franc note, the so-called 'blue' note, introduced in 1864. Notes also existed in the following denominations: 100, 200, 500, 1,000 francs. The wage of a male artisan was roughly 25 francs a week, a female artisan usually earning less than half this amount, and an apprentice much less still. Félicien's most generous gift (in the shape of the 'bank note') appears to be equivalent to two weeks' wages for an artisan.

78 *shaded gold*: a painstaking embroidery technique which Zola details below, closely following Saint-Aubin's description (*AE*, 31–2).

79 *two thousand francs*: this represents almost twice the yearly wage of the average artisan.

81 *book of hours*: a small, elaborately illustrated book, containing prayers to be said at the canonical hours, popular in the Middle Ages.

82 *masterpiece*: 'a piece of work by a craftsman accepted as qualification for membership of a guild as an acknowledged master' (*ODE*).

a sixth of an ell in height: an ell in France generally measured a little under 120 centimetres (see note to p. 41); a sixth of an ell is thus just under 20 centimetres. In one of Zola's sources, the masterpiece is described as being square in shape; that is, it would be approximately 20 by 20 centimetres (Alfred Franklin, *Les Corporations ouvrières de Paris, du XIIe au XVIIIe siècle: Histoire, statuts, armoiries, d'après des documents originaux ou inédits* (Paris: Firmin-Didot, 1884), 11).

83 *cope of Charlemagne*: this garment is alleged to have been given by the caliph Harun al-Rashid (766–809) to Charlemagne (*c*.742–814), and is kept in the treasury of Metz Cathedral. It dates, in fact, from after Charlemagne's lifetime.

Syon cope: a cope (see note to p. 34) embroidered around 1300–20 and later named for the Bridgettine convent of Syon in Middlesex, founded in 1414–15 by Henry V. It is preserved in the Victoria and Albert Museum, London.

the imperial dalmatic: this dalmatic (see note to p. 35), supposedly worn by Charlemagne at his coronation on Christmas Day in 800, is, in fact, a Byzantine vestment dating from around the fourteenth century. It is housed in the treasury of St Peter's Basilica, Rome.

Jesse tree: a tree representing the genealogy of Christ, so named because it usually emerges from the reclining figure of Jesse, the father of King David in the Old Testament. Intermediate forebears throng its branches, and the figures of Jesus or the Virgin and Child appear at the top.

83 *Christ on the cross*: a chasuble made possibly in Cologne in the fifteenth century, and held in the Hochon Collection in Paris in the late nineteenth century.

Naintré chasuble: a chasuble dating possibly from the fifteenth century, held in the church of Naintré, near Poitiers. Zola's source material emphasized that the Virgin was represented on it with 'her feet shod, as her iconography requires' (Ernest Lefébure, *Broderie et dentelles* (Paris: Quantin, 1887), 106).

84 *Simonne de Gaules, Colin Jolye*: embroiderers who worked for Charles VII (1403–61), king of France, while he held court at Bourges. The archaic spelling of the name 'Simon' seems to have led Zola to believe that this particular embroiderer was a woman; however, Lefébure indicates that both were male (*Broderie et dentelles*, 106).

86 *split silk*: embroiderers would use their fingers to split flat silk threads into narrower strands that were used for embroidering pictures (*AE*, 49).

99 *ceremoniarius*: 'An official who superintends the ceremonies and assists the ministers in a liturgical service' (*OED*).

Blessed Sacrament: the consecrated elements of the Eucharist, especially the host.

101 *foulard*: 'A thin flexible material of silk, or of silk mixed with cotton' (*OED*).

102 *tunicle*: 'A close-fitting vestment [. . .] with a fringed border and narrow sleeves [that] reaches below the knees' (*GT*). Shorter than a dalmatic, it is worn by subdeacons over the alb (a long white vestment reaching to the ankles).

sheepskin: a traditional attribute of John the Baptist (d. *c*.30), associated with him perhaps because of the life he led in the desert.

103 *surplices*: a surplice is a loose white linen vestment 'varying from hip-length to calf-length, worn over a cassock' (*ODE*).

birettas: square caps worn by Roman Catholic clergy, which have three flat projections on top and a tuft. Priests wear black birettas.

beneficiaries of the cathedral: a beneficiary of a cathedral is 'an inferior, non-capitular member of a cathedral [. . .] possessing a benefice or endowment in the church' (*GT*).

pluvials: a pluvial is a type of long cloak. 'Copes were formerly of two kinds: the *cappa pluvialis* [rain cape], a large mantle with a hood to it, used out of doors, and the choir cope, or cope canonical, such as is now used in churches' (*GT*). For the latter kind see note to p. 34.

Pange lingua: 'Sing, my tongue', the first words of a Latin hymn by St Thomas Aquinas (*c*.1225–74) written for the feast of Corpus Christi. Its opening lines can be translated as: 'Sing, my tongue, the mystery of the glorious body and the precious blood'.

104 *great golden sunburst*: the monstrance, used to display the consecrated host for veneration, typically took the form of a sunburst made out of precious

metals, and had a small round piece of glass or crystal in the centre, in which the host was placed.

109 *Monseigneur's son*: the French (*le fils de Monseigneur*) contains an untranslatable play on words: it can be heard also as *le fils de Mon Seigneur* ('the son of My Lord'), reinforcing the identification between Félicien and Christ that appears elsewhere in the novel.

111 *Tantum ergo*: 'Therefore so great', the opening words of the first of the final two verses of Aquinas's hymn *Pange lingua* (see note to p. 103), which are sung during the veneration and benediction of the Blessed Sacrament.

116 *muffle kiln*: a kiln containing a chamber (or muffle) that protects the glass from flames, smoke, and ash as paint or enamel is baked onto it at low temperature.

glass . . . coloured in the paste: glass that takes its colour during firing, rather than having colours baked onto it later.

131 *Norbert . . . boar*: at the suggestion of his friend Henry Céard, Zola modelled these titles in part after those of Charles-François-Frédéric de Montmorency-Luxembourg (1662–1726), duke of Beaufort-Montmorency.

132 *old missals*: a missal is a book containing the texts used at the Mass throughout the year; missals often contained illuminations depicting the saints celebrated on certain days in the calendar.

133 *prie-dieu*: 'A piece of furniture for use during prayer, consisting of a kneeling surface and a narrow upright front with a rest for the elbows or for books' (*ODE*).

137 *low-relief embroidery*: a style of embroidery in which layers of thick waxed thread or pieces of felt are used to supply volume to a figure, which is then covered over with gold thread (*AE*, 29–30).

Brittany thread: a type of thick, strong thread. White or yellow Brittany thread was sometimes used to create a foundation over which decorations were embroidered in gold thread.

142 *colours*: by the mid-thirteenth century, only a limited range of colours and patterns was permitted in heraldic designs. The palette consisted of the five colours (azure, gules, purpure, sable, vert), two metals (or, argent) and two furs (ermine, vair).

144 *'My God, why have you forsaken me?'*: words uttered by Jesus on the cross (Matthew 27:46; Mark 15:34).

145 *the wound in her side*: another reminder of Jesus on the cross: a soldier pierced his side with a spear after he was dead, and blood and water flowed from the wound (John 19:34).

160 *holy viaticum*: the Eucharist administered to a person near death.

aspergillum: an implement for sprinkling holy water, taking the form of a brush or a hollow metal ball pierced with holes and attached to a shaft.

161 *rochet*: 'An alb [see note to p. 102], only shorter and with tighter sleeves' (*GT*), reserved usually for bishops and abbots.

161 *ritual*: a book such as the *Rituale Romanum* ('Roman ritual'), or another regional variant, containing rites of the Catholic Church.

'*Pax . . . ea*': 'Peace be to this house.' 'And to all who dwell in it.' These Latin phrases, and those that follow in this chapter, appear in the liturgy of extreme unction, a sacrament in which a sick or dying person is anointed with holy oils.

164 '*Asperges me . . . dealbabor*': 'You shall sprinkle me with hyssop, Lord, and I shall be cleansed; you shall wash me, and I shall be whiter than snow' (incorporated into the liturgy from Psalm 51:7). Hyssop is a shrub mentioned in the Bible, whose twigs were used for sprinkling water or blood in rites of purification (Exodus 12:22, Numbers 19:18, etc.).

165 '*Exaudi nos*': 'Hear us', the opening words of a prayer that calls on God to send down an angel from heaven to protect those present.

'*Credo in unum Deum*': 'I believe in one God', the first words of the Nicene Creed.

Kyrie eleisons: The Greek words *Kyrie eleison* ('Lord have mercy') also feature in the rite of extreme unction.

166 '*Per istam . . . visum deliquisti*': 'By this holy unction, and through his great mercy, may the Lord forgive you whatever sins you have committed through the sense of sight.' Somewhat similar scenes of extreme unction occur in Flaubert's *Madame Bovary* (1856) and Sainte-Beuve's *Pleasure* (1834), in which those authors also describe sins associated with the different senses. In his notes, Zola remarks on the ironic distance between Angélique's limited experiences and the sins she is accused of here (Paris, BNF, nouv. acq. fr, MS 10324, f. 224). The same rite features in Zola's later novels *Lourdes* (1894) and *Rome* (1896).

'*Per istam . . . auditum deliquisti*': 'By this holy unction, and through his great mercy, may the Lord forgive you whatever sins you have committed through the sense of hearing.'

167 '*Per istam . . . odoratum deliquisti*': 'By this holy unction, and through his great mercy, may the Lord forgive you whatever sins you have committed through the sense of smell.'

'*Per istam . . . gustum deliquisti*': 'By this holy unction, and through his great mercy, may the Lord forgive you whatever sins you have committed through the sense of taste.'

168 '*Per istam . . . tactum deliquisti*': 'By this holy unction, and through his great mercy, may the Lord forgive you whatever sins you have committed through the sense of touch.'

169 *figures of donors*: in religious artworks of the Middle Ages and the Renaissance, those who commissioned or paid for the works were sometimes depicted as observers of the events unfolding in the image.

'*Accipe . . . saeculorum*': 'Receive this burning light, and retain your anointing, so that when the Lord shall come to judgment, you may meet him with all the saints, and live for ever and ever.' The placing of the lit candle in the dying person's hands is intended to mirror the baptismal ceremony. These lines, adapted from that ceremony, may be appended to the liturgy of extreme unction as a means of reminding the dying person of his or her baptismal innocence.

175 *English point*: after the English parliament prohibited the import of fine Flemish lace in 1662, merchants smuggled it into the country from markets in Brussels. They then exported some of their stock to France under the name *point d'Angleterre* ('English point'), where the new name caught on, and the old one, *point de Bruxelles* ('Brussels point'), fell out of use (F. B. Palliser, *A History of Lace*, 2nd edn (London: Sampson Low, Marston, Low and Searle, 1875), 93).

177 *'Ego . . . Sancti'*: 'I join you in matrimony, in the name of the Father, and of the Son, and of the Holy Spirit.'

'Benedic . . . hunc': 'Bless, Lord, this ring.'

179 *the Epistle side*: the side of the church on which the Epistle is read, to the right of the altar, from the point of view of the congregation in the nave; the Gospel side is on the left.

MORE ABOUT   **OXFORD WORLD'S CLASSICS**

The Oxford World's Classics Website

www.worldsclassics.co.uk

- Browse the full range of Oxford World's Classics online
- Sign up for our monthly e-alert to receive information on new titles
- Read extracts from the Introductions
- Listen to our editors and translators talk about the world's greatest literature with our Oxford World's Classics audio guides
- Join the conversation, follow us on Twitter at OWC_Oxford
- Teachers and lecturers can order inspection copies quickly and simply via our website

www.worldsclassics.co.uk

American Literature

British and Irish Literature

Children's Literature

Classics and Ancient Literature

Colonial Literature

Eastern Literature

European Literature

Gothic Literature

History

Medieval Literature

Oxford English Drama

Philosophy

Poetry

Politics

Religion

The Oxford Shakespeare

A complete list of Oxford World's Classics, including Authors in Context, Oxford English Drama, and the Oxford Shakespeare, is available in the UK from the Marketing Services Department, Oxford University Press, Great Clarendon Street, Oxford OX2 6DP, or visit the website at www.oup.com/uk/worldsclassics.

In the USA, visit www.oup.com/us/owc for a complete title list.

Oxford World's Classics are available from all good bookshops. In case of difficulty, customers in the UK should contact Oxford University Press Bookshop, 116 High Street, Oxford OX1 4BR.

	French Decadent Tales
	Six French Poets of the Nineteenth Century
Honoré de Balzac	**Cousin Bette**
	Eugénie Grandet
	Père Goriot
	The Wild Ass's Skin
Charles Baudelaire	**The Flowers of Evil**
	The Prose Poems and Fanfarlo
Denis Diderot	**Jacques the Fatalist**
	The Nun
Alexandre Dumas (père)	**The Black Tulip**
	The Count of Monte Cristo
	Louise de la Vallière
	The Man in the Iron Mask
	La Reine Margot
	The Three Musketeers
	Twenty Years After
	The Vicomte de Bragelonne
Alexandre Dumas (fils)	**La Dame aux Camélias**
Gustave Flaubert	**Madame Bovary**
	A Sentimental Education
	Three Tales
Victor Hugo	**Notre-Dame de Paris**
J.-K. Huysmans	**Against Nature**
Pierre Choderlos de Laclos	**Les Liaisons dangereuses**
Mme de Lafayette	**The Princesse de Clèves**
Guillaume du Lorris and Jean de Meun	**The Romance of the Rose**

GUY DE MAUPASSANT	**A Day in the Country and Other Stories** **A Life** **Bel-Ami**
PROSPER MÉRIMÉE	**Carmen and Other Stories**
MOLIÈRE	**Don Juan and Other Plays** **The Misanthrope, Tartuffe, and Other** **Plays**
BLAISE PASCAL	**Pensées and Other Writings**
ABBÉ PRÉVOST	**Manon Lescaut**
JEAN RACINE	**Britannicus, Phaedra, and Athaliah**
ARTHUR RIMBAUD	**Collected Poems**
EDMOND ROSTAND	**Cyrano de Bergerac**
MARQUIS DE SADE	**The Crimes of Love** **Justine** **The Misfortunes of Virtue and Other** **Early Tales**
GEORGE SAND	**Indiana**
MME DE STAËL	**Corinne**
STENDHAL	**The Red and the Black** **The Charterhouse of Parma**
PAUL VERLAINE	**Selected Poems**
JULES VERNE	**Around the World in Eighty Days** **Journey to the Centre of the Earth** **Twenty Thousand Leagues under the Seas**
VOLTAIRE	**Candide and Other Stories** **Letters concerning the English Nation** **A Pocket Philosophical Dictionary**

ÉMILE ZOLA

L'Assommoir
The Belly of Paris
La Bête humaine
The Conquest of Plassans
The Fortune of the Rougons
Germinal
The Kill
The Ladies' Paradise
The Masterpiece
Money
Nana
Pot Luck
Thérèse Raquin

	Eirik the Red and Other Icelandic Sagas
	The Kalevala
	The Poetic Edda
LUDOVICO ARIOSTO	Orlando Furioso
GIOVANNI BOCCACCIO	The Decameron
GEORG BÜCHNER	Danton's Death, Leonce and Lena, and Woyzeck
LUIS VAZ DE CAMÕES	The Lusiads
C. P. CAVAFY	The Collected Poems
MIGUEL DE CERVANTES	Don Quixote
	Exemplary Stories
CARLO COLLODI	The Adventures of Pinocchio
DANTE ALIGHIERI	The Divine Comedy
	Vita Nuova
J. W. VON GOETHE	Elective Affinities
	Erotic Poems
	Faust: Part One and Part Two
	The Sorrows of Young Werther
JACOB and WILHELM GRIMM	Selected Tales
E. T. A. HOFFMANN	The Golden Pot and Other Tales
HENRIK IBSEN	An Enemy of the People, The Wild Duck, Rosmersholm
	Four Major Plays
	Peer Gynt
FRANZ KAFKA	The Castle
	A Hunger Artist and Other Stories
	The Man who Disappeared (America)
	The Metamorphosis and Other Stories
	The Trial
LEONARDO DA VINCI	Selections from the Notebooks
LOPE DE VEGA	Three Major Plays

A SELECTION OF   **OXFORD WORLD'S CLASSICS**

ANTON CHEKHOV

About Love and Other Stories
Early Stories
Five Plays
The Princess and Other Stories
The Russian Master and Other Stories
The Steppe and Other Stories
Twelve Plays
Ward Number Six and Other Stories

FYODOR DOSTOEVSKY

Crime and Punishment
Devils
A Gentle Creature and Other Stories
The Idiot
The Karamazov Brothers
Memoirs from the House of the Dead
Notes from the Underground and
    The Gambler

NIKOLAI GOGOL

Dead Souls
Plays and Petersburg Tales

MIKHAIL LERMONTOV

A Hero of Our Time

ALEXANDER PUSHKIN

Boris Godunov
Eugene Onegin
The Queen of Spades and Other Stories

LEO TOLSTOY

Anna Karenina
The Kreutzer Sonata and Other Stories
The Raid and Other Stories
Resurrection
War and Peace

IVAN TURGENEV

Fathers and Sons
First Love and Other Stories
A Month in the Country

Late Victorian Gothic Tales
Literature and Science in the
    Nineteenth Century

JANE AUSTEN
Emma
Mansfield Park
Persuasion
Pride and Prejudice
Selected Letters
Sense and Sensibility

MRS BEETON
Book of Household Management

MARY ELIZABETH BRADDON
Lady Audley's Secret

ANNE BRONTË
The Tenant of Wildfell Hall

CHARLOTTE BRONTË
Jane Eyre
Shirley
Villette

EMILY BRONTË
Wuthering Heights

ROBERT BROWNING
The Major Works

JOHN CLARE
The Major Works

SAMUEL TAYLOR COLERIDGE
The Major Works

WILKIE COLLINS
The Moonstone
No Name
The Woman in White

CHARLES DARWIN
The Origin of Species

THOMAS DE QUINCEY
The Confessions of an English
    Opium-Eater
On Murder

CHARLES DICKENS
The Adventures of Oliver Twist
Barnaby Rudge
Bleak House
David Copperfield
Great Expectations
Nicholas Nickleby

A SELECTION OF   **OXFORD WORLD'S CLASSICS**

WILLIAM MORRIS   News from Nowhere

JOHN RUSKIN   Praeterita
                      Selected Writings

WALTER SCOTT   Ivanhoe
                      Rob Roy
                      Waverley

MARY SHELLEY   Frankenstein
                      The Last Man

ROBERT LOUIS STEVENSON Strange Case of Dr Jekyll and Mr Hyde
                          and Other Tales
                        Treasure Island

BRAM STOKER   Dracula

W. M. THACKERAY   Vanity Fair

FRANCES TROLLOPE   Domestic Manners of the Americans

OSCAR WILDE   The Importance of Being Earnest
                        and Other Plays
                      The Major Works
                      The Picture of Dorian Gray

ELLEN WOOD   East Lynne

DOROTHY WORDSWORTH   The Grasmere and Alfoxden Journals

WILLIAM WORDSWORTH   The Major Works

WORDSWORTH and   Lyrical Ballads
COLERIDGE